DATE DUE

Hope's Highway

Also by Dorothy Garlock
in Large Print:

Place Called Rainwater
The Edge of Town
River of Tomorrow
With Heart
Dream River
With Song
With Hope
Lonesome River
Yesteryear
Wild Sweet Wilderness
Annie Lash

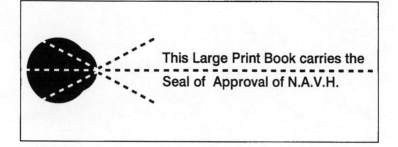

This Large Print Book carries the
Seal of Approval of N.A.V.H.

DOROTHY GARLOCK

Hope's Highway

Thorndike Press • Waterville, Maine

Published in 2004 by arrangement with Warner Books, Inc.

Thorndike Press® Large Print Core.

The tree indicium is a trademark of Thorndike Press.

The text of this Large Print edition is unabridged.
Other aspects of the book may vary from the original edition.

Set in 16 pt. Plantin by Liana M. Walker.

Printed in the United States on permanent paper.

Library of Congress Cataloging-in-Publication Data

Garlock, Dorothy.
    Hope's highway / Dorothy Garlock.
        p. cm.
    ISBN 0-7862-6180-3 (lg. print : hc : alk. paper)
    1. Triangles (Interpersonal relations) — Fiction.
2. United States Highway 66 — Fiction. 3. Women
travelers — Fiction. 4. Young women — Fiction.
5. California — Fiction. 6. Oklahoma — Fiction.
7. Large type books. I. Title.
PS3557.A71645H67 2004b
    813′.54—dc22   2004043989

Dedicated with love to
ALEX (Hemmy) LEMON,
professor, poet, eligible bachelor.
And if he doesn't behave himself,
I'll tell his students
how he got his nickname.

As the Founder/CEO of NAVH, the only national health agency solely devoted to those who, although not totally blind, have an eye disease which could lead to serious visual impairment, I am pleased to recognize Thorndike Press* as one of the leading publishers in the large print field.

Founded in 1954 in San Francisco to prepare large print textbooks for partially seeing children, NAVH became the pioneer and standard setting agency in the preparation of large type.

Today, those publishers who meet our standards carry the prestigious "Seal of Approval" indicating high quality large print. We are delighted that Thorndike Press is one of the publishers whose titles meet these standards. We are also pleased to recognize the significant contribution Thorndike Press is making in this important and growing field.

Lorraine H. Marchi, L.H.D.
Founder/CEO
NAVH

* Thorndike Press encompasses the following imprints: Thorndike, Wheeler, Walker and Large Print Press.

Rusty's song

What I See

I was alone on the Mother Road
Prospectin' for love like the Mother Lode.
I did not know that was what I sought.
I just knew that I hurt a lot.

They are blind who will not see,
None so blind as a man like me.

You were there, watchin' over me
With gentle touch and sweet sympathy,
With tender care like a gift so free,
You were there giving strength to me.

Now I know what you tried to share.
Now I see what was always there.
For my embrace you waited patiently
But I never saw what you meant to me.

They are blind who will not see,
None so blind as a man like me.

Come back, love, to my eager arms.
Come back, love, with your magic charms.
Give me love or I'll change to stone,
Give me hope or I'll die alone.

— F.S.I.

Prologue

1933
Hilton, Kansas

Brady stepped up onto the porch just as the door was shoved open. His brother came from the house carrying his wife, Becky. Her head lolled against his shoulder; blood covered her upper body and ran down the arm that swung limply. She was naked.

"Good Lord! What happened?" Brady croaked.

Although the brothers hadn't seen each other for six months, Brian, in his dazed state, seemed not in the least surprised to see him.

"I can't leave her in there with . . . him." Brian kissed Becky's forehead, cuddled her body close and stepped off the porch. Without another word he headed down the path to the barn. It was then that Brady saw

9

the butt of a gun protruding from his brother's pocket.

"What happened?" Brady managed to say again. He took a few running steps to follow his brother, then stopped. "Oh, Lord! Anna Marie —"

He dashed back up onto the porch and into the house. "Anna!" His voice was loud, as were the sounds of his boot heels on the bare floors as he hurriedly searched the rooms. He took the stairs two at a time to reach the bedrooms. The first one was empty, but the second one —

A man, naked except for his socks, lay sprawled on the blood-soaked bed. His male sex was still in its aroused state, his face destroyed. Brady paused only briefly in the doorway, then raced down the stairs. Satisfied that Anna Marie was not in the house, he ran toward the barn.

Brian sat weeping on a pile of hay in one of the stalls, Becky on his lap.

"I killed . . . my . . . Becky! Why did she do that in our bed? Why did she want to hurt me? What did I do wrong?"

"You didn't do anything wrong. She . . . Maybe he was forcing her —" Brady said the words certain they were not true.

"I killed . . . the son of a bitch and . . . I killed my Becky —" Brian lifted his right hand, the one holding the revolver, and pressed the cold tip to his head.

"Brian! For God's sake! Don't! Think of your little girl." Brady almost choked on his fear.

"She'll be better off . . . with you."

The cocking of the revolver split the silence in the barn. Brady caught his breath, then willed himself to start breathing again.

"Put down the gun, brother. Put it down and let's talk about it." Brady forced himself to speak calmly, though every nerve in his body was screaming.

"Tell Anna Marie I love her. Tell her I loved her mama . . . and that I'm sorry." In a daze of pain and confusion, Brian hugged his wife's bloody body to him. "Go, Brady. I don't want you to see this."

Too frightened to think clearly, Brady struggled for words.

"Give me the gun, Brian! Please."

Cautiously and with much trepidation Brady inched closer to his twin. His heart felt like a runaway train in his chest.

"I just went crazy." Brian's tear-filled eyes pleaded for understanding. "I loved her so much. It tore the heart right out of me to see her with him like that." He rocked back and forth, cradling his wife. He was laboring just to breathe.

"We'll go out to Colorado, Brian. We'll leave here. Just you and I and Anna Marie," Brady begged. "Put down the gun so we can talk."

"The neighbors knew he was there. They tried to keep me from goin' into the house. The sheriff will be here soon. I don't deserve to live . . . don't want to live. Take my little girl away from here . . . to where no one will know her daddy killed her . . . mama . . ." The words were hardly audible, scarcely more than a whisper.

"Oh, God, Brian, stop and think of what you're doing to the child. Now, dammit to hell! Put down the gun!"

Brady had never felt so helpless in his life. *O Lord, what can I do?* He was afraid to make a sudden move while the barrel of the gun was pressed against his brother's temple. He knew that there was a time when a human being has taken all that he can endure, a time when strength and logic were burned away. Was this the moment for his brother, his twin, who had been closer to him than his mother?

Snatches of scenes from their lives together flashed before Brady's eyes.

The two of them, young boys of sixteen, standing beside the grave of their mother and then a year later beside that of their father,

12

vowing always to take care of each other.

Working with a thrashing crew and later in the oil fields . . . always together.

Their first barn dance. How excited they had been! Brian had taken Becky. He had taken Lucy Waters.

Becky, her pink dress unbelted to hide her pregnancy, standing before the preacher, a proud and beaming Brian at her side.

The birth of little Anna Marie. Brian, smiling for days, blissfully unaware that Becky was not as happy with the child as he was.

Coming home from Colorado after receiving several letters from Brian and realizing that his brother was in a terrible state of depression. Arriving a day late.

Now, more terrified than he had ever been in his life, Brady moved closer to his brother, tears streaming unheeded down his cheeks. *Dear God, help me do and say the right thing.*

"What will I tell Anna Marie, Brian? Don't do this to your little girl . . . to me."

"You'd rather that she see me hang? I'll not put her through that." Brian's eyes were those of a man who was lost, beyond hope and willing to do anything just to make the pain go away.

"You'll not hang," Brady argued. "You'll

still be alive in the pen and able to see Anna Marie."

Brian seemed not to hear him, but he harkened to the sound of a motorcar. His eyes darted to the doorway.

"It's the sheriff. Tell him to stay away! Go tell him!"

"I'll tell him. Give me the gun first."

"No! Do this for me, Brady. Go tell him."

"I'll tell him, but stay calm. Be careful with that gun. I'll be right back."

Brady ran to the front of the barn. The sheriff and his deputy were getting out of the car. And a small girl in a blue dress and white stockings was skipping down the street toward the house. Brady had just stepped out of the barn to tell the sheriff to head her off when he heard the cry.

"Becky! Becky!"

It was a sound Brady would remember until his dying day. It filled every crevice of the dimly lit barn and spilled over into the bright Kansas sunshine. It sent a shiver of terror all through him.

Boom!

Brady staggered. The sound of the gunshot brought physical pain so intense that it was scarcely to be borne.

"No!" he shouted, and ran back down the aisle toward his brother. "Oh, Brian,

Brian —" The words burst from his throat as he gazed down at the body at his feet.

His beloved brother, his twin, was gone from him forever.

Brady turned and stumbled back to the barn door. He blinked in the brilliant sunlight as he saw his brother's child walking toward the front porch of the house.

"Anna," he shouted.

The little girl paused.

"Daddy! You're home!" With a happy smile on her little face she ran to Brady. He grabbed her up in his arms. "Uncle Brady! I thought you were Daddy" — she giggled — "till I saw your boots."

Holding her protectively close, Brady walked away from the house.

Chapter 1

1933
Route 66 — Missouri

She was on her way to California.

Margie couldn't help smiling. She would endure whatever came her way just to re- alize her dream of going to Hollywood, seeing the stars, and maybe, just maybe, get- ting a part in a movie. Not a big part. She'd never acted except in a high-school play, but everyone said she was so good she carried the performance.

Her father shifted the gears, the truck jerked and they moved down the dirt road to the highway designated as Route 66, the Mother Road, the highway that would take them all the way to California.

Margie said good-bye for the second time to Conway, Missouri, the town where she had been born and raised and where her dreams of being a movie star had made the long, lonely winter months tolerable.

She turned her thoughts to the events of the days following her father's surprising visit to the café where she worked.

"I'm goin' to California. You can come if you behave yourself," he had announced.

Margie had continued to swipe at the counter with a damp cloth. She was shocked . . . then angry at him for implying that she was in the habit of misbehaving. He had not spoken to her since her return to Conway last fall. She hadn't expected him to welcome her back with open arms or an offer of sympathy, but he could have come around to see if she was all right.

Now here he was inviting her to go with him to California, just weeks after his wife had run off and left him.

Irked by his remark, she couldn't let it go. "What do you mean, behave myself?"

"I ain't takin' ya if you're goin' to run off with every Tom, Dick or Harry that comes along."

"That wasn't what I did, and you know it." Margie kept her head down lest he see how much his words angered her. And how much they hurt.

"Well, are you comin' or not?"

"When are you leaving?"

"Thursday."

"That's day after tomorrow. What part of California?"

"Bakersfield."

"Why Bakersfield?"

"Because I want to. Are you comin' or not?" He inched toward the door, almost as if he couldn't wait to get away from her.

"I'll let you know tomorrow."

"Goddammit! I want to know now. You were eager enough to run off with that fly-by-night last summer."

"That's why I'm being cautious. That fly-by-night stole my money and left me stranded down in Oklahoma."

"I could of told you he was a no-good shyster. But you didn't ask me. You just took the bit in your teeth like you always do. I'm surprised you had enough sense to find your way back."

"You knew I was going with him. Everyone in town knew I was going. Why didn't you come tell me Ernie Harding wasn't dependable?"

" 'Cause you'd not of paid me no mind. That's why. You never did." He went to the door of the café. "Sundown tonight. If you're going, come out to the icehouse. If you're not there, I'll take Potter Jenkins or Mack Dertile."

That morning Margie had watched her father get into his truck. She knew that he would not take one of the town drunks. He had nothing but contempt for them and wouldn't give them an ice chip if they were dying of thirst.

Margie's father, Elmer Kinnard, was a short man with broad shoulders and arms thickened by years of lifting heavy blocks of ice. His light hair was thinning on top. For all his bluster Margie knew he wanted her to go because he lacked the confidence to make the trip alone.

Was he going to see Robert's family? He'd not cared anything for his son while he was growing up and hadn't seen him in years. Some of Robert's relatives on his mother's side had reported that he had done pretty well for himself in California real estate but had died a year ago of a heart attack. Margie guessed Elmer might have heard that his own wife, Goldie, had headed out there. If she had, she would soon discover that being married to Elmer wouldn't get her special treatment from his son's family.

Elmer had married Goldie six months earlier, just weeks after she had come to town to visit a cousin. She had set her cap for him. He appeared to be a good catch. Brazen, with sweet smiles and soft touches, she had cooked for him and cleaned his house while the whole town of Conway watched and wondered if she was going to hook him. She had.

At first, Elmer had been generous with Goldie. She was pretty, though a little plump. He had been flattered by her attention. After they had settled into marriage, his true tightfisted nature came to the fore. It was rumored that Goldie had become increasingly discontent with him and with their life in the small Missouri town. She left suddenly.

Elmer had never shown much interest in his only daughter. After her mother's death, Margie had gone to live with her maternal grandmother on the other side of the small town divided right down the middle by Route 66. She had never received a Christmas or a birthday present from him in all the years that followed, nor had he come to see her act in the school play or graduate from high school. And he usually avoided the café where she worked.

Margie's grandmother died the previous spring and left her a small inheritance. One hundred eighteen dollars seemed like a fortune, and Margie could see her dream of going to Hollywood becoming a reality. The dream, however, turned into a nightmare when the man she hired to take her stole her money, and she had to return to her old job at the diner in Conway. Because she was a good worker and the customers liked her, the owner was glad to have her back.

Bertha, the cook and wife of the owner, leaned in through the window that fronted the kitchen. "You're goin', ain't ya?"

"I want to."

"Then go, honey. There ain't nothin' here for ya. Go and see the sights before yo're tied down with babies and didies."

"Not much chance of that 'round here."

"Gettin' babies? Flitter! Let it be known ya want one and ever' horny man in the county would be here eatin' three squares a day and pinchin' yore cute little butt ever' time ya passed by."

"You and Harry have been awfully good to me. I don't know what I would have done if you hadn't given me my job back."

"You thinkin' Elmer wouldn'ta helped ya?"

"He never has."

"You've been good for us too, hon. It's why I don't want to see ya slingin' hash for the rest of yore life."

"I've always dreamed of going to Hollywood to see the stars."

"Yo're pretty enough to be one. Now,

21

you'd better not tell Harry yo're leavin' until you know for sure Elmer's goin'. Be just like that rascal to get yore hopes up, then fizzle out."

"Rosemary wants to come back to work."

"Her old man broke her arm is the main reason ya got yore job back. She was good help."

"If I give notice and Papa changes his mind about going, I'd be out of a job."

"I heard he sold the icehouse."

"You did? Who'd he sell it to?"

"The bank. Who else has any money?"

"What do they want with it?"

"Who knows? I'd bet my bottom dollar that Goldie Kinnard didn't leave town broke. She might of got the bank to loan her money against the icehouse, and Elmer has to turn it over or pay the debt."

"He'd come out all right. One thing about my father, he knows how to hold on to his money. Grandma used to say that he saved ninety cents out of every dollar he made."

"Yeah, he's a skinflint. Ain't no doubt about that."

An hour before sunset Margie had walked the six blocks from the café to the icehouse. She was not a tall girl and was so slender as to appear fragile, yet she walked

22

with her head up and back straight as if she were used to walking long distances. Her face was an oval frame for large light brown eyes, a straight nose and full, expressive lips. A barrette held her thick dark blond hair at the side. On first glance she did not seem a beautiful girl. But with a chin held high, bright interested eyes and lips that tilted at the corners in an almost constant smile, she nearly always got second and third glances.

As she approached the icehouse, her father came out onto the loading platform carrying a block of ice on his back, protected by his heavy leather shield. He eased the ice into a coaster wagon pulled by a barefoot boy, collected the money and stood waiting for her to say something.

"What car are you going in? Are you going to camp along the way?" Margie asked the questions as if continuing their earlier conversation.

"I'm goin' in my truck and I'm sure as hell not payin' the price for lodgin' from here to California. You figure you're too good to camp out?"

Margie ignored his sarcasm. "What do you expect of me?"

"I expect you to cook, tend the camp and keep your mouth shut."

"Where will I sleep?"

"In the truck."

You're so stingy even with your words. Is that why Goldie left you?

Pretending indifference so that he'd not know how eager she was to go with him, she let a long time elapse before she said anything more. As she waited, she thought about the times when she was younger that she had stood down the street and looked with longing at this building and wondered why her father didn't want her. She had dropped in on him once when she was twelve years old. His harsh words had sent her scurrying back to her grandmother, and she had never ventured near him again . . . until now.

"I heard you sold the icehouse."

"This is my last day."

"Will you miss it?"

"What do you care?"

"I don't."

There was silence while Elmer removed the leather shield from his back and emptied the water from the pocket on the bottom.

"All right. I'll go with you." Margie blurted the words.

"I leave on Thursday."

"Do you need help getting the truck ready?"

"No. It's ready."

"Then why are you waiting until Thursday to go?"

"I got my reasons."

"Are you waiting to see if Goldie comes back so you won't have to take me?"

"I don't have to take you, girlie," he answered sharply.

"I'm not a girlie. I'm a grown woman, in case you haven't noticed. I'm twenty-three years old." Margie couldn't keep the bite out of her voice.

"Then you're old enough to keep your nose out of things that ain't none of your business," he said in the harsh voice she remembered from her childhood.

"I'm not foolish enough to quit my job until I'm sure that you're going. If I don't work, I don't eat." *And I sure can't depend on you for any help.*

"Quit. I'm leaving Thursday," he barked. Then he added, "Sunup." He went back into the icehouse before she could say anything more.

Margie couldn't remember ever having had a civil conversation with her father, and she was not upset over this one. She was too excited. She hardly felt her feet hitting the rough roadbed as she walked back to her rooming house to get ready for the trip and dream of Hollywood.

25

★ ★ ★

At sunup on Thursday Margie waited in front of the rooming house with everything she owned in a suitcase and a cardboard box.

It was the talk of the town that Elmer Kinnard was pulling up stakes and going to California. But the big news, a surprise to all, was that he was taking Margie with him. Nearly all the citizens of Conway knew Elmer and had done business with him. Most of them had watched his daughter grow up and wondered why it was that Elmer didn't seem to know that she was alive.

In a little corner of Margie's mind, as she waited, was the fear that her father might change his mind about taking her. As far as she knew, he had never been more than a hundred miles from Conway.

"Your papa not here yet?" The man who came out of the rooming house was the printer at the newspaper.

"Not yet. But he'll be along."

"Good-bye and good luck in California."

"Thank you."

A few minutes later a truck rounded the corner and stopped. It was the truck Elmer used to haul ice. The sturdy sides rose up a foot higher than the cab. A heavy tarp was stretched across the top and tied down. Extra tires were secured to the sides.

Elmer came to the back and, without a greeting of any kind, let down the tailgate and waited for Margie to lift her suitcase and then her box into the truck. He shoved them back under the tarp, raised the tailgate and fastened it.

"Let's go."

Now as the truck moved smoothly along the newly paved highway, Margie reflected on how little she knew about her father. She was reasonably sure that he wouldn't harm her, but she was also sure that she couldn't rely on him for protection. Harry and Bertha had seen to it that she would be able to protect herself. Before she left the café, Harry had given her a little pistol and taught her to load and shoot it.

"Ya can be sure of one thing, girl. If a man pushes himself on ya, he's goin' to do his damnedest to get in yore pants. Shoot the fucker, 'cause he won't leave ya alive to tell about it!" The pistol was tucked in her box, where it would be easy to get if she needed it.

Elmer Kinnard had never been an easy man to live with, and Margie wondered how he had managed to marry three women in his less than fifty years. His first wife died

27

shortly after giving birth to Robert. Elmer turned the boy over to his wife's parents, which was understandable: He couldn't work and care for an infant. What was not understandable, however, was that after he had given the child away, he showed no more interest in him. In the early 1920s Robert went to California with his widowed grandmother, to live with her brother and his wife.

When Elmer was left with Margie, he turned her over to her grandmother. After he married Goldie, it was easy to see that he was fascinated with his new young wife. For a few months he was rather jovial in his quiet way, but it didn't last.

Now he was alone again.

Was he going to California thinking Goldie was there? Did he expect Robert's family to welcome him?

Miles passed in silence. Margie was content to gaze out the window and daydream. She was on her way again . . . to Hollywood. It was too good to be true. For years she had collected *Silver Screen* and several other movie magazines and thumbed through the pages until they were dog-eared.

She seldom had the chance to see a movie, but when she had, it had provided her with dreams for weeks. She was enchanted by the glamour of the stars. She imagined herself wearing the slinky evening gowns, feathery boas, beaded slippers and sparkling jewelry.

Most of all she dreamed of meeting a man like John Gilbert, George Raft or Ronald Colman who would sweep her off her feet and carry her away to a mansion surrounded by a big stone fence with an iron gate. There he would keep her for days and days making passionate love to her.

Back in 1926 she cried along with thousands of other fifteen-year-old girls when Rudolph Valentino died, and devoured all the news about the funeral and the mysterious woman who visited his tomb daily. Was she his secret lover, the love of his life? Had he loved —

"You got any money, girl?" Elmer asked, breaking into her daydreams.

"A little — and my name is Margie."

"I know what your name is. How much you got?"

"How much do you have?" she countered in the same tone of voice.

They were on their way. There was not much chance he would take her back. And if he stopped to put her out, she would reach for the pistol!

"If you got cash money, you'd best not carry it on you."

"It's safer on me than in my suitcase or my box."

"Do you think I'm goin' to steal it?"

"It was taken out of my suitcase before. I'm taking no chances this time."

Silence.

The pavement ended. They drove onto the gravel road and into the dust stirred up by a car ahead. Margie cranked up the window. She kept her nose pressed to the glass and watched the landscape go by. When they passed men working on the road, they slowed until they were barely creeping along, and Margie waved. Several of the men waved back.

It seemed to her that they traveled miles and miles before they came to the pavement again. What a relief it was to be off the gravel road and away from the dust. She rolled down the window again and breathed in the warm clean air.

Elmer resumed a speed of between twenty-five and thirty miles per hour. Her father was a good driver; she had to give him that. *But how was she going to endure weeks of confinement in this truck with this silent, cynical man?*

The sun was directly overhead when Elmer pulled the truck into a grove beside the road and stopped. Margie got out, stretched her arms and legs and looked around for a place to relieve herself. She found cover in a heavy stand of bushes amid the trees.

On the way back to the truck she stopped and watched her father pouring water from a bucket into the radiator. He was a puzzle to her and had been since she was old enough to know that he was not in the least like other girls' fathers. He was a neat-appearing man: clean-shaven, and he'd recently had a haircut. His overalls and shirt looked to be new. She knew that she would never *love* him, but she wished that she could *like* him.

Elmer dropped the tailgate, reached for a wooden box and dropped it on the ground. She took it to be an invitation to step up into the back of the truck. She was surprised at how compact and efficiently arranged it was. Close to the end on one side was a water barrel and next to it a cabinet with two doors. Tight against the cabinet was a small upright icebox fastened to the side of the truck. She didn't look, but was reasonably sure a small hole had been drilled in the bed of the truck beneath the icebox because there was no pan underneath to empty.

On the other side was a long bench piled high with bedding and boxes. Beneath it, she could see a camp stove and what appeared to be a small rolled-up pup tent. Across the front, next to the cab, her father had built in a heavy wooden box with a padlocked lid. On this was a thin pad.

Every foot of space in the truck bed had been utilized.

Margie looked at her father standing at the end of the truck and smiled to let him know how pleased she was with what he had done.

He grunted and walked away.

Chapter 2

Fortified with a meat sandwich and with a fruit jar of water on the seat beside her, Margie silently watched the fields and farms they passed. She laughed aloud when she read the Burma-Shave sign: IF WIFEY SHUNS YOUR FOND EMBRACE — DON'T SHOOT THE ICEMAN — FEEL YOUR FACE. She glanced at Elmer, thinking that the jingle would surely bring a smile to his face, but he was staring straight ahead.

He appeared to be a bit nervous driving in the Springfield traffic. It made Margie wonder how he would handle the traffic in places like Oklahoma City and Amarillo.

In late afternoon she became aware that he was searching for something as they approached a side road. When they came to a corner where a three-sided log shed sat back from the road, he turned. They traveled for several minutes down a rutted path before pulling into a cleared area amid a stand of blackjack trees.

A truck somewhat like the one they were in was parked there. A man sat in a chair beside it with his hand on a big black dog. A woman tended a campfire. When Elmer stopped and stepped out of the cab, a man in overalls and wide-brimmed straw hat came from behind the raised hood of the truck to meet him.

"Howdy," he called. "Did you have any trouble finding the place?"

"No." Elmer moved away from the truck and stretched. "Came right to it."

The man shook hands with Elmer, then looked questioningly at Margie. When it became apparent to her that Elmer wasn't going to introduce her, Margie rounded the front of the truck and held out her hand.

"Hello. I'm Margie Kinnard. Elmer's daughter."

"Alvin Putman, little lady. I've known Elmer for a spell. Didn't even know he had a daughter. Come meet the wife. If we're goin' to be travelin' together, you'd better be gettin' acquainted. Grace will be downright glad to have a woman to visit with. Come on, Elmer," Alvin said when Elmer headed for the back of the truck. "You've not met my wife and son."

The woman, red-faced from bending over the fire, came toward Margie while wiping her hands on the apron tied around her waist. She had a pleasant smile. Mr. Putman introduced her with pride.

"My wife, Grace. Hon, this is Mr. Kinnard and his daughter, Margie."

Grace shook hands with Margie, then held her hand out to Elmer. "Alvin has told me about you, Mr. Kinnard, but he failed to mention that you had such a pretty daughter."

"Howdy do, ma'am."

"Come meet our son, Margie. Alvin and your pa will want to chew the fat. Mr. Kinnard can meet Rusty later." Grace took her hand and pulled her toward the man who had been sitting beside the truck. He stood beside the chair now, one hand on the back.

"Son, Mr. Kinnard brought his daughter. Her name is Margie. Margie, our son, Rusty."

"Hello, Margie," he said softly.

"Hello." Margie held out her hand. Grace moved to nudge the young man's arm. He lifted his hand. Margie grasped it, suddenly realizing that Rusty was blind. Her eyes went quickly to Grace, who was watching her closely.

"She's about your age, Rusty. Pretty too. Blond hair, brown eyes, not quite as tall as I am."

"Don't believe her," Margie said with a nervous laugh. "I'm not pretty. I'm too skinny, my mouth is too big and my hair looks like a haystack after a cyclone."

Rusty had a nice smile. It was hard for Margie to believe that the eyes that were turned toward her were not seeing her. He was medium height, thin, and had on striped overalls like his father wore. His thick dark auburn hair fell across his forehead. He was clean-shaven and, although not handsome, was nice-looking in a boyish kind of way

"This is Blackie," Rusty said, bending down to scratch the ears of a big black dog who watched her with dark intelligent eyes.

Margie laughed. "Hello, Blackie. It's not hard to figure out how you got your name."

"Mother wanted to call him Whitey, but he wouldn't answer to it."

"I don't blame you," Margie said to the dog. "Blackie is a perfect name for you." She looked up to see that Rusty was still smiling. "How long have you had him?"

"Since he was a pup. About six years now."

"I've always wanted a dog, but I've never lived in a place where I could have one. See you later, Rusty. I'd better get back and help set up camp."

"Nice meeting you, Margie."

Grace walked back with her. "Rusty gets lonely for someone his own age to talk to," she said softly. "I'm glad you'll be traveling with us."

"Is he completely blind?"

"Almost. He sees shadows. He came down with a high fever when he was ten years old. We still don't know what it was. He plays the violin and the guitar and is terribly smart. I tell him something or read something to him and he never forgets it." Grace's hand clasped Margie's arm. "I don't want you to think he's a dummy."

"I didn't for a minute think he was a dummy."

"Some folks think that because he can't see, he can't hear. They'll talk to him real loud or ignore him. I hope the Lukers are as nice as you."

"Lukers?"

"Foley Luker, his wife and two kids. Didn't your pa tell you that we're going to travel in a caravan?"

"No. He's pretty close-mouthed."

"Mr. Luker was in the ice business too. That's how Alvin got to know him . . . and your pa. They hatched it up to travel together for safety reasons and to hang together when we get to California."

"I guess there is safety in numbers."

"We've heard that bad things can happen in a campground if you're alone."

"Are the Lukers to meet us here?"

"Alvin thought they would be here by now. I'd better get back and see to my pot of beans. My cousin made the trip to California two years ago. She wrote to tell me to cook up a mess of beans when I got a chance. When Alvin saw that pot of beans, he said there was enough gas there to blow us all the way to the west coast." Grace giggled, squeezed Margie's arm and left her laughing.

Grace had given Margie surprising news. Evidently her father had planned this trip to California with others who had been in the ice business. He had given considerable thought to making the trip as comfortable as possible, probably thinking that Goldie would be going with him. Not many journeyed the highway with their own iceboxes. Margie felt better about being with Elmer now that they would be traveling with the Putmans.

Margie stepped up into the truck and rummaged through the supplies. There was an assortment of canned goods as well as dried foods such as beans, rice and crackers. A large tin contained flour, another cornmeal and yet another sugar. In the icebox were milk and eggs and some of the meat left over from their sandwiches at noon. She reasoned that they should use the perishable items first.

When the tailgate of the truck was let down and hooked to leather straps attached to each side of the truck, it served as a work counter. Margie was forced to admire her father's ingenuity.

While Elmer and Alvin Putman worked beneath the hood of Alvin's truck, Margie built a small campfire and set over it a heavy wire rack she found under the bench. She made milk gravy, and into it she chipped the remainder of the meat. She would serve this on bread she toasted on a small square grill. When the meal was ready, she set it aside, climbed back up into the truck and rearranged the items beneath the shelf to make room for her suitcase and box.

The Lukers arrived while Margie and her father were eating supper. Elmer sat on a canvas camp stool, his plate on his lap. He didn't comment on the food he was served, but he ate three helpings, then set his plate on the tailgate and walked away to meet the new arrivals.

Margie heated water in a teakettle to wash the dishes, and when that was done, she crawled up into the truck, gave herself a sponge bath, then placed the washdish on an upturned box along with soap and a towel for Elmer. After combing her hair and tying it back with a ribbon, she headed for the Luker camp thinking she would get the introductions over with.

Most of the work at the Luker camp was being done by a tall, lanky boy and a young girl while a woman who didn't appear to be much older than Margie looked on.

"Hello," Margie called as she neared. The boy stopped working and returned her greeting. The young girl ignored her and continued to take things from the two-wheeled trailer behind the car.

"I'm Margie Kinnard." Margie extended her hand to the boy.

"Jody. Jody Luker."

"Glad to meet you, Jody Luker."

"I'm Mrs. Luker." The woman's clear blue eyes looked Margie over with frank female curiosity. With black curly hair, milk-white skin and lips bright red with lipstick, she was pretty and well aware of it. She preened and flashed even white teeth. Dimples appeared in each cheek. "I'm their stepmama. I guess you can tell I'm not old enough to be their real mama." She laughed and held out her hand. "Sugar. My name has been Sugar for so long I've almost forgotten my real name is Selma."

"Sugar!" the young girl snorted. "Should be Vinegar."

"Don't pay any attention to Mona. She's had her fat tail over the line all day. When her father isn't around, she says things she'd be slapped silly for if he heard them."

"And you don't?" The girl curled her lips in a sneer. "You act so nasty nice around him that it makes me want to puke."

"I apologize for the girl's behavior. The poor little thing can't help it if *she's* fat and as ugly as a mud fence." There was viciousness in Mrs. Luker's voice, and to Margie her face was no longer pretty.

"Quit pickin' on her!" Jody said sharply.

Sugar grinned at the boy and made a kissing motion with her puckered lips. He scowled and turned back to the trailer to lift out a heavy box for his sister. Mrs. Luker put her hands beneath the heavy hair at the nape of her neck, lifted it and thrust out her pointed breasts.

Margie was stunned into silence. *Oh, boy! What do we have here?* The girl, Mona, looked to be a couple of years younger than her brother and was far from ugly. She was not as slender as Sugar, but she was not fat. Margie was sure the girl was hiding hurt feelings behind her belligerent attitude.

"I must go. I'll see you again."

"There's no doubt 'bout that if you're going to be traveling with us." Sugar shrugged and raised her brows while looking Margie up and down. Her expression changed suddenly when she looked past her at the men who were approaching. A dazzling smile appeared on her face.

"I'll have something for you to eat, darlin', as soon as I get the camp set up." Sugar went to her husband and took his hand. She leaned her head against his shoulder before looking up at him.

"You mean as soon as the fat, ugly kid gets the camp set up," Mona mumbled.

Jody grunted a warning to his sister.

"This is Mr. Putman and Mr. Kinnard," Mr. Luker said to his wife, and placed his hand on her shoulder. "My wife, Sugar."

"Hello." Sugar offered her hand to each of the men, then snuggled against her husband.

Embarrassed, Alvin Putman shifted his

feet uneasily. Elmer's expression was as blank as always, and it was difficult to gauge his reaction to the woman.

Mr. Luker had near-black hair brushed back from his forehead, wide shoulders, big hands and narrow hips. Except for the slightly chipped front tooth, he was a grown-up version of his son, Jody. Warm brown eyes settled on Margie. Knowing that Elmer would not introduce her, she held out her hand.

"Margie Kinnard. Elmer's daughter."

He gripped her hand and gave her a friendly smile. "Foley Luker. Pleased to meet you, ma'am."

Sugar's eyes narrowed. She gripped the front of her husband's shirt with a tight fist to bring his attention back to her.

Margie glanced back at Jody and his sister. They stood together beside the trailer they were unloading. He was talking urgently to her, his back shielding her from the others. Margie decided then and there that she would keep her distance from Sugar. She had seen her kind before. The woman was trouble.

"What are the other folks like, Ma?"

"I'm not sure yet, son." Grace stood beside her son's chair with her hand on his

43

shoulder. "Mr. Luker's wife isn't much older than his kids. The boy is seventeen or thereabout, I'd guess. He's tall like his pa. The girl is younger by a year or two. Something's not quite right there. Mrs. Luker said to call her Sugar, as if I would. She bosses the kids around like she was queen of the May. She wasn't at all kind to the girl while I was there. I guess they'd had a set-to. The girl had been crying."

"Pa said Mr. Luker married recently. His new wife talked him into selling his ice business. She's the one who wants to go to California."

"Would you like to walk around for a while?"

"Do you mind if we wait until dark?"

"Now, son, I've told you this a hundred times." Grace knew what was in her son's mind. "Bein' blind ain't nothin' to be ashamed of. You can do some things better than some folks that can see."

"Stop kiddin' yourself, Ma. I can't even go to the outhouse unless Pa takes me."

"Not in a strange place, but you did when we were home. You will again. We'll get a place where you'll learn your way around, and you'll have a job on the radio singin' and playin' your own songs. I just know it."

44

Rusty chuckled. "My mother the eternal optimist."

"Optimist? What's that? Oh, never mind. That's one of them words you learned from that high-toned teacher."

"Is it dark?"

"It's dark enough. Let's walk to the road and back. Do you want your cane?"

"No." Rusty placed his hand on his mother's shoulder and walked beside her. They made a wide circle around the Luker camp. Blackie ran ahead, enjoying the scents he found along the way.

"Margie already knows that you can't see. She seems nice. I wonder why her pa didn't tell Alvin that he was bringing her along?"

"Maybe she didn't decide to come along until the last minute."

"I'm glad she did. She's someone we can visit with. I doubt Mrs. Luker will want to have much to do with us."

"Don't be pushing me on Margie." Rusty's voice was stern.

"What a thing to say! I wouldn't do such a thing!"

He laughed and squeezed the shoulder beneath his hand. "You don't fool me for a minute, Mother mine."

"I'm not trying to fool you," she protested. "I just want you to know people your age and —"

"Girls," he interrupted. "You want me to have a girl."

"What's wrong with that?"

"You know what's wrong."

"You . . . could be friends."

"Women don't want to be just *friends* with a man, Ma. They want a husband who can take care of them. How would I take care of a wife? I can't take care of myself."

"You will. When we get to California, you'll get a job on the radio. Cousin Oletta says there's a radio station in almost every town."

"I hope that isn't the only reason you and Pa pulled up stakes to go to California."

"You know it isn't. Your pa thinks he can start an ice business in California, where it's warm all year long. Winters here in Missouri are cold, and folks don't need ice from November to March. Blackie," Grace called. "Come back here."

"He isn't bothering, Mrs. Putman," Margie called. "He just came to say hello."

"Ma?" Rusty hissed a warning.

"We're out stretching our legs. A body stiffens up sitting in that truck all day."

"Do you mind if I walk with you? I need to get the kinks out of my legs too."

46

"Course not. We thought we'd walk out to the road and back. It's more for my benefit than Rusty's. A friend showed him how to stand in one place and run and how to use a bar to pull himself up and down. He did it every morning back home. Glory be. It made me tired just watching him. He worked in the icehouse helpin' his pa and —"

"Ma! Margie doesn't want to hear my life story."

"Yes, I do," Margie said quickly. "Then you'll have to listen while I tell you about working in the café and about the time I paid a no-good man to take me to California and he stole my money. He left me stranded down in Oklahoma, and I had to come home with my tail between my legs."

"Nothing that exciting has happened to me." Rusty laughed again.

In spite of his blindness, he laughs easily, Margie thought before she turned her attention to what his mother was saying.

"How about the time you were playing your fiddle for a barn dance and a couple of drunks rode their horses right into the barn while you were calling a square? That was exciting."

"Oh, no!" Margie exclaimed. "What happened?"

47

"Blackie took after the horses, nipping at their legs," Rusty said. "One of the riders got bucked off and broke his arm."

"Served him right."

"We all thought that was the end of the dance. Know what Rusty did?" Grace said. "He yelled for the folks to grab a partner. 'Here comes "Little Brown Jug" especially for those old boys who can't hold their liquor,' he said. Ever'body laughed and began to dance again."

"Good for Blackie. I hope he got a nice bone when he got home." Margie glanced at Rusty as she spoke, and saw that his face was turned toward her. He walked alongside them as if he could see each and every step he took.

"Blackie knows that I don't see . . . well. One time he got between me and a grass fire. I knew it was there, but didn't know how close it was until Blackie tugged on my pant leg. That was the first time we realized that my dog was aware that I couldn't see."

"That's truly remarkable," Margie exclaimed. "I heard about a dog who led a man out of a burning house and about a dog who jumped into a pond and rescued a baby."

"Dogs are smarter than some people think they are. Back home Blackie knew words like 'post office,' 'barbershop' and 'meat market.' He could lead me there."

"Will you play your fiddle for us some night?"

"Course he will." Grace didn't give Rusty a chance to answer. "He not only plays the fiddle, he plays the guitar, sings and writes his own songs. He's working on one called 'What I See.' "

"Ma!"

"He doesn't like for me to brag on him. He's goin' to give me holy heck when we get back to camp."

"When I was little," Margie said, "my granny used to brag on me. It embarrassed me then, but now I realize that she did it because she loved me. Will you sing your song for me sometime?"

"Sometime," Rusty replied.

"Were you raised by your grandma?" Grace asked.

"My mother died when I was small. Do you like writing songs, Rusty?" she asked, in order to change the subject.

"When I'm in the right mood. I'm going to miss listening to the radio while on this trip."

"His songs are good, Margie. Wait until you hear them. They'll bring tears to your eyes."

Rusty waited until they were headed back

to camp before he spoke again.

"You have to take what my mother says with a grain of salt, Margie. What mother would tell her son that his songs are not worth a cup of spit?"

"Some mothers or fathers would."

They walked on in silence back to where Margie had joined them. "I'll leave you here," she said. "Maybe we can do this again sometime. It's not much fun walking by yourself."

"Sure we can," Grace said.

"Good night, Margie."

"Good night, Rusty."

Chapter 3

Pale streaks of light were showing in the east when Margie heard a noise at the end of the truck. Elmer was building a breakfast fire. The blankets he had used to make a pallet were folded and stacked on the camp chair.

"Morning," she called, and went to the basin she had left on the box overnight. After washing and running the comb through her hair, she filled the coffeepot with water from the keg and set it over the blaze. While the water was heating, she lined a skillet with bacon strips, enough for both breakfast and the noon meal, and set it over the fire.

On her way to the pantry in the truck to get eggs and coffee, she glanced at the other camps. The Putmans were eating breakfast.

Jody Luker was building a fire. Foley Luker came out of a small tent that had been set up near the edge of the woods.

It was daylight by the time breakfast was over and Margie had washed and put away the utensils. Elmer came around to check the tarp that covered the truck bed and to tie down the back flap.

The Putmans left the campsite ahead of them. Grace waved. Alvin tooted the horn. As Elmer drove out to the road, Foley Luker was taking down the tent. Jody and Mona were working at the campfire.

Because they had pulled out and left them, Margie wanted to ask Elmer if the Lukers would still be part of the caravan; but he had not said a word to her, and she had said nothing to him, since the morning greeting that he had ignored. She decided to ask him anyway, and if he didn't want to answer, he wouldn't.

"Are the Lukers still part of the caravan?"

"They'll be along." He pulled his pipe from the bib of his overalls, struck a match on the steering wheel and lit it.

"Where is the next campsite?"

"Oklahoma."

"How far is that?"

"About a hundred miles."

"Is it the goal to make a hundred miles a day?"

"On the flatland. Might not in the mountains."

"I like the Putmans."

"Don't be flirtin' with that blind boy, gettin' him all hot for ya," he said sternly. "His pa won't stand for it." He spoke around the pipe stem in his mouth.

When the import of his words soaked into Margie's mind, she closed her eyes and fought a sharp battle to get her anger under control. But it blossomed.

"What do you mean by that?" she demanded.

"Just what I said. Stay away from him. He'd not understand a woman like you."

"What do you mean, a woman like me? Do you think I'm some cheap floozy who's out to get him in bed?"

"Yeah, I think that."

"What!" she exploded. "Why you nasty, dirty-minded old reprobate. I wish I'd known what you thought of me before we left Conway. I'd not have ridden a mile with you."

"Say the word. I'll pull over and let you out."

"You'd like that! And that's just the reason I'm going to stick with you all the way to California."

"Maybe you will and maybe you won't."

"You'd not dare put me out. What would your friends the Putmans think? Or the Lukers? That Sugar Luker is a floozy, if I ever saw one."

"It takes one to know one."

Angry, unguarded words spewed from Margie's mouth. "I suppose you know about floozies. The one you married left you."

"I married two," he said calmly.

"Are you saying that my mother was a floozy?"

"She was a whore."

Margie's breath left her. When she was finally able to speak, she said two words. "You're lying."

He shrugged.

"You're lying!" She shouted it this time.

He ignored her outburst and pulled into a filling station, got out and slammed the door. Margie was shaking. All her life she had heard little rumors that her mother had sown some wild oats before she married Elmer and settled down. No one had even hinted that she was anything but a pretty girl who attracted men like flies to a honey pot. Her granny had even said that her daughter was too pretty for her own good.

Unanswered questions floated around in

Margie's mind. If Elmer thought her mother a whore, he might be thinking that Margie wasn't his daughter. Was that why he had been so indifferent to her all these years? Oh, Lord! Here she was at the mercy of a man who cared no more for her than he did for the old dog he'd left behind.

Margie stared out the window and waited for Elmer to finish paying for the gas and get back into the truck. She intended to take up the conversation where it had left off. Minutes after they left the gas station, the paving ended and they were once again on a gravel road. Traveling this one was like riding on a washboard. Dust flew up from the car ahead. She rolled up the window to keep from breathing it and decided to wait until they were on a smoother road and it wasn't so noisy before she questioned him further.

It was almost noon when they passed off the gravel and onto the smooth paving. It was a blessed relief. Margie cranked down the window and enjoyed the breeze hitting her face. She was debating with herself on how to open the conversation with Elmer about her mother when she realized that the truck ahead was the Putmans'.

At the top of a small rise the Putmans pulled to the side of the road. Elmer stopped a few dozen feet behind them. As if she weren't there, he got out of the truck and walked off into the woods with Alvin and Rusty. Blackie trailed along behind.

Grace came to where Margie stood beside the truck. "That washboardy road 'bout shook me to pieces." She massaged the small of her back as they walked away together.

"I've traveled this road as far as Sayre, Oklahoma," Margie said. "It's mostly paved from Tulsa on through Oklahoma. We came to spots where bridges weren't finished and we had to go around. In some places the creek was dry with a good sandy bottom, and we crossed without detouring."

"Well, looky who's here." Grace nudged Margie with her elbow when the Lukers pulled up and stopped. "They got such a late start I was sure that we'd not see them all day. But they didn't have to stop for gas. Foley told Alvin they filled up last night before they got to the campground."

All the Lukers except Sugar piled out of the car and stood beside the road. Mona walked back down the road, then toward the woods. Jody called to her, but she kept going. Grace commented on it when she and Margie took their turn in the woods.

"There seems to be bad feelings between

the girl and Mrs. Luker."

"I noticed that. Jody takes up for his sister. It must be hard for both of them. I wonder how long since they lost their mother."

"Foley said two years. He married this one a few months ago."

When they were out of sight, Margie handed Grace a square of newspaper that she had softened by crushing and rubbing. She smiled at the woman's quizzical look.

"It's better than nothing. My granny taught me how to do that. She used to cut the paper in squares, crush and rub it to soften it, fold it and put it in the outhouse. It works with pages from a catalog if it's not slick paper."

Grace laughed. "Wait until I tell Alvin and Rusty —"

"Don't you dare! If you do, I'll not be able to face either one of them."

"I was funnin' you."

Later Grace clicked her tongue when she saw Mona Luker coming up the road. "I'd of give a pretty penny to have a girl, but the good Lord didn't see fit to give us one. He must have figured he gave us the best he had when he gave us Rusty, and saved the girl for someone else."

"What a sweet thing to say. Rusty is lucky the Lord gave him to you."

Grace laughed. "We'd of loved him if he'd been dumb as a pile of rocks."

Jody Luker was talking to Rusty, who leaned against the side of the Putman truck, Blackie beside him. The hood of the Luker car was up, and Alvin, Foley and Elmer were huddled around it. Alvin went to his truck, returned with a bucket of water and poured it into the radiator.

Margie climbed into Elmer's truck and made sandwiches from the bacon and eggs she had cooked that morning. She took her sandwich, along with a fruit jar of water, and went to sit on the grass beside the road, leaving Elmer's meal on the tailgate. She wasn't in a mood to talk and was glad Grace was busy making the noon meal for her family.

When Jody passed on his way back to the Luker car, Margie smiled and lifted a hand in greeting. Sugar Luker, who was sitting in the car, said something to him as he came even with it. He didn't pause or answer, but continued on to where his sister was at the back of the trailer.

Was Foley Luker so blind that he couldn't see how unhappy his wife was making his children? Or was he so fascinated with his Sugar that he didn't care?

Margie's mind was still in a turmoil over

the conversation she'd had with her father. She had opened a dialogue with her questions and was determined to know why he considered her mother a whore.

When it came time to pull out again, they fell in behind the Putmans. The highway was smooth. Margie waited until after Elmer had lit his pipe before she spoke.

"I want to know why you called my mother a whore."

He was silent for a moment, then said, "You don't want to know."

"I do," she replied staunchly. "Do you think that I'm not your daughter? Is that the reason you have ignored me all these years and why you can't bring yourself to introduce me to your friends?"

"Drop it, girl. What's done is done. No sense dragging up the past."

"I can't drop something as important as this is to me. All my life I've wondered why you didn't like me. I turned myself inside out trying to please you and get you to notice me. I *wanted* a father."

"No fault of mine. I provided for you till you were grown. I gave the old woman money every month."

"Why did you say my mother was a whore?" she insisted. "Why do you have such a low opinion of me? Tell me."

"Goddammit!" he shouted. "Let it go or I'll pull over and put you out."

Margie burst into tears. She cried softly for miles. When the scalding tears abated, she wiped her eyes on the hem of her dress and rested her head against the back of the seat. One thought sustained her: She was on her way to California and Hollywood. Tonight she would get out her movie magazines. Looking through them always gave her something new to dream about. As far as Elmer was concerned, she vowed not to say another word to him until they reached California. And that word would be "goodbye."

Margie was staring out the window when they reached Miami, Oklahoma. They passed the Coleman Theater, said to be one of the most beautiful theaters in the Southwest. She had heard that Will Rogers and many other famous people had made appearances there. No wonder Miami was proud of its theater.

On leaving Miami they were again on a rough gravel road that went on for mile after mile. They crossed the Neosho River and passed through endless prairie land. About the time that Margie was sure her rear was numb, they followed the Putmans off the highway and into a cleared area where a ve-

60

hicle was parked and a saddled buckskin horse, its reins trailing, grazed on the early summer grass. Two men stood beside a big black car with a carrier rack, and a little girl jumped rope nearby.

One of the men went to speak to the Putmans, then waited for Elmer to move forward.

"Howdy," the man said to Elmer, then tipped his hat to Margie. "Ma'am." He was young and dark-haired, with an obvious Indian heritage. "This is my land, but you're welcome to camp here. Be careful with your fire. A grass fire could easily spread to the hay crop I have just through that thin patch of woods."

"I'll watch the fire."

As they passed the car with the carrier rack on top, Margie glanced at the other man leaning against it, his arms folded across his chest. He was tall, big-framed and lean. All she could see of his face beneath the pulled-down, big-brimmed hat was his firm, unsmiling mouth. After they had passed him, she realized that he wore an air of authority. Was he a lawman?

Elmer stopped the truck near a circle of rocks that held the remains of previous fires, leaving a space of a couple hundred feet between their camp and the Putmans'.

Margie felt wrung out. She wanted to hurry and get supper over with. She had decided that she would ask Rusty to go for a walk with her.

Let Elmer make something of that.

She quickly set out the box with the washdish, soap and towel. Elmer came out of the woods with an armload of dead wood and built the cook fire.

When the fire was going, he left to speak to Foley Luker, who had driven into the campground. The radiator on the Luker car was steaming. Margie was climbing out of the truck with potatoes to peel when the man who had greeted them when they drove in approached with a large fish hanging from a stringer.

"Ma'am, could you use a catfish? I caught more than I can use." He had tipped his hat back, and she could see a few silver streaks in his hair.

"We sure could. There's nothing better than fried catfish."

"Rolled in cornmeal?" He smiled, creases appearing on each side of his wide mouth.

"Absolutely!" Margie returned the smile.

While he was removing the fish from the string, it began to flop. Margie let out a little squeal of alarm.

"I'll whack him on the head for you,

ma'am. Your man will have to skin him for you."

"My father," Margie corrected.

"On second thought, if you have something I can lay him on, I can skin him for you in half a minute."

"Half a minute," she echoed teasingly. "Now, that, I'll have to see." She removed the washdish from the box. "Mister, will this do?"

"Name's Payne, ma'am."

He circled the head of the fish with a sharp knife, then with the pliers he took from his pocket, he pulled off the skin. It took a little longer than half a minute, but there was no wasted motion. It was as if he had done it a million times before.

"It's good of you to let us camp here."

"My pleasure. I enjoy the chance to meet folks. Most of them are good people." He quickly sliced the fish down one side and then the other. After laying aside slabs of boneless fish, he tossed the long spiny bone into the campfire.

"Thank you. I'll get water so you can wash your hands." Margie ladled water into the washdish from the water keg and set it on the tailgate. "You're welcome to stay and eat with us."

"Thanks, but my friend over there" — he

jerked his head toward the big heavy car with the rack on the top — "is frying up a batch."

"Thank you, Mr. Payne, for the fish and for allowing us to camp here."

"You're welcome."

While the fish fried, Margie mixed a batch of corn bread to cook like pancakes on the griddle. She didn't know what Elmer liked to eat and she didn't care. If he didn't like the fish and corn bread, he could go eat with Sugar, she thought spitefully.

While she was bending over the cook fire, Jody Luker stopped by. "The fish smells good. Mona's cooking ours."

"Can't Sugar cook?"

"Not much." Jody didn't seem to notice the sarcasm in her voice. "I just never thought I'd meet Andy Payne. He's shook hands with the president and everythin'."

"This Mr. Payne? The one who let us camp here and gave us the fish?"

"Haven't you heard of him? Pa said he lived around here. He's the one who won the Bunion Derby. He ran from Los Angeles to New York and beat out over two hundred other runners to win."

"He *ran* from Los Angeles to New York? I can't believe it."

"He did. Back in 1928."

"I've never heard the like."

"Pa said they called the race the International Transcontinental Foot Marathon, but that's such a tongue twister it was just called the Bunion Derby. The race was thirty-four hundred miles long."

"And this Mr. Payne won it? Well, whatta ya know!"

"He's Cherokee. Pa said running is in their blood. I don't know if that had anything to do with him winning, but he did, and got money enough to buy his ranch. It's about a half mile from here. He said he came down to spend the day fishing with his friend, who is passing through."

"He certainly knows how to clean fish. I'll give him that."

Elmer had no complaints about the meal. He said nothing. Not even about the man who had so generously given them the fish — cleaned and boned. When Margie sat down to eat, he appeared and filled his plate and moved away. When he finished eating, he set his plate on the tailgate of the truck, sank down in the canvas chair and lit his pipe.

Margie wrapped the leftover fish and corn bread in waxed bread wrappers, then washed the dishes. When she finished, she filled the washdish with warm water and took it to the truck. She lit the lantern and brought down the end flap for privacy. The emotional confrontation with her father had worn her out. She would like nothing better than to go straight to bed, but she felt too dirty for that. After washing herself from head to toe, she put her clothes back on. She had worn them for two days and decided she would wear them one more day. She had three skirts and three blouses that she thought were suitable for travel. Her one dress and another skirt and blouse would be kept in reserve should she need to dress up.

She debated about staying in the truck with the lantern and thumbing through her movie magazines. That usually soothed her, but it was too hot in the truck with the end flap down. Besides, Elmer might complain about the use of the kerosene. She would reserve that pleasure for another time.

Elmer was not in sight when she rolled up the end flap and got out of the truck. The day was near an end. Only a few faint streaks showed in the western sky. A few lightning bugs flitted about.

"My ball is under your car." The voice came from a little girl who stood with her shoulders hunched up to her ears as if trying to hide.

"Hello. You lost your ball? Which end of the truck is it under?"

"I don't know."

"I'll take a look." Margie got down on her hands and knees and peered under the truck. "Is it a white ball?"

"It's red."

"Red? Ah . . . that'll make it harder to see in the dark. Hallelujah! There it is." Margie lay flat on the ground and scooted under the truck until she reached the small rubber ball. "I've got it," she called, and began to wiggle her way out.

There was no way she could keep her skirt from moving up to her thighs as she wiggled out from under the truck. When her head cleared the running board, she turned to sit up and her eyes collided with those of the man squatting down holding a lantern. She had never seen such incredible eyes: light green, like leaves in the early spring, cool and secret and surrounded with thick dark lashes.

"Oh . . . oh —" Still holding the ball, Margie grabbed to pull her skirt down to her knees. "Here's your ball," she said, and shoved it into the child's hands.

"Thank you."

Margie rolled over onto her knees to get up and felt the man's hand on her arm to help her. She was hoisted to her feet by hands strong enough to toss her across the truck. Hot with embarrassment, she swiped at her skirt to rid it of the dried grass and looked at the child standing beside the tall man. Her eyes were green like his; her dark hair was parted in the middle, and two fat braids rested on her chest.

Finally there was nothing to do but look up at the man again, her composure completely disrupted, the telltale color of embarrassment on her cheeks.

Chapter 4

She lifted her eyelids, and something about her pulled at him. There was sadness in her eyes as well as intelligence and maturity. Beneath her fragile exterior were strength and determination. He didn't know how he knew this, but he did. The large light brown eyes, flicked with amber, reminded him of the eyes of a doe who was alert and a little bit afraid.

He was not, as a rule, shy around women, but he remained quiet, hoping his nerves would settle down before he had to speak to her.

He swept the wide-brimmed hat from his head, revealing hair as black as midnight. It was thick, shiny, straight as a string, and covered the tips of his ears. He credited his reaction to her to the fact he'd not been around a pretty girl on a one-to-one basis for several months. Relieved to come to that conclusion, he continued to look at the girl who now had a bit of hostility in her expression.

Brady had learned that remaining silent gave him an edge, and for some reason unknown to him, he felt that he needed one now. Most people were uncomfortable with silence, especially women. They sought to fill it with silly chatter. Not so, this young woman. She stared at him coolly, just as silent, waiting for him to speak.

"Thanks for getting the ball." He spoke with a definite Oklahoma drawl.

Margie nodded.

"Uncle Brady told me not to throw it this way."

Her eyes left him and went to the child. "It's all right. I'm glad it wasn't lost."

He was her uncle. They looked enough alike to be father and daughter.

"You got dirty." The little girl's hair was dark, but not as dark as her uncle's, her eyes anxious.

"Don't worry about that," Margie scoffed. "This old skirt will wash."

"Brady Hoyt." The man held out his hand. Margie put hers into it. With a firm grip on her hand he introduced the little girl. "My niece, Anna Marie."

"Margie Kinnard."

"My mama and daddy went to heaven. Uncle Brady is taking me to California to live with my Aunt Opal. Uncle Brady calls me Punkie, but I don't like it much."

Brady released Margie's hand and tilted his head toward his niece. "You never told me that."

"He hasn't noticed that I don't answer when he calls me that." Big dark eyes looked up at Margie. "He wants me to cut off my braids 'cause they're too much trouble. But I'm not going to. Granny Maude, who looked after me sometimes, rolled my hair in rags and made me pretty curls like the little girl in the movies. I'll wait and see if Aunt Opal will do it."

"I bet that little girl was Shirley Temple. I've got a picture of her in one of my magazines. You'd be pretty in curls, even prettier than you already are."

"Mr. Payne gave us a fish without bones in it. Before he went home, he let me ride on his horse. He said he knew my daddy and Uncle Brady when they were just snot-nosed kids."

"Uh-oh. We'd better go before she tells you our family history."

"My daddy was Uncle Brady's twin. He

looked like him 'cepts part of my daddy's eyebrow was gone. He said an Indian tried to scalp him, but he was just funnin' me. Uncle Brady said he fell on a plow when he was little."

"You're a lucky little girl to have an uncle. I never had one, but I had a grandma."

"I don't have a grandma —"

"See what I mean," Brady broke in. "You'll soon know about how Grandpa Hoyt helped Teddy Roosevelt win the war in Cuba. Come on, Punkie."

Margie was aware that Elmer was standing in front of the truck with his hands in the bib of his overalls listening to the conversation. Damn him! *He was waiting to see if she was going to flirt with Mr. Hoyt.*

She tried hard to keep a lid on her temper and debated whether or not to introduce them. She decided that not to do so would be rude.

She gestured toward the silent man. "Mr. Hoyt, this is my father, Elmer Kinnard." Whether she liked it or not, he was her father. She couldn't change that, although she was beginning to hate saying the word.

Elmer met the extended hand. "Howdy."

"And his niece, Anna Marie Hoyt." Margie was determined not to let Elmer ignore the child.

He answered Anna Marie's "Hello" with another "Howdy."

Brady debated about trying to make conversation. When he spoke to the man earlier, he received only a grunt in reply. But what the hell —

"Did the fellow get his radiator fixed?"

"Naw. One of us will have to tow him to Claremore tomorrow."

"I've had some experience with radiators. I'll be glad to take a look at it."

Elmer shrugged.

"I can tell him right off if it's fixable or if he'll have to have a new radiator. I've got a flashlight in my car."

"Anna Marie," Margie said, "would you like to stay with me while your uncle works on the car? We'll walk down and talk to Mrs. Putman." Margie sent a defiant glance in Elmer's direction. "Just this morning she was telling me how much she liked little girls."

"Can I, Uncle Brady?"

"Sure. The lady invited you. Don't throw the ball again. We might not be able to find it in the dark."

"I won't." The child's little hand burrowed into Margie's. "I like you."

"I'm glad, because I like you too."

Brady walked toward his car wondering

73

why he was feeling so elated to discover that the sullen man was the girl's father and not her husband. He had felt the tension between the two. She never looked at him, and he never looked at her. Could it be that he was not her father and they were pretending to be father and daughter for appearance's sake?

Brady was twenty-nine years old and had never even considered the idea of marrying. When the need for sex was on him, there were a couple of women he knew who were glad to oblige him. They were not exactly whores, and he paid them in different ways. A cord of stovewood, a young, dressed-out deer, a couple of fat geese.

One of the women and her husband had been his good friends for a long time. After her husband had been killed, she had a hard time making ends meet. He knew that she would marry him at the drop of a hat, so he was careful not to let the hat drop.

The other woman . . . well, he guessed she was a good friend too. He had been surprised when she asked him to come to bed with her. She was lonely, and they had simply shared mutual pleasure.

His father had grieved himself to death over the loss of their mother. *Then Brian. O Lord! Brian.* Brady choked up when he thought of his twin. His smart, easygoing brother hadn't been able to endure the loss of his Becky to another man and had died a murderer. Knowing of his father's grief and his brother's despair, Brady swore that he would never love a woman like that. He would not allow one to get so embedded in his heart and mind that he couldn't live without her.

He clenched his teeth. There was still the problem of his spontaneous reaction to Margie Kinnard. He didn't understand the sudden urge to reach for her, hold her, cover her mouth with his, take comfort from her and give comfort in return. Sex had always been something that was important, pleasant, but not all-consuming.

Holy hell. Had grief over his twin and the added responsibility of his twin's five-year-old daughter caused him to lose his reasoning? One thing was sure: He couldn't get involved with a woman until he had Anna Marie settled. A friendly neighbor had cared for her until Brady was ready to take her. Now, two days into the journey west, Brady, unfamiliar with the needs of a little girl, was awkwardly trying to manage.

Holding hands, Margie and Anna Marie walked toward the Putman camp. A blazing campfire lit the area. Grace sat on a chair beside the truck, and nearby, sitting cross-legged on the grass, were Rusty and the Luker kids. Rusty had just finished telling them something that had made Jody and his sister laugh.

"My, my, who do we have here?" A smiling Grace held out her hand to the little girl.

"This is Anna Marie Hoyt. Her uncle is taking her to California. Anna Marie, Mrs. Putman." Margie gently urged the little girl forward.

"I'm Grace, honey. Mercy me, you're just as pretty as a buttercup."

"I'm not a flower," Anna Marie said, and timidly moved closer to the older woman.

"Course you're not. But you're pretty as one. Come sit on my knee. It's been a long time since I've held a little girl." Grace reached out and pulled the child up onto her lap.

"I don't think I look pretty. Uncle Brady isn't very good at braiding my hair."

"Humm . . ." Grace fingered the braids. "He did pretty good for a man with big old clumsy hands."

"But it's all . . . straggily —"

"A little maybe. You need some pretty ribbon to go on the ends is all. I may have a piece or two in my sewing basket." Grace set the child on her feet and got out of the chair. "Let's go see, shall we?"

Margie wandered over to where Jody was adding more wood to the campfire. His sister was sitting beside Rusty.

"Hello, Rusty."

"Margie. I thought that was you. Do you know Mona?"

"I've met her. Hello, Mona."

"Hello."

Margie got her first good look at the girl's face. Mona had dark brown hair that reached her shoulders, large, expressive eyes and a wide, unsmiling mouth. She would be quite pretty without the sour look on her face. And she was older than Margie had at first believed. She was built solidly, not fat as her stepmother had described. The blouse she wore showed well-developed girlish breasts.

"Did you get to talk to Andy Payne?" Rusty asked.

"Just briefly. I didn't know he was the famous runner until Jody came by and told me. How did you find out?"

"I knew who he was as soon as he said his name. I heard on the radio about the Bunion Derby, the race across the United States. I knew he was from near here. He put

Foyil, Oklahoma, on the map."

"Heck of a nice fellow." Jody sat down beside his sister. "He said that he has known Mr. Hoyt for a long time. He'da stayed at his house, but one of Mr. Payne's kids has whooping cough, and Mr. Hoyt wasn't sure if his niece had had it."

"Mr. Hoyt is working on your car." Margie volunteered the information. "He seems to know something about radiators."

"That ought to please *Mrs. Luker.*"

"Mona, don't start that!" Jody scolded.

"Well, it's true. When we drove in, she was looking him and Mr. Payne over like a starving dog looks at a meat wagon. She tried her best to get Mr. Payne to stay for supper. Daddy is so . . . dumb. She's got him twisted around her little finger so tight that he can't see anything but her."

"Sugar isn't at all nice to Mona when Daddy isn't around." Jody tried to explain his sister's dislike of their father's wife. "When he is, she's sweet as pie."

"My granny used to say that you can tell a lot about a person by the way they treat other people." Margie spoke in the silence that followed Jody's words.

Mona's head turned toward Margie. "She isn't going to like you."

Margie tossed her head. "Why would she

78

dislike me? I've hardly spoken to her."

"She doesn't like any woman unless she is old or so ugly that a dog wouldn't take a bone from her hand."

"Thanks for the compliment . . . I think."

"Someone will have to tell me about this Jezebel." Rusty laughed lightly. "I only know what my mother told me, and I think her version of Mrs. Luker was slightly colored."

Neither Mona nor her brother said anything.

"I guess it's up to me." Margie pulled her knees up under her full skirt and wrapped her arms around them. "She's pretty in a flashy sort of way: black hair, white skin. She has an air of helplessness, which appeals to some men. She's ill-mannered, or she'd not have spoken about Mona as she did to me, a total stranger. I think that she's a woman who demands attention, and not from other women.

"My father married a woman like her who flattered him until she got all she could from him, then she ran off and left him for greener pastures."

"That's about the same picture Ma painted for me." Rusty was smiling, and Margie was sure that he was enjoying the gossipy conversation.

"I forgot to say that she's a little older than I am," Margie said.

"A lot older than you," Mona said, and glanced at her brother. "She's thirty and claims to be twenty-five. That's not all. Daddy's her third or fourth husband."

"How do you know that?" Jody asked.

"I snooped in her things and found out."

"Holy smoke, sis! Don't do it again. As sure as God made little green apples, she'll tell Pa, and it'll give him all the more reason to think we're mean to her when he isn't around. It's what she wants."

"He thinks that anyway. She can make him think a cowpie is pudding once she gets him in that tent and —"

"Mona!" Jody said sharply.

Anna Marie came to where Margie was sitting and held up the ends of her long braids. "Look. Look at the ribbons Aunt Grace gave me."

"Pretty. The blue matches your dress."

"Aunt Grace said for me to untie them myself, 'cause Uncle Brady might lose them."

"He may not know how important ribbons are to little girls."

"Can I sit on your lap so I won't get my dress dirty? Uncle Brady said we can't get our clothes washed for a while."

"Sure. This old skirt washes easily."

Margie straightened her legs and pulled the child down to sit between her knees.

"Rusty, have you forgotten you promised to play your guitar for us?" Jody asked.

"No, I'll get it." Rusty started to rise.

"Sit still, son. I'm already up," his mother said.

Grace brought the guitar, and while Rusty was strumming it, she pulled her chair closer to the group sitting on the ground. He picked out a tune, played for a while, and then Grace began to sing.

"Come to the church in the wildwood,
Oh, come to the church in the dale . . ."

She had a beautiful soprano voice and clearly loved to sing. When the song ended, Rusty played a few notes of "I Dream of Jeannie with the Light Brown Hair." Grace's voice was hauntingly beautiful in the stillness of the night.

When she finished, Rusty sang in a low, husky voice so full of feeling that it almost brought tears to Margie's eyes.

"Oh, I'm thinking tonight of my blue eyes,
Who is sailing far over the seas.
I'm thinking tonight of my blue eyes,
And I wonder if she ever thinks of me."

Grace and her son took turns singing. Margie couldn't remember when she'd had a more enjoyable evening. Anna Marie had long ago fallen to sleep. Margie shifted her to a more comfortable position with the child's head on her breast and absently stroked her hair as she listened to Rusty sing a sad song about a dying cowboy.

"Oh, bury me not on the lone prair-ie,
Where the wild coy-otes will howl o'er me.
In a narrow grave . . . just six by three,
Oh, bury me not on the lone prair-ie."

Margie held her breath. Rusty's voice seemed to have the power to mesmerize her. She was so lost in the song that until it was over she was unaware that someone had squatted close behind her. Instinctively she knew who it was. Brady Hoyt was close enough for her to feel his body heat and to smell his warm male scent. She felt his eyes on the back of her neck and unconsciously straightened her shoulders.

Alvin, standing behind his wife's chair, joined his son in harmony-singing "Down in the Valley." It was obvious that Rusty had inherited his musical talent from his parents. The love between Grace, Alvin and their son was so poignant it almost brought

82

tears to Margie's eyes.

The song ended, and Rusty said, "Someone else take a turn. Tell me the tune, and I'll see if I know it." Silence. "How about you, Margie?"

"Not me. I can't carry a tune in a bucket."

"I bet that's not true," Brady murmured, his mouth close to her ear.

"But I heard," Margie added quickly, "that Mr. Hoyt sings . . . quite well."

"Really? That's good news. I don't want to hog the whole evening. What'll it be, Mr. Hoyt?"

"Name's Brady, and I don't know where Margie got that harebrained idea. I sing out only when I've mashed my finger or dropped something on my toe."

"Mona sings," Jody said.

"I do not! You just hush up, Jody." Mona stood. "I've got to go."

"Don't go, Mona," Rusty said quickly, reaching up his hand to stop her. "You don't have to sing."

"Why don't we *all* sing something? Play 'Home on the Range,' son," Grace said. "Everyone knows that."

It was Alvin who started singing the lyrics in a beautiful booming voice. "Oh, give me a home where the buffalo roam, where the deer and the antelope play . . ."

Margie was too aware of the man behind her to sing. Then, near her ear, she heard him singing softly in a surprisingly good voice. When the song ended, it was Jody who spoke.

"Mona and I had better get back, or Pa will be after us."

"Are you kiddin'?" Mona snorted. "You couldn't get him out of that tent with a team of mules if both of us were drowning in the river."

"I hope we meet up with you folks after Pa gets the radiator fixed," Jody said, ignoring his sister's comment.

"It's fixed," Alvin said. "Brady plugged up the hole with a wad of tinfoil."

Margie felt Brady get to his feet. "I don't know how long it will last," he said.

"You mean we can go with you in the morning?" Jody asked.

"That's the plan," Alvin said.

"Hot dog! I wish you were coming along with us, Mr. Hoyt." Jody was obviously pleased. "Pa knows the ice business, but he doesn't know beans about a motorcar."

"Anna Marie and I will mosey along behind you for a day or two."

"Well, now, ain't that nice to hear?" Grace exclaimed. "I'll tell ya what, Mr. Hoyt. You and that little darlin' are welcome to breakfast with us in the mornin'."

"Thank you, ma'am. I accept on behalf of myself and Anna Marie."

"It'll be a comfort having you along. And I'm a-warnin' you. I'm going to be havin' me some time with that little darlin'."

Brady squatted down in front of Margie and lifted the sleeping child up into his arms. She nestled her head contentedly on her uncle's shoulder. He stood and reached down to help Margie. She ignored his hand, rolled over onto her knees and got to her feet. She looked up to see that he was waiting for her to look at him.

"Thanks for looking after Punkie. She gets pretty tired of my company."

She nodded. "Good night, all."

Margie headed for the truck. Jody and Mona were just ahead of her talking in low tones. She was surprised when Brady appeared beside her, Anna Marie nestled on his shoulder.

"I'll walk you to your camp. It's the least I can do."

"It isn't necessary."

"I know that. I want to." After a brief silence he said, "Mr. Luker and Mr. Putman asked me to trail along with you folks."

"You said that."

"Anna Marie needs a woman to do things

85

for her that I can't do. I didn't realize that when we started out on this trip."

"Is that why you're going to travel with us?"

"I admit that it is. I worry about what I'd do if she got sick, or who would take care of her if something happened to me. She likes you and Mrs. Putman."

"How long have you been on the road?"

"This is our second day. I wanted to stop over here and see my friend Andy Payne."

"The Mr. Payne who gave us the fish?"

"Yeah. He'd rather fish than eat. I appreciate the attention you and Mrs. Putman gave Anna Marie tonight."

"Like tying ribbons on her braids?"

He chuckled. "She's a fussy little punkin. Wants to look pretty. Did you want to look pretty when you were a little girl?"

"It's been so long since I was a little girl, I've forgotten. Anna Marie is smart and sweet. It's a shame she lost her mother."

"Yeah? It's more of a shame she lost her father."

They neared the truck, and he turned toward his camp. "Good night, Margie."

"Goodnight, Mr. Hoyt."

Margie climbed into the truck, unrolled her pallet, undressed and lay down, but it was a long time before she went to sleep.

Chapter 5

Alvin came to the camp as Margie was pouring water on the breakfast fire. He had what appeared to be a map in his hand.

"Mornin'. It looks like it'll be a fine day."

"Yes, it does."

He then went to the side of the truck where Elmer was putting away his tools.

"I figure that if we get on down through Tulsa to Sapulpa, it'll be a long enough day. What do you think?"

"Fine with me, but what about Foley?"

"If his radiator lasts until Tulsa, he can get it fixed there."

"How long would we have to wait for him?"

"As long as it takes. The agreement we made when we started was that we'd stay together. He'd have to wait for one of us if something went wrong. There are four of us now. I'm glad we ran into Hoyt. It would take a brave or a foolish bunch to mess with us now."

"I don't know. Something about that fellow rubs me the wrong way," Elmer said.

On the other side of the truck, Margie became alert at the mention of Brady Hoyt's name. She had been looking off toward the Putman camp watching Rusty shave and wondering how in the world he could use a straight-edge razor without being able to see.

"What do you mean?" Alvin asked.

"He came out of nowhere. We don't know him."

"I'd met you only a few times when we decided to hook up and make this trip together."

"That's different. I knew about you for several years. Being in the ice business, you'd probably heard about me."

"Why didn't you say you were leery of Hoyt last night? The three of us discussed it and agreed to ask him to join us."

"Don't you think it's strange that a man would travel with a female kid that ain't his? It don't appear to me to be somethin' a feller on the up-and-up would do. He could be akidnapping that kid."

"Tarnation, Elmer. Andy Payne said he'd known Hoyt for years. Knew his family."

"Another thing. How do we know that fellow was Andy Payne? 'Cause he said so?"

"Why would he lie?" Alvin stepped back and looked at Elmer like he'd not seen him before. "He didn't come right out and say he was Andy Payne, the man who won the Bunion Derby. Rusty recognized the name and asked him if he was the racer. He and Rusty talked about stuff that only the real Andy Payne would know."

Elmer ignored Alvin's logic. His stubbornness began to irritate Alvin.

"Times are hard all over, Alvin. I don't need to tell you that. Boxcars are full of hoboes riding the rails looking for work. There's fellers out there that'd cut your throat for a dollar."

"I know that, Elmer. I'm glad to have another man with us," Alvin insisted. "I hope Hoyt stays with us all the way to California."

"If the kid gets sick, it'll slow us down."

"If that happens, we'll handle it when the time comes. A bank here in Oklahoma is robbed almost every day," Alvin argued. "Bootleggers are running up and down the highway day and night, hijacking cars and trucks. Alone in a campground, we would be sitting ducks. Our trucks, with their heavy springs for hauling ice, would be perfect for hauling booze."

"You don't think the three of us and the Luker boy could hold off a bunch of cowardly bootleggers?"

"I wouldn't call them cowardly. I'd call them dangerous crooks. We've got to keep together for the sake of our families."

"How many more are you going to want to take in?"

"Christ, Elmer! Don't put this on me. You could have had your say last night." Alvin folded the map and put it in his pocket. "We should stop and noon before we get to Tulsa. Do you want to take the lead?"

"No. You're doing fine. I'll look for you along the way."

"If something happens that we get separated, the next campground is west of Sapulpa after we cross the Rock Creek. The bridge has a brick deck. Turn off at the next road on your left. There's a place where we can camp, or so the man who drew me the map said. He didn't swear to it." Plainly irritated with Elmer, Alvin went on to speak to the Lukers.

Margie filled her fruit jar with water and got into the truck. Not a word had passed between her and her father since the afternoon before when he called her mother a whore. This morning he appeared when breakfast was ready, picked up his coffee mug, his plate of raw-fried potatoes and the last of the white bread she had toasted on the grill, and went to sit in his usual place on the running board of the truck.

Margie had been frying the potatoes when she saw Brady and Anna Marie going to the Putman camp. A few minutes later Grace and Anna Marie had gone to the woods. How much easier it would have been for Brady, Margie thought, if Anna Marie had been a little boy. It must be difficult for a five-year-old girl just to tell her uncle she needed to go to the outhouse or the woods.

Later Margie had heard talk and laughter coming from the Putmans' camp, and she envied the family's closeness. To go to California had been her dream; but the first attempt had ended in disaster, and now this second attempt to get there was total misery — not the hardship of the trip, but being with a father who hated her and hated having her along.

Now, as they followed the Putmans out of the campground, Brady was tossing a ball to Anna Marie. They were waiting to follow the Lukers, who were packing up to leave. They're always lagging behind, Margie thought, and wondered how long it would take Brady Hoyt to get tired of waiting for them.

By midmorning, after weaving slowly through the construction workers on the highway, they drove into Claremore, the home of the famed cowboy actor Will Rogers. Margie was well aware that he didn't live here but in California, where he made movies. She would like to see the big house where he was born and spent his childhood, she thought wistfully, but she doubted that she'd get the chance.

Elmer stopped at a gas station. After filling the gas tank, the attendant brought out a rubber hose and filled the water keg in the back of the truck. After he had paid the attendant, Elmer drove to a grocery store. He didn't say a word to Margie when he left to go inside. He returned with a paper sack, put it in the back of the truck and continued down the street to an ice dock.

Margie had debated about letting him know that they were out of ice, but she decided not to break her silence until he did. He took a pair of ice tongs from the long box attached to the side of the truck where he kept his tools and disappeared inside the icehouse. Margie got out of the truck, let down the tailgate and put down the box they used for a step. She got back into the truck telling herself she had done that to keep him from setting the block of ice on the ground and getting it dirty.

On the way out of town they passed two motor inns and a souvenir shop with a sign proclaiming it an Indian trading post. Margie remembered that when she passed through Claremore the year before with Ernie Harding, a man at a gas station told her that Claremore had been a busy Indian trading center back in the olden days and had been named for an Osage chief. He said that Will Rogers's home was between Claremore and Oologah, but that Will claimed Claremore as his home because nobody but an Indian could pronounce "Oologah."

She smiled thinking about it and remembered that Will Rogers had said that he had never met a man he didn't like. He must be a terribly nice man because she had met plenty of men she didn't like. Ernie Harding, the man who had stolen her money, for one. And, in spite of the guilty feeling about it, her father was another.

A few miles out of Claremore they stopped behind the Putmans, who had pulled off the highway and onto a space on the inside of a curve. It was flat and grassy with timber to one side. Elmer took off immediately for the patch of brush and scrub oak.

Margie had laid out the cold fish and corn bread on the tailgate when the Lukers arrived, and behind them Brady's black sedan.

"Margie! Margie!" Anna Marie called as she ran toward her. Then when she reached her: "Go to the woods with me . . . please. I gotta go . . . bad."

"Sure, honey." Margie flipped a cloth over the food on the tailgate to protect it from flies and took the child's hand. The two of them ran for the small patch of woods. They didn't speak until Anna Marie had hiked up her dress and Margie had unbuttoned the back flap of her drawers.

The child looked up at Margie with tear-filled eyes. "I had to go so bad —"

"Your uncle would have stopped."

"I didn't want to tell him. I miss Granny Maude."

"I bet she misses you too."

"Daddy took me to Granny Maude when . . . he had to work." Anna Marie choked back a sob. "I . . . don't have any . . . paper."

"I have some right here in my pocket. Do you want me to help you?"

94

"Yes, ma'am." More sobs. "I'm . . . nasty . . ."

Margie knelt down. "You're just a little nasty, honey. When we get back to the truck, we'll get inside and I'll wash you with a wet cloth." She wiped the tears from Anna Marie's face with the edge of her skirt.

Brady was waiting by the truck. "I was worried when you took off like that, Punkie." His eyes flicked to Margie, then back to his niece. He knelt down, studied her face, and saw evidence of tears. "Are you all right?"

"Uh-huh."

He stood and took her hand. "Mrs. Putman has a treat for you."

"I can't go . . . yet." The child looked pleadingly at Margie.

"I've something to show her in the truck. I'll bring her over in a few minutes." Margie held Brady's eyes with hers before taking Anna Marie's hand. "Come on, honey." She climbed into the truck and turned to help Anna Marie get in. Brady was there and lifted the child up. Their eyes caught again and held, then he nodded and walked away.

Anna Marie was in a much better mood when she and Margie walked over to where the Putmans were parked. Grace came to

95

meet them with a big smile of welcome.

"There's my pretty girl." She grabbed Anna Marie and gave her a hug, then said, "Hello, Margie. How are you standing the trip so far?"

"So far, all right."

"I'm enjoying every bit of it. I always did like to see new things. I chatter about everything to Rusty. We're about to drive Alvin wild. When he gets tired of us, he sings and drowns us out," she said with a giggle.

Lucky you, Margie thought, then said, "See you tonight, Grace."

Margie was aware that Brady was squatted on the ground beside Rusty, and Blackie lay sprawled on his belly close by. Margie could feel Brady's eyes on her. She had taken less than a dozen steps back toward the truck when he appeared beside her.

"Margie, wait a minute. What was that all about?"

"She had to go to the outhouse," Margie said without looking at him.

"Good Lord. I thought she was hurting someplace."

"She was."

"Why didn't she tell me? I would have found a place to stop."

"She was embarrassed. She . . . had a little accident."

"Good Lord. Poor kid. I don't know much about taking care of kids — never been around 'em, especially little girls."

"You'd better learn fast. It's a long way to California."

Elmer appeared from around the back of the truck and stood quietly watching them.

"Thanks, Margie." Brady tipped his hat and turned back toward the Putmans.

When they pulled onto the road again, Anna Marie was sitting between Alvin and Grace, and Rusty was riding with Brady.

"Did you see that?" Sugar Luker, waiting in the car for Jody and Foley to tie the tarp down over their two-wheel trailer, spoke over her shoulder to Mona when the Putmans passed. "The little girl is riding with the Putmans. Well, well. It looks like the blind dolt is going to ride with Brady."

"Don't call him that!" Mona said sharply.

"I'll call him whatever I want, Miss Ugly Muffin, and you'd better not talk to me in that tone of voice if you know what's good for you."

"Yeah, I suppose you'll tattle to Daddy."

"Now what's goin' on?" Foley slid in under the wheel, and Sugar moved to the middle of the seat to sit close to him.

"Nothin' important, darlin'. I was just remarking that the little girl is riding with the Putmans and their son is riding with Mr. Hoyt. Mona is having one of her grouchy spells. If you say one little thing to her, she blows up."

"She called Rusty a dolt. I told her not to call him that just because he's blind."

"I said colt." Sugar moved her hand up on the inside of her husband's thigh.

"You did not! You said dolt. You know you did. You're just trying to make me out a liar." Mona shook off her brother's warning hand.

"That's enough, Mona," Foley said sharply. He started the car and pulled out onto the highway. "I'm glad Brady knew about plugging holes in radiators. I hope it holds. I don't want to have to put in a new one."

"Did he say what he's going to do when he gets to California?" Sugar asked.

"Turn around and come back as far as Colorado. He's got some ranchland out there."

"Then what's he doing here?"

"He came to take his brother's little girl to her aunt somewhere in California."

"Couldn't he afford to take the train?"

"I didn't ask him. We're going to have to break camp earlier in the morning from now

98

on. And pack up faster." Foley looked in the mirror on the side of the car to see what was behind him. "If Hoyt is going to follow us, he isn't going to want to wait for us every morning."

"Tell that to Jody and Mona. Before we started I told you that I'd never camped out in my life and didn't know the first thing about cooking over a campfire. I wanted to go on the train. Remember?" she said with a pout in her voice.

"I know that. The train costs more. We've got to have enough money to start a business in California. This is the cheapest way for us to get there."

"You're right. You always are, darlin'." She squeezed his thigh. "I'll do the best I can."

"That's all I ask, honey."

"We should offer to let Brady's niece ride with us part of the time. Jody could ride with Brady."

"She'd ride with him if given half a chance," Mona mouthed to her brother.

"Mona would give her eyeteeth to ride with him," Sugar said to Foley in a low, confidential tone. "But, darling, we must be careful with our young lady. I think he's a little too old and too experienced for her. A footloose man will take advantage of a *green* girl if he gets a chance."

"I think you're jumping the gun, but if it will make you any happier, I'll keep an eye on her."

In the backseat Mona clenched her hands into fists. Her face was set in hard, angry lines. She rolled angry eyes toward her brother. He shook his head, silently asking her not to let Sugar goad her into another set-to that would just upset their father.

When Foley pulled over and stopped to check the radiator, Brady pulled in behind them. Foley had already lifted the hood by the time Brady got out. The stop also gave Blackie a chance to get out and sniff around.

"Lost any water?" Brady asked.

"Not a drop," Foley said, grinning.

"Then it looks like it'll hold. Save your tinfoil, though, just in case."

With the hood up so that the men couldn't see inside the car, Sugar turned and thumbed her nose at Mona.

"You're a bitch!" Mona said softly.

"Yes, I am," Sugar agreed with a wide, pleased smile. "And it's a hell of a lot of fun!"

Brady was enjoying Rusty's company. The miles flew by while they discussed everything from music to politics. Rusty was well informed.

"I'm not sure Roosevelt's New Deal is going to get the country back on its feet. I think what will do it will be the jobs created by making war supplies for England and France. That Hitler fellow has got absolute power in Germany now. He says he's going to purify Germany both ethnically and politically. What that means, I think, is that he wants to get rid of everyone who isn't a German. I'd bet my bottom dollar that he's gettin' ready to start a shootin' war."

"I've been kind of out of touch with what's going on for several months now," Brady admitted.

"I listened to all the news broadcasts when we were home. I'm missing it on this trip."

"Have you thought of getting a battery-powered radio?"

"They're big, bulky and expensive. I told Pa not to bother. I'll catch up when we get to where we're going."

"And where is that?"

"A town just south of Bakersfield. Pa, Mr. Kinnard and Foley Luker plan to start up an ice business. Out there ice sells year-round. In Missouri there's a lull during the winter months. Folks don't use much ice when it freezes every night."

"How long has Alvin known Mr. Kinnard?"

"He doesn't really know him. They met because they were in the same business and hitched up this plan with Foley Luker. Foley wasn't married then."

"He's hooked now." Brady followed his remark with a snorting sound.

"Ma gave me her version of his new wife." Rusty chuckled. "My mother can be a bit catty at times. She's got definite opinions on some things. I don't think she was far off the mark about Mrs. Luker. I asked Margie, and she said almost the same, only in a softer way."

"Luker seems to be a pretty levelheaded guy except where she's concerned. A woman who'd flirt with another man behind her husband's back isn't worth shootin', to my way of thinkin'."

"She flirt with you, did she?"

Brady nodded, then realized Rusty couldn't see him. "Yeah," he said. "And with Andy Payne too. Andy said that she reminded him of a black widow spider. She scared the crap out of him. He couldn't get away from her fast enough."

"She's sure to give Mr. Luker trouble." Rusty reached back to scratch Blackie, who was lying on a crate behind the front seat. "He doesn't know it now, or maybe he doesn't care, but he'll lose his kids over her if he doesn't change his ways soon. Neither one of them will put up with her much longer."

"Mona is a pretty girl."

"Is she?"

Brady glanced over and saw the interest on Rusty's face. "Yeah. Pretty brown hair that hangs a little down on her shoulders. Big brown eyes. Curves in all the right places. Sixteen or seventeen, I'd guess. If I was ten years younger, I'd set my cap for her." He continued to glance at Rusty and caught his smile.

"How old are you, Brady? Do you mind my asking?"

"Naw, I don't mind. I'm twenty-nine."

"I'm twenty-two. I've been blind for twelve years."

"You've not let it stop you."

"It's stopped me on this trip. At home I knew my way around. I could go to town, to the barbershop, the post office and the grocery store. When we settle, it'll take me a while to learn my way around again, but I can do it."

"Alvin told me that you write songs. I'd like to hear some of them sometime. I listen to *Grand Ole Opry* from Nashville every chance I get, but I've never met a songwriter."

"You just haven't been in the right places. Before we get to California you'll be wanting to slam my guitar against a tree trunk." Rusty chuckled. "My folks think I can get a job singing on the radio. You know the old saying, a mother's love is blind? Well, in this case it's also deaf."

Brady laughed. He was surprised at how easy it was to visit with a blind person. He found himself describing things he had barely noticed before.

"We're crossing the Arkansas. I'm surprised they don't have a toll on this bridge. The river is wide at this point, but there's not much water down there."

Later he said, "Almost every other building is empty in these little towns we've been going through. There's a dirt road a little way over from the highway. I'm seeing several wagons. We just passed one piled high with household furniture and with a cow tied on behind. The folks must be moving on. I wonder how they got across the river. Maybe they came down from the north.

"I was damn lucky." Brady maneuvered the car around a stripped-down Model T that was barely moving. "I worked over near Rainwater and Ponca City when the oil first came in. They were paying good wages, and I saved enough to get a little start or I'd be riding the rails looking for a job."

"Pa said you're a rancher."

"Yeah. Me and another fellow have a little ranch in Colorado. My partner is Cherokee. There isn't anything about a horse, wild or tame, that he doesn't know about. He graduated from the Cherokee Seminary down at Tahlequah and is smart enough to do anything he sets his mind to. But all he wants to do is raise horses, which is fine with me. I met him through his sister and her husband while I was in Rainwater. Radna and Randolph Bluefeather are an unforgettable pair. Sometime I'll tell you about them — that is, if you're not already tired of hearing my voice. I don't know when I've talked this much."

"I appreciate every word. You paint a good picture. I've been able to see in my mind what you've been telling me."

"It looks like this is where we'll stop for the night." Brady followed the Lukers off the highway. "I bought a hunk of meat back there at the store. Do you reckon your mother would make us a stew?"

Chapter 6

The sun was dropping behind the western horizon when Elmer followed Alvin into the camping area west of Sapulpa. A rattletrap car, the two front doors missing, was already there, and three men were sitting or squatting on the grass nearby. Alvin drove to the far side of the area before stopping, leaving room for Elmer, Foley and Brady to pull in behind him.

Elmer stopped a good fifty feet behind Alvin, got out and stood watching Alvin motion for him to move closer. When he made no move to get back into the truck, Alvin came to speak to him.

"I think we should be closer tonight, Elmer. There's three men over there, and it looks to me like they're boozin' it up."

"They're not camping. They'll move on out pretty soon."

On hearing Elmer's curt words, Alvin opened his mouth, closed it, glanced at the three men on the other side of the campground, then spoke with exaggerated calm.

"Well, I just thought I'd mention it."

Margie got out of the truck. Elmer Kinnard was stubborn as a mule! Frustration rolled through her. During the hours she had been cooped up in the truck with him he had not said one word. She had made up her mind during the afternoon that she would endure whatever she had to endure because every day brought her closer to California.

But how long would Alvin put up with Elmer being so obstinate? Her fear was that the others would cut them loose and leave her alone with him. Oh, Lord! What would she do?

She would sacrifice her pride and beg Brady Hoyt to take her with him and Anna Marie, if it came to that.

Margie had tried to look at one of her movie magazines during the afternoon, but the jolting in the truck gave her a headache, and she had to lay it aside and sit silently watching the landscape go by. It had been a long, cheerless afternoon, and she was glad

107

it was time to stop for the night.

Desperately needing a little conversation, and caring not a whit if Elmer liked it or not, Margie headed for the Putman truck to speak to Grace and Anna Marie.

"Margie, guess what?" Anna Marie, clinging tightly to Grace's hand, called as she approached.

"What? Tell me quick." Margie hadn't spoken a word since noon, and her voice seemed rough to her when she answered the child.

"Aunt Grace is teaching me the ABC song."

"Forevermore! I'll have to hear it," Margie exclaimed. "Your uncle will be surprised."

"We were just talking about that, wasn't we, Annie?" Grace cupped the child's head and held it to her side. "When I told her that our son's name was Russell Allen, but we call him Rusty, she decided that she'd like to be called Annie."

"Oh, but Anna Marie is such a pretty name."

"You can still call me Anna Marie, Margie."

"I think I will, if you don't mind."

"I don't mind. I like to ride with Aunt Grace. Can I ride with you sometime?"

Margie didn't know what to say. She was afraid of what Elmer's reaction would be if she invited the child to ride with them. Anna Marie wouldn't understand his refusal to talk to her.

The Lukers came in and parked close behind Elmer's truck, and Brady's car moved around to close the space between Elmer's truck and the Putmans'. Brady was taking a bundle off the top carrier on his Model A Ford when Anna Marie broke loose and ran to him.

"Uncle Brady! Want to hear me sing the ABC song?"

"Sure! Punkie, let her rip."

"A B C D E F G, H I J — that's all I know. Aunt Grace said I learned fast. Mr. Putman sang with me."

"He did, huh?"

"He knows lots of songs. He knows one about old MacDonald. And he knows how to go hee-haw, hee-haw. Maybe he'll show you."

"I've always wanted to know how to go hee-haw." Brady smiled down at the child. At times she reminded him so much of his lighthearted brother that his heart would stumble and almost stop.

"I'm goin' to play with Blackie."

"Stay close, Punkie."

"I will." Anna Marie ran toward the Putman camp, and Brady wondered how he had ever thought he could make the trip alone with a five-year-old girl. He thanked God for the kindness of Mrs. Putman and for Margie. He wanted to talk to her and waited until he saw Elmer walk off toward the woods.

Brady went to the back of Elmer's truck. Margie was inside kneeling beside the cupboard. "Margie —" It startled her when he spoke her name. She rose to step from the truck. Brady reached in and grasped her around the waist. Before she could protest, he had lifted her down as easily as if she were no heavier than Anna Marie.

"Oh, my! I'm too big for that!"

"Big? I doubt you weigh much over a hundred pounds dripping wet."

"I do. About ten or fifteen pounds over."

"That still isn't very big." He stood there looking down at her with his remarkable green eyes squinted. "I'm leery of that group parked over there." He jerked his head toward the parked car and the men lounging on the grass beside it.

"Is that why you're wearing a gun?"

"It's best to be prepared," he said by way of an answer.

"Mr. Putman said as much."

"If they're going to pull something, they'll wait until dark."

"What could we do if they did? There's three of them."

"There are five of us counting Jody."

"Six counting me."

He grinned. "Does Elmer have a gun?"

"I don't know, but I do. It's just a little one, but I know how to shoot it."

"But would you?"

"Doggone right," she said staunchly. "A friend gave it to me before I left home. He took me out into the woods and showed me how to use it." She smiled into his eyes. "I confess that I can't shoot the eye out of a running jackrabbit, but I did hit a barn door a few feet away."

The twinkle in his eyes caused a blush to redden her face. "Will it fit in your pocket?"

"In my apron pocket." She glanced toward the Lukers' trailer, which Jody and Mona were unloading. "Do you think there'll be trouble?"

"I don't know. But it's best to look for it and be pleasantly surprised when you don't find it."

"Are you and Anna Marie eating with the Putmans?"

"We've struck a deal. I'll help furnish the grub, and Mrs. Putman will cook it." Brady looked past Margie to see Elmer at the front of the truck watching them. He spoke to him. "I was just telling your daughter that we'd better keep an eye on that bunch over there by the other car. Do you have a gun?"

"My squirrel rifle."

"Sometimes just a show of strength will cause a bunch bent on robbery to back off."

"What makes ya think they're goin' to rob us? They don't look dangerous to me."

"They may be just good old boys out boozin' it up. But I don't plan to be caught with my pants down if they've got something else in mind." Brady turned, then said, "See you, Margie."

Unable to understand Elmer's reasoning, Margie climbed back into the truck again and began to lay out the supplies for supper.

While Foley was putting up the pup tent, Jody built a cook fire. Sugar complained to Foley that the tent was too close to the trailer and car where Jody and Mona slept.

"They'll hear everything we say and . . . do," she whispered seductively. "They're with us all day. I want you all to myself at night."

"Just for tonight. Those fellows over there may spend the night here, and we shouldn't be too far away from the others."

"Whose idea is that? Alvin Putman's? He's an old fuddy-duddy, and his wife doesn't give me the time of day." Sugar knew how to use her voice. She had let it drop into a sorrowful tone.

"You might like her if you got to know her," Foley said. "Don't you think it's worth trying?"

"No, I don't. I only want you." Sugar hugged his arm and pressed her taut breasts against him.

"We have a long trip ahead of us. It will be more pleasant for all of us if we could be sociable."

"She don't like me."

"You don't know that."

"I wasn't going to tell you, darlin', but Mr. Hoyt keeps looking at me. He was stealing glances all the time he was fixing the radiator."

"I can't blame him for that, Sugar. I like to look at you too."

"But, darlin', he looks at me like . . . like he wants to see me without my clothes on."

"If he bothers you, I'll put a stop to it."

"But . . . but he scares me."

"Don't worry. I'll watch him."

"I'm glad, so glad, I've got you to take care of me." Sugar knew when to back off after she had planted her little seed of distrust, and changed the subject. "I'm trying so hard to make Mona into a young woman you'll be proud of, but every time I open my mouth she cuts me off." Sugar pouted and snuggled against Foley.

"She'll come around. By the end of this trip the two of you will be the best of friends. I'm counting on it."

"I hope so, darlin'. I really do. Jody takes her side. He spoils her. I like Jody. I really do. He's such a sweet boy."

Mona stirred the burning embers of the campfire before she placed the kettle of beans her brother had cooked the night before on the grate. She glanced with resentment at the tent where she could hear the low voice of her father and the giggles of her stepmother.

Embarrassed that her father would be such a fool over a woman so shallow and conniving, Mona sought to busy herself to keep from thinking about what was going on in the tent. She had begun to ladle the corn bread batter into the skillet when she looked up to see two men approaching. She glanced quickly over her shoulder. Jody wasn't in sight.

"Somethin' smells mighty good." The man who spoke had a pleasant, clean-shaven face. He was younger than his companion and wore a billed cap.

Mona stood with the pancake turner in her hand. Jody came from around the trailer and placed the bowls he carried on a box near the fire.

"What do you want?" he demanded.

"We were wonderin' if ya could spare a meal? We ain't et all day, and what you got there looks and smells larrupin.' " The man eyed Mona in such a way that his words had a double meaning.

Jody's eyes went from one man to the other and didn't like what he saw. Somehow the smile on the younger man's face struck him as being as false as a three-dollar bill.

"Pa," he called. When there was no answer, he called again, urgently. "Pa, come out here."

A full minute went by before his father came out of the tent, followed closely by Sugar. On seeing the men she tossed her hair back over her shoulders, pulled her shirt tightly down over her breasts and tucked it into the waistband of her skirt.

"Howdy, folks." The young man spoke to both, but his bold eyes were on Sugar.

"Where did you come from?" she asked, as if she hadn't already spotted the three men in the car at the end of the campground.

"We're from over there." The man gestured toward the car.

Sugar flounced over and took the turner from Mona's hand. "Haven't you ever seen a man before?" she whispered irritably. "You're burning the corn bread!"

Jody gave Sugar an angry glance, then spoke to his father. "They want a meal, Pa."

"Give it to them. Mona, dish them up a plate of beans. We have plenty."

"That's mighty good of ya, mister."

"Doesn't your friend want to eat?" Sugar asked, nodding her head toward the car where the other man sat on the running board.

"No, ma'am. He's kind of under the weather."

Mona ladled beans into two bowls and stuck in spoons. It was Jody who handed them to the men. The young one hadn't taken his eyes off Sugar, and she was well aware of it.

"Here's a nice, hot corn bread pancake." Sugar scooped up the bread and took it to the younger man, who had squatted on his heels to eat. When she leaned over to put it on his bowl, he looked down at her cleavage and boldly winked at her.

"Where you folks goin'?" The older man's eyes moved constantly.

"California," Sugar answered while giving him the corn bread. "We're in the ice business. We're going to build an icehouse in California."

"That right? I've not known anyone in the ice business."

Sugar laughed. "You should have come up to Joplin. We had a big icehouse up there."

"I suppose you sold it."

"Of course. How do you think we got the money to build another one."

"Sugar —," Foley admonished, and shook his head.

Jody's anxious eyes went to his father. *The stupid woman would get them killed.*

"Where's the corn bread batter, Mona?" Sugar was enjoying the stranger's attention. "And get a bowl for your father."

Mona ladled the batter into the skillet, then retreated. Jody had filled a bowl with beans for his father. He tried and failed to catch his eye when he took it to him. He was sure the bulge beneath the shirt of the older of the two men was a gun.

"Where are you fellows headed?" Foley asked.

"Here and there. Lookin' for work."

"You'll not find work sitting out here in a campground," Jody said, and nudged his sister back toward the trailer.

"Jody," Sugar scolded, "that wasn't very nice."

The younger man stood and placed his empty bowl on the box, then went back and sat down.

"That was a mighty good supper, ma'am. A good cup of coffee would top it off."

"We're short of coffee," Jody said.

"Since when?" Sugar asked. "Fill the coffeepot, Jody. I'd like a cup myself."

"If Pa don't catch on to her now, he never will," Mona whispered to Jody when they went to the back of the trailer where they stored the foodstuffs.

"The old one has a gun. Slip around to the other side and go tell Brady."

Jody rummaged in the trailer for a while to give Mona time to get past the Kinnards. He filled the pot with water from their water barrel and set it on the rack over the fire. He poked more sticks into the blaze and decided that he could use one for a weapon if it came to that.

"Where's Mona?" Sugar demanded. "This is her job."

"She went to the woods." Jody filled a bowl for himself and backed away from the fire so that he could watch both men.

"What do you know of the highway ahead?" Foley asked.

"Sixty-six is paved to Chandler." The younger man leaned back on his elbow, leered at Sugar and spoke to Foley. "Is she your wife?"

"She is."

"Thought maybe she was your daughter. She's pretty and kind of . . . young, ain't she? I'd give a pretty penny to get me a woman like that."

"Watch your manners," Foley snarled, and got to his feet.

"Can't blame a feller for lookin' and . . . hopin'."

Jody lifted the lid on the coffeepot and poured in a scoop of coffee. When he stepped back from the fire, he was relieved to see Brady Hoyt approaching.

"Ma'am." Brady tipped his hat toward Sugar. "Howdy, Foley."

"Howdy, Brady. Coffee'll be ready in a minute."

"Thanks." Brady stood with his thumbs hooked in his belt, his hand just inches away from the butt of his gun. "Where are you fellows headed?"

"That's what ever'body wants to know these days." The older man stood and backed up a couple of steps.

"Yeah." The younger man was still leaning on his elbow, stretched out on his side on the ground. "What would ya say if we told ya we ain't goin' nowhere? We're waitin' here to rob a train. Haw, haw, haw."

Brady's cold eyes settled on the man's face. "You're going to get mighty hungry before one comes along. Move on. You'll have better luck catching a train down by the railroad tracks."

"Are ya tellin' us to leave?"

"You heard me."

The older man's eyes flicked to Sugar, who was hanging on to Foley's arm. "The pretty woman give us beans and corn bread and invited us to stay for coffee."

"Is this a social visit, Mr. Hoyt?" Sugar asked frostily.

"I guess you could say that, Mrs. Luker."

"Then I suggest that you tend to your own business. We don't have to get your permission to invite folks to have supper with us. I don't appreciate you coming into our camp and telling our guests to move on."

"I'm sorry if I offended you."

"I asked Mr. Hoyt to come down," Mona said. "This is just as much my camp as yours. I've a right to invite him to come for coffee."

Sugar, forgetting herself and the role she

played, retorted angrily. "You think so? You're just a snot-nosed kid. You weren't getting any attention, so you switched your fat butt up there to get him."

The young stranger chuckled. He was enjoying the situation. His eyes darted to Foley, who had gripped his wife's arm and was frowning down at her. The older man continued to move back, one small step at a time. Jody scooped up an armload of sticks and dropped them on the fire. It blazed up, lighting the area and allowing them to see Alvin coming toward them, his shotgun in the back of the third man.

The older man made a move to grasp his own gun through his shirt.

"Don't," Brady said sharply, and drew his gun from the holster. "I've seen that trick before. Drop your hands. Get up and get over there beside him," Brady said to the younger man. "I can shoot both of you before you can reach the gun strapped to your leg."

Sugar shrieked and clung to Foley, making it impossible to depend on him for help.

"Put your hands on the top of your heads. Both of you." There was a ring of authority in Brady's voice. "Jody, get the gun under the shirt first. The bastard thought to turn sideways and shoot me through his shirt. The laughing jackass was going to lie on the ground, lift his leg and shoot. Nice dinner guests you have, Mrs. Luker."

Alvin urged the third man forward. "This one was creeping up on Kinnard's camp."

Sugar was wailing and hanging on to Foley. Brady gave her a look of disgust. When Jody handed him the gun he took from under the older man's shirt, Brady checked to see if it was loaded, then holstered his own gun.

"Come here, Jody. Take his gun and shoot 'em if they make a move. I'll get the gun off the braying jackass."

Brady walked over and swiftly kicked the man's feet out from under him. The would-be robber hit the ground. A stream of foul words came from his mouth.

"Watch your mouth. There's ladies present."

"Ladies? That hot tamale ain't no lady." He jerked his head toward Sugar. "She's a whore if I ever saw one. Give me five minutes with her, and she'd be on her back spreadin' and beggin'."

"Hush your filthy mouth!" Foley snarled.

Brady palmed the small gun he took from the holster strapped to the man's leg. "Turn over on your belly, put your hands behind you and keep them there."

"What'll we do with them?" Alvin, ignoring Foley, spoke to Brady.

"Tie 'em up. Got any rope, Jody?"

"Not much."

"I have some. Keep them covered, Alvin. I'll get it."

"Don't worry. This old scattergun would take all three of them down with just one little twitch of my finger."

As Brady passed Elmer's truck on his way to his car, Margie stepped out and confronted him. She had been standing behind the truck watching what was going on in the Luker camp.

"You were right," she said.

"They're a dumb bunch."

"What are you going to do?"

"Tie them up for the night. Before we leave in the morning we'll turn them loose or send the sheriff out for them."

"What'd they do?" Elmer's voice startled Margie. She hadn't known he was near.

"They had robbery on their minds. Alvin caught one of them sneaking up on you with a gun in his hand."

"Fiddlesticks! I've been keepin' my eyes open. I didn't see anything. They're just down-and-outters wantin' a meal."

The man was an idiot.

Brady shook his head in dismay and moved so that his body blocked Elmer from seeing him pat the pocket on Margie's apron to assure himself the pistol was there.

"I'll talk to you later. Okay?" he whispered, then squeezed her arm and moved on.

Chapter 7

"What would they have done after they robbed us?" Jody asked.

The would-be robbers had been bound hand and foot and each tied to a wheel of their old car.

"My guess would be that they'd have disabled the other cars, taken mine and left with one of the women as a hostage, most likely Mona," Brady replied.

"Why Mona?" Jody asked, glancing at his sister, who stood beside Rusty and Blackie. "Why not Sugar? She was the one playing up to them. She told them that Pa had sold his icehouse, letting them know he had money to start another business."

"Your pa better put a muzzle on her, or he'll never make it to California." Alvin spoke firmly, and all eyes went to him. He moved to stand behind his wife, who had a sleeping Anna Marie cuddled in her lap. He put his hand on her shoulder, then said, "With shenanigans like that, she could get us all killed."

"The young one flirted with Sugar," Jody said, "but he was watchin' Mona."

Mona gasped and began to sputter. "Well . . . why, that gutter trash! I . . . I wouldn't look at him if he had gold and silver hanging all over him!"

A nervous little laugh came from Jody. "Sugar would be mad as hops if she knew there was a man alive that preferred Mona over her."

Elmer had let the campfire die down and had taken his blankets to the edge of the woods and bedded down. Margie was embarrassed that he hadn't offered to take part in securing the would-be robbers. Not that he had been needed. Brady had been very efficient in handling the situation, giving Margie cause to believe that he had done something like this before.

"I'll keep an eye out tonight," Brady was saying. "Not that I think those fellows are going anywhere."

"I'll spell you in taking a watch." Alvin's statement was echoed by Jody.

"Blackie and I can take a turn," Rusty offered. "Nothing moves that he doesn't know about."

"That makes four of us," Brady said, accepting Rusty's help. "Assign us two-hour shifts, Alvin."

"Thanks for what you did," Grace said. "I thank my lucky stars we ran into you, Brady Hoyt."

"It's a two-way street, ma'am." Brady went to where Grace sat with Anna Marie. He lifted the child in his arms. "Thanks for looking after her. I'll bed her down in the car."

One of Anna Marie's shoes slipped off. Margie picked it up, followed Brady to his car and opened the door. The space between the two seats had been filled with their belongings, and on them was what appeared to be a mattress from a crib. Brady placed the child on the bed and removed her other shoe and her stockings. After flipping a sheet over her he softly closed the door.

"I throw a bedroll down here beside the car in case she wakes up in the night. The first night, she woke up crying for her daddy. It about busted my heart." He reached for Margie's arm when she turned to leave. "Stay with me for a while. It isn't late."

"I could take a watch —"

"No. I don't want you sitting here in the dark by yourself with everyone else asleep."

"We can build up the fire."

"Those fellows are puredee trash. They have filthy mouths. There's enough men to keep watch."

"Brady," Foley Luker called as he approached. "I didn't get a chance to thank you and tell you that Sugar is sorry for the way she spoke to you. She felt sorry for the men."

"It's quite all right, Foley. We've got them trussed up. Each had a gun, and I found a shotgun in their car. I think they were waiting here for someone to rob. Four of us were a little more than they wanted to take on all at once, so they thought to rob you and get a hostage."

"I'da helped, but Sugar was upset —"

"Jody and Mona kept their heads and were a big help."

"Hey, cowboy," the voice of one of their prisoners came out of the darkness. Brady didn't answer, and the man called again. "Cowboy, I gotta piss."

Brady ignored him and spoke to Foley. "Maybe you should speak to Mrs. Luker and tell her that she should be more careful with the men she meets on the highway. Some of them are good, hardworking men down on their luck, but some are outlaws: bootleggers, thieves and hijackers."

"I've already told her that and cautioned her about mentioning we were going to California to start a business. She'll be careful from now on."

Margie closed her eyes and gritted her teeth. *Dear God, never, please never let me fall so desperately in love that I make a complete fool of myself like this man is doing.*

Brady's thoughts echoed Margie's. *You poor besotted fool.*

"I've got to shit too, cowboy." The voice was followed by laughter. "Can that pretty little gal take me to the woods?"

"Jody is taking one of the watches tonight," Brady said to Foley.

"Is that necessary?"

"I think it is."

"You've got them tied up, haven't you?"

"We want to make sure they stay that way."

"It's goin' to be a long night, cowboy. Where's that pretty little brown-haired gal? How about lettin' me fuck her to pass away the time? Trussed up like I am, she can give me a good ride."

Brady's patience came to an explosive end. "That came from one of your wife's supper guests, and he's talking about your daughter, Mr. Luker," he said with heavy sarcasm, and placed his hand on Margie's arm. "Stay while I take care of this. I don't want Punkie to wake up and find herself alone."

"Chester says he'll fuck the blonde with the titties if she'll help him get it up." Raunchy laughter came out of the darkness.

Brady went swiftly to the Putman camp and pulled a long stick out of the blazing fire.

Holding it like a torch, he carried it ahead of him to where the three men were tied.

"All right, smart-mouth," he snarled. "Repeat what you just said. Come on, say it again if you've got the guts. Say it so I can shove this torch down your throat." He swung the blazing stick so close to the man's face it singed his eyebrows.

"Hey, cut it out! I was just . . . jokin'. Hey!" he yelled again. "Yo're burnin' me."

"Not so brave now, are you, horseshit? Listen up. I'm saying this one time. If any more filth comes from your mouth, I'll shove this fire stick up your ass. Understand?" The man silently cringed away from the blaze. Brady swung it back and forth in front of his face. "Understand?" he said again.

"Yeah! Yeah! Are ya crazy? Ya burned me!"

130

"I meant to. What's your name? Give it to me straight, or I'll burn every hair off that bump on your shoulders."

"Persy. Homer Persy."

"Homer Pussy. Suits you. You're messin' with a real hard-ass when you mess with me, Pussy. You think you're tough. Where I come from you wouldn't last five minutes."

"Name's Persy. You . . . burnt me —"

"That little singe is just a start. I don't mess around with piles of shit like you. I could sit here and whistle 'Yankee Doodle' while you burn to a crisp and warm myself at the fire." Brady stood and looked down at the other two men. "That goes for all of you. If you want to see daylight, keep your mouths shut."

"We've not said nothin'," one of the men muttered.

"A word of warning. If this shithead gets me riled up enough, he'll be greeting the devil before morning. And naturally I'll not leave any witnesses. It'll be to your advantage to keep him quiet."

Brady gave each man a long, hard stare, then walked away before he allowed himself to grin. He returned the stick to the campfire.

"They'll be quiet."

"I don't like what he was saying," Jody said.

"Don't let it bother you. It's what you'd expect from their kind."

"Rusty is going to take the first watch," Alvin explained. "Mona said she'd like to stay awhile. When Rusty's time is up, Jody will take a turn. He'll wake me, and I'll wake you near morning."

"I'm sorry Pa isn't . . . able to help." Jody stumbled over the words. "He's not been the same since he met . . . her."

"Don't worry about it, son." Alvin put a hand on the boy's shoulder. "Maybe it's best that he stay and keep an eye on her. She might get to feeling sorry for them and cut them loose."

Brady went back to his car. Margie had opened the front door and was sitting sideways on the seat, her feet on the running board. She slid out of the car as he approached and stood beside it.

"Don't go." It seemed to Brady that he was always saying that to her. "Rusty and Mona are taking the first watch. Then Jody. Alvin is next, and he'll wake me for the early morning watch."

"Then you'd better get some sleep."

"I'd rather talk to you. Let's sit in the car for a while."

"I'm sorry about Elmer. I could take his place," Margie said after she had gotten back into the car and moved over on the seat to make room for him.

"I thought we'd covered that."

"We're part of this caravan. We should do our part."

"I'll do your part. You're helping me with Punkie." He turned sideways to look at her. His arm went over her head to rest on the back of the seat behind her. "Tell me to mind my own business if I'm speaking out of turn. But you and Elmer don't seem like a father and daughter to me."

"He is my father! Do you and the others think that there's something fishy about me being with him? You can ask anyone back in Conway, Missouri, and they will tell you that Elmer Kinnard is my father."

"Hold on. I didn't mean to get you riled up. It's just . . . well, forget it."

"No, I won't forget it. My mother was Elmer's second wife. She died when I was little. He sent me to live with my grandmother and had nothing more to do with me. We lived in the same town, but I might as well have lived at the North Pole as far as he was concerned."

Once she started talking, the words poured out. She told him about her dream to go to California and about the disastrous trip the year before.

"Elmer's third wife left him a month or so ago. He came to the café where I worked and said he'd sold his ice business and was going to California and I could go with him. Here I am. I didn't know how much he disliked me until we were on the way. I want to see Hollywood. I'm determined to put up with him until I get there."

While she was talking Brady's hand had slipped off the seat behind her and gripped her shoulder. Neither one of them seemed to be aware of it.

"Then what will you do?"

"Get a job."

"It may not be easy finding a job that will support you."

"I'll find one."

"If Elmer dislikes you, why did he ask you to come with him?"

"I've wondered about that. It may be because he wasn't sure if he would stick with Mr. Putman and Mr. Luker, and he'd rather have me with him than to go on alone. I just found out that he dislikes me because of my mother."

"That seems unfair."

"Not to Elmer. I don't know what has made him so cantankerous, so cynical. I'm afraid that the others will get so disgusted with him that they'll cut us out of the caravan."

"If that should happen, we'll find a place for you."

"I have some money —" She turned to find his face close to hers and pulled back. "I've been running off at the mouth, haven't I? You've hardly said a word."

"It must be a long day riding in a car without someone to talk to. I have Punkie. I'm getting used to carrying on a conversation with a five-year-old."

"It's not so bad. I have plenty of time to daydream."

"What do you dream about?" His hand now was stroking her shoulder and arm.

"Oh, this and that. Mostly about Hollywood. I just want to see it and . . . the movie stars." Her heart was beating too fast. It was making her breathless. "Enough about me. What will you do when you get to California?"

"I'll take Punkie to her Aunt Opal and hope that Becky's sister wants her."

"Oh, she will. How could she not want her sister's little girl?"

"I sent her a wire. She said to bring her, but they may not take to each other. Opal may be like Punkie's mother."

"Oh."

"Yes, oh. You're too polite to ask, so I'll tell you that Punkie's mother was . . . not

135

very motherly. My brother was both mama and daddy to her."

"That's too bad. She loves you. Can't you take her to your home and keep her if you're not sure that Opal will be a good mother to her?"

"I can't keep her on a horse ranch ten miles from a town without a woman to take care of her. And she needs to be where she can go to school. I have the money from my brother's house, and this car belonged to him. I'll sell it when we get to California and leave the money with Opal. Then I'll send a little now and then, to help out."

"My grandmother said that children need love or they'll grow up like weeds and not flowers."

"What are you? A rose? A daisy? I know, you're a Missouri bluebonnet." When he chuckled, she felt the vibration against her arm.

"I didn't mean that I'm a flower. I'm more like a weed. A pesky one that pops up among the petunias!"

"I don't believe that for a minute." He sniffed. "You smell like a honeysuckle vine." His arm tightened.

Margie's heart fluttered like a hummingbird loose in her chest. Her shoulder was tucked under his arm. She was pressed to his warm, hard body from hip to knee.

He reached for the hand in her lap. "If I kiss you, will you slap me or yell? I prefer the slap. You'll wake Punkie if you yell."

Surprised, she turned to look at him. His lips swooped down on hers. His kiss was hard and quick. A groan came from him when he lifted his head.

He pressed his forehead to hers. "Ah . . . sweet girl! It didn't do the trick." He spoke in an agonized whisper.

Unable to utter a sound, she waited for him to explain.

"I've wanted to do that since I first saw you. I thought that once I'd kissed you, I'd get you out of my system." He lifted her hand and pressed it palm-down over his heart. "Feel that? When I'm near you, it takes off like a wild mustang." *And sweetheart, that's not all that comes to attention, but I can't tell you about that now.*

"Maybe if I kissed you again, slowly, the ache would go away." His whispered words were seductive, his breath warm on her wet lips.

"You could try . . . it."

He turned her so that her breasts flattened against his chest, and he skipped his fingers up and down her spine. He ran his tongue over her lips, then kissed her

137

soundly, deeply, passionately. His lips left her mouth, moved to her cheek, her closed eyes, her brow. Then, as if he couldn't stay away, he kissed her parted lips again, knowing in some far corner of his mind that this wasn't going to banish his thoughts of her.

He suddenly feared that he would never grow tired of kissing her. Liking to kiss her was one thing, he told himself. Being wildly in love with her was another. Loving a woman would be more dangerous to his peace of mind than falling into a bed of rattlesnakes. He'd not make the same mistake his brother made. Nosiree! He had learned firsthand what comes from a man giving a woman his heart and soul.

He lifted his head and laughed a little, afraid for her to know just how near he had come to falling in love with her. It was foolish to even think that they would hitch together even if he did decide that she was the one to share his life, but not his heart. All he had was half of a ragtag horse ranch, and she had dreams of Hollywood — of all places! He loosened his arms to allow her to lean back away from him.

"Well, now. We've got that out of the way."

His words were like a dash of icy water. She felt them all the way to the tips of her toes. She took a deep breath before she could speak.

"Yeah, we did. Now I've got to get back."

Brady got out of the car and took her hand to help her out. "Thanks for staying with Punkie."

"You're welcome. Good night." Margie hurried away, tears of disappointment blinding her.

Now that she and Rusty were alone, Mona could think of nothing to say. Her tongue clung to the roof of her mouth. She hugged her sweater around her, for the evening breeze was still cool, and looked her fill of him, knowing that he wouldn't know — or at least she didn't think he would. He sat quietly with the shotgun beside him and Blackie's head beneath his hand. Jody had built up the campfire before he left, and in the flickering light she could see Rusty's eyes turn in her direction.

"Mona? Tell me what you see." His voice was little more than a whisper. "You were looking at me."

"How did you know?"

"I'd be looking at you . . . if I could see."

"Your hair is dark red and . . . your hands are . . . nice."

He held his hand out toward her. "Come

closer. I don't want our staked-out friends to hear what we say."

She moved across the blanket to sit close, but not touching him. His hand came in contact with her upper arm. He moved it after he had touched her.

"Tell me what you look like. I already know that you're pretty."

"Who told you that?"

"Brady. He said if he was younger, he'd set his cap for you."

"You're kiddin'! He didn't say that."

"He did. He said you have brown hair. Do you mind if I touch it?"

"Ah . . . no."

He took a strand of her hair and rubbed it between his thumb and forefinger. Then with the palm of his hand he stroked her hair from the crown of her head to the ends.

"It's soft," he said as if to himself. "And thick."

"I usually wash it in rainwater." Her heart was beating so fast she feared it would jump out of her chest.

"It feels like silk. May I touch your face?" he asked after he had threaded his forked fingers through her hair at the nape of her neck.

He touched her cheek and paused, waiting for permission to continue. She turned on her knees facing him and lifted his other hand to her face. Her breath caught as he ran his fingers over her chin, along her jaw, and stopped at her lips.

"Full on the bottom, thin on the top," he whispered. "And unsmiling." Then, "Ah . . . that's how I imagined you. Lips tilting at the corners. Open your mouth . . . please." He moved the knuckle of his forefinger along the edge of her teeth. "Nice and even," he murmured.

His fingertips moved up the hollows of her cheeks and rested on the cheekbones. He trailed his fingers over her eyes and up to her brows, thick and straight.

"Big brown eyes," he murmured.

"How do you know?"

"Brady said they were brown. I can feel that they are big." With fingers from both hands at her temples he combed through her hair. "Thank you for letting me see you." His hands moved over her shoulders and down her arms. "You're not very tall."

"How do you know?" She released a giddy laugh. *How many times had she said that?*

"I just know. Your head will fit under my chin."

"I'm taller than that."

"Stand up and we'll see. And don't stand

on your toes. That would be cheating." After they had stood he grasped her upper arms and pulled her against him. Her chin touched his chest; his chin rested on the top of her head. She closed her eyes for one delicious moment. "See there," he said. "I was right."

Mona stepped back. "Brady told you."

"No. Your shoulder touched mine about halfway between the top of my shoulder and my elbow that first night. I knew then about how tall you were." He grasped her hand, and they sank back down onto the blanket.

"That's remarkable! I don't know how you know these things."

"It's not remarkable. When you can't see, your other senses, such as touch and smell, kick in. I can tell by the smell of vanilla when Ma is stirring up a cake and from the yeast when she sets bread to rise. I can tell by holding your hand that in the past you've worked hard, but not recently, because the roughness on your palm is softening. I know the things your stepmother says to you hurt you and are lowering your self-esteem. Don't let her do that to you."

"I don't know how to stop her," she confessed. "Pa is so smitten with her."

"He's bound to come to his senses soon.

Don't let her get your goat. If you do, she's won."

Mona said nothing. She knew that what he said was true. They sat quietly while minutes passed, their clasped hands resting on the blanket between them. She wished that she had something interesting to say, but could not think of a thing. When she realized that she was holding on to his hand as if it were a lifeline keeping her from being swept away by a flood, she was embarrassed and relaxed her grip a little.

"How old are you, Mona?" His voice was soft and even. No wonder he sang so beautifully.

"Seventeen. I'll be eighteen by the time we get to California. Jody is twenty."

"Brady thought you were about sixteen."

"I look young for my age because I don't wear a lot of rouge and lipstick."

"Paint? I've never seen a painted woman. If I have, I've forgotten about it."

"How long have you . . ."

"Go ahead and say it. How long have I been blind? Since I was ten. I'm twenty-two now."

"Then you remember what a lot of things look like."

He smiled. "Yes, and it gives me an advantage. When something is described to me, I see it in color. My mother and father will never grow old. In my mind I see them as they were twelve years ago."

"What do you miss the most?"

He thought for a minute before he answered. "I'd like to drive a car. I know I never will. I'm resigned to it. I'd like to *see* a picture show. I've *heard* a few. I went to 'hear' *King Kong*. A friend and I sat up in the balcony, and he described it to me. It was exciting. Especially the last part when the ape was on the Empire State Building and the airplane was flying around. I'd sure like to know how the filmmaker did that."

"I've not been to many picture shows."

"I listen to the radio a lot. It puts me in contact with the whole world." He pulled a heavy pocket watch from the bib of his overalls and held it to his ear. "I heard it chime the half hour a while ago. The time has gone fast. Our two hours are almost up."

"I didn't know there was such a thing as a chiming pocket watch."

"I saved the money I earned playing my fiddle and singing for dances, weddings and even funerals. We ordered it from a company that imports from Germany. I doubt we'll get much more from there, except maybe trouble now that fellow Hitler has taken over."

"You know about a lot of things."

"I've been showing off for you." He laughed, his eyes on her face as if he were seeing her. "Do you think we can do this again?"

"What?" she said, pretending not to know. "Sit up and guard badmen?"

"You're smiling."

"You know everything!"

He tilted his head. "I know someone is coming toward us. I bet it's Jody." He held tightly to her hand and whispered as they stood. "Will you talk with me again?"

"Uh-huh."

"It's time I took over," Jody said. "I set my alarm. I'll walk you back to the car, sis."

"Thanks for staying with me, Mona."

"You're welcome," she murmured. Then nervousness struck her. She felt almost giddy. "Does Sugar know I stayed with him?" she asked her brother as they walked away.

"What do you care if she knows?"

"She'll have something nasty to say about it."

"Ignore her."

"That's easy for you to say. She's not on you like she is on me."

"Give her enough rope and she might hang herself. Pa will get his fill of her and come to his senses. If he doesn't, I'll get a job when we get to California, and we'll strike out on our own."

"He expects you to work in his ice business."

"I'll not work for him with her there."

"Oh, Jody, what can we do?"

"Nothing right now. But a lot can happen between here and California."

Chapter 8

The early morning sun was sending long fingers of light through the tops of the trees and shedding a pattern of lacy shadows on the campground when the three-car caravan pulled out. Anna Marie was with the Putmans again. Brady and Rusty stayed behind to wait for the sheriff. Grace's worried eyes stayed on her son for as long as she could see him.

"Stop worrying," Alvin urged.

"I can't help it."

"You're the one who insisted that we not coddle him. He's a man now, Gracie, not a boy. You've got to start treating him like one."

"But we don't know Brady very well. He's never been around a person who's blind. He told me so."

"We've got to trust him to look after Rusty just like he's trusting us to take care of Anna Marie."

Grace looked down at the sleeping child in her lap, and the thought came to her that if Brady wanted to be rid of the little girl, this was his chance. He knew that she and Alvin would take her as their own. Oh, Lord! What if he drove off and left Rusty in that campground?

"He's crazy about that kid," Alvin was saying, as if he knew what was in her mind. "She's the daughter of his twin. Did you know that?"

"She told me." Grace stroked the hair back from the child's face. "She said he looks just like her daddy and talks like him."

"Poor little tyke."

"She said sometimes she forgets he's her uncle and not her daddy."

"I wonder what happened to her parents. Brady hasn't said."

Grace placed her hand on her husband's thigh. "I can't help worrying about Rusty."

"Well, stop it." Alvin's hand left the wheel and patted hers to soften his command.

"We both know that he'll never be able to be completely on his own."

"I've heard of other blind people who are, and he's smart as any of them," Alvin said defensively. "He should marry and have a family like any normal man."

"He likes the Luker girl."

"That's a good sign. He likes Margie too."

"Not like he likes Mona."

"How do you know that, Miss Know-It-All?" Alvin teased.

"I just do. That's all. I don't want him to fall for her and have her break his heart."

"Don't borrow trouble. People don't die of a broken heart. My hope is that he finds a nice girl, marries and has kids who will love him and look after him when we're gone."

"I wish he liked Margie. She's a steady, sensible girl."

"Don't push the girl onto him, Grace."

"I won't, but I can wish, can't I?"

"He'll make that decision for himself. Brady accepted him in spite of his limitations, just as others have done. The right woman will see beyond his blindness and love him in spite of it."

They rode without speaking for a while. Then Alvin's chuckle broke the silence. He asked with a touch of pride in his voice, "Did you see how he handled the shotgun I put in his hands? The crooks didn't know he was blind."

"Why couldn't Brady have left the crooks tied up out there? The sheriff would get them. It's his job."

"Because he was afraid that if people came along and turned them loose, the crooks might kill them for their money and car," Alvin said patiently. "When we get to Sapulpa, I'll go straight to the sheriff's office. I told Brady we'd stop alongside the highway in Davenport. He'll meet us there."

"Mr. Kinnard is strange," Grace remarked after Alvin had turned to go into town and she looked back to see that Elmer had pulled to the side of the highway to wait. "I wonder why he's so unfriendly. His daughter is nothin' like him."

"Unfriendly? He's been downright ornery the last few days. He wasn't that way when we first talked of taking this trip."

"I've never heard him say a word to Margie. He acts like she isn't even there."

"That's their business, Gracie, and has nothing to do with us. Here we are at Sapulpa. Now, where is the sheriff's office?"

"Why do we have to wait here?" Sugar complained when Foley pulled over to the side of the highway and stopped. "Why do we always have to follow along behind the Putmans?"

"We agreed when we planned this trip that Alvin would lead the way. He knows where the campsites are."

"We could find them if he gave us the maps. Where's he going?"

"He's going into Sapulpa to tell the sheriff what happened and that Brady is waiting for him at the campground with the men who woulda robbed us."

"They looked so pitiful. I just thought they were hungry. I still don't think that they were going to rob us." Sugar let her lower lip tremble. "I guess everybody hates me."

"Nobody hates you." Foley wrapped his arm around the steering wheel and stared out the windshield.

"Yes, they do. I hate her guts!" Mona, in the backseat, mouthed silently to her brother.

"I explained to Brady and Alvin that you felt sorry for those guys and wanted to give them a meal." Foley turned to look long and hard at his wife.

Mona made a gagging gesture with her finger in her mouth. Jody shook his head at her, but he was grinning.

"I wish we could go on by ourselves. Just our little family." Sugar snuggled her face against Foley's neck.

"We can't do that. If we had been alone last night, the robbers would have taken everything we have. They might have killed us.

I'll not take that risk with my family."

"But, darlin' . . . I'm tired of traveling."

"Already? We've been gone only ten days."

"I want a bath. And I want to sleep in a real bed. With you," she added in a whisper.

"I explained that it would be a rough trip."

Sugar sniffed. "It's worse than I thought it would be."

"When we get to Oklahoma City, I'll see about getting a motor cabin for the night. How's that?"

"Would you? Oh, darlin', you are the sweetest thing." Sugar threw her arms around his neck and covered his face with kisses.

Mona looked at her brother and crossed her eyes. He burst out laughing.

Foley looked over his shoulder. "What tickled your funny bone?"

"Mona yawned and a fly flew into her mouth." Jody tried to keep a straight face while telling the lie to his father.

When Foley turned back to Sugar, who was snuggled against him, Jody winked at his sister. She put her hand over her mouth to control her giggles.

While waiting for the Putmans to come

152

back to the highway, Margie passed the time looking at her movie magazines. When Elmer got out of the truck and leaned against the fender to watch the traffic go by, her hands stilled on the magazine and she looked at him through the truck's dusty windshield. He stood with his arms folded across his chest, his old felt hat pulled down, shielding a face that, no doubt, showed not a trace of expression.

How could he be her father? Could her mother have had a secret lover? No, she told herself. If her granny had had the slightest suspicion that Elmer was not her father, she would have told her, because she had no use for the man at all. Oh, but she wished he were not so uncompromising and obstinate.

She had been embarrassed last night when he hadn't offered any assistance. And again this morning when he never thanked Alvin or Brady for removing the threat to all of them. She had no doubt that if she mentioned it to him, he would dump her out along the highway like so much garbage.

What would he say if he knew that Brady had kissed her? She answered her own question. Plenty. It would prove to him that she was the slut he believed her to be.

She had relived those kisses a hundred times. Brady's mouth had been warm and firm and had moved over hers with familiar ease. There had been nothing tentative or hesitant about the kiss. When he raised his head, his eyes had searched hers before he kissed her again. She had been stunned by his brazen action.

It hurt her that he considered kissing her as something to "get out of the way." She had walked away feeling as if her heart had been stomped on. But during the long sleepless night she had come to realize that she had only herself to blame. He was a man, after all, a very virile man. To be loved by a man like Brady Hoyt would be any girl's dream.

She could have protested. She could have slapped him as he suggested. Instead she had sat there and let him have his way with her.

It was going to be hard facing him in the light of day, but face him she must. The best way to handle the situation would be to act as if it had meant nothing at all to her. It had happened. There was nothing she could do about it now. But she could make sure that it didn't happen again and that he never know how his kisses had thrilled her to her curled-up toes.

Margie saw the Putman truck coming back to the highway and behind it a sheriff's car. Alvin stuck out his arm to signal a left turn. The Sapulpa sheriff turned right to go toward the campground. Elmer got back into the truck, and they were on their way again.

They passed through the towns of Kellyville, Bristow and Depew. The highway between Depew and Stroud was under construction, and Elmer had to dodge around the graders working to prepare it for paving. Stroud was a sleepy little town, but it had once been a tough, prosperous place. The Great Depression and Dust Bowl conditions were leaving deep scars on the towns and emotional wounds on the folks who lived in them.

A dozen years before, cattle drovers had shipped their animals from Stroud, but the bars that had made money selling illegal whiskey were gone, as were most of the businesses on the main street. The worst drought in recent history had reduced the price of wheat to thirty-three cents a bushel. The banks had foreclosed, and the families were moving on.

Davenport was merely a wide spot in the road. Alvin pulled over beneath a row of oak trees and stopped. To Margie's surprise, Elmer went on around him and pulled into a gas station. A big yellow dog got up, stared at them, then walked a few feet and flopped down again. After the man in grease-covered overalls put gas in the truck, Elmer followed him inside the small brick building, digging into his pocket for money to pay for the gas.

Margie looked back down the highway. Anna Marie and Grace were standing beside the truck. The Lukers were behind the Putmans. There was no sign of Brady's black sedan.

It was hot inside the cab of the truck even with the windows down and the windshield tilted to let in a breeze. A big blowfly came in the window, and Margie fanned it away with a movie magazine. Soon it got tired and flew out again. Minutes passed. She craned her neck to see inside the station. Elmer was sitting down, his legs stretched out in front of him, his hands clasped across his midsection, as if he planned to stay there awhile.

Margie needed to use the outhouse. She waited for what seemed to her a quarter of an hour before she got out of the truck and went to the door of the station.

"Mister," she said, and waited until the man acknowledged her. "May I use your outhouse?"

"Yes, ma'am. Ya just go right ahead and help yoreself."

"Thank you."

Margie was in the two-hole outhouse before it occurred to her that Elmer might go off and leave her, as Ernie Harding had done when she went to the outhouse at Andy's campground down near Sayre. She hurriedly finished what she had come to do and went back to the truck. She climbed into the back and filled a fruit jar with water from the keg. It was warm but wet, and soothed her scratchy throat. When she returned to the cab of the truck, she brought a handful of crackers and a hunk of cheese.

She ate slowly, and when she finished, Elmer still lounged in the chair inside the station. Margie suspected that he planned to spend the noon stop there so as to avoid talking to the others in the caravan. She went to the back of the truck again and wet a cloth to wipe her face, after which she spread on a layer of Pond's cream, enjoying the soothing effect on her windburned skin.

Later she fanned her face with the movie magazine, trying to brace up her sagging eyelids. But she fell asleep with her head resting against the back of the seat. When Elmer got into the truck and slammed the door, she woke with a start. He was eating a hot dog he must have bought at the small café across the street. Alvin's truck passed, and Elmer pulled out onto the highway and fell in line behind it. Margie looked back and was relieved to see Brady's sedan following the Lukers.

The afternoon passed slowly. After Chandler they went through several small towns. Near Arcadia, Margie spied the old round barn she had seen when she passed this way before and wondered what advantage it had over the rectangular barns with the big haylofts.

On the outer edge of Oklahoma City, they turned off the highway and followed Alvin into a field already occupied by four other campers. Elmer swung out and away from the others and parked with the back of the truck facing the campground. Margie got out and stretched. Brady passed and waved. She lifted a casual hand and began gathering firewood left by another camper.

Jody Luker came by while Margie was slicing potatoes into a skillet.

"Hi, Margie. I don't think we'll have any trouble tonight." He gestured toward the other campers. "They've all got kids."

"Have you heard what the sheriff had to say this morning when Brady turned over the men who might have robbed us?"

"No, but I'm on my way to find out."

She was opening a can of corn to serve over the fried potatoes when Jody came back by.

"Brady said the sheriff couldn't hold them because they hadn't actually committed the robbery, but he said he'd keep them there until we got on down the highway. Brady took some parts off their old car. He said it'd not be running anytime soon."

"I'm glad of that."

"Pa's unhooking the trailer. He promised Sugar they'd stay in a motor cabin tonight."

"You and Mona will stay here?"

"Yeah. I'll put up the tent for Mona. I just hope Sugar don't run Pa out of money before we get to California."

Margie watched Jody walk away and thought that he was a son a man should be proud of. Mona was lucky to have a brother like him to look out for her. Foley Luker was ten times a fool, but, then, most of the men she had come in contact with were, including Ernie Harding and her own father. She could even add Brady Hoyt to the list. *He had kissed her as if it were a chore to get out of the way!*

On the other side of the list were Mr.

159

Putman and Rusty. They seemed nice and trustworthy. On further thought she added Yates and the funny little man called Deke at Andy's Garage in Sayre . . . and Harry back at the café in Conway. He had thought enough of her to give her the pistol and show her how to use it.

"I can't be cynical like Elmer," she murmured to herself. "I got into this mess because I wanted to go to California. I'll stick it out if it kills me."

Homer Persy watched Brady and then the sheriff drive away from the campground. He went behind the car, dropped his drawers, removed his underwear and attempted to clean himself.

He swore using every foul word he'd ever heard.

"I'll get that son of a bitch if it takes the rest of my life." He burned with the desire for revenge.

The hick sheriff had *laughed* and held his nose when he discovered that Homer had messed on himself. The cowboy had sneered at him. "If I'd known he wasn't housebroke, I'd of put a diaper on him."

He'd get even. Nobody treated Homer Persy like that and got away with it.

Homer threw his soiled underwear in the

bushes and put on his britches. He had caught a grin on the face of Ross, the man his Uncle Chester had brought along. It hadn't sat well.

"If not for yore bungling, we'da had a hostage and been long gone. You let that hick get the drop on you."

"I told you I wasn't for takin' a hostage. Kidnappin' ain't somethin' folks sneeze at," Ross shot back.

"Well, you can just get yoreself on down the road. Ya ain't ridin' back in this car." Homer was itching for a fight.

"Neither are you," Ross growled. "Unless you know how to put it back together."

"I suppose you do."

"Yeah, I do. I've already picked up the parts that cowboy threw in the bushes."

"Well, get at it. That cowboy and them women are headed for California. There ain't but one way to get there — down old Highway 66."

"I'll fix your car, but I ain't havin' no part in hurtin' no women."

"I ain't heared nobody askin' ya to be part. Did you, Uncle Chester? Did you ask him to come with us?"

Chester Ford grinned and shook his head at his nephew. "Yo're more like yore grandpa ever'day." Chester took pride in his

161

infamous relative, Bob Ford, who had killed Jesse James.

"And just as sneaky as the back-shootin' bastard," Ross muttered under his breath, and lifted the hood on the old car.

Chapter 9

Brady followed the Lukers into the campground near Oklahoma City. He was irritated with the sheriff back in Sapulpa.

"I've got a jailhouse full of bootleggers and bank robbers. I've not got time to mess with petty crooks."

"Well, dammit, they wouldn't have been 'petty crooks' if we hadn't got the jump on them."

"I know. Aggravatin' as hell, ain't it? Happens every day. I get my hands on a piece of shit that hasn't done quite enough to be sent up for; but you know he's goin' to, and you got to wait for it."

Homer Persy had been so angry he was practically frothing at the mouth and, before the sheriff got there, had threatened to get

163

even. Brady and Rusty had sat in the car, laughing and holding their noses to further irritate him. Homer had calmed down, however, by the time the sheriff arrived, and vigorously denied the robbery attempt.

"I'll sign a complaint if you want," Brady had said.

"Wouldn't stick. This one" — the sheriff indicated Homer — "smells like a privy. I don't want him stinkin' up my jailhouse."

"Then we'll be on our way."

Both Brady and Rusty had taken delight in the fact that neither the crooks nor the sheriff was aware that Rusty couldn't see.

Now with his hand on Rusty's back Brady guided him to where Alvin had stopped the truck. Blackie followed. Brady had had only a glimpse of Margie when he drove in. She had answered his wave halfheartedly and disappeared in the back of the truck.

"Uncle Brady!" Anna Marie ran to meet him. "Guess what?"

"You learned another song." He grabbed her up in his arms. She planted a kiss on his cheek.

"How did you know?"

"A little bird told me."

"Did it, Rusty? Did a bird tell him?"

"I might remember if I got a hug."

Brady moved so that Anna Marie's arms

could circle Rusty's neck. Rusty held the child while she kissed him on the cheek. With Brady's hand against his back they walked on.

"I've not ever been kissed by such a pretty girl."

"How do you know?" Anna Marie asked with the frankness of a child. "You can't see me."

"No, but as sweet as you are, you've just got to be pretty."

He put his nose against her face. "And you *smell* pretty."

"I like you, Rusty. Almost as much as Uncle Brady. Will you sing songs tonight?"

"How could I refuse? And I like you too." A tug on his shirt told Rusty they had reached the camp. He stopped and set the child on her feet. She ran to the car to get her jump rope.

Jody joined them, and while Grace prepared the evening meal, Rusty and Brady took turns telling what happened after the sheriff had arrived.

"Do you think they will follow?" Alvin asked.

"I didn't see any sign in their car that they're prepared for a long trip. It'll take them a while to fix it unless one of them is a crackerjack mechanic."

"Speaking of mechanics," Alvin said to Jody, "how's your pa's radiator?"

"It's still holding. He's takin' his Sugar to a motor cabin tonight."

"You and Mona are staying here?"

"We'll be all right. Pa can't afford two cabins."

"Then, come eat with us tonight." Grace came to stand beside her husband. "I cooked a pot of stew last night."

"We . . . couldn't impose. Pa's leaving the trailer. We'll find something."

"Won't do. You'll eat with us." Grace glanced at her son. He was combing the burs out of Blackie's fur, but he was listening intensely. "Scoot now. Go fetch your sister."

"Well, if you're sure."

"I'm sure. Mona can help me clear up afterward. I think we should have a singing tonight, Alvin. Maybe some of the other campers will join us. Why don't you invite 'em? They look like decent folks."

While eating, Brady sat where he could see the Kinnard camp. Margie fixed herself a plate of food, then moved around to the other side of the truck, where he couldn't see her. Elmer sat on the canvas chair beside the cab of the truck.

If he was smart, Brady told himself, he

wouldn't get to within ten feet of Margie Kinnard lest she become too important to him. He could like her, be interested in her welfare, without falling in love with her. He didn't want to love her or any woman right now. The time wasn't right for him.

Besides, he'd seen what love could do to a man. Love with the wrong woman was having your heart and soul twisted, tied and knotted and then . . . stomped on. Even as he thought this, he was planning on how he could get Margie to come over to the Putman camp for the get-together.

It had seemed reasonable to him, at the time, that once he'd kissed her, she would become just another pretty girl. He was dead wrong. He'd thought of her sweet mouth and soft body all day. Thank the good Lord she was a girl whose dreams didn't include a piss-poor cowboy, a girl who had set her sights on Hollywood; otherwise he'd be in deep trouble.

While Mona and Grace were washing the supper dishes, Alvin, holding Anna Marie's hand, walked over to visit with the other campers. Soon he was squatted down talking to a man in a battered straw hat and Anna Marie was running and playing with the children.

Brady made a quick decision. He went to

his car to check the water and the oil. When he finished, he headed for the Kinnard camp.

"Evenin'," he said to Elmer, who sat back in his canvas chair, his arms folded across his chest, eyeing Brady as if he had just crawled out from under a rock. Margie was washing dishes on the tailgate of the truck.

"If all goes well, we'll be in Amarillo in a couple of days." Brady squatted on his heels and poked a stick into the campfire.

Elmer grunted.

"Truck runnin' all right?"

Silence. Brady sat back to wait him out.

Finally Elmer said, "I ain't goin' to hold you up, if that's what's worryin' you."

"I'm not losing any sleep over it. Foley's radiator is sure to blow soon. I'm hopin' it happens before we get to where the towns are a hundred miles apart."

Elmer grunted an incoherent reply.

"Alvin keeps his truck in good shape; checks oil and water regularly."

"You think I don't?"

"Didn't give it a thought." It was a challenge for Brady to force Elmer to carry on this conversation. He wasn't going to let him freeze him out. The bastard. He'd like nothing better than to put his fist through the man's face. "Been in the ice business long?"

"You plannin' on sellin' ice?"

"No. I raise horses."

"Then whater ya wantin' to know for?"

"Well . . ." Brady scratched his head and spoke casually. "I guess I was wondering if it was the ice business that turned you into such an ornery son of a bitch."

Elmer didn't turn a hair.

"And the more I talk to you, the less I give a damn," Brady added.

"I ain't no fool. You didn't come to talk to me. You're sniffin' after the female."

"Something wrong with that? She's a nice girl and she's pretty."

"Nice? She's a thief is what she is!"

Brady stood. He had never wanted to hit a man so badly in all his life. "That's a hell of a thing to say about your daughter." His voice was low and angry.

A sound like a snort came from Elmer, and he got to his feet. Standing with his hands tucked into the bib of his overalls, he looked Brady in the eye.

"Ya ain't knowin' what she is. She run off with a feller last year and stole his money. Name was Ernie Harding from Conway. He dumped her. She come a-crawlin' back to town with her tail 'tween her legs."

"You took his word that she stole his money?"

"Damn right. It's in her blood. She's set her sights on seein' Hollywood, bein' a *movie star.* Don't that beat all? She's got about as much chance a bein' a movie star as I have pissin' from here to California."

"I don't understand how a girl like Margie would be related to *you.*"

"I ain't a hundred percent sure she is. Take my advice. Stay away from her, or she'll sucker ya in and take everythin' ya got."

"I've not got much."

"Then ya ain't got nothin' to worry 'bout except maybe catchin' the clap." Elmer walked away.

Brady watched him leave. There were no words to describe the contempt he felt for the man. If Margie was what her father said she was, she was sure to land a job in Hollywood, because she was a damn fine actress.

Margie had heard every word that passed between Brady and Elmer.

Damn, damn, damn him! she thought. *I wish to God I was anywhere but here.*

Ernie Harding had gone back to Conway and spread the story that she had taken his money in order to excuse his going off and

170

leaving her stranded in Oklahoma. Elmer had believed him.

Margie pressed her palms to her hot cheeks and scooted around to the other side of the truck. She leaned against it and hid her face against her bent arm. Too humiliated to even cry, she stood there, stiffening the legs that wanted to sag from the weight of her heavy heart.

She hoped and prayed that Brady would leave. To have him look at her with contempt would be more than she could endure.

Her prayers were not answered. She felt a gentle hand on her shoulder. It was the final straw. A tremor shook her. She swallowed repeatedly to hold back the agonizing sobs that refused to be controlled. Silently they bubbled up. She cried as she had never cried before, tears wetting her arm.

"Hey, don't cry."

It seemed to take all her natural strength to say, "Go away . . . please."

"I don't believe what he said. I'm smarter than that."

"He . . . said that I'm a — he said I took Ernie's money. He believes — he'll tell everybody."

"They won't believe it either." Brady tried to turn her into his arms. She resisted.

"Go away. Please. I wish . . . I wish I'd never come on this blasted . . . trip."

"What kind of man is he to say these things about his daughter —"

"Unless they're true? Is that what you think?"

"No, it isn't what I think. I think he's an embittered, sick man who doesn't even like himself."

"He . . . hates me because of my mother."

"He must have loved her once."

"No. There's no love in him."

"Hold your head up, Margie girl. Don't give him anything to gloat over."

"Please go. I've got to finish the dishes."

"The Putmans are inviting all the campers to a singing. Will you come over?"

"No!" she answered quickly. "I'm going to bed."

"If you don't come, I'll come after you." He looped her hair over her ear and massaged the nape of her neck.

"Don't come back. It'll just make things worse."

"Are you afraid of him?"

"No. He'll not . . . hurt me that way. He has other ways."

"Finish the dishes. Then come over."

"Please go before he comes back."

"All right. But if you don't come over, I'll

be back; and if he says anything, I just might knock his block off." He patted her on the back and walked away.

She waited until she was sure that he was gone before she lifted her head from her arm. Oh, Lord. How could she ever face him or the others? Elmer had branded her a thief, made fun of her for wanting to see Hollywood. He had insinuated that she was a loose woman. He had probably said the same to Alvin and Grace and the Lukers. He must really hate her. She wiped her face on the hem of her skirt and went back to the dishpan.

Margie had planned all day to tell Alvin about the campsite at Andy's Garage just this side of Sayre, where Ernie had taken her money and deserted her. It was probably called Deke's Garage by now. In the one letter she received from Leona after she had married, she said that Andy had sold the garage to Deke, the man who sometimes helped him, and that he and the girls were moving with her and Yates to a ranch in Texas.

If Alvin would agree to camp there for the night, Deke would tell them that she hadn't stolen money from Ernie, that it was the other way around. The only way she was going to be able to speak to Alvin before they pulled out in the morning would be to go over there tonight.

Once she came to a decision, she hurriedly finished the evening chores, then climbed into the truck with a pan of water. The first thing she did was hold a damp cloth to her puffy eyes, hoping to erase the results of her tears. After washing she put on her blue-checked gingham skirt and blouse. It was her second-best dress. Soon she would have to find a place to wash her underwear and the two skirts and blouses she had worn all week.

Her heart felt like a rock in her chest as she brushed her hair and added a touch of color to her lips. She wanted to leave the truck before Elmer returned. She jumped down and hurried over to Brady's car before she lost her courage. Pausing there, she was assailed by sickening doubts. What if she was ignored? What if Grace no longer wanted to associate with her? What if Brady had second thoughts about what Elmer had said?

Her eyes searched for him. Rusty was playing a rousing tune on his fiddle while Alvin piled wood on the bonfire, and Grace, holding on to Anna Marie, greeted the people coming from the other camps. They came with stools and chairs and quilts for the little ones to sit on.

Brady and Jody appeared out of the darkness carrying a heavy log. When they dropped it on the fire, sparks flew in all directions. Brady paused, kicked at the log with his booted foot, then turned and came toward her.

"How did you know I was here?"

"I've been watching for you." He held out his hand. Mindlessly she reached for it, but held back when he tried to pull her toward the gathering.

"No. I'll wait here. I'm only going to stay long enough to talk to Mr. Putman."

"You're coming with me."

"No. Please —"

"You're coming. Must I remind you that I'm bigger than you are?"

Brady reached into the car for a blanket, then, holding her hand tightly, pulled her along with him. He skirted the crowd to a place out of the direct light of the campfire and spread the blanket. Margie sat down quickly, hoping not to attract any attention. Brady sat close, but not touching her.

Tilting his head so that he could see her profile, he studied the lines of her face. Brady felt that he was a fairly good judge of character, and he couldn't, for the life of him, associate her with the description her father had given him. It just wasn't possible.

He saw the trembling of her lips just before she turned to glare at him. "Stop looking at me!"

"I like looking at you. You're pretty."

"Yeah. Sure. You think I'll be an easy tumble after what Elmer said. Well, because I let you kiss me doesn't mean it'll go any further."

"We kissed each other. Remember?"

"I remember, and that's the end of it."

"I'm not asking for more."

"Thank you." She turned her face away, but not before he saw the moisture in her eyes.

"You can ride the rest of the way with me and Punkie if you want. I'd appreciate the help."

"You don't need my help. Grace will help with Anna Marie."

"Even so. You've got a place with me if you want it."

"And you'd expect payment. How? On my back?" She bit the words out angrily.

He didn't reply. A strained minute passed before she looked at him. He had turned away from her, but she could see the muscle flex in his cheek as he clenched his teeth.

"Brady? I'm sorry," she said in an agonized whisper, and placed her hand on his arm. "Please — I'm sorry."

He looked at her then. His eyes were shadowed by the thick, stubby lashes, but the set of his mouth told her that he was not pleased.

"You'd best be careful, Margie, that some of Elmer's cynicism doesn't rub off on you."

"Oh, Lord! You're right. I can't let that happen. But it's so hard when he says . . . those things." Her eyes were torn away from his face when Anna Marie ran to her and threw herself in her arms.

"Margie! I haven't seen you all day. Can I give you a hug?"

"There's nothing in the world I want more than a hug from you right now." She wrapped her arms around the child, closed her eyes and breathed in the sweet, innocent smell. "I've missed you."

"I 'bout know the rest of my ABCs."

"Forevermore! When did all of this happen?"

"While I was riding with Aunt Grace. She likes me."

"I'm not a bit surprised at that."

"Do you like me?" Anna Marie's arms were tight around her neck.

"More than you know." Margie glanced at Brady and found him gazing at her. She hugged the child and closed her eyes as her mind went back to when she had asked her granny why her daddy didn't like her.

He likes you, honey, He just doesn't know how to show it. That had satisfied her for a while, but later she had known differently.

Margie opened her eyes to see Brady still watching her. One long leg was stretched out, the other bent at the knee, his arms resting on it. She pulled her eyes away from his quiet face and tickled Anna Marie's nose with the end of her braid. The child giggled happily and hid her face against Margie's shoulder.

"Can I ride with you tomorrow? I'll sing my ABCs."

"Ah . . . I don't know, honey. We'll have to talk that over with your uncle."

"Can I, Uncle Brady? Please. I'll be nice."

"I'm feeling left out, Punkie. It's my turn to have you ride with me. I want to hear the songs you've learned and hear you sing the ABCs."

"Maybe Margie can ride with us. Can you, Margie?"

"I don't know about that either, Punkie," she said, using Brady's pet name for his niece. "Look now, Rusty has the guitar, and Mr. Putman is going to play the fiddle."

"All right, folks." Alvin's booming voice reached out over the campground. "Let's sing a few hymns. We'll start out with 'The Old Rugged Cross.' I think everyone knows that one. If anyone has a favorite, holler it out."

Alvin waved the bow of the fiddle like a baton. He and Grace started the singing, and as soon as the crowd gathered around the campfire joined in, he played the tune on the fiddle. Rusty picked chords on the guitar.

When the song ended, they sang "Shall We Gather at the River" and "In the Sweet Bye and Bye." Then someone suggested "Red River Valley." Alvin passed the fiddle to Rusty, then pulled Grace up beside him, and they sang the ballad in harmony.

When they finished, Jody called out, "Sing a cowboy song, Rusty."

"Which one?" he asked, and he and his father changed instruments again.

"How about 'Strawberry Roan'?"

Rusty sat down and casually let his hand drop to Mona's shoulder to make sure she was still beside him. The touch was noticed only by his mother. When he began to strum the strings of the guitar with slender, knowing fingers, all conversation ceased. He lifted his head and flashed a sudden bright smile around the circle and began to sing.

"Oh, that strawberry roan, oh,
* that strawberry roan,*
He goes up in the east,
* comes down in the west,*
To stay in his middle, I'm doin' my best,
Stay on that strawberry roan, stay on.
Stay on that strawberry roan!"

Rusty was a natural entertainer. His voice had a husky throb that drifted gently on the night breeze. The crowd was enthralled. When he finished the song, they clapped and shouted, "More, more!"

"All right." Rusty was smiling. There was no doubt that he was enjoying himself immensely. "How about 'The Cowboy's Lament'? It's got a lot of verses, if you can put up with them." Laughter followed his words, and he began the sad song.

"As I walked down the streets of Laredo,
As I walked out in Laredo one day,
I spied a poor cowboy
* wrapped up in white linen,*
Wrapped up in white linen
* as cold as the clay."*

Even the excited children were quiet as Rusty sang verse after verse of the sad song about a cowboy who had done wrong. When he finished, they were silent for a few seconds, then clapped their appreciation.

Chapter 10

"Rusty has an amazing memory," Margie said. "Imagine being able to play the violin and the guitar without being able to see them."

Brady grinned. "I think he has a crush on Mona."

"Goodness. I hope that she'll be kind to him if she can't return his affection."

"She seems to be taken with him."

"I hate to think of what Sugar would say to that." Margie snuggled the sleeping child close to her.

"Because he's blind?" There was resentment in the softly spoken words.

"She calls him a dummy."

"Dummy? He's got more brains in his little finger than she's got in that head of hers."

"Maybe, but it's a pretty head. You have to admit to that."

"Mrs. Luker is a different breed of cat."

"What do you mean?"

"She's like an alley cat. She'll never be satisfied with one man. My guess is that she's using Foley to get to California and will dump him as soon as they get there."

"He seems to be completely in love with her."

"She's got him bamboozled, all right. He'll wake up and find himself alone, broke and depending on his kids in his old age." Brady moved to take Anna Marie from Margie's lap. "Punkie's asleep. I'll lay her down here on the blanket."

"No. Let me hold her." Margie pulled Anna Marie's dress down over her thin little legs and cuddled the warm, trusting little body. "I hope her aunt will love her and give her a good home."

"I'll not leave her until I'm sure she'll be all right." He turned his face away, but not before Margie saw that his eyes were bleak and bitter.

"Is the aunt married?"

"She was. I don't know if they're still together. Brian said something about her husband being a fly-by-night."

"A child needs a mother and a father."

"My brother doted on her, but she never had much of a mother. Becky was the most selfish, self-centered person I've ever known." His eyes had turned hard. There was not a flicker of kindness in their depths.

"Elmer never had any use for me. I was lucky to have my grandmother."

"Have you noticed how Punkie's always asking people if they like her? I suspect that Becky told her many times that she didn't even like her."

"How could she have been so cruel?"

"When Punkie was just a little tot, Becky got mad at her for some little thing and told her that she hated her. Brian slapped Becky then. And he loved that woman with every breath in his body." He bit out the words, low, husky, angrily.

Margie turned questioning eyes to him, but he was looking toward the campfire. At the memory of Anna Marie's mother, he had bristled like an enraged porcupine. He turned to Margie, and their eyes clung for a breathless moment. Strange sensations went zigzagging along her nerves.

"Poor little thing," she said almost to herself.

The campfire was dying down and the gathering breaking up. Folks were picking up their sleeping children and calling to

184

those who had been too excited to sit still.

"Don't look so worried. I'll bring Alvin over," Brady said as he saw the expression of anxiety move over her face when she lost sight of the man she had come to talk to. His voice was sincere and had almost the same tone he used when talking to Anna Marie. He got to his feet and walked away.

Margie hadn't realized how comforting Brady's presence was until he left her sitting alone on the blanket holding the child. Grace was saying good-bye and wishing the other travelers good luck, her voice friendly as she called out that she hoped to see them again on down the line. Mona helped Rusty put the instruments in the cases, and Jody folded Grace's canvas chair and took it to the truck.

"I'll take Punkie." Brady was back beside her. "Alvin will come over to my car."

He lifted the child from her arms, stood and reached to help her up. She was grateful for the strong hand. Her legs were trembly from sitting so long. After regaining her balance, she released his hand and followed him to his car.

"She should have her little face and hands washed before she's put to bed." Margie watched as Brady removed the child's shoes and stockings.

"I've been washing her in the morning. I'm going to have to find a place soon to wash her clothes."

"Margie?" Alvin's voice came from behind her. "You wanted to see me?"

As Margie turned, Brady closed the car door and moved away. She called to him, "Brady, you don't have to go. What I have to say isn't confidential."

"If you're sure." He moved close. His hand found hers behind her back, and he interlaced her fingers with his.

"I'm sure. Mr. Putman, I traveled this road as far as Sayre, Oklahoma, last summer. Just this side of Sayre, at Andy's Garage, is where the man I had hired to take me to California stole my money and ran off and left me. The people there took me in and helped me get part of my money back — enough to get home. Andy had a nice campground, and when I was there, he even lent washtubs to people who needed to do their washing." Margie explained about Andy selling the garage and that it was probably called Deke's Garage now. "Deke is a funny little man, but oh so nice."

"Our map suggests we go on to Texola."

"Oh, well . . ." Disappointment slumped her shoulders. "Will you at least pull in

186

there so I can say hello?"

"Elmer wouldn't stop if you asked him?"

"Heavens no. If he thought it was what I wanted, he wouldn't stop if he was out of gas."

"Ride with me tomorrow," Brady said. "We'll stop so you can see your friends."

"I can't!" she exclaimed fearfully. "If I do, he might not let me back in the truck, even to get my things."

"Dammit to hell," Brady swore, then spoke to Alvin. "Would it not be worth a short day to have a place to wash?"

Alvin removed his hat and scratched his head. "Grace is anxious to wash and tidy up the truck. All right," he said after a few moments of silence. "If there's room for the four of us, we'll stop at the garage. It might be that Foley can get some work done on his radiator. It'll have to be done before we cross the desert."

"Oh, thank you." In her excitement Margie squeezed Brady's hand tightly.

"Do you know what has caused the change in Elmer? When I first met him, he wasn't this disagreeable." Alvin slapped his old felt hat back on his head.

"To tell you the truth, I don't know him very well. He's always been . . . ah . . . distant with me. But he had friends back in Conway

187

and was congenial with his customers at the icehouse."

"Maybe it's the strain of the trip, and he'll get into the swing of things in a day or so."

"Don't count on it, Mr. Putman," Margie said sadly.

"Well, good night. I doubt that we'll get an early start. We'll have to wait for Foley and his 'bride' to get back." Alvin walked off into the darkness, leaving Margie alone with Brady.

"I'm so glad we'll stop at Deke's. Thank you for speaking up. Deke will tell you that I didn't take Ernie's money."

"You don't have to prove that to me."

"Yes, I do. I can't bear for someone to think I'm a thief and a . . . loose woman. There's nothing I can do about the last, but I can at least prove that I'm not a thief."

He turned her toward him and tipped up her chin with his thumb. She lowered her lids and refused to look at him.

"Look at me. You've hardly glanced at me all evening. If I didn't know better, I'd think you were ashamed of something."

"I'm not!" She lifted a rebellious face to glare at him.

"Then hold up your head and act like it. You'll be stepped on if you're lying down but not if you're standing up looking folks in the eye."

"You think I'm silly for wanting to see Hollywood."

"I've not said that."

"Elmer does. He sneers every time I look at a movie magazine."

"I'm not Elmer."

His eyes searched her face. His thumbs beneath her chin refused to allow her to lower it. Suddenly he smiled. A pulse began to flutter lightly in her throat. His expression grew tender, and he reached to brush a lock of hair from her face. His hand cupped her cheek, then moved down her arm to grasp her hand and pull her around to the other side of the car.

"What are you doing?"

"I want to kiss you again."

"Why?"

"Because you're pretty and sweet and . . . I want to."

"And because you think —"

"Don't even think it!" he said quickly. The sweet softness he felt when he held her against him sent a powerful longing coursing through him.

She was drained of thought and will and just managed to whisper shakily, "Please."

Moon and sky were blotted out by his

dark face. His mouth was gentle even though he kissed her deeply, again and again, as if he had long been thirsty and was drinking at a cool well. The feel of his lips was strange and caressing. A feverish pounding in her temples spread to her stomach and lower. His hand slipped down to her buttocks, holding her there, his hard muscular thighs forcing intimate pressure upon her. Euphoria spread throughout her taut body, relaxing her painfully tensed muscles. Tomorrow she would probably hate herself and him, but that was tomorrow. Right now she felt a wondrous warmth suffusing her.

His mouth was persistent, ardent, relentless, snatching away her breath as well as her poise. There was a rightness to the sensation of his hands on her buttocks pressing her closer. Then the feeling of something rock-hard pressing against her lower stomach jerked her to awareness that this was going too far too fast. With a sob in her throat she began to struggle.

He raised his head. He was trembling. She could feel the tremor in the body pressed to hers and suddenly remembered Ernie Harding pressing her up against a tree in a dark campground —

"Stop! Please stop!"

The scared way she looked at him caused a hot flash of anger to wash over him.

Hell, it was only a kiss. He wasn't raping her!

"What's the matter?" he growled. "What's the harm in a few casual kisses? You've done it before."

Casual kisses. His words sent a cold chill throughout her body. She strove to pull back, but his grip was too strong. The thought that she had been used to provide him with a cheap thrill was so humiliating she wanted to sink into the ground. She swallowed dryly, feeling the frantic clamor of her throbbing pulses even as some devil prodded her to bait him.

"No harm at all. I've been wondering how good a kisser you were. I got only a little sample the other night. Not bad . . . for a cowboy."

"Think so?" A new wave of anger made his skin hot. He lowered his face until it was only a breath away from hers. "That wasn't even my top-of-the-line kiss." One of his hands gripped the nape of her neck; the other was flat against the small of her back. Before she could retort he clamped his lips to hers.

His mouth savaged hers relentlessly, prying her lips apart, grinding his teeth against her inner lips. She tried to drag her head back; but his hand held her in position, and she couldn't wrench it from his grasp. His teeth were biting into her lips, his fingers wound into her hair; she moaned in pain and struggled. He was taking her breath. When she thought her lungs would burst, he moved his mouth to the side of her face, and she took in great gulps of air through her open mouth.

She tried to speak, to protest, when she realized his hand was on her breast, but her voice seemed to have dried up. Her heart was racing, and she felt a sudden revulsion in the pit of her stomach.

He looked down into her face, his breath quick and warm on her wet mouth. Trembling, she shook her head in silent disappointment.

"Is that how you wanted it? Hard? Rough? Is that how Ernie kissed you before you accused him of stealing your money?" he asked in a strangely thickened voice, anger making him say things he'd later regret.

Helpless tears gathered in her eyes. The moonlight shone on her face, making them look like stars.

"So you *did* believe him." *I hate you,* she silently shrieked. Her disillusion was so complete she went cold and stiff. Through swollen lips she whispered on a ragged breath, "Get away from me."

"Gladly." He withdrew his hands from her body, held them up palms-out and stepped back. Anger at her rejection dissolved the hunger that tormented him.

He forcibly kept himself from saying anything more as he watched her move around the car and disappear in the darkness. A mix of anger and regret pervaded him. He scowled to himself and wondered what devil in him had caused him to manhandle her like that. But once he had started, he couldn't seem to stop.

Damn her!

He didn't want to feel anything for her. Pacing alongside the car restlessly, he hated the strange, twisted feeling that churned about inside of him. For a minute he had felt the twinge of desire to know love, but seconds later he discarded the idea. That wasn't what he wanted. He couldn't afford to be tied down.

Well, what the hell to do now? He'd sure made a mess of things.

Margie was weary but calm now. She had managed to stumble through the darkness to the truck, climb into her bunk and survive a horrible night. *A few casual kisses.* They had meant no more to him than that.

She had been stupid to think they might have meant more. In spite of all he had said, *he did believe Elmer's characterization of her as a thief, a shallow, silly woman with her head in the stars.*

Heartbroken, she had cried herself to sleep.

This morning, with her back to the Putman camp, where Brady and Anna Marie were having breakfast, she had fried mush and boiled coffee without breaking down.

The shock of having Elmer shred her character to Brady, followed by Brady's treatment of her, had sapped her strength and controlled her thoughts. Overnight it had worn away to some extent, and she had regained some of the use of her mind. Now, after pouring water on the campfire, she leaned against the side of the truck, ready to leave the campground when Elmer started the engine.

Elmer had appeared, eaten his breakfast and prepared for the departure without as much as acknowledging that she was there. Now he sat in the truck, waiting for Alvin to take the lead and pull out of the campground.

Foley and Sugar returned at sunup. Sugar

was not happy to see Mona and Jody with the Putmans, Mona helping Grace put away the breakfast things and Jody coming out of the woods with Rusty.

"I wanted coffee," she said in a loud, angry voice. "They've not even started a fire."

"You've had coffee, Sugar." Foley had backed the car up to the trailer and was working on the hitch.

"I wanted some to take with me." Her voice was like that of a spoiled child.

"I'll stop and get you some as we go through Oklahoma City," Foley said patiently.

"I thought we were going to have a good time last night." Sugar paced back and forth alongside the car. "The dance floor in that run-down joint you took me to was no bigger than the top of this car."

"It was the nearest one without going into town."

"The booths were full, and there was no place to sit. How did you expect me to have a good time in a ratty place like that?"

Foley straightened and looked at her. "Other folks were having a good time. You danced —"

"Only with you!" She stopped, put her fists on her hips and glared at him.

Her words brought him to his feet. He stared at her for a moment.

"Well, damn!" He turned his back and continued working on the car hitch.

"Oh, honey . . . darlin', I'm sorry." Sugar ran to him, wrapped her arms around him from behind and pressed her face to his back. "It's just that this trip isn't what I thought it would be."

Foley turned, and instead of putting his arms around her, he gripped her shoulders, held her away from him and looked down into her face.

"I told you before we started that it would be a hard trip and that we had to be saving with the money or we'd not have enough to get a start in California."

"But we're never alone, and we have to kowtow to that stiff-shirt about where we stop and how long we stay."

"Alvin organized this trip. He's doing a damn good job. Didn't you learn anything from the other night? It's safer to travel in the caravan."

"Let them go on. We could stay here for another day or two."

"And do what?"

"We'd think of something," she said coyly, and tried to snuggle close to him. "Let the kids go on with Brady. We'll catch up."

"Are you out of your mind? My kids stay with me."

She jerked away from him. "You love them more than me," she accused, and managed to put a sob in her voice.

"Of course I love them. They're my flesh and blood." Foley pulled her into his arms when she began to cry. "You'll understand when you have children. You said you wanted some."

"I . . . don't now."

"Course you do. You're just tired. In a couple days we'll be in Amarillo. Think of that. We'll go out dancing again. Now, dry up. The kids are coming."

"The kids are comin'," she echoed, then pulled away from him and got into the car.

"I did not!" Mona was laughing and protesting something her brother had said as they passed the car. They went on to where their father was attaching the trailer to the rear.

" 'Lo, Daddy. Have a good time last night?"

"Sure did, honey. How about you? Didn't you make a fire?"

"The Putmans asked me and Jody to eat with them."

"That was good of them."

"They had a singing last night, Daddy,"

Mona said. "Everyone in the campground came."

"Mr. Kinnard didn't come," Jody interjected.

"No one was surprised at that. Both Mr. Putman and Rusty played the violin and the guitar." Mona was in such a happy mood she didn't even think about her voice carrying to Sugar in the car.

"Mr. and Mrs. Putman sing harmony like you and Mama used to do," Jody said.

"Rusty sings and writes songs," Mona added. "He's writing one about the highway. Only one verse so far, but he'll finish it before we get to California."

Jody picked up the tools Foley had been using. "I bet there was forty people around the campfire last night. I wish you had been there, Pop. You like to sing."

"Sounds like you had a good time." Foley took a rag out of his hip pocket and wiped his hands as Alvin pulled up alongside.

"Ready to go? We'll stop just this side of Sayre at a place called Deke's Garage if there's room for the four of us. It's a small campground. If we take a short noon, we should get there before it fills up. We may be able to do some washing there."

"I reckon the womenfolks will like that."

"How's the radiator?"

"Sproutin' another leak."

"Let's hope it holds out until we get to the garage. Maybe you can get it fixed there."

"Maybe so."

"Bye, Grace. Bye, Rusty," Mona called. "See you tonight."

Alvin waved and drove on.

"Looks like Mrs. Luker was poutin' again," Grace said. "I reckon she didn't have a good time at the honky-tonk last night."

Chapter 11

There was nothing about the day that was different from the day before except that the wind was stronger, flinging up fine particles of sand and grit. But not even a beautiful, quiet day could have erased Brady's black mood.

Nothing eats at a man more than realizing he has made a complete ass of himself.

It started during breakfast when Grace made a teasing remark about him and Margie sitting together during the singing and then walking off into the dark together. Brady didn't know what to say, so he said nothing.

Margie had not even glanced at him as he passed on his way to speak to Foley and had managed to be on the other side of the truck when he returned to his car. He sat in it and waited for the Lukers to pull out, then followed the car and trailer down the ribbon of highway.

As soon as Anna Marie awakened, she had gone to a makeshift outhouse with Mona, then came back to the car. Now she slept curled up beside him in the front seat, her head on the pillow he had dragged up from her bed in the back.

On the outer edge of Oklahoma City the two trucks and the cars stopped for gas at different stations. Alvin waited along the shoulder of the road until they were lined up again, then pulled out onto the highway.

The land west of the city was flat and green from spring rains. They passed through the small town of Bethany, then crossed the Canadian River. After Yukon, the next town was El Reno.

Brady regretted that there would not be time to visit Fort Reno, where the Remount units of the United States Cavalry, essentially cowboys, broke and trained horses and mules. Some of the stock was shipped to such faraway places as the South Pacific, Burma and China, where Americans were stationed.

The Kinnard truck was a hundred feet or so ahead of Foley Luker. Brady could see it up ahead and envisioned Margie silently looking at the same landscape he was seeing.

He had decided last night, while he tossed and turned on the bedroll he had thrown out beside the car, that he didn't have good sense when he was around that woman. It was why, he reasoned, he couldn't keep his hands off her.

Why in the hell hadn't he just let her go instead of dragging her behind the car to kiss her?

If he had half the brains he was born with, he'd sell the car when they reached Amarillo, the next large town, and take Anna Marie to California on the train. After she was settled with Opal, he'd hitch a ride back to Colorado and work like hell to build up his ranch.

While Brady was deep in thought, Foley slowed suddenly. Brady's hand shot down to keep Anna Marie from rolling off the seat when he was forced to slam on the brakes to keep from smashing into the back of the trailer hitched to Foley's car.

"Damn! What's goin' on up there?"

"That's enough," Foley shouted, and looked over his shoulder to glare at his daughter. "I'm sick and tired of this bickering between you two. It's going to stop! Hear?"

"I've had about all of her I can take!" Mona's shout was as loud as her father's. "I can never do anything to suit her."

"Mona . . . this isn't the time," Jody said.

"It'll never be the right time with her," Mona retorted, and shook her arm out of her brother's grasp. "Know what, Daddy? I had a good time at the singing last night, and I just . . . I just wanted to tell *you* about it. She had to chime in and ruin it." Angry, reckless words poured from the girl. "And she has no right to call Rusty a dummy."

"She didn't mean it the way you took it." Foley sent another glance over his shoulder.

"Yes, she did. She thinks everyone is a dummy but her! Even you, Daddy, if you want to know the truth."

"I'm warnin' you, Mona!"

"Rusty's smarter than she'll be if she lives to be a hundred. Can she play the violin? The guitar? Does she know anything about President Roosevelt's New Deal or that German overseas who's stirring things up? Rusty can talk about a lot of things. All she knows is how to make life miserable for me and Jody and how to butter you up." Frustrations of the last few months bubbled up and came spewing out of Mona's mouth like a fountain.

"This constant bickering between you two is driving me crazy!" Foley slammed on the brakes and slowed the car to a mere crawl.

"I'm sorry, darlin'. I'm sorry." Sugar ran her hand up and down the inside of Foley's thigh. "I worry that Mona is becoming too attached to a hopeless cripple. The man will have to be taken care of for the rest of his life. Do we want our girl tied to a man like that?"

"*Our* girl?" Mona yelled. "I'm not your girl just because my daddy married you. I had a mother who never said unkind things. She never called me a warthog or told me I was ugly and would never get a man. And Rusty is not a helpless cripple!"

"See there, darlin'? They've already got her hooked into feeling sorry for him. How else will they get a woman to take care of a blind —"

"Just . . . shut up!" Mona yelled, and burst into tears.

"She'll never let me be a mother to her," Sugar whispered to Foley with a broken sob. "The Putmans have turned her against me."

"Mona, you will have respect for my wife —"

"How about her having respect for . . .

me?" Mona's voice broke as she sobbed.

"I never called her fat and ugly," Sugar whispered, desperate to get Foley's attention.

"Yes, she did, Pop." Jody leaned forward. "She's been on Mona's back since the week after you married her. More so since we started on this trip."

"It was for her own good, darlin'. I wanted her to take pride in herself and be *pretty*."

"Shut up!" Foley shouted. "All of you, just shut up!" He slammed his foot down on the gas pedal, and the car shot ahead.

Behind Brady, in a Model A Ford coupe with a rumble seat, the driver swore.

"What the hell they slow down for?"

"Hell, I dunno. Stay back a ways. I ain't wantin' that asshole cowboy knowin' we're behind him." Homer Persy sat with his booted foot up on the dashboard.

Homer's Uncle Chester had borrowed the car, or rather taken the car, from his mother's barn, where it had been sitting since his father's death a year ago.

"I ain't knowin' why yo're all put out 'bout taking Granny's car." Homer let his arm dangle out the window. "She can't drive it nohow."

"It was Pa's. She's got a fondness for it,

and she's still grievin'."

"How long's she goin' to grieve, fer God's sake?"

"Ma'll be back from Sister's in a week. I got to have the car back 'fore then."

"Don't worry, Uncle Chester."

"I'm worried and I'm tired. We drove like hell to catch up with these yahoos. Where we goin' to get gas money to get back home?"

"The one with the slutty woman has money. She said he sold his ice business. He'da not put it in the bank the way they're goin' bust."

"How you figure to get it?"

"The time will come."

"It better come soon."

"I got it all figured out, Uncle."

"Stop callin' me that. Makes me feel like I got one foot in the grave already. I ain't but eight years older than you."

"Lordy. You must be damn near thirty. That's older than dirt. Are ya too old to get it up, *Uncle?* Is your pleasurin' days over, *Uncle?*" Homer pushed his hat back on his head and let his foot drop to the floor of the car.

Chester ignored the jabs. "Whatta ya mean you got somethin' figured out?"

"I ain't got but ten dollars in my pocket.

How much you got?"

"Not that much. Ya said ya had money."

"I didn't say I had it. I said I know where to get it. And I do."

"You'll not be gettin' any more from your pa. That's certain."

"I'll never ask that tight-ass for another dime. There's folks along this highway just sitting there askin' for their money to be took."

"And there's police along this road just waiting for them that take it. We was lucky back at that campground. I still ain't figured why that sheriff let us go."

"We didn't rob anybody, that's why. He couldn't arrest us 'cause someone *thought* we was goin' to rob them. 'Sides, he took our guns. The asshole will sell 'em and make a little extra money. All them lawmen are crooked as a snake's back. But I'm well-heeled. I got me a shotgun in the rumble seat and a forty-five right here in my coat pocket."

"Well, I don't want to tangle with that cowboy. He don't look like he's got no quit a-tall. He's all yours."

"I ain't no fool. I won't go against him head-on. When his tires get slashed, he ain't goin' to know who done it. When he gets bashed in the head some dark night, he ain't goin' to know who done it. When I screw the eyeballs out of that blonde, he ain't goin' to know who done it."

"You better hope he don't. You can get yoreself killed screwin' a woman who don't want to be screwed."

"Ah, shit! I've screwed plenty a women that didn't want it. I put the fear in 'em, and they never let out a peep 'bout it after I got done with 'em."

"He might not care if ya screw her eyeballs out."

"He'll care. He stopped and patted her up the night he went to get the rope to tie us up. He'd care even if he didn't like her. Big, upstanding man like him has got to be a hero."

"Do as you want, but I ain't rapin' no women."

"Ain't ya got the balls for it no more, *Uncle* Chester?"

"I ain't wantin' my neck stretched."

"I'm goin' to do whatever'll piss off that cowboy the most before I bash his head in. He ain't gettin' away with what he done to me. I aim to see that he pays." Homer's young face turned hard.

He didn't shit in your pants. You did.

Chester had always known his sister's oldest boy was wild. Now he wondered if he wasn't a little crazy. Robbing a store was one thing; wanting to kill someone was another. This was the first he'd heard him talk about raping and killing. It made him nervous. He took a drink out of a quart fruit jar that sat on the seat beside him. His face twisted.

"Where did you get this rotgut anyway?"

"Ain't nothing wrong with this rotgut. It kicks like a mule. It's supposed to."

"We're passing Fort Reno, Rusty," Grace said. "This is where they break and train wild horses for the army. My, my. There must be a hundred horses in that field. All kinds: pintos, roans, buckskins, blacks, browns, all colors but pink. All look to me like range horses. Course, I ain't never seen a range horse but once. That poor thing was wilder than a turpentined cat. They got good fence around the fields so the stock can't get out. There's men on horseback bringin' in another batch."

Grace continued to talk, painting pictures with words for Rusty. "Lots of buildings here, big barns and quarters for the men. Pretty place, trees and bushes a-growing along the walks. Oh, my, there's two cowboys right there by the fence holdin' on to a mule that's buckin' like crazy.

"What do you reckon they're doin', Alvin?"

"I ain't knowin', sugar foot. But I bet they be knowin'."

"Did you see that, Alvin? That cowboy was a-holdin' on to that mule's ear with his teeth!"

"Doggone if he wasn't."

"Phew! Bet a dirty old ear wouldn't taste good!"

"Sure is flat country out here in west Oklahoma," Alvin commented after they passed the fort. "Not at all like our hills back home."

"Out here is where they're having the dust storms," Rusty said. "I can kind of smell dust in the air."

"I hope we don't have one while we're passin' through. There's a cloud bank in the southwest. Could be bad weather is comin' this way."

Alvin took his eyes off the road long enough to glance at his wife and son. He was a lucky man. They were his life. He'd do whatever he had to do to give them a better future in California. He felt sorry for Foley, the poor bastard. He would never know love and contentment with that baggage he married.

"You've been quiet, son. Have you got something on your mind?"

"No, Ma. Well, yes. I'm thinking about a

song I'm writing. The lines 'They are blind that will not see, none so blind as a man like me,' keep going over and over in my mind. I'm trying to put them in a song."

"Oh, son," Grace exclaimed. "That's not like you. It's so sad."

"Folks like sad songs now'days, Ma. The chorus will go something like this:

"Come back, love, to my eager arms.
Come back, love, with your magic charms.
Give me hope or I'll change to stone,
Give me love or I'll die alone."

When he finished singing, Grace grabbed his arm. "That was beautiful. Wasn't it, Alvin? It just made me want to cry."

Rusty laughed. "A good song should make you laugh, cry, or put you in a romantic mood. I'm working on another song. The words will be something like this:

"Though my heart is sometimes heavy,
My blind eyes filled with tears,
I only have to know you're near,
And my heartache disappears."

"That's pretty too. Have you picked out a tune to go with it?" Grace asked.

"Not yet."

"What are you going to call it?" Alvin asked.

"I've not decided, but I may call the first one 'What I See.' I've not decided a title for the second one."

"Call it 'Mona,' " Alvin teased.

"Alvin!"

"It's all right, Ma. That's not a bad idea. I'll tell her you said so, Pa."

"She's pretty. Not a painted-up hussy like her pa married." Grace sent a sideways glance at her son. "Pretty brown hair and eyes and a sweet girl —"

"You don't have to sell me, Ma. Brady already told me."

"Now, when did he do that?"

"While I was riding with him. We had some good talks. Brady knows a lot about a lot of things."

"I thought he was gettin' sweet on Margie. But when I mentioned her this morning, he turned colder than a North Pole well driller. Didn't say another word."

"He was all right with her last night," Alvin said.

"Poor girl. I pity her having to ride all day beside that grouchy father of hers." Grace shook her head and clicked her tongue. "Never did see a pair like 'em. You'd think he'd be proud as punch to have a pretty girl like her for a daughter."

"Well, he ain't. Margie told me last night that she didn't even know him very well."

"What will she do when she gets to California?" There was concern in Rusty's voice. "She surely won't stay with him."

In the truck behind them Margie was worrying about the same thing. What would she do when they reached Bakersfield? She still had to get down to Los Angeles if she was going to see the Hollywood she had dreamed about for so long. She had looked it up on the map. It was a little more than a hundred miles from Bakersfield. If she couldn't get a ride, she'd have to take the bus, which would take a big bite out of the money she had saved to live on.

Would she be able to get a job that paid enough to support her? She had only enough money for a couple of weeks if prices weren't high. Surely she could find a job in that length of time. One thing was sure: She'd lie down on the highway and let the cars drive over her before she'd ask Elmer for help.

All morning he had ignored her as if she weren't there, just as he had done for the past week. When he stopped for gas, he came out of the filling station drinking a bottle of orange soda pop. When the bottle was empty, he put it on the floor and pushed it under the seat.

Brady had been a dark blot on her mind all day. The humiliation of hearing her father tell him she was a whore paled in comparison to having Brady treat her like one. Seeing the cowboys on the horses as they passed Fort Reno brought to mind the fact that Brady wouldn't stay long in California. He would dump Anna Marie on her Aunt Opal and be gone despite his pretending to care for the child.

He had seemed to like and respect her at first. And she had liked him . . . a little too much. It was going to take all the courage she could rake up to endure the rest of the trip knowing that he and Elmer believed her to be a thief and a woman of loose morals.

Well, what did she care? She was going to Hollywood.

But she did care. She cared a lot.

Brady had said for her to hold up her head and if anyone gave her any sass to spit in their eye.

Oh, Lord, she hoped that she would be able to do that when they camped at Deke's. She would never spit at anyone, but she prayed that she would be able to hold up her head.

Deke Bales was a little man who wore cowboy boots and a big hat. He had been in love with Leona, the woman who lived in the house beside the garage and took care of Andy Connors's girls. While Andy was in the hospital, a big Texan took over the garage and he and Leona fell in love. When Andy got out of the hospital, Yates took him, Leona and the girls to his ranch in Texas.

Margie hoped that they were happy.

The day passed slowly. They paused only briefly at noon because they wanted to get to Deke's before other campers occupied the campground. They passed Weatherford, Clinton and a little place called Foss. When they reached Elk City, Margie knew that they were close.

After leaving Elk City they began to see the signs: CAR TROUBLE? NEED GAS? DEKE'S GARAGE AHEAD. A big yellow sign with black letters read SEE THE WORLD'S LARGEST RATTLESNAKE. DEKE'S GARAGE AHEAD. Another read SEE TRAINED BUFFALO AND THREE-LEGGED CHICKEN. CAMPGROUND FOR A FEW GOOD FOLKS.

When they came up over the hill and Margie glimpsed the nest of small buildings beside the highway, she became misty-eyed. Beside the garage was the house with porches on front and back, a small barn and shed behind it and a privy to the side. As they neared, she could see the campground.

Thank the Lord. It was empty.

Chapter 12

Alvin pulled his truck off the highway and stopped in front of the garage. Elmer followed. Deke came out wiping his hands on a greasy rag.

"Howdy."

Margie fought nervousness and tried to settle her breathing. Alvin's big body obscured her view of Deke. Seconds turned into minutes. Was Deke not going to let them stay? If Alvin got back into the truck to drive on, she vowed to jump out before Elmer drove away. She was determined to say hello to the man who had helped her when Ernie took her money even if Elmer drove off and left her here. She was sure that Alvin or Brady would come back for her. Then Alvin was coming toward the truck.

"We can camp here," he said to Elmer. "He asks that we leave the campground as we find it. I assured him that we would and said that some of us would buy gas before we left. Is that all right with you?"

"Guess it's got to be."

Relief made Margie giddy. She flung the door open and got out of the truck. Deke was standing in the open doors of the garage. He was just as she remembered him: bowed legs, buckteeth, a small pug nose, hair like a straw stack and practically no chin. He was near Margie's age and several inches shorter. After she had become acquainted with him, and after he had jumped to her defense heedless of the odds against him, she no longer considered him ugly.

She hurried across the hard-packed drive to the garage.

"Deke! Remember me? Margie."

The little man cocked his head, then opened his arms.

"Margie! Darlin'. Course I remember you." He hugged her, then held her away from him with his hands at her waist. "I wondered 'bout ya, darlin'."

"I wondered 'bout you too, Deke. I'm so glad to see you." The warm welcome brought tears to her eyes.

"I'm glad to see you too, darlin'. Come sit

here in the shade and tell me how ya been. I'll get ya a bottle of soda pop. Orange all right?"

Margie sat on the bench. She was aware that Elmer's truck was following Alvin to the far end of the campground, then turned toward the woods in order to make room for the Lukers and Brady. Brady's car passed slowly. Margie didn't look up even though Anna Marie called to her. To Brady and Elmer, Deke's display of affection would just be further proof of her loose morals.

She didn't care.

"Here ya are, darlin'." Deke wiped the water off the bottle of pop with his hand before handing it over to Margie.

"Thank you." Margie tipped the bottle to her lips and took a long swallow. "Oh, this is so good. I was thirsty. Tell me the news, Deke. What do you hear from Leona? Whatever happened to her brother's boys after Virgil was killed?"

"Leona's doin' fine. The girls love livin' on the ranch. Virgil's boys proved to be pretty good kids. One of 'em is working in the oil field. Another helps me out here once in a while. They're keepin' the family together. But how about you, darlin'? Whoer ya with?" Deke asked bluntly. "Is he treatin' ya right?"

"I'm riding with my father."

"Well, now, that's good to hear."

"Deke, would you believe that Ernie Harding went back home and told everybody that I had stolen his money? My father believes it."

"Why, the sneakin', lyin' polecat! Don't worry, darlin'. I'll set your pa straight on that. I'll take him in to see the records at the courthouse if I have to."

"No. Don't talk to him, Deke. He won't believe you. He wants to think the worst of me. But I would appreciate it if you would tell Mr. Putman how it was. He's very nice. So are his wife and son. I don't want them to think I'm a thief."

"I'll do that. I'll make a point of it. What's goin' on 'tween ya and your pa, darlin'? Yo're not happy, are ya?"

"No. This trip has been a nightmare."

They stood, and Deke slipped the empty pop bottle into a rack. "Come to the house. I want ya to meet my mama."

"Deke, I wanted to stop here so bad I told Mr. Putman that you might let us do some washing. Will it be all right if we heat water in your iron washpot?"

Margie was aware that Brady had come up behind her. She refused to turn and acknowledge him. Her heart jumped out of

220

rhythm, but there was no stress on the face she presented to Deke.

"Course it's all right. For you, darlin', I'd do their washin' myself." He looked beyond Margie. "Howdy, mister."

"Howdy. I was just going to ask if I could draw water from your well."

"Sure ya can. Name's Deke Bales." Deke stuck out his hand.

"Brady Hoyt. Glad to meet you."

After Deke had shaken Brady's hand he said, "It's kind of late in the day to be startin' a washin', but yo're welcome to do it. Them clouds in the southwest looks to me like they may be kickin' up a storm."

Brady tilted his hat and surveyed the clouds. "You may be right. Clouds with a tinge of green sometimes mean hail. I'll speak to Mrs. Putman."

"Margie!" Anna Marie ran to Margie and grabbed her hand. "Guess what? Aunt Grace took me to the privy. It's clean like the one back home."

"Well, that's nice."

"Come on, Punkie. Let's go see Grace."

"I want to stay with Margie. Mister, can I see the chicken with three legs? And the snake?" Anna Marie gave Deke a pleading smile. "Uncle Brady read the signs."

"The snake is in that tank at the side of

the garage, little sweetheart. Your daddy will have to hold you up."

"Daddy's in heaven. This is my Uncle Brady, but he looks just like my daddy. How did you catch him?"

"Darlin', I'm the best snake catcher in Oklahoma. I just grabbed hold of that snake, pulled him up out of a hole, threw him over my shoulder and put him in the tank."

Anna Marie looked at him with round, puzzled eyes. "Did he bite you?"

"If he had, I'd justa bit him back."

Margie smiled. "Honey, Mr. Bales likes to tease little girls."

"You're a little honey, that's sure. You go on and look at Mr. Hoover. I call him that 'cause he was the snake in the grass that got us into the Depression. Later I'll take you out to see Mr. Roosevelt, my buffalo, and Mrs. Roosevelt, my chicken. I'm takin' Margie in to see my mama. She's waitin' there on the porch."

Brady took Anna Marie's hand. "We'll see the snake later. We need to go talk to Aunt Grace."

Margie went up the path to the house with Deke. They were met on the porch by a short, heavyset woman with white hair coiled and pinned to the top of her head.

She wore a granny dress that fell from her shoulders to her ankles. It was easy to picture her as Deke's mother.

"Mama, this is Margie. Remember me telling you about the girl that was dumped here by that slimy little piece of horse dung who took her money?"

"That was last summer, wasn't it? Hello, Margie. Deke was ready to tear that man up."

"Hello, Mrs. Bales. *That man* left me in the best possible place."

"Come in, dear. I'll make you a glass of tea."

"Uh-oh. I've got a customer. Make yourself at home, Margie." Deke took off down the path to the garage.

"I can't stay long." Margie followed Deke's mother into the house. "I'll have to get back to the truck and fix supper."

"I was going to ask you to eat with us, dear. You and Deke can visit."

"I'd love to, but I'll have to prepare something for my father."

"He's welcome to come too."

"He wouldn't come, Mrs. Bales. He's kind of . . . difficult."

"All right. After supper you and Deke can visit. Have a seat and tell me about the trip so far."

Margie told Mrs. Bales about meeting Andy Payne, the man who ran from Los Angeles to New York.

"We camped on his land. He came down and gave each of us a big fish."

"I get hungry for fish, but Deke has no time to go fishing these days."

"Mr. Putman mapped out our trip. They had a singing at the camp last night in Oklahoma City. There must have been thirty or forty people there. Both Mr. Putman and his son play the violin and the guitar.

"The night before that, three men intended to rob us but were caught and turned over to the sheriff."

"Oh me, oh my. There's a lot of badmen along the highway now'days. Bootleggers come through here all the time. The bank in Sayre was robbed a few months ago. I worry about Deke. I say, 'Son, if they want your money, give it to them.' But knowing Deke, he'd not do that. He'd fight 'em."

"I'm afraid you're right."

"I tell him that if somethin' happens to him, I'd be all alone. I want to make him think before doin' somethin' foolish."

Margie spent a pleasant half hour with Deke's mother, then declined a second glass of tea.

"I must go and fix a meal for my father. It was one of the things I agreed to do if he would let me come with him."

"There is a tank out back, dear. Deke filled it this morning so the sun would take the chill off. You're welcome to use it."

"Oh, thank you. I remember bathing in it when I was here before. There's nothing I've been wanting more."

"When you're ready, tell Deke. He'll see to it that no one comes near."

"Will it be all right if I bathe a little girl?"

"Of course. Anyone you want. Deke will empty it and fill it again in the morning."

As Margie passed the garage, she saw that the Luker car had been pulled inside and the front end jacked up. Deke was standing on a box so he could lean in under the hood. She walked on, dreading to pass Brady's car, and was relieved when she didn't see him.

Jody was building a fire beside the Luker trailer. Sugar's tent was up. She wasn't in sight, so Margie assumed that she was in it. Mona was tossing the ball to Anna Marie.

"Mona, Mrs. Bales said that we can bathe in the tank out back. I used it when I was here before."

"You've been here before?"

"This is the place where the man stole my money and ran off and left me. I'll forever be grateful to Mr. Bales for helping to get part of my money back so I could go home."

"He's strange-looking."

"That may be," Margie snapped. "But he's a lot nicer than some *big, so-called handsome men* I've known."

Mona noticed the dull red that covered Margie's cheeks and wondered what she had said to cause it.

"I wasn't saying anything against him, just that he's strange-looking."

"Not after you get to know him."

"Can I go with you and Mona?" Anna Marie swung on Margie's hand.

"We're going to take a bath in a tank. You can go if it's all right with your uncle."

"I'll ask him," Mona said. "Mr. Bales is going to put a new radiator in Daddy's car. That means that we'll stay here all day tomorrow. We'll have time to do the wash and for it to dry. I'll wash my clothes and Jody's, but I'm not washing Sugar's."

"We'll go to the tank right after supper."

Margie made egg toast. She beat eggs, dipped in slices of bread and fried them in the big iron skillet. After she'd stacked a half dozen slices on a plate, Elmer miraculously appeared with his knife and fork in hand.

"Gettin' kind of hard up, ain't ya?" he said as he picked up the plate.

Margie was stunned. He hadn't spoken to her in days. It took a few seconds for his words to sink in.

"What do you mean?" She knew what he meant, but she wanted to hear him say it.

"I saw ya lovin' up to that ugly little freak."

"Don't you dare call Deke a freak. He's more of a man than you'll ever be."

Elmer's mouth made a thin line. He glared at her with cold eyes but didn't retort. Margie was suddenly awash with anger. Loud, reckless words poured from her mouth.

"He's got more decency in his little toe than you've got in your whole damn body. He's a kind, decent human being. Something that you're not!"

"Watch your mouth —"

"Then watch yours. I heard you shredding my reputation. You want people to think I'm a loose woman, a strumpet. You know it isn't true."

"Bullfoot. All I know points to it." Elmer went to the other side of the truck. She followed.

"Since we started on this trip you've treated me like I was something that had just crawled out from under a rock. I'm tired of riding all day with a mean, grouchy, self-centered old penny-pincher who doesn't have enough manners to fill a thimble."

"Then get your stuff and get out."

"Oh, no! You're taking me to California like you promised. I've lived up to my part of the agreement, you'll live up to yours."

Margie climbed into the truck, despising the tears that flooded her eyes and desperately wishing she were anywhere but here. Not wanting anyone to see her give way to tears, she pulled the rope that dropped the tarp at the end of the truck bed. Everyone in camp must have heard her shouting. It would only confirm what Elmer had said about her. It would give them all something to talk about.

She sat down on the bunk and let the tears flow. After a few minutes she straightened her shoulders, pushed her hair back and wiped her eyes. She would gain nothing by sitting here feeling sorry for herself. She would go take a bath, hold up her head, and if anyone gave her any sass, she would spit in his eye! That went for Mr. Brady Hoyt too.

Margie cleared up the supper dishes, then climbed into the truck to get a clean towel and soap. When she got out, Brady was waiting with Anna Marie.

"Ready to go, honey." Margie ignored

Brady and smiled at the child.

"I got soap."

"So do I. Let's go get Mona." She held her hand.

"Margie —"

"Yes." Her voice was as cold as she could possibly make it.

"Will you wash her hair?"

"Of course. Come on, honey."

Margie thought she heard him mutter something as they walked away. But she didn't care to hear what it was. Her attention centered on the four Lukers standing beside the camping trailer.

"Why didn't you tell me that there was a bath facility here?" Sugar demanded. She stood apart, accusing all of them.

"I didn't know," Mona said. "Margie told me." With a towel over her arm Mona turned as Margie approached. "Didn't you?"

"Yes, I did. Are you ready to go?"

Sugar whirled around and headed for the garage. "Well, I guess I'll just have to go ask that pig-ugly little monster myself."

Margie stepped in front of her. "I'm in no mood to put up with your hateful attitude, Mrs. Luker. Don't insult my friend again unless you want a handful of that dyed hair pulled out of your mean, stupid head!"

"Well, who do you think you are?" Sugar sputtered.

"I know who I am. Hasn't anyone ever told you who you are? You're a self-centered bitch. And you've got the manners of a guttersnipe. Come on, girls."

"Ha, ha, ha." Mona chortled softly as they walked toward the garage. "You sure told her, and I'm glad you did it in front of Daddy."

"I get tired of always trying to do the right and polite thing and letting bitches like Sugar walk over me. I guess you heard me yelling at Elmer. He'll probably leave me here."

"You could ride with Brady."

"I would not ride with Brady. He —" Margie would have said more, but she looked down to see Anna Marie tilt her head to look up at her. The child was drinking in every word that was said and no doubt would repeat them to her uncle.

Deke was squatted beside the radiator he had taken from the Luker car.

"Will you be able to fix it?" Margie asked.

" 'Fraid not, darlin'. I'll have to get another one from Elk City. I know a fellow over there who does salvage work. He'll have one or know where I can get one." He stood wiping his hands. "Ready to jump in the tank? I put a tarp around it since you was here. I'll go let it down."

"This is Mona Luker, Deke. Mrs. Bales said she and Anna Marie could bathe with me."

"Howdy, ma'am."

They followed Deke to the tank beside the barn where he pulled on a tarp he had strung on a wire.

"Ain't nobody out back to see ya, darlin', but Mr. Roosevelt and a couple of horses."

"Who's Mr. Roosevelt?" Mona asked.

"My buffalo. I'm not sure he knows he's a buffalo. He's been making eyes at Mama's milk cow." Deke pulled a small platform up beside the tank. "Something for you to step out on to keep your feet from getting dirty. I had to build this for Mama so she could get in the tank."

"Thanks, Deke. It's going to be a treat to take a bath."

"Take your time. Nobody will bother you."

The next thirty minutes were pure pleasure. When Margie sat down, the water covered her breasts. After she had scrubbed herself and washed her hair, she held Anna Marie on her lap while Mona washed the girl's hair, then held her over the water while she rinsed it. Margie loved the feel of the little arms around her neck and the sound of her childish laughter.

After they had all bathed, Margie climbed out, put on her dress and lifted Anna Marie out onto the platform. While Mona was dressing she asked a startling question.

"What are you wearing tonight when Brady takes us to town?"

Margie didn't answer until after she had pulled Anna Marie's dress over her head.

"I'm not going to town."

"Huh? Brady said that —"

"Brady doesn't speak for me." Her tone was sharp.

"Don't you like Uncle Brady anymore?" Anna Marie asked while Margie was tying her shoe.

"I never said anything about not liking your uncle, honey. I'm just not going with them to town."

"Will you stay with me and Aunt Grace?"

"We'll see."

"I know what that means. It means no. Uncle Brady says it sometimes."

When they stepped from behind the tarp and headed back to the campground, Rusty and Jody were sitting on the bench behind the garage.

"You girls took your time," Jody called. "Deke said Rusty and I could be next."

"If I'da known that, I'da picked up a cowpie and put it in the tank," Mona retorted. Her cheeks had turned rosy. Her eyes were on Rusty's smiling face as, with his hand resting lightly on Jody's shoulder, they came toward her.

"See what I have to put up with, Rusty? Let me have that bar of good-smellin' soap, sis. Me and Rusty might want to catch us a girl tonight."

"I left it in the tank."

"No, you didn't. I know you better than that."

"Oh, all right. But it'll take all of it to clean you two up."

"Count me out," Rusty said. "I brought my own."

"Bet it isn't lilac like mine."

"No, it's a plain old bar of P&G."

"Save some for the washpot tomorrow."

As they passed by the garage, Brady was there with Deke.

"Hey there, darlin'," Deke called. "Ever'thin' all right?"

"Fine. The bath was wonderful."

"Get yourself all pretty, we'll go to town tonight."

"Oh, Deke, I don't think so. Not tonight."

"I want to show off my best girl, darlin'." Deke put his arm around her. "When I come waltzin' into the PowWow with you on my arm, old Booger's eyes is goin' to pop right out."

Margie refused to look at Brady when he came out to pick Anna Marie up in his arms. He didn't move away, so she knew that he had to be listening.

"There's a drawing tonight at the picture show if you'd rather go there," Deke said.

"I'll be ready. You decide where we'll go."

"It'll be a while, darlin'."

"Thanks for bathing Punkie." Brady walked away with the child in his arms.

"Are you going with . . . *him?*" Mona asked as they neared the campground.

"Him? You mean Deke? Yes, I'm going with *him*."

Chapter 13

Chester stopped the Ford coupe on the top of the hill when the lead car of the caravan pulled into the space in front of the garage.

"*She-et!*" Homer snorted when the two trucks and the cars followed. "Hell. Looks like they're goin' to camp there. I thought they'd at least pull off the highway onto a back road."

"Whater ya goin' to do now?"

"Shit! Shit! Shit! Drive on. We can't be but a mile or two from a little burg called Sayre."

"How do you know that?"

"Dammit to hell! I can read. The sign way back there said five miles."

"Ya don't have to be so shitty 'bout it," Chester grumbled.

"Things ain't goin' right. I wanted to get at that cowboy tonight."

"Maybe we can go on past and come back through the woods when it's dark."

"I want the car close by."

"Sometimes ya don't get ever'thin' ya want. We're 'bout outta gas."

"We'll get some in Sayre, then go back to Elk City. I saw somethin' back there that looked good."

"I'm hungry too. We ain't et since mornin'."

"If what looks good turns out to be good, ya can have ya a big old fat steak — later on."

"We goin' to hold up somebody?"

"Ain't sayin' till I size the place up."

She needed a haircut. Margie bent over. With her hair hanging from the top of her head, she brushed it vigorously. Then while it was still slightly damp, she parted it on the side, brushed it over and held it back with a shiny clasp.

A dark blue jersey skirt gathered on a wide band and the white blouse that went with it were the only things she owned that didn't need ironing. She dressed, pulled on her stockings and slipped her feet into black pumps. She hated wearing black in the spring, but her white shoes were so run-down at the heels she was ashamed of them.

After touching up her eyelashes with Maybelline mascara she tinted her cheeks with a little rouge and put on her lipstick. Margie studied her face in the small, round hand mirror and wished that she could see the overall effect. Then, again, maybe she was better off not seeing the overall effect, she told herself, and put away the mirror.

The last things she did before leaving the truck were to dab a little Evening in Paris perfume behind her ears and to make sure the three twenty-dollar bills, all the money she had in the world, were secured with a big brass safety pin to her brassiere.

Elmer was sitting in his canvas chair when she climbed down. Ignoring him, she walked across the campground and up the path to the house. It was almost dark. A bird wheeled overhead, searching for one last meal before seeking its nest for the night. The chubby figure of Mrs. Bales occupied the porch swing.

"Come on up, my dear, and have a seat. My, don't you look pretty."

"Thank you. It's hard to look presentable when everything you have to wear is crammed in a suitcase."

"Deke will be out in a minute. I'm glad

he's gettin' away from here for a while. He sticks close because he doesn't want to leave me alone."

"I've no idea where we'll be going."

"That nice Mr. Putman put Deke's mind at ease. He said he'd keep an eye on things while he's gone."

"And he will. He's very reliable."

"Deke jumped into the tank. That tank's had a workout since suppertime. After the two young fellows, that tall one with the little girl got in, then Deke. Deke will pull the plug and let the water out tonight. It'll be good on the garden."

"I thought we were in for a little rain tonight. I'm afraid of storms especially while camping."

"We've got a good storm cellar. A few weeks ago Deke thought sure a cyclone was comin'. He took me and two camper families to the cellar. It blowed real good, but we only got a dab of rain out of it."

As Mrs. Bales talked, Margie saw the headlights of Brady's car flash on. The car backed up even with the garage and stopped. Deke came out of the house, the screen door slamming behind him.

"I thought I heard you out here, darlin'." He was wearing a white shirt with a string tie. His coarse, straw-colored hair had been slicked down. "Mama, Mr. Putman is goin' to keep an eye out. Switch the porch light on and off several times if you think there's somethin' he needs to know."

"I'll be just fine. Go on with Margie and have a good time."

"Ready, darlin'?"

After saying good night to Mrs. Bales, Margie took Deke's arm and they walked down the path to the garage. When they appeared to be headed for Brady's car, Margie pulled back on Deke's arm.

"Deke? We're not going with them, are we?"

"Darlin', you wouldn't want to ride to town on my cycle. Brady's takin' the kids to town and invited us to go along."

"I want time to visit . . . just with you."

"That makes me feel ten feet tall, darlin'. Come on now, I want to show you off."

Brady sat silently behind the wheel. Mona sat in the backseat between Rusty and Jody.

"Get in, darlin'. Not too close to that old boy. You're my girl tonight."

Margie moved across the seat to make room for Deke. It was impossible not to come up against Brady's long, hard body. She heard him draw in a harsh breath as if being close to her were as unpleasant to him as it was to her. Deke crowded in beside her

239

and slammed the car door.

"All set?" Brady asked.

"All set," Deke agreed, and put his arm across the back of the seat. Margie moved close to him to allow as little contact with Brady as possible. "There's a picture show and a roller-skating rink in Elk City along with a few honky-tonks. In Sayre we have the PowWow right in town and the Starlight farther on down the highway."

"Don't let me keep you from going to the picture show," Rusty said. "I'll enjoy hearing it, and Mona can whisper in my ear and tell me what's going on."

Deke looked over his shoulder as they pulled out onto the highway. "You can't see?" he asked bluntly.

"With my eyes I see a few shadows and a flickering light now and then. But I can hear a cloud passing overhead, so be careful what you say."

"Well, I'll be hornswaggled. I talked to you when you and the young fellow got out of the tank, but I didn't know you were . . . that you were blind."

"Thank you," Rusty said cheerfully. "I've had a lot of practice foolin' folks into thinking I can see."

"Let's stop in down here at the PowWow, Brady, and see what's goin' on. That all right with you, darlin'?" Deke's arm tightened around Margie. "When you get to Main Street, turn left. It's on the next corner. They've got a dance floor and one of them new jukeboxes you put a nickel in. Bootlegger money paid for it, but that ain't none of my business."

Lord, help me get through this evening. Margie was so miserable by the time they parked in front of the PowWow that she wanted to cry. Brady had said a total of two words. In the backseat Mona giggled, Jody teased and Rusty seemed to be enjoying himself.

The outside of the honky-tonk was decorated with wagon wheels and steer horns. Margie vaguely wondered what they had to do with a place named the PowWow. There was, however, a painted wooden Indian beside the door.

Several cars and two motorcycles were parked in front. Three horses were tied to a rail on the side of the building.

"Some of the boys from the ranch where I used to work are here. Their eyes will bug out when they see ya, darlin'." Deke led the way, with Margie anchored firmly to his side. She was uncomfortably conscious of Brady behind them.

Rusty's arm was tucked inside Mona's,

their fingers entwined. "One step up," she whispered when they reached the door.

The large room had booths down two sides of the dance floor and a bar across the far end. On the jukebox Gene Autry was singing "That Silver-Haired Daddy of Mine." Half of the booths were occupied and nearly all of the barstools.

"Hey, Deke. Who opened the gate and let you out?"

"Same damn fool that let you out, cowboy."

"Howdy, Deke. Introduce me to your lady."

"Not on your life, Bulldog. She's not for the likes of you."

Deke was greeted boisterously by friends as he led the way to a booth in the back. It was evident that he was well liked and that he was enjoying the spectacle he was creating.

As she slid into the booth, Margie looked up to see Brady heading toward the bar.

"I'll get us somethin' to drink," Deke said. "What'll ya have, darlin'?"

"Cola, if they have it."

"How about you, Mona?" Rusty asked.

"Cola for me too."

"Lead the way, Jody." Rusty placed his hand on Jody's shoulder. "I'm buying for my girl tonight. You too, if you behave yourself."

They followed Deke back up the line of booths to the bar. Deke stopped along the way to talk to several men wearing big, Texas-style hats.

Mona's eyes were shining. "Isn't Rusty something? I never thought I'd ever meet anyone like him. He called me his girl because that's what Deke called you."

"Don't be too sure. He likes you . . . a lot."

"Do you think so? Sugar is being mean about me and Jody spending time with the Putmans."

"What does your father say?"

"Nothing."

"Then what do you care what she thinks?"

"I'm afraid of what she'll say in front of Rusty. She has no sense at all when she's on one of her tears. She'll have it in for *you* now. Watch out for her."

"There isn't anything she can do to me that hasn't already been done."

"What happened between you and Brady?" Mona asked with the frankness of youth.

"Nothing. There's nothing between me and Brady."

"I thought you liked each other . . . a little."

"No more than I like you and Jody and Rusty."

The music changed on the jukebox. Someone was singing, "I don't know why I love you like I do." Two couples were dancing on the small floor.

"Here they come. Just look at him." Mona's eyes were on Rusty. "You'd never know that he's blind. He's cheerful all the time and so . . . smart."

"Uh-oh. I think you're falling for him."

"I can't help it, Margie."

Deke set a bottle of cola and a glass on the table and then slid in beside Margie with a bottle of beer. Rusty moved over close to Mona to make room for her brother.

"You should've seen Rusty, darlin'. Booger didn't know he couldn't see. Rusty pulled a handful of change from his pocket and counted out the coins just pretty as ya please."

"How do you do that?" Margie asked.

"Easy." Rusty reached into his pocket and put a handful of coins on the table. "The dime is the smallest and usually the thinnest. The penny is next, then the nickel and the quarter."

"Well, doggone if ya ain't right."

Rusty slid the coins off the table into the palm of his hand and put them back into his pocket as a dark-whiskered man stopped at the booth.

"Ya goin' to let me dance with yore woman, Deke?" His watery eyes honed in on Margie and he winked.

"Hell no! You're drunk, Hooter."

"I ain't that drunk."

"Yeah, ya are. 'Sides, I'm goin' to dance with her. Ain't that right, darlin'?"

"Right." Margie gave him her hand. He helped her slide out of the booth. "This is one of my favorite songs."

"Mine too." Deke put his arm around her and pulled her close. She was surprised how smoothly he moved. She hardly noticed that he was a couple inches shorter than she was. He sang softly with his cheek pressed to hers. "On a day like today, we pass the time away, writing love letters in the sand."

"I didn't know you sang, Deke. You should get together with Rusty before we move on."

"The blind boy?"

"He plays the violin and the guitar."

"It'll be a day or two before I can get that radiator fixed. We'll have us a singin' before you go."

When they finished the dance and went back to the booth, Jody jumped up before Margie could sit down.

"May I dance with your girl, Deke?"

"If it's all right with her and if ya promise not to get fresh."

"I swear it. Margie?"

Again Margie was surprised. "Where did you learn to dance, Jody?"

"We danced at home. The folks took us with them when they went to dances, mostly in the homes of their friends. And we had a Victrola. Mama danced with me, and Pop danced with Mona."

"How nice."

"Yeah. I look back and wonder how things can change in such a hurry."

"Maybe they won't be so bad when you get to California and are settled again."

"Sugar had a fit when we left tonight. She wanted to come, but with you and Deke there wasn't room in Brady's car. She accused Pa of letting Deke take the radiator out of their car so he wouldn't have to take her out someplace tonight. I keep wondering how long he'll put up with it."

"I take it she's different from your mother."

"As different as night and day. Mona and I still don't understand how Sugar got her hooks in Pop, but he may be starting to see that she isn't all she pretends."

"He was probably lonely when he met her."

"He had me and Mona."

"That isn't the same. My goodness. Look, Jody. Rusty and Mona are going to dance."

"She probably talked him into it. She likes him a lot."

"I can see that she would. He's a really nice person."

"I can't imagine what it would be like to be blind."

"Especially after being able to see."

"Mona will keep them from plowing into anyone. I'll move up over a little closer so if they bump into someone, it'll be us."

"Jody, if I had a brother, I'd want him to be just like you."

"Thank you, Miss Kinnard," he said, and whirled her around to come beside Rusty and Mona. "Hello, kids. Your mama let you out tonight?"

"We're doin' the town. Can't you tell? Has he gotten fresh yet, Margie?" Rusty asked.

"No, and I don't expect him to, doggone it."

"I could put a bug in his ear."

"I don't need your help, Romeo." Jody flashed him a grin. "And don't get fresh with my sister."

"Jody!" Mona hit her brother on the arm. "Tend to your own business."

Margie's eyes locked with Brady's as they

passed near to the bar. He stood with his back to it, his arms folded over his chest. The scowl on his face goaded her into a slow smile.

The cowboy was not having a good time!

They were in the middle of the dance floor when the music ended.

"My turn."

Before Margie's mind could jerk awake to what was happening, Brady had her hand and was pulling her out onto the dance floor and into his arms. She was too surprised to speak and totally unaware the song coming from the jukebox was one of her favorites, "You Made Me Love You."

They swayed to the music for a short while before they began to dance. He turned so that his big body shielded her from those in the booth, held her firmly, lowered his head and pressed his cheek to hers.

"Stop playing up to Deke. He's crazy about you." The words were growled in her ear. She pulled back so that she could see his face.

"He is not. That's just the way he is with everyone. But if he wants his friends to think I'm his girl, it's all right with me," she snapped.

"What will he tell them after you leave to chase your rainbow in Hollywood?"

"*My* rainbow? What about *your* rainbow, cowboy?" She tried to move away from him, but he was holding her so tightly against him that she could only tilt her head back and glare at him.

"What about it?"

"You want to palm a sweet little girl off on someone she doesn't even know so you can go on your merry way free of responsibility."

"You know nothing about it."

"Don't tell me I don't know what it's like to be dumped. It's the story of my life."

"What's put your back up?"

"You don't know? You're the most insensitive clod I've ever met."

"There's a limit to how far you can push me, little tease."

"Your threats just scare me to death."

"I mean it when I say stop playing up to Deke. He'll begin to think you mean it. I doubt he's had many women as good-looking as you pay attention to him."

"Maybe I do mean it. What's it to you? Deke and I understand each other. I don't need you telling me what to do."

"You need someone, you little twit, or you'd not be in the mess you're in." The hand holding hers came to her chin and lifted it. Light green eyes as cold as ice glared down at her.

"Whatever mess I'm in has nothing to do with you, Mr. Know-It-All Hoyt."

"I'm warning you, Margie. Climb down off your high horse or —"

"Or what? Now, let go of me before I kick you. I don't want to dance with you. I don't want anything to do with you."

"Too bad, Miss Mule-Headed Kinnard. We're finishing this dance. And if you kick me, I'll swat your butt right here on the dance floor."

"I'm surprised that the upright Mr. Hoyt would dance in public with a thief and a strumpet."

"Hush up!"

"I won't —"

"You'd better hush or I'll whirl you right out the door and lay my hand down hard on your rear end."

Margie missed a step and stumbled. "And I'd scream 'rape' so loud every man in this place would be on you like a duck on a June bug."

He said nothing, but she knew he was angry. The arms encircling her pulled her so close her breasts were crushed against his chest. She had to admit that she and Brady fit perfectly against each other. She could feel the warmth of his body through her dress, and the wild beating of her heart against his. Was his breath coming faster than usual, or was it just wishful thinking on her part that she had disturbed him just a little?

If I could be with you one hour tonight. If I was free to do the things I might . . .

Margie floated along in a haze, only vaguely aware of the crooning voice coming from the jukebox or that the arms holding her had loosened and now held her gently. Brady pressed his cheek to hers. Her steps matched his as if they had been dancing together forever. She closed her eyes and wished just for an instant that the song would never end. But it did.

Brady took her arm and led her back to the table and shoved her at Deke when he stood.

"Here's your girl. Thanks for the loan."

With a feeling of anger and frustration Brady strode back along the booths toward the bar. As he approached it, he was suddenly knocked off his feet by a meaty fist that slammed into his face.

Chapter 14

While Brady was dancing with Margie, two men had come into the PowWow and moved down the bar to stand behind a big, rough man in a billed cap.

"That was a shitty thin' to do," one of the men said to the other. "Slashin' a man's truck tires is low as ya can get."

"Yeah, 'specially when he's got a load in the back."

The man in the billed cap turned slowly around. "Whater ya talkin' 'bout?"

"We was sittin' out front and seen that feller there dancing with the blonde in the blue dress come out and slash a tire on a Model A truck with a side door off. I was sayin' it was a shitty thin' to do."

"Sounds like my truck." The big man slid

off the stool. "If it was, I'm tearin' his head off. Back in a minute," he said to the barkeep.

Homer and Chester followed the man outside and heard his roar of rage when he saw his tire.

"That's a damn shame," Chester exclaimed.

"Can we help ya change the tire, mister?" Homer asked.

"I'll change the damn tire after I take the head off that son of a bitch!" The big man headed back into the bar.

Homer and Chester followed. The trucker waited until Brady left the dance floor and approached the bar before he stepped out and planted his heavy fist in his face.

The unexpected blow caught Brady flatfooted. He scarcely saw the man as he backpedaled to gain his balance. The next blow knocked him to the floor. He bounced to his feet like a cat.

"What the hell is the matter with you?"

Brady threw up an arm to weather the windmilling attack of arms and fists. He sidestepped and swung a jarring right to the mouth of his assailant. The blow would have stopped a bigger man, but it merely slowed down the trucker, who let out a bellow of rage and came at Brady again.

"Out! Get the hell out!" The shout came from the barkeep, Booger, who waded in between them swinging a shotgun. "Take your fight outside."

"I don't know what's got his ass up, but if he wants to fight, we'll fight." Brady wiped the blood from his mouth on his shirtsleeve.

"Ya know, ya goddamn tire slasher!" the trucker shouted.

Brady backed out of the doorway and into the space in front of the honky-tonk. While he eyed the man who wanted to whip him, a fierce love of battle welled up inside him. It had been a year or two since he had a good fight, and he was in the mood for it. He didn't know and didn't care what the man's bitch was. If he wanted a fight, he'd get one.

The trucker, tall as Brady but outweighing him by forty pounds, rolled up his sleeves. His friends gathered around him shouting encouragement.

Deke, Jody behind him, spilled out the door and hurried to him. "What's going on?" Deke asked Brady.

"I've no idea. The man wants a fight."

"Get outta the way, Deke. No need you gettin' hurt."

"Brady's with me, Booger. Ya think I'll stand back and let that bunch beat him up?"

"It'll be one-on-one. We'll see it's a fair fight — fer yore sake, Deke, 'cause he came here with ya." Booger cradled his shotgun in his arms. "If it was my tire he slashed, I'd stomp his ass in the ground."

"Whatta ya mean? Slashed whose tires?"

"The low-down polecat was seen slashin' Miller Evans's tire."

"That's a damn lie." Brady stepped out and pushed Deke behind him. "Who says they saw me?"

"Two fellers came in and told me they saw ya doin' it," Evans said, "and I'm taking the price of that tire outta yore hide."

"They lied, but if you want a fight, come on, ya big blowhard." Brady's eyes blazed with a leaping light, and his teeth bared a little.

"Wait, Brady! Wait!" Jody was tugging on Brady's arm. "Your tires have been slashed too."

"What?" Turning his back on the trucker, Brady went to where he had parked his car. All four tires were flat. The car was sitting on the rims. "Son of a bitch!"

"Here's the sheriff. Take over here, McChesney," Booger called. "I've got to get back inside."

"What's the problem?"

"How ya doin', Rex?" Deke said.

"Miller Evans come plowin' into my friend here accusin' him of tire slashin'. His truck wasn't even here when we got here. Brady was in the PowWow with me all the blessed time. 'Sides, his tires were slashed too."

"What makes you think this fellow slashed your tire, Evans?"

"He was seen doin' it, Sheriff. Some fellers came in the bar and told me."

"Loaded pretty heavy tonight, aren't you?"

"No more than usual. Got some feed to take to the ranch."

"Got anything under the feed, Evans?"

"Ah, hell, Rex. Maybe a bottle or two. Ain't nothin' to get in a sweat over."

"Where are the men who told you they saw this man slash your tire?"

"I don't know. 'Round here somewheres."

"Find them."

"Hell, Rex. You takin' his side?"

"I'm not takin' any side. Find the men." The sheriff, a tall, thin man with sharp blue eyes, focused them on Brady. "Who are you?"

"Brady Hoyt. Just passing through."

"He's staying at the campground, Rex," Deke said.

"Yeah? Don't suppose anyone saw who

slashed *his* tires. It isn't likely he did it himself."

Miller Evans came out of the bar. He eyed Brady but spoke to the sheriff. "The fellers who told me left when the fight started."

"Someone around here got a grudge against you, Mr. Hoyt?"

"I only got here today. I don't know anyone except Deke."

The sheriff took off his hat and scratched his head. "What'd these fellows look like, Evans?"

"I don't know. One was young, other'n a little older. Offered to help me change the tire. Seemed nice."

"If they were pulling a fast one, they would be. It appears to me that they wanted to stir up a little excitement, and both of you got suckered into it."

"Suckered, hell! I'm out four good tires and tubes," Brady said angrily. "And I owe that hotheaded dungheap a sock in the mouth." He glared at the trucker, who stood slightly behind the sheriff.

"Then come on and give it your best shot!" Evans stepped out, stood on spread feet and glared at Brady.

"Calm down." McChesney stepped between the two men. "You should have asked a few questions, Evans, before you started swinging your fists."

"Well, hell. You'da done the same. Fellers said that they saw him do it."

"I wouldn't have gone off half-cocked like you did. You owe the man an apology."

"Apology? Hell, I'll not be belly-crawlin' for nobody. But . . . I'll help ya change the tires if ya got any to change to."

"I'm not be needin' help from the likes of you," Brady growled.

"Evans, I'll help ya put your spare on, then ya can take me back to the garage," Deke said. "We'll pick up some tires for Brady."

"The son of a bitch even ruined my spare," Brady exclaimed.

Now that the excitement was over, the onlookers wandered back into the bar. The sheriff was speaking to his deputy, who had driven up. When he finished, he turned to Brady.

"My deputy said that two fellows in a coupe hightailed it out of town a while ago. If they are Evans's witnesses, they're long gone by now. Sorry this happened to you in our town, Hoyt."

"Yeah, well, so am I."

McChesney turned to the trucker. "This settled, Evans?"

"Hell no. It won't be settled till I get my

hands on those two shitheads that did this."

"Good luck."

While Deke helped Evans get his spare tire and wheel out of the truck, Brady squatted beside his front tire and wondered if any of the tires would be usable even with a heavy boot placed inside over the hole. If he had to buy four new tires and four new tubes, it was going to take a big bite out of his travel money. When he stood, Margie was beside him holding out a wet towel.

"Thanks." He held it to his face, wiped his cut chin, then his hands. Margie avoided his eyes. He continued to wipe his hands and look at her.

Thinking that she must say something, she said, "I asked the bartender for it."

"You went up to the bar?"

"Sure," she said, raising her chin. "I know my way around bars and speakeasies. Even brothels."

In spite of his cut lip, Brady had to grin.

"Don't go back in there by yourself." He waited a minute, his eyes holding her defiant ones. "You're not going to argue?"

"No. I've taken care of myself for a long time. I don't need your advice."

"Where's Mona and Rusty?"

"Over there." She jerked her head to the

259

side of the building where the couple were standing face-to-face, Rusty's hands on her shoulders.

"Smoochin'?"

"And if they are?"

"I'm jealous."

"Of . . . Rusty?"

"No, because I'm not smoochin' with you. Don't," he said when she turned away. "Give them a little time alone. Do you want to wait in the car?"

"We're goin' back to the garage, darlin'," Deke said before she could answer. "Do you want to go or stay here?"

"I'll stay with Mona and Rusty."

"Keep an eye on her, Brady. I'll bring back boots for the tires and tubes that will get you back to the campground."

"I'll jack up the front end and get the wheels off."

"The trucker is taking Deke back to the garage. Jody's helping Brady take the wheels off the front of his car."

"Anyone paying attention to us?" Rusty whispered close to Mona's ear.

"Brady and Margie looked our way a while ago. But he's busy now, and she's watching him and Jody."

"Will you scream if I kiss you?" Rusty

leaned against the building, drew her close and buried his nose in her hair.

"You won't know unless you try."

"I think I will."

"I'll not argue . . ." Her voice was a mere whisper against his mouth.

The warm pressure of his lips sent her senses spinning. They covered hers lightly, his tongue caressing the edge of her mouth. Her arms slid around his neck.

"Soft, sweet, delicious." His voice was no more than a sigh.

"Hummm . . ." A sweet, almost unbearable pain unfolded in Mona's stomach.

"Did you like that, sweet girl?"

"I love it. I've only kissed one other boy, and I . . . didn't like it much."

"He probably wasn't as good a kisser as I am."

"I suppose you've had a lot of practice."

"Yeah, lots." He laughed. "One time. I missed the mark and kissed her eye."

She giggled softly. "I'm glad you're not an expert. I might not be able to stand it."

"I never thought I'd ever meet a girl like you. I hoped I would."

She lifted her palms and caressed his face. "Then you like me . . . a little?"

"More than a little, sweet girl. But I don't want you to get too fond of me. I'm never going to see, Mona."

"I wish you could, even though you might not like me if you could see me and compare me to other girls."

"Don't say that," he scolded, and hugged her tightly to him. "I see you in my mind. Sweetheart, fifty years from now when I'm bald and have lost my teeth, you'll look the same to me."

"Do you think we'll know each other then?"

"I would like to think so. Do I dare kiss you again? Is anyone looking?"

"Jody, but he knows —"

"Knows what?"

"That I . . . like you."

"Do you go around kissing fellows you *don't* like?"

"All the time."

They laughed joyfully and decided that this was the happiest night of their lives.

"Let's get out of here. If that cowboy sees yore face, he'll know it was you who slashed his tires." Chester drove down the dusty road and pulled out onto the highway five miles west of town.

"All right. I've had my fun for now. We'll wait for them in Amarillo."

"I'm not going to Amarillo," Chester said

angrily. "I've got to get this car home to Mama."

"We'll send her a telegram. Tell her that you had a call to come to Amarillo. Gordon needed you."

"Gordon? Hell, we've not heard from him in ten years."

"That's why I said Gordon. She said at Grandpa's burial she had a longin' to see her oldest boy."

"Gordon's probably dead by now."

"Don't matter. It'll give us time in Amarillo to hit a few places and wait for the cowboy. Granny'll think yore out doin' good work helpin' her long-lost boy."

"I shouldn't've took her car."

"You still moanin' 'bout that?"

"I ain't anxious to be robbin' more stores either. I ain't wantin' to do no jail time, and I ain't wantin' to get shot."

"Christ, Uncle Chester. What money we got in Elk City ain't goin' to last hardly no time a-tall."

"Ya got more'n fifty from that grocery store."

Homer laughed. "That was slicker than snot. The fool never knowed what hit him. I was in and outta there like a scalded cat."

"Ya'd better not hurt nobody too bad. I ain't for hurtin' anybody."

"Shitfire, Uncle Chester. Ya got no more guts than a crawly worm. Ya got to hurt folks once in a while, or they ain't goin' to respect ya."

"Yo're crazy."

"Might be, but I'm havin' a hell of a lot of fun. After I get a bit more money in my pocket, I'm goin' to find me a woman and have me a high old time. I ain't forgot the cowboy's blond babe, mind ya. I can wait. When the time is right, I'll screw her into the ground."

"All ya got on yore mind is that cowboy and screwin' women. Beats all I ever did see."

Chapter 15

She heard a rooster crowing.

Margie flipped the sheet up over her head. She didn't want to open her eyes and start another day. They had returned to camp last night after midnight, and sleep hadn't come until several hours later. She had lain wide awake for what seemed hours trying to sort out the emotions that were pressing down on her. The events of the past few days were crushing her spirit.

She was disgusted with herself. She was a fool. She was so mad she could scream. She stifled a groan as her mind began summoning back, in feverish detail, the feel of Brady's breath on her face, his arms and how she had melted into them, letting the music wash over her. She had wanted to stay there in his arms forever.

How she could have these thoughts about a man who thought so little of her was the most demoralizing of all.

Margie's common sense told her what she should do, but she seriously doubted that she had the nerve to do it. When they reached Amarillo, she should ask Elmer to let her off in the downtown area. She had no doubt that he would do it. She'd take a bus to California. Then let him explain where she was to the Putmans and to Brady, if they should ask.

She thought briefly of asking Deke if she could stay a few days, help his mother in the garden, then take the bus to California. On second thought, she realized that she couldn't impose on their hospitality.

Right now she had to figure out how to get through the day while avoiding Brady and keeping the others from knowing how really desperate she was.

After breakfast she approached the back of Deke's house, where Alvin was heating water in the iron pot for Grace to do her washing. Margie was relieved to learn that Brady had driven with Deke and Foley to Elk City to find a radiator for Foley's car and tires for his. Jody and Rusty had been left in charge of the gas pump and sat on a bench in front of the garage. Rusty was brushing the burs out of Blackie's thick coat of fur.

After washing her own clothes in a bucket and hanging them on the line, Margie pitched in to help Grace, who had not only her family's wash but Anna Marie's and Brady's as well.

Grace washed the clothes in the iron tub with a scrubboard, all the while chatting with Mrs. Bales.

"My watermelon pickles are good. I won a blue ribbon at the fair one year, a red the next. I'll be hornswoggled if I know what happened that time. Do you soak the rind in lime and cold water to crisp them up before you cook them?"

"Always. Do you add ground cloves or whole?"

"Whole. Stick cinnamon too."

The two talked as if they had known each other forever.

After she had washed a piece of clothing, Grace wrung it out and dropped it in the rinse water. Margie rinsed each piece, wrung it out and hung it on the line.

Anna Marie played happily on the porch, basking in the attention of Mrs. Bales, who had cut a string of paper dolls out of newspaper.

"I saw the chicken with three legs," Anna Marie called out to Margie. "One leg is little and just hangs down. Wanna see? I know where it is."

"As soon as we get through here, honey, we'll take a look at it. Are these yours too?" Margie asked Grace, indicating a pile of clothes on the end of the porch.

"They're Mona's. She's washing for herself and Jody. There was a fuss raised when *Miss Sugar* tried to add hers to the pile. Mona told her daddy in no uncertain terms that she was not washing Sugar's clothes. That man has sure got himself into a mess with that one."

"Good for Mona. I've not seen Sugar lift a hand to do anything but primp."

"She was honeyin' up to Brady this morning. I think she wanted to go to Elk City with the men."

"Did she go?"

"No. For once Foley put his foot down."

Margie rinsed one of Brady's shirts, then took it to the far end of the line and hung it up by the tail so that it would flop in the breeze. It was the blue one he wore the night they sat on the blanket and listened to the music.

"It's a shame about Mr. Hoyt's tires," Mrs. Bales said when Margie came back to the porch. "Deke seems to think it was someone wanting to cause a fight to create a little excitement."

"It did that, all right. When Brady hit the floor, Deke shot out of the booth yelling for Jody to come on and for Rusty to stay and take care of us girls."

"Oh, my. Did he really say that?" Grace asked. "I thank God for men who don't make my son feel useless."

"When everyone went outside, Rusty, Mona and I went along to see what was going on. Deke was right in the middle, between those two big men."

"That boy will tackle anything if he's mad enough. When he's mad, he thinks he's six feet tall," Mrs. Bales said with a click of her tongue.

Margie smiled. "I remember how he went after the man who took my money. He didn't wait for help from anyone."

"Uncle Brady was mad about his tires. He even said a . . . nasty word. He didn't know I was listening."

Grace caught Margie's eye. "Big ears," she mouthed.

"She doesn't miss much," Margie murmured.

"She's smart as a whip." Grace followed Margie to the pump, where she was filling a bucket of water to pour into the iron pot. "I wish I could keep her."

"He'd probably give her to you if you ask. He's going to palm her off on a woman he doesn't even know."

"Brady said he was taking her to her mother's sister."

"Yeah, he said that and that he doesn't know what kind of woman she is. Hasn't he told you about Anna's mother?"

"Not much."

"She wasn't much of a mother, according to Brady. The sister may be the same."

Grace frowned. "He wouldn't leave her with someone unless he was sure she really wanted her and would take good care of her. He cares a lot for that child."

"He puts up a good front. I'll give him that."

"Forevermore! Why do you say that? You liked him . . . at first."

"Never trust first impressions. It takes a while to get to know a person, especially a smooth-talkin' man. I've been burnt before. It'll not happen again."

Margie dumped the bucket of water into the iron pot, then poked a few sticks of wood in the fire beneath it.

"The water will be hot for Mona in no time at all."

"Aunty Grace, Margie — I gotta go."

"Come on, puddin'." Margie grabbed Anna Marie's hand, and they ran toward the outhouse.

When they came out, they were both laughing. "We made it just in time," Margie called to Grace. "We'll go tell Mona she'd better shake a leg and get her wash on the line so it can dry." Swinging hands, they headed for the campground.

At first Margie didn't notice, but when she did, she stopped dead still and a feeling of déjà vu washed over her.

Elmer's truck was gone.

Was history repeating itself? Had he left her here and taken everything she had in the world except the sixty dollars she had pinned in her brassiere and the clothes she had drying on the line?

"Honey," she said to Anna Marie, "go to Mona. She's there in front of the garage." Feeling as if a rock had fallen into the pit of her stomach, she hurried down into the campground where Alvin was tinkering with the motor on his truck. "Mr. Put . . . man?" Her voice cracked.

"Hello, Margie." Alvin brought his head up from under the hood of the car.

"Where did Elmer go?"

"He didn't say." Alvin wiped his hands on

271

a rag. "I heard the truck start up and thought he was working on the motor. Then he pulled out and headed down the highway toward Sayre."

"He didn't say anything?"

"Not to me. And as far as I know he didn't go near Rusty and Jody. He probably went into town to get a few groceries or some ice."

She shook her head. "He heard Deke say the iceman comes today."

"Are you thinkin' he might not come back?"

"I'd not put it past him. He'd think it's what I deserved."

"For what?"

"For being born," she said bitterly.

"He'll be back. I can't believe he'd just go off and leave you or us without some explanation."

"You don't know him like I do."

"I guess I never knew him at all. He was very congenial while we were planning this trip. I haven't been able to get a decent word out of him since that first night up in Missouri. I decided that the best way to get along with him was to leave him alone."

"Everyone probably heard me screaming at him last night. I just lost my patience."

"We heard and . . . frankly Grace and I

wanted to give you a pat on the back."

"I'm taking my things out of the truck. That is, if he comes back. Deke will help me get to a bus station. I can't continue on with him. His constant disapproving silence and his sly remarks are making a nervous wreck out of me."

"You could make arrangements to ride with Brady —"

"No!" Margie shook her head vigorously. "Elmer told Brady that I'm a . . . a thief. I'm surprised he hasn't told the rest of you that I'm not fit company for decent folks."

"Brady hasn't said anything. I'm sure he didn't believe —"

"Oh, but he did. But that's . . . Never mind about that. I'm sorry I interrupted your work. I'd better go look after Anna Marie so Mona can do her wash."

"There's a cloud bank building in the southwest. It could mean rain or could be a dust storm."

"Grace has her clothes on the line. It won't take long for them to dry."

"Don't worry, Margie. You've got friends here."

"Thank you, Mr. Putman."

As she passed the Luker tent, she glanced in to see Sugar sitting on the mattress plucking her eyebrows. She was leaning back against a box, her feet on the mattress and her thighs spread, exposing herself all the way up to her crotch. A large bottle of NeHi soda pop sat beside her. Shocked at the vulgar display, Margie hurried on by.

Margie was sitting on the bench with Rusty, and Jody was putting gas in a car that had pulled in off the highway, when Brady's car turned in and stopped in front of the garage. His eyes caught hers as soon as he stepped from the car. His bitter stare made the color rise to flood her face. Margie managed to turn and smile at Rusty, although she didn't have the slightest idea what he had said.

"Howdy, darlin'. How's my girl?" Deke came and nudged her chin with his fist.

"Did you get what you went after?" She felt that she had to say something. Brady was listening.

"Sure did. Brady's fixed up with tires, and we got a radiator for Foley's car. It'll take us the rest of the day to put it in."

"We sold ten gallons of gas, Mr. Bales." Jody dug into his pocket and brought out a few bills and some change.

"Tell you what, son. Keep a dollar of that and hang here for the rest of the day so I can work on your pa's car."

"No, I'll watch the pump and do anything else I can to help, but I'll not take your money."

"Well, hold on to it for now."

Margie, feeling out of place among the men, inched by Deke and slipped around the side of the garage. Once out of sight, she walked faster. Then a hand on her arm pulled her to a stop. She knew who it was without turning around.

"Where'd Elmer go?"

"How would I know?" She tried to pull away from him. "Let go of my arm. I need to help Grace get the clothes off the line."

"Deke told me what happened when you were here before."

"So? I'm supposed to be thrilled about that?"

"I didn't believe what Elmer said."

"That just plumb tickles me to death." She drew in her lower lip, her face stiff with brittle cynicism.

"How many times do I have to say it?"

"Actions speak louder than words, Mr. Hoyt."

"I was rough when I kissed you. I admit it."

"I've forgotten all about *that*. Now, let go of me." Her voice had savage, raw feeling in it.

"You haven't forgotten it, and neither have I."

"Why would I remember the kiss of a footloose cowboy? I've kissed hundreds —"

"Shut-up lyin'. You've done no such thing."

"Ask Elmer. He'll tell you, if he comes back, about all the men in Conway, Missouri, that I serviced. I had a real good business going, but decided business would be better in California."

"I could shake you." He looked at her set face and blazing eyes for a long time. Then he muttered, "To hell with it."

The instant his hand left her arm, Margie walked quickly away before the tears she fought so hard to hold back disgraced her.

Noon came, and still Elmer hadn't returned. Embarrassed to be at loose ends while everyone was preparing the noon meal, Margie found a hoe in the shed and went out to Deke's garden patch. She was sure Grace would invite her to eat with them, and she didn't think she would be able to bear the clicking tongues, the pitying glances and the unspoken questions about what she would do if her father had gone off and left her.

She had cleared weeds from one row of

beans when Deke came to the edge of the garden and called to her.

"Darlin', whater ya doin' out here?"

"Clearing out some weeds. I love working in a garden. When I was here before, Leona and I canned a bushel of beans and one of tomatoes from this patch."

"Mama sent me to find you. She's cooked up some ham and beans and made a bread puddin'."

"I had a big breakfast, Deke."

"I ain't takin' a no, darlin'. Come talk to me while I eat."

She batted her eyes continually as she walked back down the row toward him. The closer she got to him, the harder it was to keep the tears at bay.

He knew, and held out his arms.

"Oh, Deke, what'll I do?" It was all she could get through the sobs that clogged her throat. She leaned her forehead on his shoulder and let the tears flow. He stood silently holding her, his hand stroking her back.

Neither of them was aware that Brady had come around the corner of the barn and was watching them, his eyes hard, his mouth grim.

"I'm sorry, Deke."

"Don't be sorry, darlin'. Do you think

277

your pa has gone off and left you?"

"I don't know. He's so . . . ornery."

"Tell ya what, darlin'. We'll cross that bridge when we come to it. Come on now, let's go have a nice cold glass of tea."

Deke carried the hoe and put it in the shed on their way to the house. The cozy kitchen was as she remembered it. The table was set for three, and Mrs. Bales was taking a pan of corn bread from the oven.

"You can wash up there at the washstand, Margie. Deke washed on the porch."

Margie ate. She enjoyed the meal after a week of food cooked over a campfire. When it was over, Deke went back to the garage and Margie stayed to help Mrs. Bales do the dishes.

"If you have anything you want to iron, dear, we'll just set the sad iron on the stove and put up the ironing board."

"Thank you. I'm grateful to have washed clothes; to have ironed ones will be a real treat."

"I'll be surprised if we don't get a storm out of those clouds." Mrs. Bales came in after throwing the dishwater off the end of the porch. "It's been trying to storm off and on for a week."

"I hope not. It's not even rained since we left home."

"We've got a good storm cellar. We've been in it once already this spring."

Deke came into the house in the middle of the afternoon to get a rag to tie around a cut on his hand. Margie held it over the washdish while his mother dabbed it with iodine.

"That hurts!"

"Too bad." Mrs. Bales continued to dab. "I keep this on hand because he's always getting cut. He'd just tie a dirty rag around it and go on if I didn't watch him," she scolded.

"Mama likes to fuss." Deke looked at Margie and winked.

"How's the work going?" she asked.

"Good. That big cowboy knows about as much about it as I do. He's a big help. We'd be farther along than we are if Foley's wife would stop prancin' around gettin' in the way. I wasn't surprised a-tall to learn she ain't the mother of his kids. They're two damn nice kids."

"Why, Deke, I thought you'd be bowled over by Sugar," Margie teased.

"You know better'n that, darlin'. She flirts with Brady right under her husband's nose."

"Brady could put a stop to it if he wanted to."

"He's between a rock and a hard place,

darlin'. The woman's a barracuda."

"What's that?"

"It's a little fish that eats everything in sight."

"Ugh!" Margie made a face. "If he keeps messing around with her, her husband will knock his block off."

"Darlin', I didn't say that *he* was doin' the flirtin'."

"Now, don't let that come off." Mrs. Bales finished tying a clean cloth around Deke's hand.

The afternoon wore on. Margie did her best to stay busy. She ironed a couple of dresses for Anna Marie and a blouse for Mona. Every so often she would look toward the campground to see if Elmer's truck was there.

By late afternoon she had resigned herself to the fact he was not coming back and that when the caravan left tomorrow she would not be with it. She knew that she would be welcome to stay with Deke and his mother until she could get a small suitcase for her meager possessions and make arrangements for a bus ticket. It hurt to think of the box of treasured keepsakes in Elmer's truck. But, she reasoned, they were only *things*.

Knowing that Brady was still in the garage with Deke, and wanting to get the dresses she'd ironed for Anna Marie to Grace before suppertime, Margie folded them over her arm and left the kitchen. She rounded the end of the house to see Elmer's truck turn into the drive and proceed on to the campground and park.

Margie stopped beside the garage. Her feet refused to carry her any farther. Sudden anger raged through her like a forest fire scorching everything in its path. She began to tremble.

The lousy, conniving horse's ass had deliberately stayed away all day in order to worry her. He wanted to make her so angry that she would stay here when they pulled out in the morning.

He wanted to be rid of her without his losing face with the others.

Chapter 16

Elmer was sitting in his canvas chair beside his truck, his hands tucked into the bib of his overalls, his feet stretched out in front of him, when Margie passed by carrying the dresses she had ironed for Anna Marie. Refusing to give him the satisfaction of even looking at him, she went on to the Putmans' camp and placed them on the back of the straight chair.

"He came back." Grace spoke in low tones. "Alvin wasn't sure he would."

"Neither was I. Where's Anna Marie?"

"She and Mona went to look at the chicken again. She thinks it's grand."

"It is strange. Several carloads of people stopped today to look at the snake, the chicken and the buffalo. All but one of them bought gas."

Grace's laugh was soft . . . and nice. "Mona won't go near the snake. She made Jody lift Anna Marie up so she could see it."

"Mona and Rusty danced last night. You would have been so proud of him."

"I am proud of him. It's been good for him to be with young folks."

"I guess you know that Mona has a crush on him."

"Yes, and I hope to God she don't break his heart."

"Or he hers. Young girls can be hurt easily."

"I know."

Grace watched Margie walk back past her father without giving him as much as a glance and wondered how she could put up with that cantankerous man.

Under lowering clouds darkness came early. It was nearly dark when Margie returned to the truck with her neatly folded clean clothes. She laid out the clothes she would wear the next day and repacked her suitcase. After mulling it over in her mind she had decided to ride with Elmer until they reached a town where she could catch a bus. It would be a clean break from the others in the caravan. There would be no explaining to do and no good-byes.

She would ask Deke to keep her box of

"keepsakes" until she could send for them. She sat on the bunk and waited for the light to go off in the garage and for Brady to go to the Putman camp before she carried the box up to the house.

Weariness overcame her. After a while she lay down and pillowed her head on her bent arm. She was tired not only in body but in mind. It had been a stressful day, not knowing if she had been abandoned here . . . again. She dozed fitfully, aroused briefly, then fell into a deep sleep.

She awakened with a startled cry and became instantly alert. Strong gusts of wind rocked the truck, and she heard the insistent rumble of thunder. She sat up in total darkness clutching the edge of the bunk. The back flap had been let down and tied. As a rule she was not afraid of storms, but sitting here alone in the darkness unable to see what was going on outside, she was desperately afraid and began to tremble violently as she dressed.

It seemed to her that she had been sitting there for hours when she heard a voice over the roar of the thunder.

"Margie! Margie, are you in there?"

"Yes, I'm here." She made her way to the end of the truck and began to claw at the rope holding down the flap. A corner of it opened suddenly. Brady stood there.

"We're going to the cellar." He reached for her and lifted her out over the tailgate, then quickly retied the flap.

Glancing upward, Margie glimpsed during the flashes of lightning a blanket of dark, rolling clouds. A gust of wind came up under her full skirt and wrapped it around her thighs. She fought to hold it down while the wind whipped her hair around her face.

"Anna Marie?" The wind whipped her words away, but he must have heard them.

"With Alvin," he shouted. "Deke is taking his mother to the cellar, and the Lukers are on their way. Where's Elmer?"

Margie pointed toward the cab of the truck, where she supposed he would be unless he had put up his pup tent in this wind. Holding her hand tightly, Brady pulled her around the truck until he could reach the door of the cab and yank it open.

"Come to the cellar," he shouted over the rumbling thunder, the roar of the wind and the rippling of the canvas covering the truck bed. "There could be a twister up there."

Elmer shook his head.

"Come on. We'll be safe in the cellar," Brady shouted angrily.

For an answer Elmer reached over and pulled the door shut.

Brady cursed. "Damn stubborn fool."

Wrapping an arm around her, Brady urged Margie up the path. Drops of wind-driven rain lashed them like pine needles. The door to the cellar was open, and the glow of a lantern came from within. Alvin stood on the steps, took Margie's arm and helped her scramble down the stairwell.

"Did you find Elmer?" Alvin shouted over the deafening noise of the approaching storm.

"He won't come."

"Darn fool. Where is he?"

"The cab of his truck."

"I'll go."

"He won't come, Mr. Putman," Margie said quickly.

"I'll go anyway."

Grace got up to protest, but Alvin was up the stairs and out, running toward the campground.

Benches lined the walls of the cellar. The Lukers sat on one of them; Grace, Rusty and Mona sat across from them on another. Anna Marie was cuddled in Rusty's lap, Blackie at his feet. Mrs. Bales sat on a wooden folding chair beside a box that held the lantern.

"Where's Deke?"

"He went to see about his animals," Mrs.

Bales said calmly. "He'll be here."

And he was. Minutes later the little man, his hair swirling wildly around his head, bounded down the uneven steps as agilely as a young fawn. And on his heels came Alvin.

"The stubborn fool wouldn't come," he told Margie.

"Thank you for trying."

Brady and Deke battled to close the door. Summoning all their strength, they managed to get the door up off the ground, then ducked into the stairwell as the wind caught it and slammed it shut. Deke produced a flashlight so that he could see to shoot the bolt that would keep it closed.

Now the noise of the storm was muffled.

Margie sat down on the end of the bench where the Lukers were. Alvin went to sit by Grace and put his arm around her. Brady, stooping to keep his head from hitting the cellar ceiling, sat beside Margie. Deke hung the lantern on a nail in one of the ceiling beams and sat down on the box.

Anna Marie slid off Rusty's lap and went to Margie, bringing a scrap of blanket with her. Margie lifted her up to sit on her lap, put her arms around her and snuggled her close.

"Are ya scared, Margie?"

"No, puddin'. I'm not scared. We'll be just fine down here." She covered the child with the blanket, tucking it in around her legs.

"I was scared. Uncle Alvin carried me so Uncle Brady could go get you. Then Rusty held me. Rusty likes me."

"Of course he does. We all like you, very much."

"*She* don't." Anna Marie lifted her head so she could see Sugar Luker. "She said, 'Go away, pest.'"

Margie's eyes collided with Sugar Luker's. If looks could kill, Sugar would have dropped dead.

"We don't pay any attention to her," Margie was goaded to say loudly enough for all to hear.

Silence followed. A chunk of something hit the cellar door.

"Let's hope that's not a limb from your peach tree, Mama." Deke put a reassuring hand on his mother's shoulder. "I thought we were only going to get a good thunderstorm until the wind came up and I saw those rolling clouds. They're the kind a twister could drop out of."

"I've heard that this is tornado country," Foley said. "Ever been in one?"

"Close, but not head-on. We sight a few

every year; usually in late summer."

"I'm glad we're here and not in some other campground," Alvin said. "We thank you for invitin' us down here."

Deke shrugged and after a long silent period, looked at Margie. "How ya doin', darlin'?"

"All right." She couldn't think of anything else to say. She hated the quiet within the cellar. She wished someone would say something so that she wouldn't be so conscious of Brady's hard body close to hers, or the big hand resting on his thigh, the hand that had cupped her head when he kissed her. She tried to concentrate on something else.

Mona, sitting close to Rusty, was glaring at her stepmother, daring her to make one of her sarcastic comments. Sugar was cuddled against Foley, her hand clutching the front of his shirt. Tension between Mona and Sugar was sharp as a knife.

Then Alvin began to sing.

> *"Give me that old-time religion,*
> *Give me that old-time religion,*
> *Give me that old-time religion;*
> *It's good enough for me."*

Grace joined the singing, then Rusty and

Mrs. Bales. Soon the others joined in. After several hymns Jody urged Rusty to sing alone.

"What do you want to hear?"

"One of the ballads you sang the other night."

Even without the accompaniment of his guitar Rusty's voice was low and haunting.

> *"Standing by the water tank,*
> *Waiting for a train.*
> *I'm a thousand miles away from home,*
> *Sleeping in the rain.*
> *My pocketbook is empty,*
> *Not a penny to my name . . .*

He sang with such feeling you could almost see in your mind's eye the lonely figure waiting for the train. He sang several ballads, then after coaxing from Mona, sang her favorite.

> *"In a little rosewood casket,*
> *Sitting on a marble stand,*
> *Are a package of love letters,*
> *Written by my true love's hand."*

Rusty's hand reached for Mona's. Her fingers interlaced with his, and tears filled her eyes. He continued to sing.

290

"While I listen to you read them,
I will gently fall asleep,
Fall asleep to wake with Jesus;
Oh, dear sister, do not weep."

In the quiet after he had finished, Sugar exclaimed, "Oh, my God! That's the silliest song I ever heard. Don't you ever sing anything happy, or about good times?"

"Sure," Rusty said calmly. "How about this:

"Happy days are here again.
The skies above are clear again.
So let's sing a song of cheer again.
Happy days are here again."

"If that's the best you can do, I prefer quiet."

"Sugar!" Foley removed his arm from around her. "That wasn't called for."

"She's got no more manners than an alley cat," Mona said staunchly.

"Mona, that's enough." There was a warning tone in Foley's voice. "This is not the time or the place for a family squabble."

"Then hush *her* up!" Mona said, and whispered an apology to Rusty.

"Thank you for the songs, Rusty," Margie said. "I enjoyed every one of them."

"I've heard a lot worse than that on the radio," Deke added. "You should be on the *Grand Ole Opry*. Don't you think so, Mama? Mama and I listen to Nashville every Saturday night."

Rain pounded on the slanting plank door of the cellar.

"Could be a little hail mixed with the rain," Alvin commented.

"Yeah," Deke said. "The wind may have gone down some. The thunder seemed to be moving farther away."

Margie had no idea how long she had sat there. She knew that her bottom was numb. Anna Marie had fallen asleep while Rusty sang.

"Let me hold her for a while." The softly spoken words came suddenly. Margie turned and found Brady's face close to hers. She looked down quickly.

"All right. My arms are tired."

Brady leaned into her to lift Anna Marie from her arms. When she was settled in his lap, Margie lifted the child's feet and legs across hers and adjusted the blanket around her.

"Are you cold?" Brady asked.

"No, I'm all right."

Silence. Even Deke didn't have anything to say. Sugar's rude remarks seemed to have dried up the conversation and placed a blanket of unease over the group in the cellar. Grace's head was against Alvin's shoulder, her eyes closed. Mona and Rusty whispered in each other's ears. Margie closed her eyes and dozed.

She awoke with a start and sat up quickly when she realized her head was against Brady's shoulder. Vowing to stay awake — and in order to whip up her anger against him — she recalled to mind the night he manhandled her like the loose woman he thought she was.

But instead of thinking of the hateful kiss and the hateful words that followed, she remembered the tender kisses they shared before Elmer poisoned Brady against her. Even after their quarrel at the PowWow, he had held her gently while they danced and had pressed his cheek against hers.

After tomorrow morning she would never see him again. Thinking about it made her want to cry.

"The rain has let up." Deke was at the cellar door. He shot the bolt back, lifted the plank door and let it fall back. "It's only a light drizzle now." He stuck his head out and looked around. "It looks like the wind has tore up jack. Branches are down all over."

"Take her, Margie." Brady shifted Anna

Marie to Margie's lap. "I'll go out with Deke and Alvin and look around."

Foley left Sugar's clinging arms and followed the men out, stopping to put a hand on Jody's shoulder with the unspoken request that he try to keep peace between his daughter and his wife.

The damp breeze blew from the open door, and Margie shivered and hugged Anna Marie close, welcoming her warmth.

Deke went to the barn to check on his animals, the others to see what, if any, damage had been done to their cars and trucks. Then Brady saw sparks dancing along the ground in the middle of the campground.

"Hold it," he said. "The electric wires are down. Watch where you step. If you come in contact with a hot wire on this wet ground, you're a goner."

"I'll go for the lantern." Alvin backtracked quickly.

He was back in less than a minute. "I hated to leave the women in the dark."

Brady picked up a long leafless branch, one of many strewn about. They proceeded cautiously toward the downed wire that was sending sparks over the wet ground.

"There! Good Lord!" Alvin exclaimed. "That's — that's — Elmer!"

The light from the lantern shone on the

body of the man who lay crumpled in the puddle of water. Nearby, the end of the live electric wire lay on the ground.

"Stay back. I'll try to move the wire away from him." Brady, using the branch, carefully lifted the deadly wire a few feet from the end and moved it a good six feet before it slipped off the end of the branch.

Alvin and Foley knelt beside the still form, turned him over and stared into his open, vacant eyes.

"Mother of Christ," Foley murmured. "He's dead!"

"No doubt about that."

Shocked into silence, the men looked down at the man who had rejected their attempts to be friendly.

"It looks like he may have decided to come to the cellar after all. The limb from one of those trees broke off and snapped the wire. It caught him out here in the open."

The beam of Deke's flashlight danced along the ground as he approached.

"I see we got a downed wire."

"That's not all that's down." Alvin moved aside and held up the lantern.

"Godalmighty!" Deke peered closer. "Is he dead?" The question was moot, he knew, even as he asked it.

"We should get him out of this puddle," Brady said.

"Put him in the garage. I'll hop on my cycle, get the sheriff and someone out here to take care of that hot wire."

"We can take my car." Brady moved to lift Elmer beneath his arms. Foley took his feet.

"Better leave it as it is. The wind could come up and whip that wire around. I'll go on my cycle."

"Hadn't thought of that."

Deke led the way and had the garage doors open by the time they reached it. They laid Elmer down on the floor beside Foley's car. Deke covered his face with a towel.

Alvin shook his head sadly. "Poor stubborn fool. I don't know what got into him this past week."

"His stubbornness got him killed," Brady said without feeling. "I urged him to come with us to the cellar, but he'd have none of it."

"Will the sheriff bring the undertaker?" Alvin asked Deke while he was filling an extra lantern with kerosene.

"I suspect he will after I tell him what's happened. Before I go, I'll light the lamps in the house. Mama won't stay in that cellar any longer than she has to." He lit the lantern and set it on a box beside the door.

"I'll bring the women up. Do you mind if they sit on your porch?"

"Lord, no. Bring Mama and the women up to the house, Mr. Putman. Mama will fuss over 'em."

"Margie has to be told." This came from Brady after Deke's cycle had roared off down the highway toward town.

"Do you want to tell her?" Alvin asked.

"No. She'll take it better coming from you."

Chapter 17

Margie took the news of her father's death quietly. It was almost as if Alvin had told her of the death of a stranger. She was sad that it had happened, but she felt no heart-wrenching grief. The implication of what this meant for *her* would take a while longer to sink in.

Everyone had been kind. Grace had told her how sorry she was and hugged her, as had Mona and Mrs. Bales. The men had removed their hats when they spoke to her. Margie knew they were sincere in their expressions of sympathy. She also knew how each of them had felt about her father while he was alive. He was not a likable man.

The midmorning air was fresh and cool — not that she noticed as she walked down to the campground. It hit her, as she approached the truck, that now she was without kin. Elmer had not been much of a father, but he had given her life. As far as she knew, he was her only blood relative. Her half brother's family, if he had one, probably didn't even know that she was alive and wouldn't care if they did.

Earlier, feeling detached, she had sat on Deke's porch and watched the undertaker take the body away. Shortly afterward, Brady came to the porch with the contents he had taken from Elmer's pockets tied in a handkerchief.

"I told the undertaker that I'd bring down clean clothes sometime this morning."

"He kept the box locked where he kept his things."

"You have his keys. Do you want to bury him here or send him back to Conway?"

"Here. There's no one back there."

"Do you want me to take care of it?"

"I don't want to put you out —"

"I want to help."

"I'll go look for something to bury him in."

"I thought you would want to know, so I asked the undertaker how much this was going to cost. He said the grave space is five dollars, and his fee plus the casket is forty.

There is money there in Elmer's billfold. I didn't count it, but I believe it's enough."

"I guess we'll need a preacher."

"Not necessarily. Alvin will conduct a service if you want him to. The undertaker suggested ten o'clock in the morning."

"The families won't want to wait until noon to leave. Mrs. Luker is wanting to go today."

"Foley put the kibosh on that. Alvin will stay. So will I."

"I'll go to the truck and see what I can find for the burial."

"The undertaker will need some information about Elmer for the records."

"I'll write down what I know." She left the porch and started down the path toward the truck. Brady kept step with her. When they reached the truck, he took her arm.

"Margie . . . I'm sorry about what happened the other night. I shouldn't have been rough with you."

"It's all right."

"I've no excuse except to say I was frustrated . . . because you seemed to think that I would take more than I was offered."

"It doesn't matter."

"It matters to me."

"Once a stink is out of a box, it can't be put back in."

"What do you mean?"

"I understand you thought I was a silly, starstruck girl who would welcome that kind of treatment. Forget it."

She fumbled to untie the wet ropes on the flap on the back of the truck. Brady reached over her, blocking her in with his body, and pushed her hands away. He untied and rolled up the flap.

"Thank you. I appreciate your help with . . . the funeral. But if you'd rather not, I'm sure Deke would —"

"I'm sure he'd do what he could, but he doesn't need to, because I'm here." He let down the tailgate and took her arm when she stepped up onto the box to climb into the truck. "I'll be back in a little while to get whatever you want to send to the funeral home."

She nodded.

"You look worn-out. Why don't you lie down and sleep for a while?"

She nodded again, stepped up into the truck and sat down on the bunk. When she was sure that she was alone, she covered her face with her hands and allowed the tears to run between her fingers and down her cheeks. She cried silently, not from grief over Elmer, but because she felt as if she were floating on a river of unreality and there was a waterfall just ahead.

A wave of fatigue washed over her. She loosened the top buttons at the neck of her blouse and lay back on the bunk. Her spine straightened painfully. She flexed her shoulders and rolled her head from side to side to ease her tense muscles. Her body was tired to the point of collapse.

"What will happen next?" she whispered into the silence that gave no answer.

Alvin had tried to assure her that something would be worked out so that she could continue on with the caravan. Knowing how Brady felt about her made it all the more humiliating to have to accept his help.

Sometime later she heard the sound of voices coming from the Luker camp. Then a car passed on the highway. It was time to face what had to be done.

She sat up and reached for the bundle of things taken from Elmer's pockets. Inside she found a ring of keys, pocketknife, worn billfold, pocket watch and some loose change. In the billfold was fifty-eight dollars. Thank goodness it was enough for the burial. She was sure that Elmer had the money from the sale of his house and the ice company put away somewhere, but it didn't matter: She wasn't entitled to it.

When Goldie, his wife, was notified of his

death, she would search out every nook and cranny for whatever he had left. Everything he had, including the truck, now belonged to her even if she had gone off and left him.

Margie removed the pad from the box she had been sleeping on and tried each of the keys in the padlock until she found the one that opened it. Feeling jumpy, as if Elmer might come around to the back of the truck and catch her searching through his private possessions, she opened the lid.

In one end of the box were several pairs of neatly folded overalls and shirts, a black serge suit and black shoes with socks stuffed in the toes. Margie wondered if this was the suit he'd worn when he and Goldie were married. On the top of his underwear was a white shirt with a black string tie in the pocket.

At the other end of the box was a mantel clock wrapped in a piece of blanket, a square metal box secured with another padlock, a handgun and several boxes of shells. Tucked down alongside of the clock was a red Prince Albert tobacco can.

She took out the black suit, shook the coat and held it to the light. The suit appeared to be new. The white shirt was wrinkled but clean. She refolded the suit and shirt and set the shoes beside them.

Margie had the feeling of invading Elmer's privacy when she fitted a key in the lock of the metal box to open it. There wasn't much in it: two flat, round snuff cans with something heavy in them, apparently coins. A half dozen letters were tied with a string; an envelope held a cameo necklace. There was also a lady's lapel watch and a pair of baby shoes.

She pulled one of the envelopes from the stack, opened the flap and gasped in amazement. Instead of a letter, the envelope held four fifty-dollar bills. When she recovered from the surprise of finding the money, she looked in the next five envelopes. Two one-hundred-dollar bills were in each.

In the last envelope was a two-sheet letter. She put the sheets back in the envelope still so shocked she didn't bother to read the letter. With shaking hands, she retied the envelopes, put them back in the metal box and locked it.

She had never in all her life seen so much money at one time. She closed the lid on the wooden box and replaced the padlock. It didn't even occur to her to claim the money. Elmer had married, so, of course, it belonged to his wife.

Goldie would be overjoyed. Damn her!

Margie had never seen her father in anything but overalls. The shiny black shoes she had placed beside the suit that she had laid out for Brady to take to the funeral parlor looked as if they had never been worn. She pulled a sock from a shoe. Rolling the top of the sock down to turn it right side out, she felt a hard lump in the toe and pulled out two fifty-dollar bills folded in a small tight square. She stared at them dumbfounded for a long moment, then looked in the other sock and found the same. Two hundred more dollars.

Margie tucked the money in her skirt pocket and quickly searched the pockets of the suit. She found nothing but a stick of Juicy Fruit gum. She was refolding the trousers when Brady appeared. He stood at the end of the truck, his hat pulled down over his eyes.

"Margie?"

"He had a suit."

"Do you want to go to town with me?"

"No."

"I think you should. The undertaker will want to know a few things."

"I don't even know how old he was," she said irritably. "He didn't think enough of me to even tell me he had married — for the third time. I had to find it out when someone came into the café where I was working."

"The date of his birth would be on his driver's license if he had one. Did you look in his billfold?"

She held out the billfold. "I only looked to see if there was enough money to bury him." She turned her back and picked up the stack of folded clothes.

"He was born in '85," Brady said, slipping a card back in the billfold. "That makes him forty-eight."

"That sounds about right. Granny said he was twenty-five when I was born and he had already buried one wife."

"Was he born there in Conway?"

"As far as I know."

"I wish you'd come with me. You don't have to get out of the car if you don't want to."

"I don't want to go," she said stubbornly. "If you don't want to take the burial clothes, I'll ask Deke."

"It isn't that I don't want to go," he said patiently. "I think it would be good for you to get away from here for a while."

"Well, I don't. I've got thinking to do. I can do it better here by myself. I've got to decide what to do."

"Are you worried that we'll all pull out and leave you here by yourself? We'll not do that."

"I won't be by myself. Deke will help me sell the truck. The sheriff will help me locate Goldie. She'll come running if she thinks she's getting some money."

"Is that what you want to do?"

"It isn't a matter of wanting. It's what I've got to do."

Brady saw the fatigue in her face, the dark circles beneath her eyes. "Why don't you lie down and sleep for a while? I'll give the undertaker the information."

"Pay him with the money in the billfold."

"You've got friends here, Margie. Don't push them away."

"I appreciate your staying for Elmer's burial."

"We're not staying for Elmer. We're staying for you."

"When he's in the ground, your obligation will be over. I've always taken care of myself, paid my own way. I've never been a burden on anyone and don't intend to start now."

Brady looked at her long and steadily. He saw her quivering lips, her chin tilted defiantly, the overbright eyes that were trying to hold back tears. She was tired and scared and, Lord, how he wanted to take her in his arms and tell her that she wasn't alone. Instead he reached for the clothes and backed away.

He had taken only a few steps when he heard the back flap on the truck drop down.

When Margie awoke, she realized that the sun had gone down and that she had slept the day away. She could smell the smoke from the supper fires. While she slept, someone had stepped up into the truck and covered her with a sheet.

She sat up on the side of the bunk and ran her forked fingers through her hair. Her stomach growled, and she had to use the outhouse. Dreading to leave the truck but knowing that she must, she ran a comb through her hair and held it back from her face by slipping a ribbon beneath it, tying it in a bow and moving the bow back to be covered by her hair.

She made it to the outhouse without being intercepted, but she wasn't so lucky on the way back. Foley Luker stopped her to invite her to eat supper with them.

"Thank you, but I've got something laid out."

"If there's anything we can do, let us know. Would you like Mona to come over and stay with you?"

"No, but thanks." Margie shook her head and looked directly at Sugar, who had come to stand beside her husband. "I'll manage just fine." She walked away, her head high.

"She don't want Mona. She wants to sleep with Brady," Sugar said spitefully and loud enough for Margie to hear.

Foley turned on his wife. "Shut up! Don't you have anything nice to say about anybody?" He stalked off and left her standing.

Margie climbed into the truck and looked in the icebox. The day before, Elmer had bought ice as well as eggs, a ring of baloney and milk. In the cupboard were bread, crackers, pork and beans and canned peaches. Margie buttered two slices of bread and cut the baloney in chunks. She sat on the bunk and ate slowly.

"Darlin'? Are you all right?" Deke came to stand at the end of the truck.

"I'm fine, Deke. I was tired and slept the day away."

"It's what ya needed, darlin'. Why don't ya come up to the house and stay with Mama? I'd stay here with ya, but I'm goin' to be workin' on a motor that was brought in from the ranch where I used to work."

"I don't need anyone with me, Deke. I'll stay right here. I've got to decide what I'm going to do."

"Ya know yo're welcome to stay here long as ya want. And if I can help in any way, ya only got to ask."

"I know that, and I'll not hesitate to ask."

"Get some rest, darlin'."

When she finished eating, Margie put the back flap down, filled the washdish with water from the barrel, washed herself from head to toe and felt considerably better.

From where he sat eating supper with the Putmans, Brady had seen Margie leave the truck, go to the outhouse and talk with Foley on the way back. He couldn't hear the conversation, but he was certain that Sugar said something after Margie had left that didn't sit well with Foley. He had stalked off leaving his wife standing with her hands on her hips glaring after him. It was about time he got that woman in line. She was a walking, talking troublemaker.

Brady brought his attention back to what Alvin was saying.

"It's too bad that Elmer went the way he did. The man turned sour the last week or so. I was having my doubts about going partners with him in the ice business when we got to California. Luker said the same."

"You don't have to worry about that now."

"Margie is as nice a girl as I've ever met, and Elmer treated her like dirt." Grace passed around boiled eggs. She had bought several dozen from Mrs. Bales. It was a treat to eat them. She usually had to save them for cooking.

"Rusty, will you take the shell off mine?" Anna Marie put the egg in Rusty's hand. It was amazing to Brady how the child had adapted to Rusty's blindness.

"Sure, little puddin'." Rusty peeled the egg and ran his sensitive fingertips over it to make sure it was free of shell pieces. "There's salt here on my plate if you want to use it."

"Thank you, Rusty. Can I give Blackie a bite of my bread?"

Once again Brady thanked his lucky stars he had met up with the Putmans. But Anna Marie was becoming so attached to them that he feared her reaction when they parted company in California.

"I'll go over and talk to Margie." Alvin placed his empty plate on the table. "Tomorrow after the service we should get on down the road."

"What will we do if she refuses what we've talked about?" There was concern in Brady's voice. He didn't understand Margie's hostility toward him. Nor did he understand why he was so concerned about that hostility. He only knew, deep down, that he wasn't going off and leaving her to flounder around by herself.

"There isn't anything we can do. She's a grown woman. Do you want to come with me, hon?" he asked Grace.

"I'll come if you want me to, but it might be better if you talked to her alone." Grace slipped her hand under his arm and hugged it to her. "You can talk the skin off a rabbit when you set your mind to it."

"Bein' able to talk comes in handy once in a while. I talked you into marryin' me even though your pa said I wasn't worth the powder it would take to blow me up. He said that if you hitched up with me, you and a passel of younguns would end up in the poorhouse."

"He was wrong, and I've not been a bit sorry I chose you over that sissified corset salesman he wanted me to marry."

Alvin laughed and hugged her. "You could have had free corsets for life."

"Who needs 'em?"

"You sure don't. Even after twenty-three years you're as trim as you were at eighteen."

"Sweet-talkin' me, ain't ya? You're not getting another egg no matter how you rattle on, if that's what you're anglin' for. They're for the noon meal tomorrow."

"You're a mean, cruel woman, Gracie

Louise Putman," Alvin said affectionately, and dropped a kiss on the top of her head.

"Go on with you. Just don't forget that Margie's got pride she hasn't used yet. Tell her I'm expecting her for breakfast in the morning. After I finish with the dishes Anna Marie and I are going up and sit on the porch with Mrs. Bales. I'm sure glad we stopped here. I've taken a likin' to that woman."

Brady watched the couple, seeing the loving, comfortable way they were with each other. It brought back deeply buried memories of his mother and father. They had loved each other, and their love had included their sons. He remembered how his father would pull his mother down on his lap and nestle his face in the curve of her neck. Poor Brian had thought he was going to share with Becky what their parents had. But it hadn't worked out that way.

Brady vowed, then and there, never to marry until he found a woman who would love him with all her heart and soul. One who would stand beside him through good times and bad, be his best friend as well as his lover.

Loud voices jarred Brady from his reverie. At the other end of the campground Sugar was arguing with Foley. He had moved the car from the garage and parked it beside their trailer. His hands were on her shoulders trying to restrain her. Suddenly she swung her hand and slapped him. When he released her, she tried to hit him again. He caught her arm and pushed her away.

Sugar stood still for a moment. Low, angry words streamed from her lips, then she turned, left the campground and walked down the highway toward town.

Chapter 18

Foley stood at the back of his car and watched Sugar leave. This trip had been an eye-opener. It suddenly occurred to him that her actions didn't hurt nearly as much as they would have a few weeks ago.

Sugar was showing an altogether different side of herself from the one she had presented when they first met and during the first few weeks after they had married. Good Lord, how can a woman be so sweet and loving one minute and a real bitch the next? Foley had begun to wonder if his loneliness and his desire for sexual satisfaction had caused him to make a complete fool out of himself. Now he no longer had to wonder.

Let a pretty young thing make up to a sex-

starved man, and he loses what few brains he ever had.

"Pa?" Jody had come up beside him. "Do you want me to go get her?"

Foley didn't answer for a moment, then said, "No, son. Let her walk off her snit. I'll go get her in a little while." He turned a tired, almost defeated face to Jody. "Thank you for your patience. My marrying her hasn't turned out like I thought it would. I know this has been hard for you and Mona, and I'm sorry, son."

"Harder on Mona than on me."

"Well, what's done is done," Foley said with resignation. "I'll keep my eyes open from now on."

"She was so different from Mama that it was hard for me and Mona to warm up to her."

"It's true. She's nothing like your mother. I wasn't looking for someone to take her place. No one will ever do that." Foley's voice became rough, and he walked quickly away.

Margie always liked the early evening hours. She loved to watch the setting sun change the colors of the sky and to inhale the cool, fresh air, with the smell of the greening pastures, as it swept across the land.

When she was younger and her granny was alive, everything had been easy. She had never imagined that life would be so hard, so lonely, so full of disappointments, and could end so quickly. Like any young girl, she had dreamed of meeting a strong man who would love her with all his heart. And, as couples did in the movies, they would build a life together, fill a home with children and laughter and live happily ever after.

She supposed that was what was the matter with her now. There was an emptiness within her, a yearning that still begged for that fairy-tale dream. She was a woman with a woman's love to give; and in her ignorance she had reached out to Brady Hoyt because he was handsome and had been kind and attentive when she so badly needed a friend.

She had been blinded by loneliness. What a fool she was, and how he must have secretly laughed at the naive small-town girl with the big dreams.

"Evenin', Margie." Alvin approached as Margie stepped down from the truck.

"Hello, Mr. Putman."

"We would have had you come to supper, but Brady said you were sleeping. Grace sends an invite to breakfast in the morning."

"That's nice of her."

"Can we talk a little?"

"Sure. I'll get Elmer's folding chair for you." She reached in the truck for the chair, took it to the front of the truck, then perched herself on the fender.

"Nice evening." Alvin sat down and stretched his legs out in front of him. "I thought Missouri's weather changed fast. It can't hold a candle to Oklahoma weather. The storm we had last night was a real tail twister. I only wish Elmer had come with us to the cellar."

"It was a freaky thing that happened to him. He was in the wrong place when the electric line broke."

"I've heard of electrocution by hot wires. I never thought I'd see it firsthand. Being in water when around electricity is about the worst place you can be."

"Is this going to ruin your plans to set up your ice business?"

"I don't think so. Luker and I have talked it over. It'll mean that there will be two of us instead of three, and we'll have to try for a bigger loan from a bank."

"Elmer had a wife. She left him a few months ago and went out to California. I thought that was his reason for going out there."

"He never mentioned a wife to me. She

318

may have already left when we started talking about a partnership a couple months ago."

"Everything he had now belongs to her." She glanced toward the Putman camp and saw Brady squatting on his heels beside Rusty, but he was looking toward her.

"Do you know where his wife is?"

"No." She brought her attention back to Alvin. "I'd only seen her a couple of times — from a distance. The town was full of rumors about them. They married suddenly but were not together very long. I can't think that my father would be easy to live with. The joke around town was that he was so miserly he'd skin a mosquito for the hide."

"He may have been different with her."

"Something caused her to leave." Margie was aware that Brady was still watching. It made her nervous. "Deke will help me sell the truck. I'll give the money and what I found in his locked box to the sheriff. I don't think it's my place to find her."

"Then what will you do?"

"Get myself a bus ticket." Margie touched the two hundred dollars still in her skirt pocket. "I'm going to keep out enough money to get me to California and a little more to last until I find a job. I think he owes me that much."

"Have you considered taking the truck on to California and turning it over to Elmer's wife out there?"

"I may not be able to find her. Besides that, I can't drive this truck all the way to California."

"You can hire Jody Luker to drive. He's been drivin' Foley's ice truck for several years."

"If I pay out my money for a driver, I won't have much when I get there."

"Pay him out of Elmer's money. You'll be taking the truck to his wife. It'll save you bus fare."

"I've not the slightest idea how to take care of a car of any kind. All I know about them is that they need water and gas and air for the tires."

"We want you and your truck in the caravan, Margie." Alvin spoke earnestly. "It will be safer for all of us. Brady and I will see that the truck is kept in running order."

Margie shook her head. "I don't like having to depend —"

"You'll be doing us a favor. If you decide to come along, you can take your meals with us. Grace would welcome your help."

"No. You've already got Brady and Anna Marie."

"He pitches in on groceries. You could do the same."

"No. I thank you, but I'd rather be on my own." Margie put her hand in her pocket and fingered again the bills she had taken from Elmer's socks before she sent his clothes to the funeral home. "It would be different if I could drive."

"You can learn by doing. Along the way there will be places where there is little or no traffic. We'll help you in the evening. Then the first thing you know you'd be an old hand at it. We're all hoping you'll stay with us."

"You and Grace?"

"Me and Grace, Brady, Rusty, the Lukers."

"I don't know, Mr. Putman. I'm afraid I'll slow you down."

"Elmer, Foley and I made an agreement when we started that we would hang to-gether — for safety. It has proven to be a good idea. If one or even two of us had been in that campground the other night, we'd have been easy pickings for the robbers."

"What about Mr. Luker? Mrs. Luker doesn't like me at all."

"Mrs. Luker doesn't like any of us. Foley may be waking up to the fact that he's got to take a strong hand with her."

"I wouldn't know what to pay Jody even if his father let him drive for me."

"He may not want pay, but if he does, I'd suggest not more than a dollar a day. I figure it'll take us a little more than three weeks to get there if we don't rest on Sundays. That's somewhere around twenty-one dollars. And you'd get a better price if you sold the truck out there."

"I'm not interested in getting more money for Goldie."

"Can't say that I blame you for that."

"Elmer was tight with his money, but I can't believe that she left empty-handed."

"I'm surprised Elmer wasn't wearing a money belt."

"He had his money locked in a stout box. It would take an ax to open it without a key."

"I don't think it's wise to put all your eggs in one basket, Margie. Someone could come along and steal the truck."

Alvin took out his pipe, lit it and watched Rusty and Mona walking arm in arm out to the fenced pasture where Deke kept his buffalo and his horse.

Lord, please let my boy find a woman who will love him as I have loved his mother. If Mona isn't the one, I'm still grateful for the happiness she's brought to him.

After a while, Alvin said, "It wasn't my intention to put pressure on you, Margie. You're a grown woman and know what you want to do. Whatever it is, we will do what we can to help you."

"I'll have to talk to Jody before I know if I have a choice or not."

"All right. Let me know what you decide."

"Mr. Luker is leaving. I suppose he's going after his wife. She had one of her little tantrums, left him and walked down the highway toward town."

"The man's got his hands full with that one."

Inside the Ford coupe at the top of the hill, Homer Persy and his Uncle Chester surveyed Deke's campground.

"They still ain't got electric down there. In a while it'll be darker'n inside a black-bird's ass." Chester sent a quick look at his nephew. "You could sneak in there, cut up the cowboy's tires again, then we could go home."

"Stop bein' a nervous Nellie. Grandma's got your wire about goin' to help Uncle Gordon and won't expect us back for a month."

"She'll want news of him."

"We'll give her news. In a day or two we'll wire her and say that he's come down with

323

somethin' and we have to take care of him till he's on his feet. Don't ya have any imagination a-tall?"

"I hate lyin' to Maw."

"Why? She'll never know the difference. Gal-damn! Looks like one of the women is takin' off down the highway."

"What's she doin' that for?"

"Might of had a spat with her old man. Hot dog! We'll wait a bit, then follow 'er."

"You're goin' to get us hung," Chester moaned.

Homer was too excited to listen to his uncle's mutterings.

"Wait till she gets on down past that clump of woods."

"I'm tellin' ya, Homer. We ain't takin' no woman! We could get hung for kidnappin'."

"Trust me, Uncle Chester. It's near dark. We'll offer her a ride, politelike. She ain't goin' to recognize us."

"She will too."

"Them birds in the campground don't know this car either. So ease on down there."

Muttering that Homer had no more sense than a pie-eyed mule, Chester started the car and drove on down the hill.

"Get up to twenty-five when we pass the garage. We don't want them to think we're pokin' along. Then slow when we get by."

"Do this, do that. Yo're good at givin' orders."

Homer paid no attention to his uncle's grumbling. His eyes were on the woman walking at the edge of the road.

"Ease up on her — by damn, I think it's the hot-blooded, black-haired bitch that give us supper. Howdy," he said when they were even with Sugar. "You needin' a ride somers?"

"What's it to you?"

"Nothin'. Just offerin' ya a ride. Be glad to take ya where yo're goin'."

"I'm goin' to town."

"So are we, ma'am. No sense in a lady walkin' when she can ride."

Sugar stopped. The car moved past her before Chester could stop. Homer opened the door, stepped out and made a courtly bow.

"We're harmless and at yore service, pretty lady," he said with a charming grin.

"You'll take me to town?"

"Sure will. It's just down the road a mile or two."

Sugar hesitated only a moment, then stepped up onto the running board. She sat down, then moved over into the middle of the seat. Homer got in and slammed the door.

"My name is Homer. His is Chester. He don't talk much."

"My name is Selma, but I'm called Sugar."

"Fittin' name for a pretty lady." Homer put his arm across the back of the seat. Chester stepped on the gas, and the car shot off down the highway. "Whyer ya goin' to town, Sugar?"

" 'Cause I'm sick and tired of being in an old campground with a bunch of old farts whose idea of havin' fun is singin' hymns. Hey, wait a minute. You're . . . you're — Godalmighty! The other night you had a cap on!" To the surprise of both Homer and Chester, Sugar laughed, loud and long. "Now, ain't this rich? Whater you doin' here?"

"We wasn't goin' to rob ya, ya know. We was just havin' us a little fun when that cowboy poked his nose in." Homer's arm on the back of the seat slid down and hugged her to him. When she offered no resistance, he hugged her tighter.

"How come you're here? Are you goin' to California?"

"To tell you the truth, sweet little Sugar, we're pokin' along to get even with that cowboy who tied us up all night. The sheriff let us go 'cause we hadn't done nothin'.

What do you think of that?"

"You rascals you! You slashed his tires the other night!"

"Now, why would you go and think a thin' like that?"

"Because it's what I'd have done."

"Whee! Hot doggie-dog-dog! Uncle Chester, this is the woman I've been lookin' for all my life." He hugged her briefly with both arms.

"Hey, look. I've not forgotten what you said about me that night at the camp-ground." Sugar stuck her lip out in a pout.

"About ya being a bitch and all? I was tryin' to rile yore old man and the cowboy into doin' something foolish. I knew they both thought ya was the cat's meow. Honey, ya got to use yore old noggin when yo're in a fix like that. I knew sayin' that 'bout you would rile 'em more'n anythin', and they might drop their guard so we could get the hell out of there."

"You're as full of shit as a young robin."

Homer's laugh rang out. Sugar tilted her head so that she could see his face. He was young and full of life. Not bad-looking either.

"Where ya been all my life, sugar teat?"

"Lookin' for someone to put a little fun in mine."

"Ya found him, sweet thin'."

"That depends . . . sweet thin'." Her voice was a breathy whisper. She leaned forward to look out the windshield "We're in town. God, what a dead place."

"We can go on up to Elk City. There's a couple hot honky-tonks up there. Have we got enough gas, Chester?"

"Yeah. But I don't think we ort to go there."

"Go to Elk City? Why not? We got us a good-time lady here who wants to go honky-tonkin'."

"You know why we shouldn't go there."

"Forget that. I want to show this sweet little thin' a good time. How 'bout it, sugar doll?"

"Got any money?"

"Some."

"Then let's go!"

"Will yore old man be after ya?"

"Probably."

"I would too, if'n ya was mine."

"He *adores* me! Take me someplace where he can't find me. I've had 'bout all of him and his damn kids I can take."

"Why'd a good-lookin' woman like you marry a clod like him?"

"Money, honey. He's got some, but he's not turnin' loose of it till he gets to California."

"A lot of it?"

"Enough."

"Maybe we can help ya pry some of it away from him."

"Maybe." Sugar looked at him and made a kissing movement with her lips. "I'll think on it."

"By damn, Uncle Chester. I'm fallin' in love with this woman."

Chapter 19

"Do you want me to go with you, Pa?"

"No, son." Foley slid in under the wheel of his car. "I'll go get her. She's goin' to be madder than a wet hen. You don't need to listen to her rant and rave. Hopefully she'll be calmed down by the time we get back."

Margie joined Jody. They stood together and watched his father leave the campground.

"Is he going to get Sugar?"

"Yeah. She got mad and walked off. It don't take much to set her off."

Margie walked beside him back to the Luker camp.

"Mona and Rusty are out walking," Jody remarked.

"Does that set all right with you and your father?"

He turned to look at her. "Because Rusty's blind?"

"Almost every time I see them they've got their heads together."

"Yeah." He smiled.

"You approve?"

"Sure, but it isn't for me to approve or to disapprove. It's all right with me as long as Mona is happy. If they love each other, it'll work out."

Margie tilted her head and looked up at the tall boy. "Mona is lucky. If I'd had a brother, Jody, I would want him to be just like you."

Jody laughed nervously and kicked a dirt clod with the toe of his shoe.

Margie took a deep breath, then said, "Jody, I've got to decide what I'm going to do. As I see it, I could turn the truck over to the sheriff until my father's wife can claim it. Or, as Mr. Putman suggested, I could hire a driver and take the truck to Goldie in California, if I could find her."

"I didn't know Mr. Kinnard was married."

"He married Goldie Johnson. It didn't last. She ran off and went to California, or so her cousin said. What Elmer left is hers now."

"I take it you don't drive."

"No. I've not had a reason to learn."

"I taught Mona to drive a few years ago. She would go on ice deliveries with me, and I'd let her drive some until she got pretty good."

"Would you be interested in driving the truck? I would pay you of course."

"Drive you to California?"

"Uh-huh. Mr. Putman suggested that I pay you a dollar a day."

"I'll drive the truck for you, but I won't take your money."

"Oh, but I couldn't let you do it otherwise."

"We can talk later about pay."

"Shouldn't you talk it over with your father before you decide?"

"I don't think so. Pa wouldn't object."

"Would you be able to stand my company all day, every day, for more than three weeks?"

"That won't be any trouble at all." Jody smiled. "Could Mona ride with us part of the time? It would make things a little easier for Pa."

"Why not? And, Jody, will you teach me to drive? Of course, I'll not have anything to drive once I turn the truck over to Goldie."

"Sure. If we stop at a campground where

there's room, I'll show you how to start and stop and use the hand signals. The rest is just steering."

"Oh, thank you." Margie was so relieved she put her hand on Jody's arm and smiled at him. When she became aware that Brady and Anna Marie had come up beside them, her first smile of the day faded.

"Margie, Uncle Brady is going to get me a soda pop."

"That's nice. What kind?" Margie's eyes went down to the child. All she could see of Brady was from his knees to his dusty boots.

"I don't know. Strawberry or orange."

"Both are good."

"He'll get one for *you*." Anna Marie giggled. "If you've been good."

Margie's eyes flew up to collide with squinted green ones, then back to Anna Marie.

Margie's pretty and proud and has had more trouble this past week than some women have in half a lifetime. These thoughts went through Brady's head as he looked at her. Her face, he noticed, had tanned from the sun, and her hair was becoming sun-bleached. She was capable and strong-minded, despite looking so fragile that a man would automatically want to protect her. She had demonstrated that strength when told of her father's sudden death.

Edgy under Brady's scrutiny, Margie stooped and straightened the collar of the child's dress.

"I just finished a big glass of iced tea, honey."

"I haven't thanked you for ironing Anna Marie's dresses." Brady's voice was a little rough.

"I had nothing else to do." Margie turned and headed for the truck. "I'll talk to you later, Jody," she called over her shoulder.

Brady waited until Margie reached the truck and sat down in the canvas chair before he spoke to Jody.

"Did she ask you to drive?"

"Yeah. She wants to pay me, but I couldn't take her money."

"Maybe you should. That way she'll feel that she's paying her way. She's doesn't want to be obligated to anyone." He said the last dryly.

"She wouldn't be."

"She would think she was, and that's what counts."

"Mr. Kinnard wasn't a nice man, but at least she wasn't alone. I feel sorry for her."

"Don't let her know that," Brady was quick to suggest. "That would get her back up in a hurry. She'd take off like a wild goose if she thought we asked her to come along because we feel sorry for her."

"Why else do you want her along?" Brady heard a small note of irritation in the boy's voice.

Uh-oh. The frown on Jody's young face triggered a warning signal. Did the boy have a crush on Margie? God, he hoped not. At his age unrequited love was painful.

"We don't have to pity her to want to help her. But it'll not hurt at all to have another truck in our caravan." When Jody said nothing more, Brady asked, "Did Foley go after Sugar?"

"Yeah. She wanted him to take her honky-tonkin'. He told her he was tired from working on the car all day and that when we got to Amarillo they would go out one night. She got in a snit and walked off down the highway."

"That wasn't too smart. There's nothing between here and town but woods on both sides of the highway."

"Can we get the pop now?" Anna Marie tugged on Brady's hand.

"Sure, Punkie. Let's go get it before Deke locks up for the night."

Brady and Anna Marie were sitting on the bench in front of the garage when Foley

Luker drove in. Jody hurried to the car when he saw that he was alone. Foley got out and spoke to his son. Snatches of words drifted to Brady.

"Can't find her."

"Did you look in the PowWow?"

"Not many there. It's early."

"She couldn't have walked to town in that length of time."

"Are you sure she didn't come back through the woods? I looked all over town. I don't know what the hell to do."

"Is this all the pop you want, Punkie?" Brady held the bottle of NeHi.

"I'm full."

"Mind if I have the rest?"

"Huh-uh."

Brady emptied the bottle in a few gulps and left it in the wooden case. Picking up the tired little girl, he carried her to where Foley was leaning against his car.

"I'll be glad to take my car and help hunt for her."

"I'd be obliged, Brady. I don't know where to look next."

"Deke might have an idea," Jody suggested.

"We should let Alvin know that we're leaving."

"While you're letting him know, I'll leave

336

Anna Marie with Margie and be right back."

He stopped a few feet from where Margie sat in the canvas chair. "Can Punkie stay with you while I help Foley look for his wife?"

"Sure. Stand her in the truck. I'll wash her face and hands, and when she gets sleepy, she can lie down on the bunk."

"Grace and Alvin are visiting with Mrs. Bales and Deke. Mona and Rusty are out spoonin'."

"And I'm all that's left."

"I didn't mean to imply that," he said sharply.

"I don't care how you meant it."

When Margie climbed into the truck and turned to take the child, she found her eyes locked with a pair of startling green ones. Brady looked at her as if he were reading each and every thought that passed through her mind. She kept her features composed, but a little shock went through her when she realized how hardened she had become since she left home.

She wasn't bowing her head to anyone ever again.

"I don't know how long I'll be gone."

"It doesn't matter. She can sleep here. Come on, puddin'." Margie turned her back to Brady and lifted the child to sit on the bunk. "We'll wash your face and hands and take off your shoes."

"I got mud on 'em."

"That's all right. We can take care of that."

Brady lingered for a few seconds, then walked away.

Anna Marie whispered, "Is he gone?"

"He's gone."

"I got to pee-pee. Real bad."

"That's no problem, honey." Margie climbed out of the truck and held up her arms. "Everyone is gone. We'll just go around here on the other side of the truck where no one can see us." She unbuttoned the back of the child's underpants and held up her dress while she squatted beside the truck.

"I like you, Margie."

Every time Anna Marie said that, Margie wanted to slap the mother who had told her child she didn't like her.

"I like you too, puddin'. I more than like you. I think you're the sweetest, prettiest little girl I've ever known."

"You do?"

"I sure do. Let's get back in the truck. I'll light the lantern, and after we take off your muddy shoes I'll wash your face and hands.

Then we'll look at the pictures in a movie magazine."

"Can I see a picture of the little girl with the curls?"

"I know right where to find one."

"Where's the man who sat out there in the chair every night? He didn't like me. I said hello to him and he went like this." Anna Marie drew her eyebrows together and turned down her lips.

"It wasn't that he didn't like you, honey. He was unhappy and . . . thinking about things."

"Is he comin' back?"

"Ah . . . no. He went to where your mama and daddy went."

"Oh. I'm glad he's not comin' back," she said with a child's honesty.

Sometime later Anna Marie fell asleep cuddled against Margie. Putting aside the magazine, Margie eased the child down on the bunk. Poor little girl, going to live with strangers. Margie wished with all her heart that she had the means to keep her and give her the love she never had from her mother.

Margie made a pad of blankets on Elmer's strongbox at the front of the truck and moved Anna Marie there so she could lie down on the bunk. After covering the child with a light sheet she stooped and kissed her cheek.

A wave of fatigue washed over her. She blew out the lantern and sank down on the bunk. She felt her stomach drop away when she thought of the burial tomorrow. She had tried, really tried, to grieve for her father. Long ago she had relegated him to a special place in her mind — the place where she put unpleasant things she didn't like to think about. Now she was ashamed to admit that she would grieve more if it had been Alvin Putman who came in fatal contact with the electric wire.

What kind of a person have I turned out to be?

Lying there in the dark, she would occasionally hear a car pass on the highway. She didn't allow herself to think about Brady Hoyt. Giving in to him had been an even bigger mistake than thinking that Ernie Harding was an honorable man and going off with him. She vowed silently never to put her blind trust in anyone again.

The people who thought they knew her had the notion that her big dream was to see Hollywood. She had wanted to see it since she saw her first movie, but more than that, she wanted a home and to belong to someone who needed her as much as she needed him. She wanted to love and be loved. She wanted a man who thought she was grand, the way that Alvin thought Grace was grand. She wanted *roots*. She wanted a little girl like Anna Marie to love and fuss over. She wanted, she wanted —

She made no attempt to wipe away the tears. She would indulge herself tonight . . . tomorrow would be another day.

It was near midnight when Brady stopped his car in front of the post office and waited for Foley to pull alongside.

"Jody and I went as far west as Texola. There wasn't anything there. I doubt that whoever picked her up would have backtracked to Elk City."

"Deke talked to the bartender at the PowWow. He said there had been very few ladies in there tonight and none fitted her description. Do you want to notify the sheriff?"

"If she isn't back by morning, we'll have to. I believe that she was picked up on the highway by someone she thought would show her a good time. She hadn't had time to get very far before I went out looking for her." Foley rubbed his hand over his face. "She has a suitcase in the trailer. She may come back for it."

341

"Are you thinking that she got a chance to go with someone and left you?"

"In the back of my mind I knew it would happen someday. I just didn't expect it so soon."

"Hell. I'm sorry."

"Let's get on back," Foley said tiredly. "No use burning up more gas looking for her. It would be like her to worry me by hiding out all night, then come trottin' in in the morning."

On the way back to the campground Deke said, "It didn't take long for me to figure out that woman wasn't ever goin' to be anythin' but trouble to Luker. I'm a-wonderin' why he married her."

"He was lonely and horny." Brady looked at the little man and grinned.

"Godalmighty. There's easier ways of gettin' your rocks hauled than marryin' up with a floozy."

"I agree. My brother married a woman who gave him a merry chase. I learned a lesson there. I'm going to be damn careful who I tie up with."

"You said young Luker was goin' to drive Margie's truck. I'm right glad she's not goin' to strike out on her own. She's too nice, too trusting."

"We'll look after her."

"Hell I hope so. Mama'd be glad for her to stay here till she got on her feet, but she didn't want to put us out. As if having that little thin' around would be anything but pure pleasure."

"She wants to see Hollywood," Brady said irritably.

Deke glanced at Brady's set features. "I hope she sees it and gets it out of her system. Then she'll settle down."

"To what? Workin' in a laundry washin' someone's dirty drawers?"

"She's pretty enough to be in the movies. Maybe some high muckety-muck will take one look at her, sign her up, and we'll see that pretty little face on the screen."

"More than likely she'll take up with some no-good jelly bean who'll use her like the bastard that left her here last year."

Deke turned his head and smiled when he heard the irritation in Brady's voice. *The man had a yen for little Margie!* He decided to goad him a little.

"Yep, that's about what'll happen to her. She'll find herself tied down with a bunch of kids and a life of pickin' oranges or hoein' cotton to feed 'em. A lot of no-good bums out there are just waitin' to latch onto a woman like Margie who's sweet and loving and loyal. She deserves more, by golly."

Brady's silence spoke louder than words. Hearing Deke's prediction of Margie's future had set his teeth on edge and a muscle dancing in his jaw. Deke kind of wished they'd stay around so he could find out what would happen between them.

When Deke and Brady turned into the campground, the car headlights shone on Mona, Rusty and Jody standing beside the Lukers' trailer. Jody, no doubt, was telling them of the search for Sugar. Brady let Deke out, then parked his car behind the Kinnard truck. He sat there for a minute or two before going to the end of the truck to get Anna Marie.

"Did you find her?" Margie's voice came out of the dark interior.

"No. Foley says she'll either come back or she won't."

"I suppose he's all torn up about her leaving."

"Didn't seem to be. I think he finally got his eyes opened to the kind of woman she was."

"I'm glad. I hate to think of him hurting."

"I'll take Anna Marie."

"Don't wake her. She's all right."

"Sure you don't mind?"

"Would I have said, 'Don't wake her,' if I minded?"

"Guess not. Well, thanks and good night."

Margie stared into the darkness. Sleep now evaded her. After a while she heard Jody's voice just outside the truck telling Mona to go on and that he would wait for her.

Mona was walking Rusty to the Putman camp, and Jody didn't want his sister coming back through the darkness alone. Margie decided that although Foley Luker hadn't used much judgment in choosing a second wife, he must have done something right. He had two really nice kids.

In a motor court cabin near Elk City, Sugar and Homer Persy lay in a tangle of bedsheets. Sugar giggled happily.

"Spread yore legs, slut!" he demanded.

"We've done it three times, you horny little stud!"

"I can go three more." Homer sucked on a spot beneath her ear and rocked himself against her naked thigh.

"Save some of it, lover. I don't want you to go dry on me."

"Don't worry about it. You've got the hottest little pussy I've ever had. Know that?"

Sugar sank her teeth in his shoulder. She loved it when he called her a slut, a hot pussy. She loved it when he drank bootleg whiskey out of her navel.

"Whater we going to do about Uncle Chester? He didn't like having to sleep in the car."

"Nothin' right now. I got other things on my mind."

"He don't like it that you're in here with me. I heard him call me a bangtail."

"Well, ya are, ain't ya? I aim to bang yore tail all the way to California."

Sugar giggled, wiggled against him and stroked his erection.

"I'll send him back home." Homer worried her earlobe between his lips. "Then it'll be just you and me, baby doll. We'll honky-tonk, screw and raise holy hell all the way to California."

"I want to get my suitcase —"

"We'll get it." Homer moved over between her spread legs. "Is yore old man goin' to kick up a fuss?"

"What if he does? There's nothin' he can do."

"Godalmighty. You musta been desperate to wed up with a clod old enough to have grown kids."

"It seemed like a good way to get to California."

Homer slid into her. "Goddamn. I been waitin' all my life for a hot-and-ready woman."

"Ya found her, Stud."

"We'll make a damn good team. Stud and Sugar. Sugar and Stud."

"Whater we goin' to do, Stud, after we get rid of Uncle Chester?" Sugar wrapped her legs around him.

"We'll get us some money. You said you could drive."

"Anything that's got four wheels. Will we —"

"Shut up talkin' and move yore ass! Ya've got me big as a fence post and harder'n a rock —"

Chapter 20

Sugar Luker had not returned when the group gathered to go to the cemetery for the burial. Foley looked haggard and tired after spending a sleepless night. He and Jody had gone on ahead to report to the sheriff that Sugar was missing, and would meet them later at the cemetery.

Alvin suggested that he and Grace go in his truck and Brady's car would carry the rest. Anna Marie would stay with Mrs. Bales. When Brady brought the car around to the front of the garage, Margie got in the backseat with Deke. Mona sat in front between Brady and Rusty. Rusty put his arm on the back of the seat. His hand cupped Mona's shoulder and pulled her close to him.

"You all right, darlin'?" Deke asked Margie as they pulled into the lonely-looking treeless cemetery where two workers in overalls stood back from a mound of red Oklahoma dirt. The casket containing her father's body sat on the ground beside an open hole. Deke reached for her hand and held it tightly.

"I'm all right. It was good of you to come, Deke. You'll lose business with the garage closed."

"Only for an hour, darlin'. Ole Deke wouldn't let ya go through this without bein' with ya."

"Both times I've been here, I've been trouble to you."

"It wasn't of your makin', darlin'. None of it."

"Thank you for being with me today."

When Foley and Jody drove up and parked behind them, they got out of the car. Somberly they walked through the sparse prairie grass and stood at the grave site. Before the service began Alvin asked Margie if she wanted the casket opened so that she could see her father for the last time. She shook her head. Deke stayed beside her, his arm around her.

Alvin spoke about how they had started on this trip and how Elmer's life had ended before they completed a third of it. After a sketchy background of Elmer's life, Rusty began to strum on his guitar, then sang "Rock of Ages." Alvin read from his Bible. When he closed it, he, Grace and Rusty sang "Nearer My God to Thee."

The service was short but decent and respectful. When it was over, Deke turned Margie away from the grave and led her back to the car while the casket was being lowered into the ground. Brady watched Deke lead Margie away and felt a surge of primitive jealousy. *He* should have been the one to be with her when they buried her father.

Brady hid his feelings when Alvin moved up beside him, but that didn't make them go away. He knew what was the matter with him, but it didn't make it any easier to tolerate. This plucky, little blond woman had gotten under his skin. He wanted her for his own. The need to have her was burning a hole in his gut. He didn't like the feeling and was impatient with himself for his restlessness.

Foley, who was the last to arrive at the cemetery, led the way back down the highway to the garage. As soon as they pulled into the campground, he saw that the ropes holding the cover on his trailer had been cut and the canvas thrown back. He knew before he looked that Sugar's suitcase would be gone. She and whoever she was with had sneaked in here to get it, knowing that he would be at the cemetery burying Elmer Kinnard.

Now he felt like a fool for reporting her as missing to the sheriff. She had left him for someone who had picked her up on the highway. Foley was relieved in a way that she hadn't been kidnapped, that she was evidently where she wanted to be. He didn't wish her to be harmed. But, Lord, what a chance she was taking. Didn't she have any sense at all? Then he thought that he had no right to question *her* reasoning when *he* hadn't shown any at all when he married her.

He glanced at his children. Jody and Mona were waiting to see what he was going to do. He owed them far more than he owed the woman he had known only a couple of weeks when he took her for his wife. He would try to make it up to them for the time they'd had to spend with Sugar.

"Daddy?" Mona came to look in the trailer, then up at her father. "She took her suitcase. I'm sorry, Daddy."

Foley put his arm around his daughter. "I'm the one who's sorry, honey. I knew even before we started on this trip that I shouldn't have married her."

"You were lonesome and . . . missed Mama." Mona put her arms around her father and hugged him. "What will we do now? Do we have to stay here and wait for her?" she asked anxiously.

"Well . . ." Foley loosened her arms and stepped back. "There's not much use in hanging around here. We'll go on. Jody is going to drive for Margie. If we don't go on, she won't have a driver."

"We can stay if you want to. Margie will wait with us." Mona was compelled to say it even though it would break her heart to have to part from Rusty.

"No. Sugar broke from us. She won't be back."

"But what if you never see her again?"

"Right now, honey, that would be all right with me."

"But you'll still be married to her."

"That worries me. If something happened to me, she would get everything. You and Jody would be left in the same fix as Margie." Foley knotted the cut rope and tied down the canvas.

"Isn't there something you can do?"

"I've already given Jody some of my cash money to keep. As soon as you can rig up a way to carry it, I'll divide what I have left with you. It's what Alvin did. He divided his money between the three of them. He said that way if he's robbed, they wouldn't lose everything."

"Do you think we might be robbed?"

"I don't know, honey. Sugar has hooked up with someone. I can't think a decent sort would pick a woman up off the highway, keep her out all night, then sneak her in here to get her suitcase. She may have dropped a hint that I'm carrying money."

"Pa." Jody came to where Foley was checking the air in his tires. "I need to tell Margie if we're goin' or stayin'."

"We're going."

"You don't want to wait —"

"No. We'll go on."

"Deke talked to his mother. She didn't see anyone drive in while we were gone."

"I'm not surprised they didn't drive in." Foley kept his head down.

"Brady is filling his gas tank. Margie wants me to move the truck up to the gas pump. She's wondering if she should buy extra tubes or anything before we go."

"Tell her to ask Deke. He'll know."

A knowing look that said "stay with Pa" passed from brother to sister before Jody hurried away.

He drove the truck up to the gas pump, and while he was putting gas in the overly large gas tank, Deke was checking the water and the oil. Brady with a pump in his hand was inspecting the tires with a gauge he put on the air valve.

"Ever'thing's up to snuff, darlin'," Deke said to Margie.

"Is there anything I should get now to have on hand?"

"I'm not tryin' to make a sale, but you should have an extra fan belt in case you get off in the desert and break one."

"Do I need tire tubes?"

Brady spoke up. "She's got two that haven't been used and extra boots in case she gets a hole in a tire."

"Then you don't need 'em now, darlin'. I'll get you a spare fan belt." He spoke to Brady as he passed. "Y'all got the tools to put it on?"

Brady nodded, then called out to Jody, "Look in the toolbox and hand me an oilcan."

Margie followed Deke into the garage. "Deke, do you know what it would cost to put some kind of marker on my father's grave?"

"Honey, it'd cost fifteen or twenty dollars to put a marker there that would last."

Margie looked apologetic as she pulled a twenty-dollar bill from her pocket.

"Do you know someone who would do it? I hate to impose on you once again."

"The undertaker will take care of it. Just write down what you want on the marker. I'll see that he gets it, and I'll see that it's done." He tore a sheet from the back of a tablet and handed her a pencil.

"I'll write down his name, his age and the date. I think that will be enough, don't you? I hate to think of years going by and no one knowing who is buried there."

"Don't ya worry none about it. It'll be done."

"Oh, Deke," she said after she had put the note and the money on the shelf beside the tablet, "I've never had such a good friend." Margie put her arms around his neck and laid her head on his shoulder.

"Now, now, darlin'. Yo're goin' to be all right. Mr. Putman is pure hickory, and Brady's a man to ride the river with. They'll look after ya."

"I don't want to be looked after as if I was a little kid. I have to feel that I'm pulling my own weight."

"Now, darlin'." Deke saw Brady come to the garage door. "Don't ya go and get all stiff-necked with pride. Hear? These is good folks yo're with, or I'd not let ya go off with them."

"I'm afraid that I'll be nothing but trouble."

"When the time comes that ya think yo're holdin' them back, just peel off, leave the truck settin' and take the bus."

Deke was watching Brady over Margie's shoulder. Brady's scowling face spoke volumes; his eyes were so narrow Deke could scarcely see them. The big galoot was jealous of him! Deke turned his face and kissed Margie on the cheek. When he looked up, the door was empty.

"I want to tell your mother good-bye."

When Margie left the garage, Jody moved the truck to make room for his father to pull up to the gas pump. After Alvin had gassed up and was ready to go, Jody got in line behind him.

"I'm sure obliged for what you've done," Foley said as Deke filled his gas tank. "Alvin figures that we should be in Flagstaff, Arizona, in about a week and a half. If you hear anything from my wife, I would appreciate it if you'd send me a card General Delivery. Or send it to Bakersfield, California. We are going there to scout out places for our ice business. I think Alvin has relatives there. I'll ask at both places."

"I'll do that, Foley. I'm sure sorry about what happened."

"Yeah, so am I. I just hope that Sugar's with someone who will look out for her. She lived all her life in a one-horse town up in Missouri. For all her flirty ways she's dumb as a stump when it comes to taking care of herself."

When the caravan was lined up and ready to leave, they all got out to tell Deke goodbye. He squatted down so Anna Marie could hug his neck.

"We'll not forget you," Mona said, and waved to Mrs. Bales on the porch.

"And I'll not forget you, darlin'. Y'all send me a card from time to time and let me know how yo're makin' out. Just send it to Deke's Garage, Sayre, Oklahoma, and we'll get it. Bye now. Be careful with my girl, Jody."

"I will. I'm going to teach her to drive."

"Well, now, I ain't so sure *that's* a good idea," Deke teased, and winked at Margie. "Take care, darlin'. Write to me."

"I will, Deke. I promise."

Margie had tears in her eyes when they pulled away from the campground. She waved at Deke until he was lost from sight.

Margie soon discovered that Jody handled the truck even better than Elmer had.

He maintained a steady speed, not speeding up, then slowing down as Elmer had. At the end of the day Margie used to feel as if she had been on a roller coaster.

When they passed the prairie cemetery on their way out of town, Margie could see the fresh mound of red dirt that was her father's grave. He would remain there, far from home, throughout all eternity.

Good-bye, Daddy. I wish we could have loved each other like a father and daughter should.

Shortly after they had crossed into Texas they hit a patch of dirt highway. Choking dust boiled up. Jody slowed to allow the Putmans to get farther ahead. Margie rolled up the window, making it terribly hot in the truck.

"Oh, my. This is the first dirt road we've hit in a while. You're a good driver, Jody."

"Pa taught me when I was twelve. Mama had a fit. She thought I was too young. Pa put the truck out in a field and told me to go at it." He grinned at her proudly. "I started delivering ice when I was thirteen."

"Is your father heartbroken over losing Sugar?"

"He doesn't appear to be. Pa's usually very levelheaded. Marrying Sugar is the one time that I can remember when he went off kind of half-cocked."

"Most of us do that sometime in our life. I've already done it a couple of times, and I'm younger than your father."

"He's thirty-seven. He was my age when he and mama married. They were in school together. It 'bout killed him when she died. He might have thought he'd have something like he had with mama when he married Sugar."

"Some things don't work out like we plan."

"*That* sure didn't."

"Having someone to talk to makes the time go fast, Jody. How far to Amarillo?"

"From Sayre, Alvin figured about a hundred and twenty-nine miles. We won't make it tonight. None of us want to be on the road at night."

"I heard Alvin say that the trucks are loaded too heavily to make good time."

"Yeah, and they want to get them to California in good shape so they can be used in the business."

In the middle of the afternoon they came to a place where men were working on the highway. Jody slowed the truck to a crawl. Farther on down they had to stop and wait for a scoop, pulled by a team of mules, to get across the road.

Margie sat on the edge of her seat and

watched the road construction with interest. The crew used big machines that belched smoke from smokestacks, a water wagon that was pulled by horses and drags pulled by mules. Men in overalls worked with scoop shovels and rakes.

"That's a relief," Margie said an hour later when they pulled up onto the new paving. "We're spoiled." She smiled at the boy behind the wheel.

"Sure is easier driving."

"Want a drink of water out of the fruit jar?"

"Uncle Brady." Anna Marie pulled on Brady's arm. "I'm hot. I want a drink of water."

He reached over and rolled down the window. "That better? Move over away from the door, honey."

"I still want a drink."

"Hold on just a minute, Punkie. It looks like we're going to be stopping." Brady watched Alvin pull over onto a wide shoulder of the road, and Jody stopped behind him. Brady parked behind Margie and Jody.

Rusty and Grace stood beside their truck while Alvin climbed into the back. The rough road had caused some pans to fall, and they were bouncing around. Holding Anna Marie's hand, Brady walked up to where Jody and Margie stood. Jody was drinking from a fruit jar.

"Margie!" Anna Marie cried.

"Hello, puddin'."

Anna Marie pulled on her hand. Margie bent over so the girl could whisper. "I'm thirsty but . . . I got to pee-pee first."

"Well, let's see." Margie looked around the flat, treeless area conscious that Brady was watching her. Finally she said, "We'll get in the truck."

Before she could untie the ropes holding the back flap, Brady was there. He let down the tailgate, then reached in for the box Margie used to step up into the truck.

"Thank you."

She climbed up and reached for the child. Brady lifted her up. Her eyes were snared for several seconds by his, and she was surprised to see that a sadness was reflected there.

"Thank *you*," he echoed her words softly.

As soon as the flap was dropped down, Margie took the washdish from where it was wedged next to the water barrel. It was the only thing she could think of for the child to use. She would wash and scald it tonight before it was used again.

Anna Marie giggled. "I've not pee-peed in a washdish."

"Hurry, puddin'. We don't want to keep them waiting for us."

When the child was finished, Margie lifted the canvas flap. Brady stood a few feet away talking to Foley and Jody. He came and lifted Anna Marie down.

"Go to Mona, Punkie. She's waiting with a drink of water for you."

He offered his hand to Margie and helped her down. He clasped it tightly and seemed reluctant to let it go. She tugged on it, and he suddenly realized what she needed to do and went to the side of the truck. Margie reached for the washdish, emptied it quickly and shoved it back into the truck.

Brady was there seconds later, lifting the box and rolling down the flap.

"I can do it," Margie said.

"I know you can. I think you can do most anything you set your mind to, but you don't have to do this when I'm here." He finished tying the flap and turned so that his big frame blocked her view of the others. "You're still mad about . . . that night, aren't you?"

"What . . . ah . . . night?" She hated herself for stammering. "Oh, that. I've forgotten all about that."

He reached out a finger and looped a strand of hair over her ear. Time ticked away as they looked at each other. His warm fingertips touched her cheeks. Something inside Margie began to melt, spreading warmth to her toes. Finally he pulled his eyes away from hers and swung them to watch a car that passed them on the highway. When his eyes returned to hers, they held a quiet, serious look.

"Did you get all shook up on that bad stretch of road?" He drank in the sight of her pretty face.

She met his green stare with all the poise and self-control she could muster. His eyes were so narrowed she could hardly see the green glint between the thick lashes. She was more scared of his effect on her than she wanted to admit.

"Yeah, I did."

"Did what?" Watching her, he had forgotten that he had asked her a question.

"Get shook up on that rough road."

He couldn't stop looking at her. "Are you and Jody doing all right?"

"He's a good driver."

"I'm glad you didn't stay behind."

"So am I."

When she smiled, her eyes moved over him like a soft caress. Watching her lips spread and her eyes light up, he was so fascinated that he couldn't look away. His hand reached for hers and held it in his large rough one. He glanced down at their clasped hands. Hers was small, her wrists fragile. His eyes moved to her face, and he wished desperately to know what she was thinking, if she was still remembering his rough treatment of her. The thought made him weak inside.

The silence between them was beginning to be embarrassing when Anna Marie called.

"Uncle Brady. Can I ride with Aunt Grace? Rusty is goin' to ride with Mona."

"Did she ask you, honey, or did you ask her?"

"She asked me."

Before answering Anna Marie he squeezed Margie's hand and murmured, "I'll see you this evening."

Chapter 21

Chester was angry.

He drove the Ford coupe at breakneck speed toward Amarillo and hardly slowed over the rough, unpaved patch of highway. The workers jumped out of the way, cursing and shaking their fists at the car as it disappeared in the cloud of dust.

Homer and Sugar didn't appear to notice Chester's recklessness. They cuddled on the seat beside him, hugging and kissing and . . . more. At times Homer's hand was up under her dress and hers was rubbing his crotch.

The woman was a bitch.

Chester seethed with indignation. Homer had gone too far this time. Some of the men in their family were a little wild, he thought, but all of the women were decent. Every blasted one of them! Chester wanted no truck with this woman who called herself Sugar. She was the type who would eat a man alive.

Chester intended to dump Homer and his whore the first chance he got and head back home. He admitted to himself that he had done a lot of mean things, but taking his mother's car bothered him the most. He shouldn't have let the stupid little horsecock talk him into it.

He drove into Amarillo at sundown.

"Find a motor court, Uncle. We'll wait till dark, then go out and find us some money. We got to have us a good time while we wait for the road-hoppers to get here."

"They won't get here tonight," Sugar said. "Foley piddles along following the trucks and won't drive at night."

"Good. That'll give us some time. This is a good-sized town. With yore looks, baby, we ort to do pretty good here."

"I'm not goin' to rob any more stores," Chester said flatly.

"You didn't rob them, Uncle. I did. It was as easy as fallin' off a log. But I got me a idey how we can get more money faster without takin' such a risk."

"We've got enough gas money to get home."

"You still singin' that tune? I'm not through with that cowboy yet. I ain't goin' till I am."

"Homer, honey, you said we'd go to California —"

"I ain't goin' to California either!" Chester broke in angrily.

"Don't get it in yore head to run out on us, Uncle Chester." Homer's voice held a threat. Then he laughed nastily. "I bet I know what's got yore tail over the line. Yo're randy as a ruttin' moose and mad cause ya ain't gettin' any of what my Sugar's puttin' out."

"I ain't wantin' *her*."

"Well, la-di-da! You wouldn't get it if you was rich as Rockofelter — or whatever his name is," Sugar jeered.

Homer laughed and kissed her soundly. "He ain't gettin' any if he was Alfalfa Bill Murray, the great know-it-all governor of Oklahoma. This's all mine." He grabbed her between her legs.

Sugar giggled. Chester grimaced and muttered under his breath. Homer ignored him.

"Ya know what that crazy son of a bitch did?"

"Who?"

"Alfalfa Bill. He plowed up the yard at

that statehouse where he lived and planted taters. Don't that beat all?"

"Why'd he do that?"

"Hell, who knows? Whater ya mutterin' about, Uncle? Stick with us till we get enough money to get us a car and you can hightail it back to the sticks, run a little booze and take handouts from Grandma while me 'n' Sugar is livin' high on the hog."

Chester turned into a motor court with six tiny cabins lined up behind the main office.

"Find out what they got, Chester. If they got one with two beds, ya won't have to sleep in the car."

Chester got out and slammed the door.

"I don't like him none a-tall." Sugar snuggled her hand inside Homer's shirt and ran her fingernails over his chest. "And I don't want him in the room with us tonight."

"Why not, pretty little puss? If ya get him hot enough, he'll drive this car to hell and back for ya. Wouldn't ya like that?"

"Naw, I want it to be just you and me."

"We need the car right now, little pussy," he whispered in her ear, then grabbed her earlobe with his teeth and nibbled on it.

"He left the keys. We could just drive off and leave him."

Homer chuckled. "Yo're a real pisser,

sugar teat. He'd call the sheriff, and we'd have to hole up somewhere."

"He'd do that?"

"Wouldn't put it past him. Tell ya what. Get all dolled up tonight, sweet pussy, and we'll go out huntin'. Now that I've got you to partner up with, it's time we got another car. If that old lady back at the garage saw this one, she's told the cowboy and yore old man. They'll be on the lookout for it."

"She couldn't of seen it. We parked down the road and went through the woods."

"I got it all figured out how we can get our hands on some money and buy our own car."

"Foley had money, but he wouldn't give me any. He wore a money belt around his waist and wouldn't take it off for anything. No chance of us getting that."

Homer grabbed her face and turned it to his. "He wouldn't take it off even to get naked with ya?"

"No." Her lips formed the word. He was holding her face so tight she couldn't speak.

"The poor, stupid son of a bitch!" His fingers dug into her cheeks to force her to open her mouth before he kissed her as if sucking the life out of her. "Yo're a wicked little bitch with the face of an angel," he breathed. "Ya like it rough, don't ya?"

369

Her fingers dug into the back of his neck. She pinched the small nipple on his chest so hard that he grunted.

"Yeah, and so does my horny stud."

Chester jerked the car door open. They broke the kiss, and Homer said, "Well?"

"Far end. Bed and a cot."

Sugar groaned.

Homer laughed. "Don't worry, little puss. Uncle's a sound sleeper."

Later, after they had eaten at a diner, they went back to the cabin so Sugar could put on what Homer jokingly called her working clothes — a modest blue dress with a round low neckline. She brushed her hair back and fastened a blue bow at the side with a bobby pin. When she was ready for Homer's approval, he took a cloth and wiped off some of the rouge and lipstick.

"Yo're just a sweet little girl. Remember? Now, ya know what to do. We'll let you out a block from that fancy hotel. When one a them well-dressed dudes comes out, turn that sweet innocent little face up and let out a little groan. Act like yo're hurtin' real bad. He'll take ya past that alley like he had a string tied to his pecker." Homer kissed her, careful to not smear her lipstick.

"I'd like to tie a string to your pecker and lead you into a dark alley," Sugar whispered seductively, and heard Chester snort. The freedom to talk dirty was one of the things that excited her most.

Acting as if setting up a man to be robbed was something she did every day of the week, Sugar, looking beautiful and seductive, her black hair tumbling around her face and shoulders, got out of the car a block from the hotel.

She was nervous about what she was about to do but was determined that Homer not know it. She had learned a lot about herself during the past twenty-four hours. This was the exciting life she craved, far removed from that hick town in Missouri and from poor, dull Foley Luker and his two equally dull and stupid kids.

Sugar walked confidently down the street until she reached the hotel, where she pretended to stumble. She let out a little cry of pain and hobbled to the side of the building, where she stood on one foot and rubbed her ankle.

"Oh, oh!" she cried as a well-dressed man came out of the hotel.

"Miss? Miss, are you hurt?"

"I've sprained my ankle." Sugar grabbed his arm as if she were about to fall and looked pleadingly into the face of a man with gray hair who wore an expensive suit and a brown felt hat. "Oh, dear. Oh, me. I've got to get down the street to the car. If my husband comes back and I'm not there, he'll . . . be so . . . mad . . ." She let her voice fall away.

"Where is your car?"

"It's . . . it's right down there."

"I'll help you. Hold on to my arm."

"Thank you, sir. Oh, thank you." Sugar held tightly to his arm and took hopping steps.

"Will you be all right until your husband comes?"

"Yes, but it . . . hurts."

"We'll take it slow."

When they reached the alley running alongside the hotel, Homer stepped out and rapped the man smartly on the side of the head with a sap, caught him as he fell and then dragged him into the dark alley. He quickly stripped him of his wallet, a pocket watch and a ring. He stuffed them in his pocket, took Sugar's arm and walked with her leisurely down the street to where Chester waited in the car.

"How'd I do?" Sugar said after they had sped away.

"You're a natural, little puss. Let's see what we got. Whee," he said after he had counted the money he took from the bill-

372

fold. "Fifty-two dollars, the ring and the watch."

"Did you kill him?" Chester asked.

"Naw. I just gave him a little tap on the head. He'll wake up in the alley with a whale of a headache, wondering what hit him."

"It was exciting," Sugar exclaimed. "And easy. Where are we going now?"

"Ya ort to be in the movies, little puss. Head for that speakeasy we spotted a while ago, Chester. Then we'll hit a honky-tonk. Before the night's over we'll have enough money to buy a car and you'll be shed of us."

Jody and Margie followed Alvin into a treeless area at Alanreed, Texas. The ruins of a burned-out house sat in the middle of the campground. A half dozen campers were there and looked to have been there for some time. Clothes hung on lines stretched between dusty cars and trucks. Children played barefoot in the dirt while women tended campfires. Several men pulled their heads out from under the hood of a car to watch the newcomers drive in.

"They look like a real down-and-out bunch," Jody said as he followed Alvin's lead to the far side of the burned-out house. Nearby, a privy that had survived the fire leaned precariously to one side.

"They've left their homes looking for a better life. I hope they find it." Margie thought that they at least had one another. It was more than she had.

Jody drove the truck close to the Putmans', then backed up and parked, leaving no more than a car length between the two trucks. Elmer had always made sure that there was a good distance between his camp and the others. Brady stopped close beside Margie on the other side, making it plain to the campers that watched that this caravan was a close unit, probably family.

Mona and Rusty came by as Margie was working the kinks out of her shoulders.

"Eat with us tonight, Margie," Mona said. "Daddy is getting out the kerosene stove. We're going to have fried potatoes and onions."

"All right. I'll bring a can of corn."

"I haven't had fried potatoes and corn since we left home."

"She's tired of my company, Margie. She didn't ask *me* to eat with her." Rusty's hand on Mona's shoulder moved across the back of her neck to cup the other shoulder and pull her closer to him. She turned on him.

"Bullfoot! Shame on you, Rusty Putman. I did too ask you to eat with us, and you said not until I came to eat with you. You said that, and I said I didn't want to leave Daddy and Jody alone tonight."

"She's tellin' a windy, Margie." He laughed happily, his face turned to Mona. It was hard to believe that he was not seeing her.

"You certainly did, you . . . you clabberhead."

It was a pleasure, Margie thought, to see how happy they were together.

"Hi, Rusty. Hi, Mona." Anna Marie and Blackie, glad to be out of the car, came running toward them. "Guess what? Aunt Grace is goin' to let me draw faces on the eggs before we peel them."

"You can't draw a face," Rusty teased, and stooped to scratch Blackie's ears. The dog was glad to see him and had whined to let him know he was there.

"I can too. I've got a red crayon. I'm goin' to get it. Uncle Brady," Anna Marie called as she ran away.

"See what I mean, Margie? He's gettin' to be a regular smart aleck."

Margie laughed. "But he sings like a bird."

"More like a buzzard." Mona giggled and tried to move away. Rusty caught her, reached down and swung her up into his arms.

"Is there a muddy hole around here, Margie?" He swung Mona around, and Blackie, wanting to join in the merriment, raced around them and barked.

"Put me down, you knucklehead!"

"Not a muddy hole in sight, Rusty. You might consider dropping her in the ruins of that burned-out house."

"Where is it?"

"To your right."

Rusty took a few steps, stopped and let Mona slide down until her feet touched the ground.

Their laughter reached Margie as they walked away, Blackie frolicking alongside, Rusty's arm across Mona's shoulders, hers around his waist as if it were the most natural thing in the world. Without her stepmother glaring at her, waiting to find something to criticize, Mona was free to act like a young girl in love.

Suddenly Margie felt old. It had been a long time since she was young and carefree and did silly things just for the fun of it.

Since Elmer had gone to a store the day he spent away from Deke's campground, the cupboard was well stocked when Margie looked in it to find a can of corn. There was even a box of Cream of Wheat and syrup for pancakes. She made a mental note to get milk when next they stopped for ice.

She took the corn, the canvas chair, a plate and eating utensils with her when she went to the Luker camp. The get-together was enjoyable. Even Foley appeared to be more relaxed without Sugar's cloying, overpowering presence. Mona and Jody were certainly more at ease. Foley cooked the meal of fried potatoes and onions on a small kerosene stove and heated the creamed corn, Margie's contribution, right in the can.

While she and Mona washed the supper dishes, Foley, Brady and Alvin squatted on their heels with a map spread out in front of them. Jody and Rusty came from the Putman camp with Anna Marie hanging on Rusty's hand. Blackie, as usual, trailed them.

Later when Margie went back to the truck with her chair, Brady's head and shoulders were beneath the hood.

"Is something wrong?"

He raised up to look at her. "No. I was checking the oil. The motor is in good condition. It doesn't use much oil." He wiped his hands on a rag he pulled from his back pocket and shut the hood. "Alvin thinks that we should leave at dawn and make as much time as we can tomorrow on the flatland.

After we get over into New Mexico a ways, it's up one hill and down another."

"Have you been there?"

"I've been down around Albuquerque."

She could feel his gaze, hot and questing, on her face and was grateful for the evening shadows that hid the blush that crept up her throat to her cheeks. The silence between them went on and on. She was only half aware of the sound of Anna Marie calling to her.

"Margie! Margie!" Anna Marie ran to her from the Putman camp. "Aunt Grace let me keep an egg. Look." The egg had two round circles for eyes, a dot for a nose and a curved line for the mouth.

"Who is it?" Margie asked after looking at it closely.

"Uncle Brady. See his ears?" She turned the egg in her small fingers.

"It does look like him." Margie looked from the egg to Brady's smiling eyes. "When he loses his hair, you won't be able to tell them apart."

Anna Marie giggled and pulled on Margie's hand so that she would bend over.

"Ask Uncle Brady if I can sleep with you again," she whispered.

"You ask him," Margie whispered back.

"I'm 'fraid he won't let me."

"You won't know until you ask him."

Brady's eyes darted back and forth between his niece and the woman who had been in his thoughts all day.

"I'm beginning to feel like the skunk at the picnic. What are you two whispering about?"

Anna Marie had put the egg in the pocket of her dress and was holding on to Margie's hand with both of hers.

"All right. Out with it," he pressed. "What are you two hatching up?"

As his eyes roamed her face, strange feelings stirred in Margie. Her heart fluttered. She drew the tip of her tongue across dry lips.

"We-ll," she stammered. "I was just about to invite Anna Marie to sleep in the truck with me again."

Brady's eyes were fixed unwavering on her.

She has a wistfulness about her tonight. She's a woman, yet she's a girl.

She was looking at him with wide, clear eyes. And in the flickering light of the Putmans' campfire her face appeared infinitely soft and beautiful. An unexpected twinge of yearning stirred deep inside of him. Brady tore his eyes away and looked down at his niece.

"Do you want to accept Margie's invitation?"

"Does that mean yes?"

"It means yes if Margie really wants you to stay."

"She wants me. Don't you, Margie?"

"Sure I do, puddin'. You can sleep on the box again. I like the company."

"Goody, goody. I can stretch out my feet."

"You could stretch your legs out in the car."

"Huh-uh. I kicked the door."

"I didn't realize that. I'll get the mattress for you."

"Margie likes me," Anna Marie said brightly, smiling up at her uncle.

Margie saw his jaw tighten and knew that he was remembering the cruel words that Becky, the child's mother, had said to her.

"Of course I like you." Margie hugged the child to her. "Everyone likes you. You're pretty and sweet and . . . smart to draw your uncle's face on the egg."

"I gave him big ears."

"By golly, you did." Margie lifted the child up into the truck. "You've got to be washed before you can go to bed. I've got a bar of scented soap I've been saving. We'll use it and some powder to make you smell good."

Margie lit the lantern and set it on the icebox.

"I wish you were my mama." Anna Marie cuddled the boiled egg in her hand and looked at Margie with big, solemn eyes. "She was pretty, like you, but she didn't like me."

"Oh, honey. You must be mistaken."

"Huh-uh."

Wanting to change the subject, Margie said quickly, "We should have told your uncle to bring a nightgown."

"I brought one." Brady was standing at the end of the truck with the small mattress from his car. "I'll slide the mattress in. Can you take it from there? Otherwise you girls will have to get out before I can get in."

Margie had cleared off the things that rode on the box during the day. She moved the mattress over and tilted it onto the box.

"Just fits. Does she have a pillow?"

"I'll get it."

Later Brady sat beside the dark truck, smoked a cigarette and listened to Margie talking to his niece.

"When I was a little girl, my grandmother used to read to me. I liked the fairy tales best. Want me to tell you about Cinderella and the prince?"

"I like stories. Daddy told me about the three bears."

"Once upon a time there was a beautiful girl who lived with her cruel stepmother and stepsisters. They made her work from morning until night . . ."

Brady found himself listening to the story with rapt attention. It dawned on him for the hundredth time how foolish he had been to attempt to drive across the country with a five-year-old girl. God must have been watching out for the child and arranged for him to meet Margie and the Putmans. It had not even occurred to him to tell her a story. He didn't know if he even knew one.

"The prince tried the glass slipper on every girl in his kingdom, but it fit none of them. He feared that he would never find the beautiful girl who came to the ball. Then he came to the house where Cinderella lived with her stepmother and stepsisters . . ."

Silence. Brady tilted his head to listen. Would Margie come out? God, he hoped so. The heavy hand of loneliness gripped him, wrapping its icy fingers around his heart at the thought of the journey's end and never again seeing the slim, brown-eyed girl with the sweet, soft lips and the sad, shy smile.

Dear God! He was in love with her!

How had it happened? He knew that he

liked her. Liked her a lot and enjoyed being with her. He hadn't intended to fall in love until he was on his feet and could provide for a wife. Hell and damnation! He had learned that love was an intimate, gut-wrenching experience that turned a reasonably intelligent man into a blithering idiot.

Is this how poor tortured Brian felt about Becky? Is this why a sensible man like Foley Luker married a floozy like Sugar?

Inside the truck Anna Marie had gone to sleep. Margie sat on the bunk and debated about what to do. She knew that Brady was out there. If she went out, he would think that she was running after him. If she didn't, he would think that she was avoiding him because she was still angry. She wanted him to believe that she was indifferent to him, that she was no more interested in him than she was in Jody or Rusty, which meant not going out of her way to avoid him.

She climbed out of the truck.

Chapter 22

Brady got to his feet when Margie appeared. With a flick of her hand she motioned for him to sit down and went to sit on the fender of the truck.

"Does Anna Marie have a toothbrush?"

"She did when we started out. I looked for it this morning and couldn't find it."

"Even though she'll be losing her baby teeth, she should brush them at least once a day."

"I know. Brian was a stickler for that and for keeping her hands clean."

"Another thing. She's outgrown her shoes. Her little toes are red from being squeezed."

"Good Lord. I hadn't noticed that. She hasn't said anything. She's barefoot while in the car, but she puts on her shoes when we get out, because of cockleburs, nails and glass in the campgrounds."

"She wanted me to put her egg in a safe place so it wouldn't be broken."

"Not much chance of that. It's been boiled." He got to his feet. Margie thought he was leaving, but he came to where she sat on the fender and held out his hand.

"Sit in the car with me for a while. We'll leave both doors open so we can hear Anna Marie if she wakes."

She ignored his hand and said, "No," shaking her head at the same time.

"Please." The softly spoken word coming from him shocked her. She looked up at the dark blur that was his face. "I want to tell you about Brian and Becky and how I came to have Anna Marie."

"You can tell me here. I don't think it's a good idea to get in the car with you."

"Do you think that I'm going to force myself on you? I've told you that I'm sorry about what happened that night in Oklahoma City. Don't you believe me?"

"Yes, I believe that you're sorry now, but that doesn't mean it won't happen again."

"Oh, Lord. I didn't realize that I had hurt you so much."

"The words hurt more than the rough treatment."

"I don't even remember what I said. Whatever it was, I said it in the heat of anger."

"Oftentimes people blurt out their innermost feelings when they are angry."

"Can't you forget it so we can start over?"

"I can't forget it. But if you like, we can start over. I don't want to be at loggerheads with anyone as I was with Elmer all my life. And I do appreciate all that you've done to help me these last few days."

"I need no thanks for that."

"You might not need them, but I need to offer them anyway."

"Deke said that you are one of a kind, and I believe him. If we are going to let the sleeping dog lie, come sit with me. You can call it a test . . . of sorts."

She was as surprised as he was when she accepted the hand he offered. She found herself walking beside him, her hand engulfed in a large, warm one.

"What else did Deke tell you?"

"He said that you had a lot of love to give someone and the man who got it would be a lucky son of a bitch. His words exactly."

"I wish I could have loved him the way a woman loves her special man. He is one of the most caring, unselfish people I've ever known."

"He'll meet someone someday who will realize that. My mother said that God made a woman for every man and that he made her for my father."

"What a sweet thing to say."

"He loved her very much and didn't last very long after she died."

Brady opened the passenger side of his car and left the door open after Margie had gotten in. He went around to the driver's side and slid in under the wheel.

"If it gets too windy, close the door."

"I hadn't visualized the land here in the Texas Panhandle as so flat and treeless."

"It is that. I prefer mountains and valleys."

"Is your ranch on a mountain?"

"It's in a lush, green valley. The grass at times comes up to the horses' bellies."

"Who do you sell your horses to?"

"Mostly other ranchers. Some go to the army. I also run a few hundred head of steers. They are what pay the bills."

Margie was surprised that she was so comfortable with him. They were quiet for a long while before Margie spoke.

"It's been strange without Elmer. Somehow I keep thinking that he'll show up and tell me to get out of his truck."

"I know the feeling. I kept thinking that

Brian would walk in the door. It wasn't until Anna Marie and I drove away from the house that I felt that it was over, that he was really gone." He put a cigarette in his mouth, flipped the head of the match with his thumbnail and lit it.

"When we get to a town that's big enough to have a shoe store, will you help me pick out shoes for Anna Marie?"

"Sure. She's a smart little thing . . . for her age."

"Is she? I've not been around enough children to know."

"The people I worked for had a boy and a girl. They were six and eight. Anna Marie is very bright. She acts as mature as the eight-year-old."

"She talks about you a lot. She's not been around many young women her mother's age. The woman Brian hired to take care of her was a grandmother. When Anna Marie wasn't with Brian, she was with her. She may have thought all young women were mean like her mother."

"Well, for crying out loud. I certainly hope that your brother set her straight about that."

"He tried. When I think of how he died, it almost tears me apart." Brady rushed on, hurrying to say what he wanted to say. "He was my twin. We looked exactly alike except for the scar in Brian's eyebrow. That's how the teacher told us apart. We even fooled our pa sometimes. We were always together. After the folks died it was just the two of us. We worked together, had fun together, without a thought that someday there would be only one of us left.

"Then he married Becky."

Margie watched Brady's large hands grip the steering wheel and knew that talking about his brother was painful. When one of his hands left the wheel and groped for hers, she put her hand in it.

"He loved Becky with all his heart from the time we were fourteen. He could see no other girl but her. She led him a merry chase through school and afterward. She was a good-time girl: loved to go to parties, dances, smoke cigarettes and drink bootleg whiskey. But she always kept Brian on the string. I think she married him to get away from home. Her folks were clamping down on her. Brian thought that she would settle down once they had a family.

"She did for a while. She hated being pregnant. Brian did everything for her. He was thrilled over Anna Marie. Becky never wanted to have much to do with her. Brian named her Anna after our grandma and

Marie after our mother."

"Was your brother a rancher?"

"No. With the money we got from our parents and grandparents he bought a newspaper in a little town in Kansas. Becky didn't want to move, but she did; and it wasn't long until she had a circle of wild friends and fell back into her same old pattern. Foley's wife reminds me of her, but Becky wasn't as pretty or as flirty. If Brian knew she was messing around with other men, he never let on."

"What about you at that time? Did you go to Kansas?"

"No. I took my money and went west. It meant that Brian and I would be separated for the first time. But he had a wife who didn't like me much, and I couldn't abide her. It was best that I go my way and Brian go his. During the four years I was in Colorado I came back several times.

"Then I got a letter from Brian saying that he was about to lose the paper because he couldn't give it the time it needed. He didn't mention Becky, but I knew by the tone of the letter that she was at the root of his problems and that he was in a terrible state of depression. I got on the train the day I received the letter and got there an hour too late."

Margie didn't know what to say. She

heard the pain in his voice and desperately wanted to say something to comfort him. She took his hand in both of hers, drew it into her lap and held it tightly.

"Brian went home and found her in his bed with a man he thought was his friend. He killed both of them. I met him coming out of the house with Becky's body in his arms. He went to the barn and killed himself." Brady drew in a deep breath. "I never knew anything could hurt so much. It was like a knife had cut out part of my heart."

"I can imagine. It must have been unbearable."

"He asked me what he had done wrong that would cause his Becky to hurt him so. What could I tell him? He had wasted his life loving a woman who wasn't worth spit."

"Was there no one else to take Anna Marie?"

"Becky's folks had washed their hands of Becky and didn't even come to the funeral. She had one old-maid aunt. But after I looked her over I wouldn't leave a sick pup with her. So I wrote to Opal, Becky's sister. She wrote back and said to bring her out."

"She may be just the thing for Anna Marie."

"And she may not. If I remember correctly, she was a year or two younger than

Becky and had left home before she did. The aunt who gave me her address seemed to think that she was all right, although I heard Brian say something to the effect that her husband was a scalawag who couldn't hold a job. I've grown so attached to the little mite that I don't know if I'll be able to give her up even if Opal is a saint."

"When the time comes, you'll do what's best for Anna Marie."

"I'm afraid that I'll be selfish and want to keep her with me, even if I can't give her the life someone else could give her."

"Do you think someone else will love her more than you do? Take better care of her?" Margie could feel each time he looked at her and then away.

"No. She's all I have left of my brother . . . my family. But I've learned on this trip that I don't know much about how to take care of a little girl. She's even embarrassed to tell me when she needs to go to the outhouse."

"Couldn't you hire someone to take care of her? Her father did."

"I live ten miles from town. Two Indian families and one Mexican family live there on the ranch. My house is just a rough cabin. I was going to fix it up this year, but I've spent my money going back to Kansas and on this trip to California. After paying

Brian's bills, all that was left was this car."

"Anna Marie might prefer living in a rough cabin where she is loved to living in a nice house where she is an outsider."

"But she's too young to make that decision."

The logic of his statement left Margie with nothing to say. The silence between them stretched into frozen moments in time — two people sitting in the dark. She looked out the car window into a sky studded with a million stars. The moon, looking like a big yellow balloon, was hanging high above the burned-out house. The crying of a child from one of the other camps, then the barking of a dog, broke the stillness. Brady brought her hand to the seat between them and laced his fingers with hers.

"My ranch is about three hundred miles north of Albuquerque." He finally spoke, leaving his statement hanging in the air.

Margie hesitated, then said, "You could turn off there. It would save you miles and . . . time. Alvin and Grace would take Anna Marie on to her aunt in California. They are going to Bakersfield."

Slowly he turned his head and looked at her. "If I turn off at Albuquerque, Anna Marie will be with me." He continued to look at her.

Margie with the big sad eyes, I wish that I dared to ask you to go with me. But in a way you are like Becky. She had her heart set on having a good time. You've got yours set on seeing Hollywood and would laugh if I asked you to live with me on an isolated horse ranch.

"You've got two or three days to make up your mind." She wiggled her hand out of his and slid out of the car. "I'd better turn in if we're going to leave at dawn."

Brady met her in front of the car and took her arm. "Thank you for being with me and being such a patient listener."

She wasn't sure what to say, so she said nothing. At the end of the truck they stopped and looked steadily at each other. Even though it was dark, the force of his eyes held her as firmly as if he held her with his hands. It had been pleasant being with him. She had not felt in the least threatened.

He was a hard man, but he had soft spots too. He had loved his brother, and, whether he was aware of it or not, he loved his brother's child.

"Would you like me to light the lantern?"

"No." She laughed lightly. "My night vision has improved lately."

"Well, good night."

"Good night."

Margie lay awake for a long time thinking

about Brady Hoyt and what had made him the kind of man he was.

Margie was up and dressed when dawn began to light the eastern sky.

Anna Marie was still asleep when Brady came for her. Margie held her while he put her mattress back in his car. She wished with all her heart that she could keep this child with her forever. How wonderful it would be to have someone of your very own to love and to watch grow. She was unaware that Brady stood at the end of the truck until she lifted her head after placing a kiss on Anna Marie's forehead.

He stepped up on the box and reached for the child. It was too dark to see his eyes, but Margie felt them on her face. He gently lifted the little girl out of her arms, then stood for a long moment looking at her, the sleeping child between them.

"We'll stop for gas in Amarillo," he said.

"All right."

"See you then."

The headlights shone on the back of Alvin's truck as Margie and Jody left the campground. As soon as the sky was light enough that Jody could see, he turned them off.

"Brady said the lights were a drain on the battery."

"How is your father doin'?" Margie asked.

"All right. He's worried about Sugar. He doesn't want anything bad to happen to her."

"Elmer's wife ran off and left him too. I don't know what made her go, but I do know that he must have been hard to live with."

"Pa was too good to Sugar. He tried hard to give her everything she wanted. He thinks now that she was just using him to get to California."

"But he's married to her. She could step in and take everything he has if anything happened to him."

"Pa knows that. He said that when we get to California, he'll see if he can get something called an annulment because she ran off and left him."

Sugar woke to find herself alone in the small cabin. Light was streaming in through the window. She crawled out of the rumpled bed and went to look out. The car was gone!

"The dirty, low-life son of a bitch!"

She quickly searched the room. He had taken everything except her suitcase. He'd not left her a dime! She fumed as she dressed. He'd not get away with it. She'd go to the police and tell them that he not only kidnapped her, he forced her to help him rob those people. She'd see his sorry ass in jail!

She was putting on her lipstick when she heard a car stop, then the slamming of a door. A key rattled in the lock, then the door was flung open.

" 'Lo, sweet thing. Didn't expect ya to be up." Homer came to her, grabbed the hair at the back of her head and kissed her. "Why ya got them clothes on for?"

"Where the hell have you been?"

"Takin' care of a few things. Did ya think I run off and left ya? I took all the money so ya'd be here when I got back all warm, naked and sweet-smellin' —"

"Where's Chester?"

"Gone home."

"You talked him into lettin' us keep the car?"

"Yup. We'll get us another car license to put on it in a day or two."

"It's just you and me now?"

"Uh-huh."

Sugar laughed. "Glory be! I bet old Chester didn't want to get on that bus. Did he put up a fight?" She snuggled against him, bit him on the chin and rubbed against him.

"Not much of a fight at all. We gotta be out of here in an hour, or we'll have to pay again. Get outta them clothes, pretty little bitch. I'm horny as a rutting moose, hard as a rock and randy as a two-peckered mountain goat."

"I got just what ya need, my lusty stud," she said, squeezing him.

Homer put her away from him, shed his coat and unbuttoned his shirt. He took the gun that was tucked in his belt and laid it on the scarred table, then placed a pocket watch and a wad of bills beside it.

Sugar hurriedly removed her dress and slip and sprawled naked across the bed.

"Isn't that Chester's watch?"

"Yeah. He gave it to me."

Sugar waited until he was naked and crawling on top of her before she asked, "Did you do something to Chester?"

"Whatta ya care? Ya didn't like him."

"I didn't like him and I don't care."

"Then shut up and open up."

Later he lay on her, breathing heavily, and whispered, "Get up, ya damn beautiful bitch. We've got to get out to the highway so we can follow that cowboy when he comes through."

Chapter 23

The small gas station owner, on the western edge of Amarillo, couldn't believe his luck when two trucks and two cars lined up and waited patiently at the pump.

After giving Jody money to pay for their gas, Margie got out of the truck and walked back and forth to limber her legs after the long ride. Brady was getting out of his car. Anna Marie was sitting in the front seat. As Margie neared, she saw that the child's little face was wet with tears. Margie's eyes caught Brady's troubled gaze over the top of the car before she spoke to the child.

"What's the matter, honey?"

"Nothin'."

"Want a drink of water?"

"No. I want . . . I want —"

"Want what? What do you want, punkin?"

Before Anna Marie answered, Brady said, "She wants to ride with you. I told her that she should wait until she was invited."

"I'm inviting her," Margie said quickly, opened the car door and lifted the child out. When Anna Marie wrapped her arms around her neck and her legs around her waist, Margie discovered that the child's nightgown was wet. She hid her wet face against Margie's neck and sobbed out something Margie didn't understand.

"Now, now, punkin. Don't cry." Margie turned her back to Brady, hugged and murmured to the sobbing child. "What is it, darlin'? What do you want?"

"I want . . . my dad . . . dy . . ."

The tearful words tore at Margie's heart, and big tears sprang to her eyes. After a heart-stopping moment she went to the truck, which was now at the gas pump. Brady met her there, a concerned look on his face.

"Her dress is in there," Margie said, unable to hold back the tears that leaked from the corners of her eyes.

"What's the matter? Is she sick?"

"She's wet and . . . she wants her . . . daddy." Margie spoke with trembling lips.

"Oh . . . God," he breathed huskily.

Through her blurred vision Margie saw the stricken look on his face and knew that she would remember it forever. It was the look of a man in almost unbearable pain. He turned and untied the back flap on the truck.

"Do you want to get in?" he asked Anna Marie. "I'll tell Jody to go easy when he leaves the gas pump."

When she nodded, Brady pulled the box down for her to step on and lifted her from Margie's arms so she could climb into the truck. He held the little girl close, his head bent, his cheek against hers. His green eyes were shiny when he lifted his head. After setting his niece up into the truck, he quickly walked away.

By the time Anna Marie was dressed, she was in a better mood. It was exciting to her to be in the back of the truck while it was moved to make room for Brady and Foley at the gas pump. When they stopped, Margie got out and reached for the little girl, but Brady was already there.

"Feel better, Punkie?" He lifted the child in his arms, held her for a minute, then carefully set her on her feet. "Stay right here or you may step on a cocklebur. I'll carry you after I make sure the canvas is tied down."

"Margie's goin' to brush my hair."

"We'll get you some shoes the first chance we get."

He finished tying the flap, picked up Anna Marie again and set her on his arm. He looked at Margie. His gaze swept the area, then settled back on her face.

"Ride with us for a couple hours. Rusty will ride with Jody." His tone of voice revealed a touch of anxiety.

Margie tilted her head to look up at him. His face was different, uncertain. His green eyes were shadowed with sadness.

"Well . . . all right. I'll brush Anna Marie's hair. Has she had anything to eat?"

"Some dry toasties. The man here says there's a store ahead and just beyond that an ice dock."

"She should have milk."

"I'll get it at the store."

"You can put it in the icebox after I get ice."

By the time they reached Brady's car, Anna Marie's eyes were anxiously going from one to the other. "Margie?"

"She's going to ride with us, Punkie." Brady spoke with a happier note in his voice. He stood her on the seat. "Move over and make room for her."

"Goody, goody!"

Jody and Rusty had been to the outhouse

402

behind the station. Jody left Rusty at the passenger side of the truck and went around to the driver's side. Mona ran up to say something to Rusty, laughed, hit him on the arm and ran to her father's car. Rusty called out to her that she'd better behave or he'd tell Jody something she had said.

The caravan moved down the highway a half mile and stopped between the mercantile store and the ice dock.

"I'll carry Anna Marie to the porch, then go get your ice. I take it your box will hold twenty-five pounds."

"The last melted out last night. The tongs are in the toolbox there on the side of the truck. Jody has the keys."

Grace was in the store exclaiming over the variety of goods when Margie and Anna Marie entered.

"I haven't seen this much stuff since we left home. There's everything in the world over there." She had come from the dry goods side of the store.

"Do they have shoes?"

"Didn't see any. Oh, mister, do you have any dried apples? I've got a hankerin' to make fried apple pie." Grace went to the grocery side of the store, leaving Margie and Anna Marie to explore the dry goods side.

They paused at a table of dress goods

and fingered the pretty prints. There were hats, gloves, stockings, ribbons and buttons. At the far end, as they were turning to come back up the aisle, Margie spotted a table of Indian moccasins. They were different from the ones she had seen in Missouri.

"These are nice. Look at the beadwork. Do you think we could find a pair that would fit you, honey?" Margie lifted Anna Marie up onto the end of the table. "I had a pair when I was little."

"I like blue ones."

"Here's a pair with blue beads." She measured the sole of the moccasin against Anna's foot. "Too little." She delved into the pile and came out with another pair. "These look just right. Shall we try them on?"

"They're pretty."

After slipping the moccasins on Anna's small feet and tying the thong, she lifted the child down.

"How do they feel?" Down on her knees, Margie pressed her thumb on the end of the shoe to test the fit.

"Good. Can I have 'em?"

Margie looked at the sign: CHILDREN'S MOC 75 CENTS. OTHERS 1.00. She got to her feet. A dollar seventy-five if she got a pair for herself. She made the decision.

"Yes, you can, and I'll get a pair for myself."

"Like mine?"

"Like yours."

"Goody, goody!"

She wouldn't have dared to spend the money before, but she had kept the two hundred dollars she had found in Elmer's socks. It was worth every penny of the money to see the smile on Anna Marie's face and see her dance up the aisle of the store.

Grace had left before they reached the counter. Margie asked for a bottle of milk, a loaf of sliced bread and a pound of sliced meat.

"I'll have to charge you a nickel deposit on the bottle."

"Can I turn it in down the line if I buy more milk tomorrow?"

"You should be able to."

She was paying for the purchases when Brady came into the store. She hurriedly put the change in her pocket.

"Looky, Uncle Brady. Looky what I got. You don't have to carry me. They're Indian shoes."

"So they are." He knelt down and lifted her foot. "That's just the ticket, Punkie."

He stood and went to the counter, his eyes

on Margie. She avoided looking at him and picked up the sack with the milk, bread and meat. He didn't say anything until they reached the store porch.

"I'm glad you found the footwear. I'll pay you for them and for the milk."

"I'll pay you for the ice."

"It was all of fifteen cents."

"Well . . . the shoes were ten dollars," she said with a cocky smile.

At first he was taken aback, then a slow smile covered his face and his eyes lit up.

"Is that all? You should have bought two or three more pairs."

"I did buy one more." She held up the pair she had bought for herself. "I'm going to sit down right here on the steps and put them on."

"Take your time. We've decided this will be our noon stop even if it is a little early. Stay with Margie, Punkie, I'll be right back." Brady went back into the store.

When he came out, Margie and Anna Marie in their new moccasins stood at the end of the truck. Brady had tied the flap back when he put the ice in the box, but it was still as hot as an oven under the canvas.

"Stay here, honey. I'll get a cup for your milk and butter to go on our bread," Margie said.

"Can I show Aunt Grace and Mona my new shoes?"

"Wait until I come back."

Margie was ready to climb out over the tailgate when Brady reappeared. He set a sack on the ground and lifted her down as easily as if she had been Anna Marie. "Thank you."

"You're very welcome." His eyes smiled at her.

"I got bread and meat. I'll make Anna Marie a sandwich. She's eager to show her shoes to Mona and Grace."

"I got bread and meat too. And a toothbrush for Punkie."

"Put the meat in the icebox. Would you like a glass of tea? I have some made, but had no ice to go in it until now."

"I sure would. Shall I chip the ice?"

Margie glanced at him. The smile he gave her spread a warm light into his eyes. He looked years younger when he smiled. Her pulse leaped, bringing color to her face, and her flushed cheeks made her soft brown eyes seem all the warmer.

They ate the sandwiches while sitting on the fender of the truck and watched Anna Marie run around showing everyone her new footwear.

"I know now why Indians wear moccasins," Margie said, wiggling her toes. "They're comfortable. It's like going barefoot, except you don't have to worry about cockleburs."

Brady dug in his pocket, brought out two dollars and put it in her hand.

"What's this for?"

"The shoes and the milk."

"The shoes and the milk were eighty-five cents. I'll get the deposit back on the bottle." She shoved the bills back in his hand.

"I want to pay for your shoes too . . . for all you've done for Anna Marie."

"I don't expect pay for what I've done for Anna Marie." Her voice was so cold that it sent a chill down his back. "Do you want pay for what you've done for me?"

"No, of course not! Oh, Lord, I've put my foot in it again. I'm sorry. I didn't put it right. I want to give you something, and I used Anna Marie for an excuse."

"We don't know each other well enough for me to accept a present from you." She held her head high, her hard brown eyes refusing to look away from his.

The expression on her face cut him like a knife. He felt a tide of panic rise in his throat. He had to make amends, and fast.

"Margie, for the past four years I've been

on an isolated ranch, and even before I went to Colorado I didn't have all that much to do with women. I've lost touch with what's proper and what isn't. If it was forward of me to offer you a gift, I'm sorry."

"After what Elmer said about me I suppose you thought that I —"

"Believe me," he interrupted, "after getting to know you I totally disregarded what Elmer said. He was a bitter, unhappy man, and I think he resented your independence. Be patient with me, Margie. Please."

When she didn't say anything, he said anxiously, "Can't we start over again? Again?"

After a long-drawn-out silence she suddenly let out a little nervous laugh.

"I'm on kind of a short fuse. You can get my back up quicker than anyone I've ever met."

He was too stunned with relief to utter another word; his heart was drumming so hard he could hardly breathe.

"Grace is packing up. I'd better do the same." Margie stood and reached for his glass. "I hate to let this ice go to waste. I'll put it and some tea in the fruit jar. We'll drink it on the way."

He followed her to the truck. After she had filled the jar and before he tied down the flap, she reached inside for her hairbrush. "I haven't brushed Anna Marie's hair yet."

"I'm hot," Sugar complained. "Are the fools goin' to sit there all day?"

Homer had stopped the coupe beside a cluster of shops several hundred feet from where the caravan was parked. Sugar looked like a boy with her hair up under Homer's cap and in the denim pants and striped shirt they had bought this morning. Homer wore Chester's old felt hat.

Sugar had not mentioned Chester again, and neither had Homer. In the back of her mind she wondered at his sudden leaving after vowing to take the car back to his mother. Homer had handled the situation, and that was enough for her. If he had done away with his uncle, she didn't want to know it. She was happier than she'd ever been. She was free. She was doing exciting things. Now, if only Homer would forget about getting even with that damn cowboy . . .

"I see that sweet little Margie is getting in the car with Brady," Sugar said with heavy sarcasm. "The mealymouthed scrawny bitch! She'd been angling to get him between her legs since we started this trip. Now that her papa's out of the way, she'll not have to wait long. A man like Brady's used to getting his poontang. He won't go long without it."

"Scrawny? If I remember right, she had good-sized tits." Homer wore a devilish grin when he looked at her.

"Bullshit! So does a cow. Ya wanta screw a cow?" she asked shrewishly, and flounced over next to the door.

One of the best things about being with Homer was that they spoke the same language. She could use all the forbidden words she had used only in her thoughts. None of this having to be so nasty nice and having to make it right with Foley every time she slipped up. It was great to be out from under that strain and be able to be herself.

Homer let out a hoot of laughter. "Chester screwed a sheep once on a dare."

Sugar looked pained. "I'm not surprised." Then, "How was it?"

"All right, I guess. He shot his wad."

"Piddle," Sugar said with disgust. "He had sheep dung for brains anyhow."

They sat silently and watched the activity going on around the caravan. Then Homer asked, "Is the cowboy hot for the blonde?"

"She's the only one handy beside Foley's kid, and that one went gaga over the blind dummy 'cause he could sing and play the guitar."

"Who's drivin' her truck?"

"Jody, Foley's kid. That's the blind dummy getting in with him. Lordy, but it pissed her for me to call him that."

"If we get the chance, we'll run yore old man off the road."

"Don't do that!" Sugar exclaimed. "I want the money he's carryin'. I'm entitled to some of it."

"He's last in line. Before anyone misses him we'd have the money and be gone."

"He'd know it was me."

"Maybe not."

"You'd kill him?"

"Well, shit! Do you think I'm dumb enough to let him put the finger on me?"

"What about the cowboy?"

"I ain't giving up on him."

"Can't we go on ahead, lover?" Sugar moved over and worked her hand against his fly.

"Cut that out." He removed her hand. "Some jay-hawk will come out of that feedstore and see a boy with his hands in my pants. The shock might kill him."

Sugar's tinkling laugh rang out. Homer gazed at her smiling face. She was about the prettiest woman he'd ever seen, pretty and wicked, and she loved to screw. How in the hell had he had the good luck to find her? Now that they were rid of old Chester, he'd pull off the road whenever they took a notion to have a little fun and go at it.

"Hey, Stud." Sugar waved her hand in front of his face to get his attention. "When are we goin' to get more money?"

"You liked that, didn't you?"

"It was exciting."

"I'm afraid we'll have to wait until we get to a big enough town before I put my pretty little decoy out again. Meanwhile, we'll keep our eyes open for easy pickin's."

Chapter 24

The country west of Amarillo was big and open as far as the eye could see. The highway cut a path between a sea of short prairie grass, a pale gold carpet, rolled back on each side of the highway. Shadows of the low-flying clouds created dark patches on the open sun-yellowed grassy plain.

Margie thought that they might as well be traveling across a space as empty and limitless as the sky except for the skeleton of a windmill silhouetted against the blue. On the breeze that came from the south was the smell of sun-ripened grass and sage. She had the feeling that she would be like a grain of sand on a beach if she were ever lost in this vast space.

"It's a lonesome country." She spoke for

the first time since Anna Marie had fallen asleep, her head in Margie's lap, her feet in Brady's.

"Yes, it is. But hills and valleys can be lonesome too."

"Were you lonesome at your ranch?"

"Most of the time I was so busy that I didn't have time to think about it. But when I did, I wished to have someone to go home to." He glanced at her profile. "Both of the Mexicans that work there have large happy families. Ramon, my partner, married last fall."

"Ramon. Is he a Mexican?"

"No. Cherokee. He has an interesting background. His father was a teacher at the Cherokee Seminary at Tahlequah, Oklahoma. His mother was a quadroon, which makes him one-eighth colored. He's one of the smartest men I've ever known and could be teaching in a university somewhere. But he loves ranching, loves horses, hates being in town and seldom goes there."

"How did you meet him?"

"While working on a ranch. When I first went out to Colorado, I signed on to work for bed, board and ten a month. I wanted to get a little experience under my belt before I put my money down. Ramon had come out from Rainwater, Oklahoma, and didn't have a dime to his name. A few months later his sister, Radna Bluefeather, and her husband, Randolph, came to visit him. Randolph insisted on staking Ramon and put up money equal to mine. That's how I happened to be partners with him. It was one of the smartest moves I ever made."

"Is Ramon married?"

"He went to Denver to get a load of books and came back with a wife. They're well suited. Both are educated, private people and are crazy in love with each other."

"Is she an Indian?"

"No. Do you have anything against a white woman who marries a man of mixed blood?"

"No." She glanced at his sharply etched profile. He turned, and she saw a flicker of humor in his eyes as he swung them away from her and concentrated on his driving. The car picked up speed. There was something terribly attractive about him. He was totally male from the top of his thick black hair to his scuffed cowboy boots. There was no doubt that he aroused her physically. *How do I know another attractive man wouldn't do the same under the same circumstances?*

Brady Hoyt, however, was unlike any man she had ever met. He was efficient, decisive

416

and even brutal when necessary. That was demonstrated by the way he had handled men who would probably have robbed them. On the other hand, he was as gentle and as caring with Anna Marie as if she was the most precious thing in the world. Would he be the same with a woman . . . if he loved her?

Margie longed for someone who would look forward to coming home to *her*. She wanted a man she could stand beside, as a helpmate to share his joy and his sorrows, bear his children and grow old with. She gave a little involuntary shiver. In Brady she had finally met a man she could give her heart to completely, build her life around.

Her lips curled with disgust. She was too much a coward to admit that she was already in love with him, and she was afraid that if she did admit it, it would become real and would hurt much more later on. She had to be realistic about this. Brady was probably interested in her only for the duration of the trip. It would never do to let him know how much she had enjoyed being with him and Anna Marie this afternoon.

The trucks ahead slowed until they were creeping along. When they hit the dirt and gravel road, flourlike dust, stirred by the wheels, swirled up behind them. Margie rolled up the window. Brady backed away to allow more space between them and the truck ahead.

The going was slow for what seemed to be miles and miles, and the heat inside the car became wicked. Anna Marie's head was wet with sweat. Margie cooled her face with the cardboard fan Brady pulled from under the seat.

"This heat gives me a powerful thirst." Brady wiped the sweat from his forehead with the sleeve of his shirt.

Margie reached for the fruit jar she had wrapped in a towel. "The ice is gone, but there's a little tea left."

"You drink first."

Margie took a swallow and passed the jar to Brady. She watched as he tilted his head to drink. Her eyes took in every detail of his profile. When he finished, he held out the jar. Bright green eyes from beneath a brush of brows as dark as his windblown hair smiled at her. She took the jar from his hand, screwed the top back on and set it on the floor. She hoped desperately that he didn't know how her heart was behaving.

It was a blessed relief when the car bumped over a ridge and onto a patch of newly paved highway.

"I'm glad that's over," Margie said, and

rolled down the window.

"We'll hit a lot of dirt roads before we get to Albuquerque."

"Have you been over this road before?"

"Not here. I was on a little patch west of Albuquerque. We should be in Tucumcari in a couple of hours. I hope Alvin knows where to find the campground."

"Will it be dark then? The days are getting longer."

"Just about dark, I think. I was dreading this long day, but it's gone fast." He looked across the intervening space between them. "You should ride with us every day."

"That would never do, and you know it."

"Why not?"

"Well . . ." She paused and bit down on her lower lip. "Because I've got a lot of thinking to do, and so do you. You've got to decide if you're going to turn off at Albuquerque. We can't do any thinking sitting here chatting."

"What are you trying to decide? I thought you'd made up your mind to see Hollywood."

"That's what I wanted to do when I left Missouri. You think that it's a silly girl's shallow dream, don't you?"

"I don't know about that. If seeing Hollywood is something you always dreamed of, I

419

don't think it's shallow. We all have our dreams. Mine is to raise a quarter horse that is smarter than its rider. At times I've thought that wouldn't be too hard to do." His lips quirked in a smile.

"I dreamed about Hollywood because I lived in a town of three hundred stretched along the highway. I worked in a café and saw maybe two movies a year. I had to have a dream, a goal, or my dull life would have been unbearable."

"And now?"

"Now I'm facing reality. I'm alone in a strange land. I've got to think about a job. Before we left home I had the notion that if I could just get to California, a job would be waiting for me. I'd see the sights and put some excitement in my life. Now I see all these people going there with the same sort of hopes. The place must be as crowded as fleas on a dog's back. It's scary."

Margie drew in a deep breath. She was appalled that she had revealed so much to this man who would break her heart if she wasn't careful. She was too embarrassed to look at him and kept unseeing eyes turned toward the window.

"So what is it you've got to think about?"

"I've got to think about what I want to do after I find Goldie and give her Elmer's money and his truck. Do I want to stay near Bakersfield? Grace and Alvin said it would be nice if I settled near them. I would know someone. I'm not sure now that I want to use what little money I have and go on to a more uncertain future in Hollywood."

"Elmer's wife left him. Some would say that you are entitled to his money and his truck."

Margie turned, stared at his profile and spoke coolly. "And give proof to what he said about me being a thief? No, thank you."

Anna Marie stirred, then sat up. "Are we there yet?"

"Not yet, honey." Margie smoothed the hair back from her face. "You slept a long time."

"Can I sit on your lap?"

"Sure you can." After she was cuddled in Margie's lap, the child pressed her cheek against Margie's shoulder. "Don't go back to sleep, puddin', or you won't want to sleep tonight."

Brady's eyes left the road to glance at the woman bent over the little girl in her lap. She was murmuring to her and kissing her forehead. He felt a twinge in the region of his heart. Anna Marie had never known a mother's love as he and Brian had. Unlike Becky, Margie appeared to be a woman with mating and nesting instincts who would build her life around her family.

Had he been able to read Margie's thoughts, Brady would have been surprised to know that she was wishing with all her heart that this was her little girl. She would give all the love bottled up inside her to this child and to the man beside her if he wanted it. She would put her heart and soul into making a home for them, taking care of them, loving them.

Good Lord! What was she thinking? She'd better get those notions out of her head, or she was in for a rough time ahead.

She looked up to meet Brady's gaze until he focused again on the road. Each was quiet except for the turmoil going on inside. The late afternoon light illuminated Brady's tired face, showing the dark cast of a day-old beard and, in that one quick glimpse, the hungry, anxious look in his eyes. Her heart slammed against her rib cage so hard she could hardly breathe.

Even when she closed her eyes, Margie could see his face behind her eyelids. *She had to stop thinking about him as if he could even possibly be a permanent part of her life.* The chances were good that he would leave the caravan at Albuquerque and she would never see him again. A feeling of emptiness shot through her at the thought.

It was dusk when Alvin led them into a large field on the edge of Tucumcari. Margie almost groaned when she saw that it was full of campers. Cars, trucks and wagons were spread out over a couple acres. Supper fires that burned in front of some camps were sending up a trail of smoke. Other campers were using small kerosene stoves. Rocking chairs had been unloaded, and women sat in them nursing their babies while men gathered, squatted on their heels and talked of the dust storms back home and their hope of finding a better life for their families in the fertile fields of California.

When Alvin stopped, Jody parked the truck behind him. Brady pulled up and parked parallel to Alvin, and Foley parked behind Brady parallel to Jody. They were a tight group of four vehicles. It was in areas like this that Margie saw the wisdom of traveling in a caravan.

At the far end of the field were two ramshackle outhouses. To reach them, they would have to pass through the camp where men without families lounged beside low rag tents and old cars. After Grace had held a whispered conversation with Alvin, he motioned to the men and they walked a distance away, stopped and appeared to be looking things over. Grace took a granite chamber pot and a blanket from the back of the truck.

"I don't like the looks of them outhouses or where they're at." Grace wrinkled her nose. "We'll make our own right here between the cars and the trucks."

Anna Marie thought it was great fun to use the pot while Mona and Margie held up the blanket to give her privacy.

It had been the longest day of their trip. They had covered a hundred and eighty miles. Everyone was tired. It was Brady's idea to pool what they had and have a cold supper. Alvin set up the kerosene stove, and Grace made coffee. Margie and Brady supplied the meat and bread they had bought at the store in Amarillo, and Foley brought out a box of crackers and a large chunk of cheese. It was dark by the time they finished eating.

The caliber of the people at the campground made the men uneasy. They cautioned the women not to go behind the cars unless they all went. Blackie, ever watchful, growled menacingly when another dog wandered too close. Cars came and went. Two men on horseback approached, gave them the eye and moved on.

"I don't like this place." Mona sat beside Rusty on a quilt. Earlier she had described the camp to him in detail. Now, holding his hand in her lap, unconcerned that their parents were nearby, she whispered to him when there was something of interest he couldn't see.

Sneaking sly glances at the couple, Grace thanked God for the girl who was opening up a whole new world for her boy. Since meeting Mona, he seemed to have more confidence and be less self-conscious about his blindness. If they parted when they reached California, he would at least have had this happy experience.

Margie, with Anna Marie on her lap, sat in the canvas chair. Around them were the usual camp sounds: a crying child, a barking dog, drunken laughter and, occasionally, a male voice raised in anger. The group gathered beside Alvin's truck was like a family to Margie, a family she had not had since her granny died. Even then there had been only the two of them.

O Lord, I'm so glad that I'm here and not alone on a bus going to some unknown place.

Her eyes often sought Brady where he lounged on the ground beside Foley. Most of the time when she looked at him, his face was turned toward her. When she realized that he had been looking at her steadily for some time, her cheeks turned warm. She quickly looked away and made a to-do about pulling Anna Marie's dress down over her legs.

"We should keep a watch tonight." Alvin spoke softly as Blackie stood, his tail straight out, and peered off in the darkness. "Son," he said to Rusty, "better keep Blackie close. He's actin' like there's a bitch in heat nearby. He might decide to go courtin'."

"Sit, Blackie," Rusty commanded.

"There's probably fifty people in this camp, not countin' the kids. We look to be the most prosperous folks here. The trucks could be a mighty big temptation to someone with bootleggin' in mind." Brady struck a match on the sole of his boot and lit a cigarette.

"I've been thinking that we probably shouldn't set up any sleeping tents," Foley added. "I'd rather be out in the open where I can see what's going on."

Margie spoke. "Mona can sleep on the box in the truck, and we'll make a pallet of blankets and pillows beside my bunk for Anna Marie."

"That's a good idea." Grace lifted the coffeepot. "Too bad if anyone wanted more coffee. This is the last of it."

"Mona, Blackie and I will take the first watch," Rusty announced from where he sat beside Mona.

"I know what you're up to, you . . . you masher!" Jody teased. "After we've all gone to bed, you're thinkin' to neck with my sister."

"Just kiss my foot, Jody Luker! And shut up!" Mona glared at her brother, but she was grinning.

"Let the clabberhead talk." Rusty put his arm across Mona's shoulders. "He's just jealous because he doesn't have a girl to neck with unless he can talk Margie into sharing his watch."

"If Margie shares anybody's watch, it'll be mine."

There was a heavy silence after Brady had spoken, and all eyes turned on Margie. Hers flew to him. There was no mistake. He was looking directly at her. When her mind cleared and the words he had spoken registered, she was embarrassed, but elated too. She was also grateful for the dark that concealed her blush. Finally she had enough breath in her lungs to speak.

"I can take a watch —"

"No." Brady, Foley and Alvin spoke in unison.

"Why not? You men are tired from driving

427

all day. I could yell loud enough to wake you, and I have a pistol. I'm not afraid to shoot it if I have to. I need to do my part."

"I'll do your part," Brady said in a no-nonsense tone of voice. Then added as if explaining his statement, "You're looking after Anna Marie."

"I think we should pull out of here in the morning before the camp stirs," Alvin said quietly to fill the awkward silence that followed Brady's statement. "We can stop after daylight and get a bite to eat. We'll have to gas up before we leave town anyway."

"Sounds like a good idea to me." Foley stood and stretched. He felt more like himself than he had in a long time. He would never have been able to be an active part of this group if Sugar were still with him. She would be nagging him to break away, and he would be on pins and needles fearful of what she would do or say.

It had been her choice to take off, and he had been afraid that she might run into something or someone who would hurt her. But sometime during the past couple of days he had come to the conclusion that she had done him a favor by leaving.

Homer waited until the caravan was parked in the campground before he followed it in and stopped as far from it as possible. There were so many campers and so many cars going in and out that a coupe with a couple of young *men* in it was hardly noticed.

"There's yore man, little puss." Homer pointed toward the men who had walked a distance away from the trucks. "Want to wave at him?"

"No, and he's not my man. You are."

"How come ya didn't set yore sights on the cowboy, pussy-wussy? Wasn't he rough enough for ya?"

"I didn't like him; that's why," she retorted testily.

"I hate his guts!" Homer said viciously. He would never forget the humiliation of being tied up, messing in his pants, and the ridicule that followed.

"How long are we staying here? I'm tired and thirsty."

"Now, sugar teat," Homer said patiently. "I'm just gettin' the lay of the land. In just a little bit we'll go on into town, find us a room and eat a meal. We got money, honey."

"Then whater we goin' to do?"

"I know what I'm goin' to do." The hand on her leg traveled up the inside of her thigh, making his meaning clear. "I'm goin' to

429

strip ya naked as a jaybird and screw ya till yore eyes bug out."

"Promise?"

"Swear to it, little bitch. Then while yo're restin' up for the next go-round, I'll come back here and pay a call on the cowboy."

"I want to come with you."

He grabbed her chin between his thumb and forefinger and turned her face toward him.

"Ya'll do what I tell ya to do, little puss," he snarled. "I'm callin' the shots. Hear?" Then in his usual teasing tone he asked, "Is it that yo're not wantin' to let yore man outta yore sight, huh? Huh?"

"I don't want to miss out on the fun."

"Yo're wantin' to watch me screw his bitch? Is that it?"

"You mess with that snooty bitch that way, and I'll cut your pecker off with a dull knife." She grabbed his crotch, squeezing so hard that he winced. "This is mine."

Homer laughed with delight. "I'd kiss ya, but two fellows are comin' this way on horseback, and I don't want to draw their attention by kissin' a *boy*."

"I could take off the cap."

"Ya leave it on till we get outta here."

"And if I don't?"

"I'll beat yore ass."

"Try it, you'll have a fight on your hands."

Homer laughed and squeezed her cheek between his thumb and forefinger.

"Shucks. Yo're more fun than pinnin' the tail on the donkey at a kids' party. We're goin' to have to have us one of them fights soon, but not tonight, little pussy. I got to think of how I'm goin' to get even with that cowboy."

"Is that all you think about?"

"No. I'm thinkin' how we can get the money off that fool that let ya get away from him."

Chapter 25

Brady carried Anna Marie to the back of the truck and waited for Margie to climb inside, then lifted the child to her waiting arms. She laid her on her bunk and took off her moccasins. It was so dark that she had to feel her way around, but she managed to take off Anna Marie's dress and slip the nightgown over her head. She was very aware that Brady stood at the end of the truck.

"It's going to be hot in there tonight." His low voice came out of the darkness.

"I won't cover her."

"Are you going to come out for a while?"

"I . . . hadn't planned on it. You'd better get some sleep before you take your watch."

"I've got a while. I'm taking the two-to-four."

"Wake me and I'll sit with you."

"No. I don't want you out of the truck at that time of night."

"But you're wanting me out now."

"For purely selfish reasons. I want to be with you for a little while." She couldn't be sure, but she thought he grinned.

"You were with me all day. I'd think you'd be sick of my company by now."

"Are you sick of mine?" He reached for her and lifted her down, but kept her close to him.

She said nothing because she knew that she couldn't tell him that this was one of the happiest times in her life, that she had stored up memories to bring out and replay over in her mind when they were no longer together.

"Are you afraid that I'll be rough with you again?"

She tried to pull away from him, but he locked his hands behind her and refused to let her go. "I'm not afraid of that. I realize that what happened that night was as much my fault as yours."

"How so?" His hands moved to slide up and down her arms. When she didn't answer, he said, "Why do you think it was as much your fault as mine?"

"Well." She licked her lips and wondered

where to put her hands. Finally she put them on the arms holding her. "I was easy. You said there was no harm in a few casual kisses, and I just let myself —"

"They were not as casual as I led you to believe."

"It doesn't matter. I'm sorry I made such a to-do over it. I was just . . . overstrung. Elmer had rattled me by saying what he did."

"I've never done such a rotten thing in my life. Our parents raised us to be respectful of women. I want you to know that I'm sorry."

"Let's agree to forget it. We have no future together. At the end of this trip, maybe even when we reach Albuquerque, you'll go your way and I'll go mine. I don't want to do anything during this short time that I'll regret."

"Like what?"

"Like becoming too fond of Anna Marie and . . . you."

"Is there a danger of that?"

"Of course. Anna Marie is a darling little girl. If I had the means to take care of her, I'd take her in a minute and love her as my own."

Brady wanted to know badly if she could love him too, but feared to ask the question. When he hesitated, she rushed into speech.

"You've got your ranch to go to. I've got

the sights of Hollywood to see and —"

"I thought you were not so sure about that anymore."

"Well, heck. What else is there for a girl to do?" She tried to keep her voice light.

"You could come and make a home with me and Anna Marie."

Damn his heart for beating so fast and making him feel so inept. Without realizing it, his hands were pulling her closer. This feeling of being totally alive when he was with her, even butting heads with her, and seeing her face behind his closed eyelids was so damn new. Yet here he was asking this lovely, sweet girl to turn her life over to a man that she scarcely knew. It was only natural that she would have some misgivings.

The air in her lungs refused to come out. When it finally did, her voice came in a quivering whisper.

"What does the job pay?" She refused to believe that he was offering any more than a job.

"There won't be much money involved. It will be years before we do more than just make a living." His voice was husky. His hands moved up to her shoulders. "But I can guarantee you a lifetime of . . . devotion. I'll bust my butt to take care of you." He rushed on before she could say anything. "It would not be the kind of life you see in the movies. My house on the ranch is just a rough cabin right now, but it's tight and warm and we'd have plenty of beef to eat."

Margie felt the wild hammering of her pulse as she looked up into his dark face. Her heart was beating in a strange and disturbing way as she struggled to get sufficient air into her lungs. His hands had moved from her shoulders down over her arms. He was waiting for her to speak. *He had not said, "Marry me, I love you." He had offered devotion, food and shelter.*

"Is this so you won't have to leave Anna Marie with Opal?" She asked the question even as she thought it.

"It's true that I don't want to leave my brother's child with a stranger, but I'm not asking you to share my life just for that, although I know you would be a much better mother to her than the one she had. And it would please Brian to know that his little girl was with someone who loved her." He hesitated. His throat worked as he swallowed repeatedly. When he continued, his voice was hoarse. "He asked me to take care of her. I just didn't see how I could do it alone. I planned to send money to her aunt for her keep."

There was a long moment of silence,

dominated by the pounding of their hearts. She stood with her head bowed, her forehead a whisker away from his shoulder. A thin thread of panic ran through her. Was she getting in too deeply too fast? Was she setting herself up for living a lifetime with a man who only wanted her to provide a home for him and his niece? It was not the loving relationship she had dreamed about.

When she spoke, it was so softly that he couldn't hear. He lifted her chin with the tips of his fingers.

"What did you say, honey?"

"I said, can I think about it?"

"If you have to think about it, it means that you're not sure that you want to take on the two of us." He looked down into her upturned face and slowly shook his head. "You said that you'd take Anna Marie if you had the means to take care of her. I'm offering you the means. But in order to have her, you'll have to put up with me. Is that what you have to think about?" There was huskiness in his voice as if this was terribly important to him.

"No, that isn't what I have to think about." His words had ignited a spark of anger in her, and she spoke sharply. "I have to decide how having a sweet little girl who, if I'm lucky, will someday think of me as her mother compares against living my life with a man who *someday* may fall in love with a woman and leave me to fend for myself." By the time she finished speaking, tears were rolling from her eyes and she was terribly ashamed of them.

"Ah . . . honey, this can't be easy for you." There was genuine regret in his voice. "Why are you thinking that?" His hands moved to her back and pulled her up against him. The bristles on his chin caught on her hair. Her palms flattened on his chest in an attempt to hold herself away from him.

The intensity with which he longed to make her his was causing his heart to jump out of rhythm. He was sure that he had found the woman who was meant for him. He loved to look at her, to talk to her, to be with her. She had responded to his kisses. He was confident that if she didn't care for him now, she was on the verge of it. She was just confused because things were happening too fast. He had to convince her that they were meant to be together.

"Sweetheart, remember me telling you that my mother said God made a certain woman for a certain man? I'm convinced that you're the woman he made for me. I feel it in my heart, in my bones."

"You never said anything about — you

said come make a home with you and Anna Marie."

"I'd not ask you to come with me, share my life, if I didn't care deeply for you."

"I thought you wanted to hire me to take care of Anna Marie —"

"And then I'd fall in love with another woman and leave you?" he finished for her.

"Something like that. I've not known of many truly happy couples except in the movies."

"My mother and father were in love until the day they died. Look at Alvin and Grace. She's the light of his life. I'm sure she feels the same. Are you thinking of my brother and Becky?"

"And Elmer and Mr. Luker and any number of people back home who practically hated each other but stayed together either because they had kids or she had no place to go." Soft brown eyes looked pleadingly into his. "I've got to be very careful that when I give my heart, it's to a man who loves me as much as I love him."

"Honey, I understand that. All of this has happened too fast for you. I can wait for you to think about it." He folded her gently in his arms. "Sweetheart, you're a treasure, a prize at the end of the rainbow. I want to kiss you, but I haven't shaved and

I may scratch your face."

"You never let that stop you before," she said on a breath of a whisper.

With a swift look into her face he lifted her chin and fitted his lips to hers. He kissed her as openly and as intimately as a man could kiss a woman. Margie's arm moved up, and her hand caressed his nape. She had never felt anything like the sensual enjoyment she was feeling now.

When he lifted his head, he looked down at the pale, luminous oval of her face. His face was creased with smiles.

O Lord, he is so handsome, so sweet. Thank you, God, for letting me come on this trip and meet him!

"Your eyes glow in the dark. Did you know that?" The softly murmured words sent tremors of joy through her.

He pressed a gentle kiss to her lips. It was over too quickly for both of them. He lifted both her arms to encircle his neck, and his arms closed around her. There was no haste in the kiss this time. It was slow and deliberate. He took his time, with closed eyes and pounding heart. He held her so close against him that she could feel the hard bones and muscles of his body. His hoarse, ragged breathing accompanied the thunder of his heartbeat against her breasts.

With a sigh Margie gave herself up to the pure joy of kissing and being kissed, to the thrill of wanting and being wanted. She offered herself willingly. Her mouth opened under gentle pressure, yielding, molding itself to the shape of his.

He lifted his head. Hungrily his eyes slid over her upturned face. Their breaths mingled for an instant before he covered her mouth again. When next he lifted his head, he pressed his cheek to hers.

"Ah . . . sweetheart," he murmured, his hand stroking the nape of her neck. "I'm never going to get enough of kissing you." Slowly he moved his head until his lips touched hers again as if, having tasted them, he couldn't stay away. His kiss deepened, and he dropped his hand from her nape to wrap her tightly in his arms, driven by passion, sparked by the touch of her tongue on his lower lip. He wanted it to go on and on but knew it had to end.

She became conscious of his hand stroking her back and his low voice speaking in her ear. "I'll be careful with you, darlin' girl. I want more, much more, than your sweet kisses. But I can wait until you're ready to give it to me."

She tugged on his hand and lifted his knuckles to her lips. They had spoken no words of love, but something wonderful throbbed between them. He pressed her head to his shoulder, and they stood close together, he leaning against the truck and she against him, in companionable silence and sweet intimacy.

Glancing skyward, Brady was jarred out of his contentment when he glimpsed flashes of lightning.

"We may get a rain."

"Where will you go?"

"In the car."

"I don't like to think of you out in the rain. You could get in the truck."

"It would be a mite crowded, honey."

Honey. Sweetheart. Margie closed her eyes and prayed that this was real, that she wouldn't wake up and find that she had been dreaming.

"Being in this bunk reminds me of when we were first married." Grace giggled softly. "Remember that little half-bed we slept on that first year?"

"Sure do," Alvin whispered. "Some of my happiest hours were spent on that little half-bed."

"We broke the bed slats one night, and the old man downstairs came up and pounded on the door —"

"And I had a heck of a time getting untangled from the bedsheets and climbing over the bed rail to get to the door."

"We were silly happy and didn't have a dime."

"I'm still silly happy when I'm with you, love."

"Almost twenty-five years. I can't believe the time has gone so fast." She kissed him on the chin. "And you're just as randy as you were back then."

He chuckled soundlessly. "Not quite, love."

"Randy enough for me," she whispered.

"I'm glad. I was afraid you were going to trade me in for a new model."

"You were not. You know that no one would put up with me but you." She nestled her face in the curve of his neck. "Alvin? Rusty is so happy. I think he's in love with Mona."

"Puppy love, honey. I was about his age when I fell in love with you."

"She's the first girl he's spent much time with."

"Are you worried that this is just a way to pass the time for her?"

"I'm afraid he'll be brokenhearted if she leaves him." Grace ran the palm of her hand over him in the places she knew he liked.

"Maybe they won't break up, but if they do, he'll have to take it like any other man who is disappointed in love. Now, stop your fooling around, woman. I've got to get some sleep."

"Alvin, I'm afraid Brady has decided to keep Anna Marie and will leave us at Albuquerque. His ranch is straight north."

"I don't think he will unless Margie goes with him. She feels obligated to take the truck and the rest of Elmer's possessions to California and find his wife. That says a lot about the girl's character."

"Brady's crazy about her."

"Yeah, and I'm crazy about you." Alvin yawned.

"Sometimes I long for our old home, but I tell myself that home is where you and Rusty are. I hope that if Rusty ever marries, it will be to a girl who will want to be close to us."

"Honey, we'll have plenty of time to talk about this tomorrow. I've got to get some sleep. I take the watch in about four hours."

Sitting on the blanket beside the truck, with Rusty's arm around her, Mona whispered to him.

"What did you and Jody talk about today?"

"Lots of things. He told me about the time he tied a string on your loose tooth and the other end to the doorknob. He said he slammed the door ten times and every time you ran with the door."

"He was telling a big windy. I ran with the door one time. Then he grabbed the string and yanked out the tooth."

"And you cried because you couldn't find it."

"What else did he tell you?"

"He told me that when you were in the fifth grade, you played Mary in the Christmas play and you pinched the boy who played Joseph because he'd put chewing gum in your hair. He yelled, 'Damn you,' just as the Wise Men arrived."

"That blabbermouth! What else?"

"You don't want to know."

"Yes, I do. Tell me or I'll pinch you."

"I'll pinch you back. I've been wanting to anyway." His hand moved to the side of her breast and stroked gently.

"What did he say?" she asked breathlessly.

"He told me about the time you went to the outhouse and were going to stand up on the seat and your foot slipped." He could hardly talk for the laughter that bubbled up.

"I'm going to kill him," Mona said quietly.

"But before I do I'm going to cut him into little-bitty pieces."

Rusty, his hand on Blackie's back, felt the dog tense, then stand. "What is it, boy? Still got the ladies on your mind?" he whispered, and minutes later felt the swish of the dog's tail before he sank back down. "Sometimes us fellas have to just grin and bear it, huh, Blackie?"

"He wasn't thinkin' about *that*. He was looking toward the end of Margie's truck. I think she got in, and Brady went to his car for his bedroll."

"They've been there talking for a long while. I'd bet a dollar Brady's in love with her."

"From what he said tonight?"

"That, and the way he arranged for me to ride with Jody today so she would ride with him and how he's been looking out for her and trying to not overdo it."

"He may be just pretending to be interested in her to get her to look after Anna Marie. He told Daddy he was going to have a hard time parting with his twin's little girl."

"Naw. Brady strikes me as having more integrity than that. I think he's fallen for her. Just like I've fallen for you, sweet girl."

"And like I've fallen for you, sweet man."

They sat silently in the velvet darkness. Mona laid her head on his shoulder. He turned his lips to her forehead. It was quiet except for male voices and laughter coming from in front of one of the rag tents where a group of men had gathered to talk and drink bootleg whiskey. A car came in off the road, its headlights dancing over the array of cars, trucks and tents before shutting off.

"There is a little bit of lightning off in the southwest," Mona said softly.

"It doesn't smell like rain."

"Can you smell rain?"

"Sure. When you can't see, your other senses like hearing and smelling kick in. I know every time you powder your nose. This morning you were wearing a blouse that had been sun-dried and ironed." He buried his nose in her hair. "You washed your hair with castile soap."

"I'll have to be careful, or you'll think I'm dolling up for you. Rusty, you haven't sung to me since we left Deke's."

"I can't sing to you tonight, sweet girl. I'm trying to keep my ears open for any unexpected sound. If the two of us ride with Jody tomorrow, I'll sing to you all the way to Albuquerque."

"Have you worked any more on your song?"

"Our song? A little bit."

"I'd like to ride with you, even if we have to put up with Jody. It'll depend on whether or not Margie rides with Brady." She put her hand on his cheek and turned his face down to her. "When we started this trip, I hated it. Now I think if not for the trip, I'd never have met you. I'm afraid, now, that after we get to California and you get a job on the radio, you'll be so popular that you'll not want anything to do with a Missouri country girl."

"And I'm afraid that when we get to California, you'll see so many men that you'll not want anything to do with a man you have to lead around by the hand."

Mona's arms went around his neck. "Darlin' Rusty, don't ever think that," she said furiously. "You're the dearest, most wonderful man in the world, and I'll love you forever."

"Forever is a long time, little Mona. And I'm going to be like I am for all that time."

"I don't care! Oh, I do care. I wish you could see — for your sake. But . . . but if you could see me, you might not want me."

"I see you, sweet girl. I see you in my mind's eye. You're young, fresh and pretty as a buttercup. What's more, you'll never change. The years will go by, and you'll never be wrinkled or gray. You'll always be as I see you now."

"Rusty, I'm so glad you like me."

"How glad? Glad enough to kiss me?"

"A thousand times," she whispered.

"Then you'd better get started. I heard my watch chime the hour. We've only got thirty minutes until Jody comes to take over the watch."

Chapter 26

Margie would never know what had awakened her.

Perhaps, she thought later, she had not been fully asleep. Instantly alert, she slid off the bunk, slipped her skirt on over her head and buttoned it at the waist. After putting on her blouse she reached for the pistol she sometimes carried in her pocket.

Anna Marie was asleep on the end of the bunk and Mona on the box when Margie eased to the end of the truck and looked out. It was quiet and dark.

Brady had said that he would stay near the back of the truck. She thought of calling out to him, but instead she stepped over the tailgate and eased down onto the ground, holding the pistol close to her side.

Cautiously she moved around between the truck and Foley's car and trailer, wishing she had taken the time to put on her shoes. As her eyes became more accustomed to the darkness, she saw the outline of Brady's car ahead. She stopped near the cab of the truck to listen.

The unmistakable smell of gasoline caused her to wrinkle her nose. Was Brady's gas tank leaking? Then she heard a sound and recognized it. She had thrown out enough dishwater to know that what she heard was a splash of liquid.

At that moment a man rounded the back of Brady's car. She knew instantly that the short man in the cap wasn't Brady. When he was no more than a few feet away, she saw that he had a can in his hands and was splashing its contents on Brady's car. It was a few seconds before Margie's vocal cords thawed enough for her to yell.

"Stop that!"

Catlike, the man spun around. On seeing her he took a quick step toward her and drew back the can to hit her.

She pointed the gun as she had been taught and pulled the trigger.

Bang!

The man dropped the can and grabbed his arm. "Gawdamn! Bitch!" he shouted, then whirled and disappeared behind the car and down into the ditch beside the road.

Shaken by what she had done, Margie let the hand holding the pistol drop to her side. Seconds later a bare-chested Alvin was there; then Brady came running. Foley was a few steps behind him.

"He . . . he . . ." Margie tried to point to the car.

"Honey . . . sweetheart" — Brady took the pistol out of her hand — "are you all right? What were you shooting at?" He tucked the gun in his belt and put his arms around her.

"Good Lord! Smell that gas." Alvin picked up the can the man had dropped.

Margie began to shake. "I hit him. In the arm, I think."

Brady held her tightly to him. "What were you doing out here?"

"Something woke me. I was looking for you and smelled the gas before I saw him. He was going to hit me with the can."

Jody came with a lantern. "Stay back with that, son," Foley said. "There's gasoline all over."

Grace, in her nightgown, joined them. Rusty was with her. Mona climbed out of the truck, went to him and took his hand as if her place was beside him.

"Where's Blackie?" Rusty asked.

"I think he went courtin'. Don't blame him," Brady said. "The bitches in heat were too much for him."

"He wouldn't have gone off if Rusty had been out," Alvin said in defense of the faithful dog.

"I was snookered too." Brady continued to hold Margie protectively close. "I heard a woman crying. I walked down alongside the ditch a short way and saw her huddled on the ground. She called out to me, 'Help me. Please, help me.' Before I could get near her she got up and stumbled away. She was bent over and crying and mumbling about someone trying to kill her. She fell down on her knees. And again, before I could get to her she got up and ran down into the ditch. Then I heard Margie's yell followed by the shot."

"Sounds like the woman was drawing you away." Foley scratched his head.

"They probably didn't expect to find anyone up at this time of night."

"Why did they pick your car?" Alvin asked.

"I don't know anyone out this way —"

"What's goin' on? We heard a shot." Two hastily dressed men approached, the suspenders of one still hanging over his hips. The other man's shirt was loose over his pants. "There's a mighty strong smell of gasoline."

"A man was splashing the car with it," Alvin explained. "From the looks of it he was going to burn him out. As close as we are, it would have burned us all out if we weren't able to move the trucks in time."

"Son of a bitch!" The man pulled the suspenders up over his shoulders.

"A minute or two after I heard the shot, a car took off down the road."

"Did you get a look at it?" Brady asked.

"Naw. But the motor had a soft purrin' sound."

"You fellas travelin' together?" Foley asked.

"Yeah. There was three of us, but one turned back." He stuck out his hand. "Name's Taylor. My trailin' partner here is Harry Wills. We're both from over near Kingfisher, Oklahoma."

The men introduced themselves and shook hands.

"We was a mite leery of this place and glad when you folks drove in." Taylor was the more talkative of the two.

"We were leery too. It's why we posted a guard. Good thing we did," Alvin said.

"We was sleepin' with one eye open."

"It wasn't anyone from inside the camp."

Harry Wills spoke for the first time since grunting a greeting when introduced. "He'da knowed that south wind woulda spread the fire."

"Maybe he didn't care," Foley said. "We'd better get this mess cleaned up if we want to be away from here by daylight."

"Mister," Taylor said, "me and my partner would like to tag along behind you folks for a while, if ya ain't mindin' it. We ain't wantin' to be no trouble, and we ain't askin' for no help."

Alvin lifted his hands palms-out. "We couldn't stop you if we wanted to. We're stopping to gas up before we leave town."

Margie pushed away from Brady. The realization of what she had just done was taking root in her mind.

"You don't have your shoes on." Brady swung her up in his arms. "There's burs and glass and no telling what all out here." He carried her to the end of the truck and guided her feet in over the tailgate. "Put on your shoes."

Margie sat down on the end of the bunk, put her feet in her moccasins and tied them. Brady was waiting. She clung to him for a minute after he'd lifted her down.

"Do you think I killed him?"

"Probably not. It would be no great loss if

you did, though. He could have burned down the whole campground."

"Brady," Alvin called, "we're going to use the water we have in the barrels to wash the gas off your car. A spark from a backfire could set off a blaze."

Rusty drained water from the barrels in both trucks and from the small one in Foley's trailer into buckets. Brady and Foley washed down the car, diluting the gasoline with the water. Alvin moved the kerosene stove out into an open space away from the cars and trucks so Grace could make coffee.

"You women stay together," he cautioned. "As soon as it's safe to start the cars, we'll leave here."

Blackie, his tail between his legs and his coat full of cockleburs, came and sank down under the truck.

"Some watchdog you are," Alvin scolded. "Off ramming around when we needed you."

"I'm glad you shot 'em," Mona said as soon as Alvin left them. "I just wish you'd shot him in the head."

"I did it before I thought. I didn't think about anything except that he was going to hit me with the can."

"A can half full of gasoline would've knocked you cold." Mona shivered. "You'd of burnt up with the car."

Brady was wiping the windshield on his car and thinking about Margie shooting at a man holding a can of gas.

"I'm sure as hell glad that Margie hit the man and not the gas can," Foley said as if he had read Brady's thoughts.

"That's the gospel truth."

Foley mopped his forehead with his shirtsleeve. "If she'd shot into that can, it would have exploded, and pieces of her would have been scattered all over the campground."

Brady paled, then said, "I'd rather she didn't know that."

"A half can of gas is more dangerous than a full one because it's half full of fumes. I've heard it's the fumes that explode."

Brady nodded. He felt cold with fear at the thought of her coming out of the truck with that little gun and meeting up with a man rotten enough to start a fire that could have swept through a campground full of poor folk trying to get to where they could make a living. He stopped what he was doing and stared down at the ground.

Dear Lord. He had almost lost her!

Who had picked his car to set ablaze and why? It bothered him that he had been observed without his being aware of it and dumb enough to let himself be suckered away from the camp. The son of a bitch saw him there and used the woman to lure him from the car.

He searched his mind for a description of the woman who had acted as decoy. She had dark thick hair that fell over her face. He was sure of that. She could have been a Mexican, he reasoned. The only Mexicans he knew lived on the ranch, and he got along well with all of them. Something about her voice, though, rang a bell. He was fifty percent sure he'd heard that whine before. But where?

Sugar had come out of the brush and run down into the ditch when she heard the sound of a shot being fired. She ran to the car and started the motor as she had been instructed to do. Looking through the back window, she craned her neck, expecting to see the blaze of the fire. Instead she saw a shadowy figure running down the road toward the car. The door was jerked open. Homer vaulted inside.

"Get goin'! Get goin'!"

The car's wheels skidded when Sugar stomped on the gas and they shot off down the dark, dirt road that ran alongside the campground. A minute later she turned on the lights and found they were perilously close to the ditch on the other side of the road. During that minute Homer had spewed out a string of curses, some of which Sugar had never even heard before.

"Why didn't you fire the car?" she asked as soon as she got the car in the middle of the road.

"Shut up, gawddammit! Can't ya see I been shot?"

"Oh, no! Oh, Jesus!" Sugar's foot hit the brake.

"Keep goin', ya stupid bitch," Homer shouted.

"Are you hurt bad?"

"How in hell do I know? Turn right at the corner."

"Are we going back to the motor court?"

"Where else? Use yore head, for God's sake."

"You don't have to be so shitty!" Sugar shouted. "I did my part. I got him away like I said I would."

"Turn left."

"I know how to get there. Who shot you? It wasn't the cowboy."

"It was his bitch! I came around the end of the car, and there she was yellin' her fuckin' head off. Then she shot me."

"Why didn't you shoot her back?"

" 'Cause she shot my arm, ya useless fuckhead! I couldn't get my gun out."

Sugar stomped down so hard on the brakes the wheels skidded. She jerked open the door and stepped out.

"I don't have to take your shit! It wasn't my fault that you got shot."

"Get back in here, babe. I'm sorry. I hurt so damn bad."

"Whyer you taking your spite out on me? I did everything you told me to do."

"I'm hurtin' so goddamn bad I ain't got good sense."

Sugar got back in and started the car. "Are you ready to give up on the cowboy so we can go on to California?"

"Not on yore life, sugar teat! I'm gettin' him, and I'm gettin' the bitch that shot me!"

Sugar clamped her mouth shut and said not another word until they stopped in front of the cabin they had rented at the motor court.

"Give me the key," she whispered so as not to draw attention to their coming in at such a late hour.

Inside the cabin she turned on the overhead light and made sure that the blinds were tightly closed before she turned to look at Homer. His shirtsleeve was blood-soaked.

"Oh, honey, we got to get you to a hospital."

"No. Help me off with the shirt so I can see how bad it is."

The bullet had gone through the flesh on the inside of his upper arm, leaving a three-inch gash. Sugar wrapped a wet towel tightly around his arm to stem the flow of blood, then helped him out of his bloodstained britches.

"Don't you want to go to a hospital and let them sew that up?" She was gently washing the blood from between his fingers.

"As soon as the stores open, we'll go get some iodine, bandages and sticky tape. That'll hold it together long enough for it to heal. Bundle up the bloody shirt and pants, babe. We'll dump them someplace."

Homer seemed to have calmed down. He lay on the bed unashamedly naked while Sugar fussed over him. She washed him, paying particular attention to his male organs, which brought a smile to his face. After she had finished washing the bloody towels in the rust-stained lavatory, she hung them on the edge of the tub to dry.

"Come here, little puss." Homer held out his uninjured arm. "Come finish what ya started."

Sugar removed her wet skirt, took off her

blouse and looked at the man on the bed. The cocky little bastard wasn't all that much to look at, yet he set her on fire. She had lived more since she met him than in all her life put together. Of all the men she had known, he was the horniest. She didn't doubt that he could screw ten times a day. But, then, he was only twenty-three years old. He hadn't asked her her age, and if he had, she would have lied.

She was made for this kind of life with this kind of man even if he was years younger than she was. She hated to think of the years she had wasted. God, she wished that she had met someone like him ten years earlier.

Sugar had never intended to spend her life with Foley Luker. She had seduced him into marrying her while fully intending to leave him once they got to California. She readily admitted that she was a woman who loved to fornicate, but, with Foley, she'd been lucky to get a rise out of him once or twice a week after the first couple weeks of marriage.

She flashed a smile at the man on the bed and pulled her slip off over her head. She teased him by cupping her breasts before she slowly slid her panties down over her hips.

"You wicked, angel-faced bitch! Get yore sweet ass over here."

Chapter 27

The sun was peeking over the horizon when Brady lifted Anna Marie out of the truck and gently laid her on the small mattress in the backseat of his car. She snuggled down and went back to sleep. He covered her and rolled down the windows to allow the air to pass through, thankful that the windows had been rolled up when the gasoline was splashed and that there was none inside the car.

While they were packing up to leave, he had asked Margie to ride with him. She had said she would after they filled up at the gas station if Rusty would ride with Jody.

Since the early morning scare, Brady didn't want to be parted from her. The close call had made him realize, more than ever, how important she was to him, how much he loved her. Was this how Brian had felt about Becky? If so, it was no wonder he went out of his mind when he saw her in bed with another man.

Brady helped Jody tie the canvas down on all sides of the truck, then went to sit in his car until it was time to pull out. It was a hundred and fourteen miles to Albuquerque. If everything went well, they would be there by the middle of the afternoon. He wished he could take Margie and Anna Marie and head for Colorado. But after what they had encountered last night, he wouldn't feel right about leaving Alvin and Foley to finish the trip alone, even if Margie was willing.

It was hard for Brady to believe that he had been picked as the target by the person who tried to set fire to his car. Who would know him in this place besides the Putmans, the Lukers and Margie? It had to be a random act. But if not, was he putting Margie in more danger by keeping her with him? It was a thought he had wrestled with most of the night.

If this camp was an example of what they would run into the closer they came to Bakersfield, he would suggest that they avoid the public camps and camp back away from the highway in an out-of-the-way place.

The gas station where they stopped provided a welcome sight: two nearly new privies. While Jody waited behind Alvin for their turn at the gas pump, Margie came back to Brady's car with Anna Marie's dress and moccasins.

"Wake up, honey. Let's put on your dress and shoes and go to the outhouse." Brady came up behind her and ran his hand lovingly up and down her back. She smiled at him over her shoulder. "We can't afford to pass up this opportunity."

As soon as she was dressed, Anna Marie scooted out of the car and Margie took her hand. Brady's hand was still warm on her back.

"The man says we can fill the water barrels for fifteen cents. I told Jody to pull over to the hand pump after he gets gas."

"I gave him money," Margie said. "There should be enough left over for the water."

"Rusty and Mona want to be together. Rusty asked me if you were going to ride with me today. And, if so, would you mind if they rode with Jody."

"What did you tell him?"

"That I was sure you wouldn't mind if they rode with Jody. I told him that I wanted you with me, that I never want to let you out of my sight again, that I like to look at you, touch you and kiss you. I said that I'm so crazy about you that every minute I'm away from you seems like an hour." His voice was husky and tender.

"You didn't say *that!*"

"Yes, I did, and I also told him that I'm thinking about carrying you off someplace where I can have you all to myself for the next hundred years."

"Be serious."

"I am serious, sweetheart."

"Margie, let's go." Anna Marie tugged on her hand.

Margie looked down at the fidgeting child, then back at Brady with eyes that shone with pure happiness.

"Now, this is serious."

"Go on," he said softly. "I'll be waiting." Brady watched her walk away with Anna Marie's hand tucked in hers.

There goes my everything. Lord, help me to keep them safe.

When Alvin's gas tank was full, he pulled up to the water pump. Rusty worked the pump handle while he carried the buckets of water to his water keg. The women, along with those from the two families that were tagging along behind them, were in front of the outhouse.

Jody pulled Margie's truck up to the gas pump. While the tank was being filled,

Brady lifted the hood and checked the oil and the water in the radiator.

After the truck had been serviced, Rusty and Jody filled the water barrel and Alvin went over to speak with Brady.

"What do you think about the folks trailing us?" Alvin jerked his head toward the two sedans with carriers on top that were waiting along the road.

"They seem to be decent. I looked them over before we left this morning. I don't think a robber or a bootlegger would be travelin' with a woman and two little kids. The woman with Harry Wills is in the family way."

"They have pretty good outfits."

"Wills had a gun under his shirt this morning. I can't hold that against him. I may start carrying one myself."

"You've got a sharp eye. I didn't notice the gun."

"To my way of thinking, Wills is a man who won't back down. The other one follows his lead, although he does the talking."

"We might be glad to have 'em near if we get into another place like the one last night." Alvin laughed and shook his head. "Grace has the women cornered. She'll know all about them by the time we start up again."

Margie was so happy she was scared. Hovering in the back of her mind was the fear that something would happen to spoil her happiness. *Brady cared for her.* He had not said that he loved her. He'd said that he cared deeply, but he was acting as if he loved her. And he was happy. She could tell by the shine in his eyes and the smile that tilted his lips when he looked at her. And when he touched her, it was gently, as if he feared she would break.

Sitting beside him in the car, her eyes catching his each time he turned to look at her, she would have been happy to keep on going forever. They had entered low, clustering hills that promised mountains ahead. The highway wound around jutting slopes and crossed small rocky streams that divided the hills that rammed each other. At times it clung to the rocky ledges; at other times it passed through meadowland.

There were more stretches of unpaved roadway with huge chuckholes. Brady had to keep his eyes on the road. But his hand caught hers and released it only when he had to shift gears.

Anna Marie was bored and sleepy. She wanted to get in the back and lie down on her bed. Margie helped her climb over the back of the seat.

"Stay away from the door, puddin'," she cautioned. "If we hit one of these big old chuckholes, one of the doors might pop open."

After Margie had turned around, Anna Marie leaned over the seat and wrapped her arms around Margie's neck and whispered something to her.

"Oh, honey. I wish it too." Tears sprang to Margie's eyes. She stared out the side window for a long while, batting her eyes to keep the tears at bay.

Brady held her hand tightly. When she finally looked at him, she saw concern in his eyes.

"Sweetheart?"

She moved closer to him and spoke softly. "Sometimes I think that I had it bad, but I had a mother and then a grandmother who loved me."

"And now me." He lifted the hand in his and rubbed her knuckles across his lips. "What did Punkie say that caused you to cry?"

"She said . . . she said that she loved me and wished . . . that I was her mama." Her eyes filled again, and the tears spilled over to run down her cheeks. "No one has ever said,

'I love you,' to me. Not even Granny, though I know she did."

"*I* love you. I told you last night."

"You . . . didn't say the words."

"I didn't? I thought I'd made my feelings clear. I love you. I want to spend my life with you. Brian was the one good with words. He told Punkie many times that he loved her."

"I love you too. I didn't want to." Her wet eyes blurred her vision.

Brady let out a slow breath. "You didn't want to?"

"I knew that you could break my heart." Her words came out on a strangled sob. "If you didn't love me back."

He looked at her, then had to jerk the wheel to avoid a chuckhole when his eyes went back to the road.

"This is a hell of a place to have this conversation." He held her hand to his lips.

The realization that except for chance he would never have met this woman, never have known that she existed, sent a surge of emotion through him that was both tender and fierce. He longed to pull her into his arms and tell her again and again that he would never break her heart. He would guard it as carefully as he guarded his own. He loved her with a cherishing kind of love. He wanted to hold her in his arms, plant his child in her warm, fertile body and keep her at his side forever.

Dear God, help me to find the words to tell her how I feel about her.

It wasn't until they had neared the outskirts of Albuquerque that Brady spoke about his ranch being only two days north.

"You'd rather turn here than go on to California." Margie wished that she hadn't brought to light her fear. *Dear Lord, I couldn't bear to lose him now.*

"I'm going to do whatever it takes to keep you with me."

"You want me to go to Colorado?"

"More than anything in the world."

"Deke told me to just leave the truck with the authorities and let them find Goldie. I'd hate to do that. I'd never be sure if she got it or the money in Elmer's box." She tilted her head to rest for just a minute against his upper arm, then looked up into his face. "I took two hundred dollars of it. I'm calling it payment for delivering the truck."

"He was your father. He brought you on this trip and owed you enough money to see you through. How are you going to find his wife?"

"Her cousin said she went to Bakersfield."

471

"Was there an address book or any letters in Elmer's things?"

"There's a packet of envelopes. Money is in some of them."

"Maybe you should look again. You might find something that would make the hunt for her easier. Honey, I don't have money to stay in Bakersfield but a few days unless I find work."

"I have the two hundred dollars."

"Don't you want to use that to see Hollywood?"

"I want to use it to buy curtains, rugs and doodads for our cabin."

"Sweetheart! Are you giving up your dream?"

"It was a little girl's dream. Now I have a bigger, better one. To be a helpmate to the man I love. To make a home with him, have his children. I can get all the Hollywood I want in the movie magazines."

"Sweet girl. I don't want you to be sorry."

"I plan to be too busy to be sorry. If your ranch is ten miles from town, I'm going to have to be mother and teacher to Anna Marie for the first few years — that is, if we can get the books and the other things I will need."

"You can do that?"

"Sure I can. When I got out of high

school, I helped the teacher one year because the school system was so broke they couldn't hire another teacher. I got half her pay. I thought I was rich."

He glanced at her with love and pride. "Wait till I tell Ramon I've got a teacher for the kids."

"Kids? I don't speak Spanish."

"They all know a smattering of English. Uh-oh . . . I'd better pay more attention to my driving. Jody is pulling over."

Brady parked along the highway behind Jody, got out and waited for Alvin, who was walking toward him from up ahead, and Foley, coming from behind.

"The public campground ahead looks about like the one we came out of," Alvin said. "Are you willing to go on to another place even if we have to pay fifty cents or a dollar to camp?"

"Do you know of another camp?" Foley asked.

"No. But if we don't find one, I'm willing to move on out of town and find an out-of-the-way spot."

"Fine with me," Brady said.

Foley nodded.

"I'll walk back and — no need, here come Taylor and Wills." Alvin spoke to the men. "I was just coming to tell you that the public campground is ahead, but we're going on."

"Glad to hear it," Taylor said. "Harry has been warned about this place. He has directions to a place where we can camp for two bits a car. It has water and toilets. The man runs a good place, so he was told."

"Is it far off the highway?"

" 'Bout a mile." Harry was stingy with his words.

Alvin looked for approval from both Foley and Brady before he spoke.

"Sounds good. Move out in front and lead the way."

While they waited for the other two cars to pull ahead, Brady, with his arm around Margie, explained the situation.

"If this is a good place and Grace will look after Anna Marie for a while, we'll go into town and take in a picture show."

"Really?" Margie's eyes went wide with pleasure.

"Really. Just the two of us, pretty girl." He hugged her and placed a kiss on her nose. "We'll eat supper at a restaurant and go to a picture show to celebrate. It isn't every day a man meets the woman he wants to keep beside him for the rest of his life."

"Can we afford it? We've got to have money to get back to Colorado."

"This will be our one and only splurge, honey."

The campground was a shady acre enclosed with barbed wire. A man in overalls had a little stand at the gate where he was selling oranges and a few garden vegetables. After Alvin had pulled through, Jody stopped. Brady was about to get out and pay for the truck when Jody drove on into the campground.

"Howdy. Welcome to Shady Acres. Stayin' long?" The man was middle-aged, big and brawny. He looked them over, glancing at Anna Marie in the backseat.

"Just overnight." Brady dropped a coin in his hand.

"This is the best place we've stayed," Margie remarked as they passed the man at the gate. "Even if we do have to pay."

"I liked that place up in Oklahoma where I met a sassy little blonde with pretty brown eyes." Brady stopped the car alongside the truck.

Margie's eyes devoured his smiling face. She wouldn't have believed it if she had been told when she met this stern, unsmiling man who had just buried his twin brother, that in only a few short weeks he would become so dear to her.

"Margie." Anna Marie put her hand on

Margie's shoulder to get her attention. "Can I get out?"

"If you put on your shoes. There'll be cockleburs here." Margie got out and opened the back door.

"Can I play with that little girl?"

"We'll go over and talk to Mrs. Taylor and see if she wants to play. You can take your jump rope or your ball."

Margie tied Anna Marie's shoes, then leaned down to whisper to her.

"You girls are always whispering," Brady complained.

"This is something you don't need to know."

"Yeah, Uncle Brady. You don't need to know."

Later Margie was able to report to Grace and Mona that the outhouses were as clean as could be expected and that generous doses of lime had reduced the odor. Grace informed her that Brady had already asked if she and Mona would keep an eye on Anna Marie while he took Margie out for the evening.

"Go," Grace whispered. "Have a good time. Mona and I will keep an eye on Anna Marie." She tilted her head toward where Brady was talking with Foley. "If I was young and single, I'd be after him like a shot.

That is, if I hadn't met Alvin yet." She finished with one of her contagious giggles. "I think we just might invite the other folks over and have a singin' tonight. They seem to be right nice folks. It'll give Rusty a chance to sing his new song."

Excited about the prospect of going out with Brady, Margie left Anna Marie playing happily with the little Taylor girl and climbed into the truck to wash herself thoroughly and dress for her big evening.

"Shit, shit, shit!" Homer pounded on the wheel when he saw that the caravan wasn't going to stop at the crowded public campground. "Now, where the hell are they goin'?" he snarled.

When Homer had caught up with the caravan outside Tucumcari and discovered that two more cars had joined it, he had felt safe with those two cars between him and Foley Luker. Now one of those cars had taken the lead, and with only one car between him and Luker, Homer backed off.

"Does your arm hurt?" Sugar asked.

"Hell yes, it hurts."

"You should of let me drive more."

"I don't trust ya drivin' in town."

"Well, hell. You trusted me to drive in Tucumcari."

"Tucumcari ain't Albuquerque. Now, shut up!"

Sugar sulked and made no comment when the caravan turned off at the sign that said CAMPGROUND 1 MILE. Homer drove on.

"They'll be easy to find, but first we'll find us a place to spend the night." He looked over at her and grinned. "Ya got to get all gussied up, pretty puss, so we can go huntin' for easy pickin's. I'm down to a hundred bucks."

At the El Rancho Motor Court they parked the car beneath the shelter attached to the cabin. Homer unlocked the door and went inside, leaving Sugar to get the bags out of the rumble seat of the car. She pulled her case out and set it on the ground, then reached in for Homer's cloth bag. She paused. In the far corner she saw a leather belt with a big brass buckle. Chester's belt and buckle.

Had Chester taken the bus back to Oklahoma without his belt and his watch? If so — she almost giggled — what was holding his pants up? Seeing the belt only confirmed her suspicion that Homer had gotten rid of his uncle. Instead of being hor-rified at the thought, Sugar smiled. Homer knew that she didn't like Chester, and he cared enough for her that he'd gotten rid of him.

The little shit!

Homer was in a better mood after he had rested on the bed and Sugar had changed the bandage on his arm. After watching her strip and wash, he was aroused and insisted that she do something about it. She was willing to comply.

When they left the cabin to eat, Sugar was dressed as a boy, but later she wore her demure blue dress when they went to scout the hotels and fine eating places for their "easy pickin's."

By midnight they had robbed one gentleman and two drunks, and their take was a hundred and forty dollars. Sugar deemed it enough, but when Homer spotted a pool hall that was closing, he decided they'd wait until all the patrons had left and the door had been locked. After being coached by Homer, Sugar rapped on the door, and when a man came and unlocked it, she acted scared and pointed down the street. Then Homer stepped up and rapped the man smartly on the head with the butt of his gun. He shoved him out of the way and went inside.

While Sugar was bringing the car around, Homer rifled the cash register. On a shelf beneath it he found a bank bag with several days' receipts. It was their most successful take so far, four hundred and sixty dollars all told. Sugar hooted with glee when he told her.

"We're rich! Let's go honky-tonkin'!"

"Not in the town where we're doin' business, little bitch. Frank Barrow, brother of Clyde, told me that. He said, 'Strike quick, lay low and get out.' We're gettin' back to that cabin and that's that."

"Well, hell. What's the good of havin' money if ya can't spend it and have a good time?"

"We'll have us one hell of a time when we get to the next big town. Now, don't go sulkin' on me, little pussy. We're gonna have us a real slam-bang tonight. I've been holdin' back a trick or two that'll set ya to squealin' like a rabbit bein' humped by a six-foot jack."

"Don't you even want to go see where the cowboy is campin'?"

"I got time 'tween here and California to get to the cowboy and that prissy-ass bitch that shot me. What I'm wantin', pretty pussy, is to get ya naked and in bed where we can be *nasty!*"

"I'll swear to goodness you're the horniest little stud I've ever known."

Homer grinned proudly. "Thank ya kindly, little puss."

Chapter 28

At the Wagon Wheel restaurant Brady placed his hat on a hook beside the door and led Margie to a table at the end of the room. After they were seated, he handed her a menu.

"You look awfully pretty."

"So do you."

"Did you notice that I shaved?" He fingered his chin.

"Uh-huh. Did you notice that I combed my hair and put a ribbon in it?"

"You're pretty without a ribbon."

"Flattery will get you nowhere, Mr. Hoyt. I'm still going to order the most expensive thing on the menu."

Their eyes held. She was the girl of his dreams, even more wonderful than he had imagined. Her hair was the rich color of ripened wheat, her mouth wide and sweet, her eyes like stars.

She stared at him for a long silent moment. She was afraid that if she moved, he would be sure to know how happy she was being here with him. When she finally spoke, her voice caught, then came out in a husky whisper.

"I'll have beef, mashed potatoes and gravy."

"I'm going to have a steak, medium rare. I haven't had a decent one since I left the ranch."

"And I haven't had mashed potatoes since I left home." A smile tilted the corners of her mouth.

Brady chuckled. She was fun, intelligent . . . soft. When he started on this trip, he never dreamed that he would meet a woman like her.

The overweight waitress who came to take their order had eyes only for Brady. She was still looking at him when she walked away. Margie wanted to scratch her eyes out even though she couldn't blame her for looking at him.

While waiting for their order, Margie smiled into the eyes observing her. When his hand moved across the table, hers met it halfway.

"I hated leaving Anna Marie. She was afraid we wouldn't come back."

"She's grown attached to you. She'll have to learn to share you with me, honey." He watched her, and when she tried to pull her hand away, his fingers gripped hers tightly. "This is my time to claim all your attention."

Margie noticed the looks he was getting from two women who had just come in and sat down at a table not far from them. He was an exceedingly attractive man who would radiate confidence if he stood barefoot and ragged. His thick black hair sprang back from his forehead and hung to the collar of his shirt. Deep crinkly grooves marked the corners of his eyes, etched there from squinting at the sun. There were other lines too, which grief and experience had made.

How was it possible that she was here with this wonderful, handsome man? *It was a miracle!*

When the waitress brought their order, she glanced at Margie, then fixed her gaze on Brady again. Brady smiled and thanked her. They had just started to eat when the waitress came back to the table.

"We have one piece of fresh peach pie left. Want me to save it for you?" she asked Brady.

"Do you want it, honey?"

The waitress took her eyes off Brady long enough to glance at Margie.

"No. I'd rather have raisin or custard."

"We have custard." The woman spoke again to Brady.

"We'll each have the custard," he said.

After she had walked away, Margie said, "I thought she was going to sit in your lap."

He smiled broadly. "Jealous? It's a good sign."

When they left the well-lit restaurant, Margie couldn't even feel her feet on the ground. Happiness sang like a bird in her heart. She was proud to be walking beside this tall, broad-shouldered man who said he loved her. She cast a glance up at him and found him smiling down at her, his arm holding her hand tightly to his side.

"What would you like to do? If we go to a movie, we may not get out in time to get back before eleven o'clock, when the man locks the gate."

"We could sit in the car outside the gate all night." A blush covered her face.

Brady laughed. "When we spend our first night together, sweetheart, it will be in a bed where I can love you all night long." He stopped and looked down at her. "Are you blushing?"

"No! Well, yes!"

"Does it excite you to think of spending the night in bed with me?" He started walking again.

"Of course! I've . . . never spent the night — never wanted . . ." Her voice trailed off as embarrassment took control of her tongue.

"Thank God for that!" They reached the car. "Would you like to stop at that place we saw on the way in? We can get something to drink and dance for a while." He held open the door for her.

"All right," she said after he had gone around and slid under the wheel.

"The other time we danced you were so mad at me I thought you'd bite a chunk out of me." The hand at the nape of her neck brought her face toward his, then slipped down to cup her shoulder to allow her to turn away if she chose. "I want to kiss you, right here on the street. If I do, will you bite me?"

"I might. And I might yell too."

"To kiss you would be worth a bite and a hundred punches in the nose by those who come to rescue you." His voice was husky and raw, like his deep, quivering breaths.

She felt the caress of his warm breath on her cheek before his lips, with the utmost tenderness and caution, settled on hers. A warm tide of tingling excitement washed over her. Her heart beat wildly, and her mind whirled giddily. Brady moved his head and placed his cheek against hers. His arm tightened; he was as breathless as if he'd run a mile; he was stunned with happiness.

Finally she stirred and gently moved away from him. People passing on the sidewalk were gawking. She uttered a little laugh so soundless that it was no more than an exhalation of breath.

"We're putting on a show for people passing by."

He laughed intimately, joyously, and started the car.

"I don't care if the whole world is watching. I like kissing you. I'm going to kiss my wife every day for the rest of our lives."

"I'm not very good at it."

"Practice makes perfect. We'll practice some more as soon as I find a place to park the car."

The next morning at sunrise the women gathered around Grace's giant coffeepot. Margie's eyes dwelled on Brady, who was with the other men looking at a map spread out over the hood of Alvin's truck.

Her mind kept going back to the night before, trying to remember each and every word that was said. Their love was so new they had not talked about the future. They both knew that they would be together, and that was enough for now.

Margie was absolutely sure that it had been the most wonderful evening of her life. They had come back to the campground, sat in the car and in between kisses listened to the singing coming from the group gathered at the Putman camp. Rusty had sung his new song, "What I See." One of the verses stuck in Margie's mind.

> *You were there watchin' over me*
> *With gentle touch and sweet sympathy,*
> *With tender care like a gift so free,*
> *You were there givin' strength to me.*

Margie shivered recalling the chorus of the song.

> *They are blind who will not see.*
> *None so blind as a man like me.*

Rusty was so remarkable, so cheerful, loving and kind, she prayed that he had found the happiness with Mona that she had found with Brady.

Brady. The wonderful feeling of belonging to him was so new, so exciting, that at times she was giddy. A thrill spiraled down her spine when she thought of his words last night as he caressed her breasts.

"Soon I'll see them, kiss them. No man will ever touch them but me."

Her daydreaming was interrupted when Alvin folded the map and began talking.

"The man here at the campground says that most of the highway between here and Gallup is under construction. There are many rough spots, and sometimes we'll have to wait for as long as an hour before we can go on. Loaded as we are, we'll be lucky to make seventy-five miles a day for the next couple days. After that the going will be easier. I figure that we're about nine hundred miles from Bakersfield, and unless we have a breakdown, we should be there in about ten days."

"Hallelujah! I'm wantin' to sleep in a real bed and put my feet under a real table," Grace declared.

Alvin smiled at his wife. "There's a campground at Grants. It's one hundred and four miles. If we see we can't make it, we'll camp along the road. That's as much as I know. Anyone got anything to add?"

Harry Wills drank the last of the coffee and tossed the dregs from his tin cup. His main concern was the comfort and safety of his wife, who was pregnant with their first child. They had given up all hope of having a family and had decided to move to California to be near his brother and his family when she became pregnant.

He had wanted to postpone the trip until after the baby was born, but she would not hear of it. It worried him that they were bouncing along on rough, dusty roads prowled by bootleggers and outlaws who would cut your throat for a dime. The pistol in the bib of his overalls was a reassuring weight.

"Ya may have another tagalong," Harry said. "A Ford coupe was about a half mile back all day yesterday. When a car got 'tween us, he'd move up. He coulda passed all of us anytime he wanted to."

"I noticed a coupe back up the road a ways when we stopped before we got to the public campground," Foley said. "A fella was out foolin' around with somethin' in the rumble seat."

"I'm wonderin' if it's the same one that was in the campground back in Amarillo. It looked like a pretty late model." All eyes turned to Mr. Taylor. "Two young fellas was in it. Drove in, set a spell, then pulled out. Wasn't loaded with campin' gear like ya usually see."

"They may be thinkin' it's safer to tag along. I don't know what help they think they'd get from us way back there." Alvin opened the door of his truck and stuck the map inside.

Brady came to Margie, and they went to the truck, where Anna Marie was still sleeping.

"Wake up, honey. Uncle Brady is here to take you to the car." Margie led the sleepy child to the end of the truck, where Brady lifted her out and carried her to his car. She was picking up Anna Marie's clothes when Rusty and Jody arrived to check the tie-down canvases.

"I'll be out of here as soon as I find Anna Marie's shoes."

"Let me give you a hand," Jody said.

"My turn." Rusty held up his hands. Margie put hers on his shoulders, and he lifted her down.

"Thank you. You'll get me in trouble with Mona."

"And with me." Brady appeared, took Margie's hand and pulled her to him. "This woman's mine."

Rusty spoke aside to Jody. "He's gotten selfish lately."

"And grabby." Jody began tying down the canvas.

"Darn right. A man's got to be on his toes when his woman is being manhandled by a couple of young scutters."

"Manhandled? Brady, for goodness' sake," Margie scolded, but her eyes danced and her lips tilted. She pulled a bill out of her pocket. "This should be enough for gas and ten pounds of ice, Jody, if we find a place. That chunk we got yesterday is going down fast. Why don't you fix a jar of ice water for yourself and Rusty?"

"I take it I've got a steady job ridin' with Jody."

"Yeah," Brady retorted. "And your pay is getting to cuddle with Mona all day."

"What more could a man ask for?" Rusty was all smiles as he moved around the truck to the cab.

It had been a week since Sugar Luker left them at Sayre. When he stopped to think about it, Foley was surprised how seldom he thought of the woman he had been with day and night for almost three months. He admitted to having been smitten at first, flattered by the attention of a young, beautiful woman and the sex she offered. After he had married her, it hadn't taken long for him to suspect that her beauty was only skin-deep. Then, when he knew that to be true, he had

491

been too embarrassed to admit that she had made a fool of him.

He was lucky to have two wonderful kids — his and Marion's children. They had stuck with him, endured the rough times when he knew that Sugar was making them perfectly miserable.

For the past two days Mona had ridden with him for half a day and with Rusty and Jody the other half. Foley and his children were now close again, as they had been after they had lost their mother and he his beloved wife. It was as if Sugar had never been there.

His little girl was in love with a man who would forever be blind. At first he had felt keen disappointment. He wanted so much more for her: a strong man to take care of her. Then he thought of when he first met Marion. Would he have loved her had she been blind? Hell yes! He would have loved her if she had been deaf and blind and couldn't move a muscle. If it turned out that Mona and Rusty were truly in love and wanted to be together, he would be there to help them, as would Alvin and Grace.

As soon as they reached their destination, Foley planned to try to get his marriage to Sugar annulled. He was determined to break all ties with her. He suppressed the little nagging fear that he had not seen the last of the woman with the face of an angel and the soul of a wicked witch. She knew he had the money from the sale of his icehouse and was no doubt plotting how she could get it.

The stretch of highway west of Albuquerque was as they had expected. It had been start and stop since they left the campground. A stiff breeze from the south blew the dust that sprayed up from beneath the wheels. Marge pitied the construction workers who had to stand on the north side of the road while a string of cars passed.

Anna Marie was hot and tired. Margie did her best to entertain her by telling stories and teaching her to count on her fingers. The child stayed awake all day, not giving Margie and Brady a chance to talk alone, but Margie was happy just to be with him. By afternoon they'd hit a stretch of newly paved highway and reached Grants in the late evening.

The campground was a large, open field. There were about as many campers as in Tucumcari, but more families than single men. The caravan parked at one end with plenty of space around it. Foley led the other two cars to form a circle with the two trucks and Brady's car. Anna Marie waited eagerly to play with her new friend, Lucy Taylor. As soon as the Taylors stopped, Lucy jumped out and Anna Marie ran to meet her.

"Stay where I can see you, punkin," Margie called. Brady caught her hand when she attempted to follow.

"Wait a minute, honey. I've been thinking —"

Margie turned quickly to look at him. Something about the tone of his voice chilled her. *O Lord. Don't let it be that he's changed his mind!* His next words caused a flood of relief to wash over her.

"I want us to be married as soon as possible. I don't want to wait until we get to California. I want to know that you're mine."

"I . . . am yours."

He brought her hand up and rubbed her knuckles against his lips. "I want to take you home to our ranch as my wife, and Anna Marie as our daughter. You can leave the truck and the rest of Elmer's belongings with Alvin and tell him about where to look for Elmer's wife. Alvin is a good, honest man. He'll see to it that she gets it."

"All right." Tears filled her eyes.

"Darlin' girl. Don't cry about it. You want it too, don't you?"

"You know I do. More than anything."

"Tonight go through Elmer's things and see if you can find the cousin's address. He had to have some idea of where his wife was going."

"He didn't talk to me about anything, but I heard that Goldie's cousin was in a place called Victorville."

"Honey, I need to keep as much of my money as I can to get us to Colorado. If you're not dead set on going on to California, we could be married in Gallup and head home."

"I thought you'd planned on spending some time in California before you left Anna Marie with Opal."

"That was before I had a wife and daughter to take care of. I could have bummed around by myself. Things are different now."

"I'm not dead set on going on to California. I just want to be with you and Anna Marie. If you think Alvin will handle seeing that Goldie gets what was Elmer's, it's all right with me. We'll leave at Gallup, and Jody will drive the truck on to Bakersfield. Let's go through Elmer's things tonight. It would be easier if we could tell Alvin where

495

to find Goldie's cousin."

"We don't have to worry about Alvin and Foley being alone. Wills and Taylor are good, reliable men. They'll be with them for the rest of the trip."

She saw Alvin getting out the kerosene stove. "I'd better go help Grace if we are all going to eat together."

"Go on, sweetheart. We'll talk about it tonight." Brady reluctantly released her hand, and she got out of the car.

"What a dump!" Sugar's patience had almost reached its limit by the time they reached Grants. "Whater we goin' to do in this hick town? We've fiddle-farted along behind that drag-ass outfit and eaten their dust all day. We've not been dancin' or to a picture show. I doubt they even got a place to piss in this shitty burg."

Sugar had complained most of the day and wasn't aware that Homer was getting tired of it.

"Lord, what I wouldn't give for a glass of cold beer. I'm so sick of lukewarm soda pop that I could puke."

"Hush yore bitchin'," Homer shouted. "If ya don't shut up, I'll stop and put ya out. Ya can wiggle yore ass and get a ride with someone else. That clodhopper yo're married to might be sucker enough to take ya back."

Sugar had learned when to retort and when to keep quiet. She realized that she had gone a mite too far and waited for Homer's anger to cool while they cruised the streets of Grants to find a place to stay. The motor court was full. Homer stopped and went into the lobby of what appeared to be the best hotel in town. After standing at the desk waiting for a slick-haired jelly bean to tell him there were no rooms, he came back to the car, let loose a string of obscenities and drove down the street to a third-rate hotel.

"I got a room," he said when he returned to the car. "Keep yore head down and yore hat on. Ya'd be too easy to remember in this town."

Sugar was exhausted by the time she had carried her suitcase to the third-floor room. As soon as the door closed behind them, she snatched off the cap. She was hungry and dirty and tired of wearing the damn cap, but was wary of Homer's temper and kept her mouth shut.

"The bathroom is at the end of the hall. Wear the cap when you go in and have it on when you come out. I'll go out and get us something to eat."

"Can't I go with you?"

"No. I don't want anyone to remember we've been in this town. Hear? I signed in as Tom and Wilbur Smith. Yo're a boy, sugar tit." He grinned and before she could step aside, grabbed her breast and cruelly twisted the nipple. "But I'm mighty glad ya ain't one."

"Shit!" The pain caused Sugar's temper to flare. "When are you goin' to finish up with the cowboy so we can go on?" she blurted angrily.

His mood changed lightning-fast. "When I'm damn good and ready, and if ya don't like it —" He jerked his thumb toward the door. "Make up yore mind while I'm gone. If yo're stayin', be naked by the time I get back."

Sugar glared at the door for a long moment after he went out and she heard the click of the lock. *The stinkin', horny little stud wanted her with him, or he wouldn't have locked the door.*

"All he thinks about is gettin' even with the cowboy and gettin' me naked," she said aloud to the empty room. "If he wasn't so damn good in bed, the little bastard could just kiss my ass good-bye."

Chapter 29

It was dark by the time supper was over. Anna Marie, tired from vigorous play with her new friend, was ready for bed as soon as she was washed. Margie sat beside her on the bunk and told her a story about three bears. By the time she was finished, the child was asleep.

She smoothed the dark hair back from the child's face and kissed her chubby cheek. She could hardly wait until she could pick her up, hug her and tell her that she was going to be her little girl and that they would live in Colorado with her Uncle Brady. It still seemed as if this dream of marrying Brady were happening to someone else.

"Is the little tyke asleep?" Brady appeared at the end of the truck.

"Yes. She was tuckered out. Come on in. It will be crowded, but I don't mind if *you* don't."

"It couldn't be too crowded to suit me." Brady stepped up into the truck, bent over so that he could move to the front and sat down on the bunk. "Come here." He pulled her down on his lap.

"Someone will see."

"I don't care if the whole world sees. Put your arms around my neck and kiss me."

A tiny moan trembled from her throat. "Mmm . . ." Her lips moved over his in a sweet caress. His were warm and soft yet firm and insistent. A stubble of beard scraped her chin as his mouth settled on hers. He trembled, and the kiss became deeper. A ribbon of desire unfurled inside Margie. Her body was flooded with the longing that lapped at her senses whenever she was with him.

He backed away slightly. "I'd better stop while I can, sweetheart. One of these nights soon, I won't have to stop."

"Mmmm," she murmured again, kissed him quickly and slid off his lap.

She unlocked the box Elmer had built across the front of the truck and folded back the lid. Brady moved the lantern to hang directly over the box.

"I found the two hundred dollars in the toe of his socks," Margie said, taking out a stack of clothes. "The suit he was buried in was probably the one he was married in." She reached for the Prince Albert can and heard a clinking noise. "I wonder why he put his tobacco in here?" She handed the can to Brady and searched in her pocket for the key to the tin box. "The clock looks familiar. I may keep it. It'll be the only thing I'll have that came from my family."

Brady whistled through his teeth when he opened the Prince Albert can. "Look, honey, two five-dollar gold pieces and all these bills."

"Well, for goodness' sake."

"Ten one-hundred-dollar bills! Lord, that's a thousand dollars."

"My gosh! And there's more in the tin box."

Brady stuffed the bills back in the can while Margie opened the box to view again the strange assortment: a pair of baby shoes, a cameo necklace, a lady's lapel watch and the envelopes tied with string. Sitting on the floor of the truck between Brady's legs, she untied the string.

"The first envelope had four fifty-dollar bills in it. The next five have two one-hundred-dollar bills. That's twelve hundred.

With what is in the can, there's over two thousand dollars here. Goldie will think she's hit a gold mine. In the last envelope is a letter to Elmer from . . . I can't make out the postmark, can you?" She handed him the letter addressed to Mr. Elmer Kinnard, Conway, Missouri. He held it close to the lantern.

"Looks like Victorville."

"You read it."

Brady took the sheets from inside the envelope. "It's from Goldie." He scanned the pages, then held them out to Margie.

"You should read this." He reached for the lantern and held it just above her head.

Margie read the letter quickly, then went back and reread it.

Elmer,

It gives me great joy to write this. At last I will say what I've thought of you since first we met. You are without a doubt the most miserable excuse for a man that has ever lived. At first you were kind and generous, and I thought to amuse myself with you while I was there. When you thought you had me hooked to do your washing and cooking and to service you once a week in bed, you turned out to be a miserly, hateful, self-centered man. I hated every minute I

502

spent in your bed. It was like having sex with a hog. You gave no thought for anyone's pleasure but your own.

But, Elmer, I will have the last laugh. I used you to have a place to live. I made fun of you behind your back and I took three hundred dollars that you had hidden behind a dresser drawer. A whore would have charged you much more than that for the services I gave you.

I've returned to be with my husband, the love of my life. You see, I was only separated from him, and the marriage that you thought would bind me to you as your unpaid housekeeper and whore was not a marriage at all. Ha ha ha.

Goldie

"My goodness." Margie looked up at Brady. "Did you read all of this?"

"Over your shoulder, honey. It's no wonder he was such a bitter man."

"Why did she marry him when she was already married?"

"Sounds like she wanted a place to live while she was separated from her husband."

"It was mean of her to use him that way." Margie folded the letter and put it back in the envelope.

"She doesn't sound like anyone I'd like to know."

"Brady? If she and Elmer weren't married, she's not entitled to any of this, is she?"

"Not by law."

"Then I don't have to give her anything?"

"I wouldn't think so. If they were not legally married, you're Elmer's next of kin."

"I had a half brother somewhere in California. I don't ever remember seeing him. He lived with his mother's parents. I heard later that he had died, but I don't know for sure."

"I don't think you have to worry about his family coming after the estate."

"This is all mine . . . ours?"

"Yours, sweetheart. After reading this letter no one could dispute it."

"It's a lot of money. I knew he was close with his money, but I had no idea he had so much."

"You've got money now to go to Hollywood, stay as long as you want and see all the movies you want to see." It about killed Brady to say the words, but they had to be said — and said now before he lost his nerve.

She turned to look up at him. "By myself?"

"Sure, honey. It's what you planned to do

504

when you came on this trip, and I've got to get back to the ranch."

"Are you trying to say that now that I have this money and this truck, you don't want me to go home with you to . . . to Colorado?" The words caught in her throat.

"No, honey, I'm not saying that. I'm trying to say that now you have the means to fulfill your dream of seeing Hollywood without having to worry where your next meal will come from."

She got up on her knees between his legs and grasped his arms. Her eyes were so full of tears her vision was blurred.

"I woke up from that childish dream as soon as I met you. I have another now — the dream of going home, living with you in our cabin, cooking and cleaning for my husband and our little girl, giving you all the love in my heart."

He lifted her chin with his fingers and placed his lips on hers. At first his mouth brushed gently over hers in soft, lingering kisses, then his fingertips stroked the tender skin at the nape of her neck.

"You are my love," he whispered against her mouth. His hand moved down her back, pulling her closer. She could feel the pounding of his heart against her breasts. "I thank God every day that I found you."

"We've not known each other very long."

"I feel like I've known you forever. Do I seem like a stranger to you?"

"You've never seemed like a stranger to me."

"That proves it, sweetheart. You were meant for me."

"If you're going to let this money come between us, I'll . . . I'll give it away. I don't know how to handle this much money. The most I ever had at one time before I took the two hundred dollars out of Elmer's socks was the one hundred and eighteen dollars my granny left me." She wrapped her arms around his neck. "I don't even know how much is here; but if it's really mine, I want to use it for our home, for our children." She pulled away and looked at him. "You wanted me an hour ago when I only had the two hundred dollars. I'm no different now."

"I wanted you then. I want you now!" He buried his face in the curve of her neck. "I'm trying to be fair to you. All I've wanted to do since I met you was work and take care of you."

"Please, please, Brady." She cupped his face with her palms. "Don't be stiff-necked with pride. Let's think of this as a gift from Goldie. She said the last laugh was on Elmer, but it was on her. If she hadn't written that letter, all this would have been hers. Now it's ours. In a few years we might want to make our house bigger, or build a new one."

Brady hugged her to him and kissed her again and again, the money forgotten while he held this sweet woman in his arms. Her lips parted in a soft sigh. As if it were the signal he'd awaited, Brady captured her lips in a kiss that was rich and deep, a kiss she desperately welcomed.

"Nothing has changed?" she asked fearfully when he released her lips.

"Nothing's changed, sweetheart."

"You'll help me with . . . this?"

"Of course. What do you want me to do?"

"Tell me what to do with the money and the truck."

"Well the first thing we should do is lower the back flap in case someone comes by. Then we search in all the places where he may have squirreled away even more money."

A half hour later they were stunned by what they had found: one-hundred-dollar bills in the back of the clock, in the bib of a pair of rolled-up overalls, behind the wooden back of a framed picture of a farmhouse and in the drip pocket of the leather shield he wore when carrying ice. The snuff tins were full of gold pieces.

Brady counted the bills. "Nine thousand and seven hundred dollars. I don't know the value of the gold coins. It's a fortune, honey. Some men work all their lives and never earn this much. You're rich, honey. Very rich."

"We're rich. I can't imagine him having all this money, although I remember my granny saying that he was from moneyed people. She said his parents owned half of Conway at one time, and he was the only child. He may have inherited some of it. He sold the ice business and his house. With all this money he never once offered to help me when I was working twelve hours a day, in order to have food and a roof over my head. He never, ever bought me a birthday or Christmas present or helped me when Granny died."

"Don't think about it, honey."

"It's ironic, though, isn't it? I think he would hate it if he knew I had his money."

"He would hate it more for Goldie to have it. Now, what do you want to do about the truck?" Brady asked while putting the money in the tin box.

"I don't know. What do you think we should do?"

"We can't take it and my car too. I have a

good truck out at the ranch. It might be best if you sell the truck. We'll go home in the car, and later I'll teach you to drive it so that you can go to town when you want to."

"How much is the truck worth?"

"It's worth more than the car. I'd say about three hundred because of the heavy springs, tires and the heavy-duty motor."

"I'd like Jody to have it," she said without hesitation. "We could give it to him, but I'm sure he wouldn't accept it."

"How about if you tell him you'll sell it to him for a hundred dollars, and he can send you monthly payments until it's paid for?"

"That's a good idea. All I want out of here is the clock, my clothes and a box of pictures my granny gave me." She put the tin box in his hands. "What'll we do with this?"

"Put it back for now. It's as safe there as anywhere."

She laid Goldie's letter aside before she locked the tin box. "I want Alvin to see this."

While breakfast was being readied by Grace and Mona, Brady and Margie drew Alvin aside and gave him Goldie's letter to read.

"I can see now what was eating at the man," Alvin said after he had read the letter and put it back in the envelope. "As far as I

509

can tell, you've got a clear title to everything he had, Margie. And I must say that I'm glad. I hated to think of his belongings going to a woman who had run off and left him."

"We're going to be married tomorrow in Gallup and go to Colorado," Brady said. "We wanted you to know before we made the announcement to the others."

"Congratulations to both of you." Alvin held out his hand. "We'll miss you on the rest of the trip."

"From what I've seen of Wills and Taylor, you've got good men with you in case of trouble. I'd not leave you otherwise."

Alvin took off his hat and scratched his head. "Ah . . . do you plan to take the truck?"

Brady looked at Margie. "You tell him, honey."

"We don't need it. I'm going to see if Jody would like to buy it. He can use it in the ice business you and Mr. Luker will start, and he can pay me in installments."

Alvin seemed relieved. "If the Lukers can't see their way clear to buy it, I will and hire Jody to drive it the rest of the way. We were counting on having that truck when we started the business."

Jody was dumbstruck when Margie asked him if he wanted to buy the truck.

"Buy . . . the truck?" he stammered.

"I'm not a bit worried that you won't send the payments."

"Oh, I would. I want to talk to Pa. Back in a minute."

He was back in not much more than a minute with a hundred-dollar bill rolled up in his hand.

"Pa says I can borrow the money from him to pay for it and pay him back five dollars a month when I'm hired to work for him and Alvin." He had a wide grin on his face. "I can't believe that I'm the owner of a truck! I mean me and Pa are the owners until I get it paid for."

"I'm glad you will have it, Jody. Can I give you a kiss?"

"Yes, ma'am!"

"Hey, wait a minute," Brady said. "This is getting out of hand."

After congratulations had been passed around, Alvin led the caravan out of the campground. For Brady and Margie it was the last time. With Anna Marie still asleep on the backseat, Margie sat close to Brady and they talked about the trip.

"So much has happened since we all met. The best part was meeting you and falling in love." Margie turned sideways in the seat and hugged Brady's arm. "The worst part was the storm and Elmer being killed."

"Foley might have thought the worst part was Sugar running off, but I doubt that he thinks so now. He seems a different man than when we started out."

"If not for you, the men up there in Oklahoma would have robbed us and taken Mona. I wonder what happened to them?"

"They're probably still hanging around campgrounds stealing from folks who already are as poor as Job's turkey."

The sixty-three miles between Grants and Gallup went by fast even with one stretch of the highway unfinished. The caravan pulled into a campground at Gallup shortly after noon.

"This is your wedding day, sweetheart," Brady said when he parked the car behind the truck. "Will you mind being married in the courthouse?"

"We'll be just as married as if we said our vows in a great cathedral." She looked at him with tender, loving eyes.

"I told Alvin that I was getting a motor court cabin for our first night together. Grace and Mona will keep Anna Marie, so I'll have you all to myself. Why are you blushing, honey?"

"I . . . I don't know."

Brady laughed and kissed her on the nose.

"By the end of the day you will be Mrs. Brady Hoyt."

After Brady had rented a cabin in a court not far from the campground, he left Margie and Mona at a department store and went on to the courthouse to make arrangements for the wedding.

For the first time in her life Margie bought the dress she wanted without first having to consider the cost. The white dress had a full skirt, short puffed sleeves, a round neckline and a wide sash of pink satin. She bought silk stockings and white pumps. Then with Mona giggling and her blushing, she bought a white satin nightgown with a lace bodice.

When Brady picked the girls up outside the store, he'd had a haircut and shave and was wearing a new shirt and britches. His scuffed boots had been polished. The marriage license was in his pocket.

"What did you buy?"

"A dress and shoes."

"Tell him what else," Mona whispered.

"Oh, you blabbermouth."

Grace, Mrs. Taylor and Mrs. Wills were making preparations for the wedding supper when Brady and Margie took Mona back to the campground. Jody and Rusty had found a bakery and bought a cake. The

513

two of them and Mona were going to the courthouse with Margie and Brady to be witnesses.

At the cabin Brady parked at the side and produced a key to unlock the door.

"It's not fancy, sweetheart."

"It's private, and that's wonderful. We'll stay at a fancy place on our anniversary."

"Get ready, honey. I've got one more thing to do. I'll be back in about half an hour. We have to be at the courthouse before six."

Margie ran water in the bathtub for her first full bath since leaving Deke's Garage. She hurriedly bathed, dressed and added a touch of rouge to her cheeks and color to her lips. She wished she'd had time to wash her hair, but had to settle for a vigorous brushing.

She was ready when Brady knocked on the door. She opened it and backed away. He stood looking at her, a proud smile on his face.

"Ah . . . sweetheart. A man never had a prettier bride."

"Thank you. You're . . . kind of pretty yourself."

He came to her, kissed her carefully on the lips, then pulled a tiny box from his pocket, opened it and held up a chain with a small heart hanging from it.

"My gift to you on our wedding day. Turn around, darlin', so I can put it on."

Margie blinked rapidly. "I don't have anything for you."

"You're giving me you. Nothing could top that." He fastened the chain around her neck and kissed the nape.

"Thank you. I'll treasure it always." She turned and kissed his lips.

"Ready to go?" His voice was husky with emotion. "Jody's here. We're going to the courthouse in Foley's car, so I won't have to unload mine."

She gave him her hand, and they went out the door.

"Stay right there," Mona called. She was waiting by the car with a Kodak. "You've got to have a picture taken on your wedding day."

"Smile, honey. We'll have it enlarged and hang it on the wall."

"Wedding pictures are usually of the woman sitting down and the man standing behind her."

"You know why that is, don't you?"

"No. Why?"

"I'll tell you after we're married. Now smile."

Mona took several, then Brady helped

Margie into the backseat of the car, where she found a bouquet of white roses.

In the cabin next door Sugar looked over her shoulder to where Homer lay naked on the bed. They had followed the caravan to Gallup. When it stopped so early and when Brady rented a cabin at the motor court, Sugar thought that maybe someone was sick.

"Well, dog my cats. The cowboy and the bitch are getting married, or my name isn't Sugar Wadsworth Corning Hudspeth Williamson Luker. That's why they stopped early."

"What are ya talkin' 'bout?"

"Come look. She's all dolled up in a white dress."

Homer peered out the window. "Well, shit, little pussy. This couldn't be better. When he drove in here, I thought he was just goin' to shack up with her for the night." Homer got up and put his pants on.

"What are you going to do?"

"I'm goin' to shag my ass over there while they're gone and see if the key to our door fits theirs. This is a streak of luck, little puss. I'm goin' to screw his bride while ya hold the gun on him. I want to see his face when I rip into her."

"Are you out of your mind?"

"Jealous, little slut? There'll be plenty left for you."

"They'll recognize you."

"I sure as hell hope so. I want the son of a bitch to know who's screwin' his bride." He came up behind her, reached around and pinched her nipple.

"You're goin' to kill them, aren't you?"

"Sugar tittie, yo're as dumb as dogshit. Almost as dumb as old Chester." He opened the door, looked both ways, then slithered out and around the corner.

Sugar felt a tremor of fear go down her spine. At times her young lover was a cold, vicious little bastard. Even though she knew he could turn on her in a second, she also knew that she was in love for the first time in her life; and when all was said and done, she would do exactly what he told her to do.

Chapter 30

Anna Marie was a bundle of excitement when Margie and Brady returned to the campground after being married. She wore the clean dress Margie had left for her. Grace had brushed her hair and entwined ribbons in her braids.

The wedding cake sat on a cloth-covered makeshift table. Surrounding it were platters of sandwiches. On a keg beside the table was a crock of lemonade, and on the kerosene stove the large coffeepot was sending up a plume of steam. The bride and groom stepped out of the car to a round of applause. Happy to have an excuse to celebrate, other campers had joined those from the caravan to make this a festive occasion for the couple.

Happy tears flooded Margie's eyes. These people were the nearest to a family she had ever known. She glanced up to find her new husband beaming. He knelt down and opened his arms when Anna Marie ran to him.

"Uncle Brady! We're gonna have cake. Aunt Grace made lemonade. See my ribbons?"

Brady laughed, hugged her and set her on her feet. She went directly to Margie.

"Aunt Grace said you're my Aunt Margie now."

"I guess that's right. I married your Uncle Brady."

She pulled Margie down so she could whisper in her ear. "I wanted you to be my mama."

"Oh, honey. You can call me that if you want to. You and I and your Uncle Brady are going to make a home together. Tomorrow we're going to his ranch in Colorado. I'll tell you all about it later."

"Can I tell Lucy?"

"Sure you can."

Mona insisted on taking a picture of the table and one of Margie and Brady standing behind the cake before the sun went down. That done, she talked nonstop about the ceremony in the judge's chamber that made

Brady and Margie man and wife and insisted that Margie show the gold band Brady had put on her finger.

Mrs. Wills held Mrs. Taylor's baby while she helped Grace with the table. The nearby campers had been invited, and those who came brought an assortment of food: deviled eggs, potato salad, pickled peaches.

By the time the meal was over and the table cleared, it was near dark. Lanterns were hung, and a place was cleared for dancing. Alvin got out his violin and Rusty his guitar.

"I can't dance in these shoes," Margie whispered to Brady, who had not left her side.

"I'll get your moccasins out of the truck."

When Alvin's voice boomed that the first dance was for the bride and groom, Rusty began to play "I Love You Truly" on the violin. Grace and Alvin sang in perfect harmony. Smiling, Brady took Margie's hand, and they began to dance.

"I love you truly," he whispered in her ear.

"I love you too." Margie floated dreamily in the arms of her new husband.

The dance ended with more applause. When the music started again, Alvin played the violin, and several couples, including Rusty and Mona, began to dance. Later, after Rusty had danced with the bride, his mother and Mona again, he took the fiddle so Alvin could dance with the bride, then with Grace.

Harry Wills, who had brought a pillow and tucked it behind his wife's back, squatted on his heels beside her. His alert eyes swept back and forth around the area. A nagging unease was at the back of his mind, and he was determined to speak to Alvin about it as soon as the festivities were over.

Out of respect for the other campers Alvin put a stop to the party after a couple of hours.

"Many of the campers," he explained, "will be on the road before daylight and need their sleep."

With Margie's hand tucked in his, Brady stood with her beside Alvin.

"My wife and I want to thank you for the reception, for your good wishes and for helping to make our wedding day so festive. Now, as every one of you who has been a bridegroom knows — I want to be alone with my wife!"

Whoops and hollers greeted the statement. Margie hid her face against Brady's arm. Grinning broadly, Brady put his arm around her as they went to say good night to

Anna Marie before leaving for the cabin. Mona and Rusty were standing close together at the end of the truck.

"She's already asleep," Mona said.

"Thank you for looking after her tonight. Tell Jody that when we come back in the morning, I'll take my things out of the truck. Rusty, I love your new song. I'll be listening for you on the radio."

"Don't hold your breath. California is probably full of singers."

"Not as good as you."

"It's what I've been telling him," Mona said.

"Is that what you've been doing?" Brady teased. "All this time I thought you were standing over here kissing."

"I notice you've been doing your share," Rusty retorted.

"It's going to be hard to say good-bye in the morning." Margie, suddenly tearful, put an arm around Mona.

"We can keep in touch. Maybe someday Mona and I can come visit."

"Really?" Mona said. Then again, "Really?"

Rusty laughed and pulled Mona to him. "You can never tell. I know one thing: I'm not letting this woman get away from me."

"Oh, I hope you do come see us — together."

"So do I," Mona said, and laid her head on Rusty's shoulder.

"Come on, honey." Brady pulled Margie away. "We'd better go so they can smooch."

"Thanks, Brady," Rusty said. "I knew you'd understand."

"Darn right, I do. I want to smooch with my wife."

Jody, who had struck up an acquaintance with a girl from another camp, had offered to drive them to the cabin. Not wanting to cut short Jody's time with the girl, Brady and Margie had decided to walk the short distance.

"Are you tired, honey?"

"I'm too keyed up to be tired. It was nice, wasn't it?"

"Yes, it was. Alvin and Grace know how to put on a party."

"I didn't expect to get a ring. I thought maybe sometime later I'd get one."

"That ring tells the world that you're mine. I wish it had a diamond as big as a hen's egg."

"I don't. I'd feel silly trying to do the dishes with a stone as big as a hen's egg on my finger."

When they reached the motor court,

Brady noticed that all six cabins were occupied. He unlocked the door to theirs and then swung Margie up in his arms and carried her into the dark room. He kicked the door closed and kissed her before he set her on her feet. She was trembling. Brady held her for a while, then moved away, switched on the light and lowered the window shades.

"You're trembling, honey. Are you scared of me?"

"I'm just . . . excited."

"Go get ready." He pushed her gently toward the bathroom. "Is there anything in here you need?"

She shook her head. "Brady?" she said before she closed the door. "Have you done this many times before?"

"A few, but not with someone I love. That's altogether different. It's the love we share that will make it so special."

Brady began to undress but kept his trousers on. His arousal was embarrassing to him, and he feared for his bride to see it.

Lord, help me to go slow and not rush to completion. This first time for her will set the tone for our mating from now on.

He turned off the light. Standing in the nearly pitch-dark room, the only light coming through the cracks around the bathroom door, Brady felt not only a strong sexual desire for his wife, but a strange fear that he wouldn't be able to make it a pleasant experience for her. He was awed by the responsibility of introducing her to the way a man loved a woman with his body.

The door opened, making a path of light that spread out into the room. Margie came out carrying her dress and draped it over the back of a chair. Brady stood beside the bed.

"Let me look at you." His hands grasped her shoulders, his eyes boldly sweeping over her. He could see the rosy tips of her breasts through the lace bodice of her gown. "Ah . . . honey, no man ever had a prettier or sweeter bride." His voice was low, husky, and trembled with emotion.

He pulled her to him. Her arms encircled him and caressed the smooth skin of his back. He felt so good. His scent was all male, fresh and clean. His chest was warm, and she could feel the heavy beat of his heart. His arms held her tightly before he bent and pulled back the sheet on the bed.

"Get in, darlin'. I'll be right back." Brady used the bathroom, and when he came out, he left the door ajar and went to sit on the side of the bed. He bent down to kiss her. "I want you naked in my arms."

"Did I waste my money on this night-gown?" She giggled happily, wrapped her arms around his neck and pulled his head down until their lips were touching.

The door burst open.

Brady had no time to lift his head or turn before the barrel of a gun was pressed against it. Margie let out a little cry of alarm. In the light coming from the bathroom she saw the menacing figure of a man looming over them and the gun held to Brady's head. Brady threw up an arm. The man with the gun backed away.

"Close the door and turn on the light, little pussy. I want the cowboy and the bitch to see who's come callin'. What we've got here is a bride and groom gettin' ready to do the nasty. I'll just help 'em out a little — show 'em how it's done."

The light came on. Brady blinked once, then fixed his gaze on the woman leaning against the door. Sugar smiled and pursed her lips in the form of a kiss. It took Brady a little longer to recognize the man. When he did, his lips curled in a sneer, but he said nothing.

"Ain't ya got nothin' to say, cowboy?"

"Can't think of anything," Brady said easily.

"You will. Get up, slut. I want to see yore

titties, and I just might make you lick my arm where ya shot me."

"Stay where you are, honey."

"I guess ya don't know who has the upper hand here."

"Yeah, I do. A cocky little shithead who thinks he's a man because he's got a gun in his hand."

The barrel of the gun shifted to point down at Margie's face. Homer grinned, showing yellowed teeth.

"Turn around, cowboy, or I'll splatter her brains all over the pillow and screw her corpse."

Sugar stood beside the closed door, her face hard. Brady turned. His eyes caught Margie's, and he nodded slightly. She got out of bed and took a step toward him.

"Stay back," Homer yelled. "Stay back or I'll shoot him."

Margie stopped, looked at Sugar and, taking a cue from Brady, said calmly, "Hello, Sugar. Nice to see you."

Sugar laughed. "I just bet ya are, Miss Prissy Ass."

"Come here, pussy. Take the gun, and if this big, brave cowboy moves a muscle, shoot him." Homer pulled out a knife with a long thin blade. He jerked Margie to him, wrapped his arm around her waist and placed the blade at her throat. "All right, cowboy, turn around. I want you to enjoy this. Make just one little move, and I'll slit her throat." He pressed the blade to make a small cut. Margie closed her eyes but didn't let out a sound.

"What do you want?" Brady demanded.

"It's payback time, cowboy. Remember the fire stick ya were goin' to shove up my ass? Well, I got somethin' to shove up the ass of the bitch who shot me."

"You followed us all the way from Oklahoma. Slashed my tires and tried to burn my car."

"And a good time I had doin' it — especially since I met a bitch who likes her pussy scratched five times a day and six times on Sunday." He flicked his eyes to Sugar and laughed. "Ain't that right, sweet thin'?"

"Get on with it, Homer. We've not got all day."

"See what I mean?" He bit on Margie's earlobe. "My whore's wantin' her poontang."

Things came to Brady's mind to say, but he choked them back and spoke calmly.

"Let her go. I'm the one you want to get even with."

"And I'm a-doin' it. If ya ain't noticed, I can give her another little nick with this knife."

Brady knew he had to be careful if he and Margie were going to get out of this alive. He had underestimated the disgusting, smart-mouthed robber back at the campground in Oklahoma. He was like a vicious little viper, unpredictable and deadly.

"Get the bitch's stocking and tie his hands behind his back. He ain't goin' to do nothin'. He knows that one swipe of the knife will give his bride a new mouth, right here under her chin." He nicked the skin on Margie's neck again, drawing a trickle of blood.

Sugar yanked the silk stocking off the back of the chair and moved behind Brady. If he'd had a thought that she had been forced into helping Homer against her will, he was soon rid of it. She seemed to take pleasure in tying him as tightly as she could.

His bright eyes on Brady, Homer put his free hand inside the neck of Margie's gown and ripped the lace to expose her breasts. He rubbed a palm over them, pinched and pulled at the nipples.

"She got nice high titties, cowboy. Nipples is good size for suckin'. Take a look. These titties ain't never goin' to get a chance to get flat and ugly."

Margie's eyes pleaded with Brady to say nothing. He clamped his mouth shut on the rage that threatened to burn out of control.

"Have ya busted into her yet, cowboy? I bet ya ain't. Doggie! I got here in time. I figured her as one of them women that's got to have a ring on her finger or she ain't givin' out no pussy."

Brady's rage was so evident Margie feared he would do something that would cause Sugar to shoot him.

"Get somethin' to stuff in her mouth. She's goin' to be yellin' before I'm through with her." Homer, not much taller than Margie, rubbed his erection against her buttocks. "Feel that, bitch? I'm going to shove it up yore ass!"

"Goddamn you!" Brady's shout filled the room. "Get away from her." His control broke, and he took a step forward. "Cut her again and I'll kill you!"

For a second Homer's bravado left him. "Shoot the son of a bitch!" he yelled. "Shoot him!"

Suddenly the door was flung open so hard it bounced against the wall.

Harry Wills stood there with a gun in his hand. Alvin was behind him.

"Let the girl go."

Homer's back was to the door. He turned, dragging Margie with him, and lifted his arm to throw the knife. In the seconds that followed, everything seemed to happen in slow motion. Sugar, seeing the gun pointed at Homer, forgot about the gun in her own hand.

"No!" she shouted, and lunged in front of Homer just as Harry fired. The sound of the shot filled the small room. Blood sprayed, covering her neck and chest. She was thrown back against Homer, then crumpled to the floor.

Homer dropped the knife to grab for the gun when it fell from Sugar's hand. Brady's foot caught him under the chin, sending him crashing against the wall. Then Brady was on him lightning-fast, one foot on his arm, the other on his neck, holding him to the floor, where he squirmed like a poisonous little snake.

Horrified, Margie stood with her hands to her ears, her eyes wide with fear. She came out of her shock when Alvin draped Brady's shirt around her, then knelt on the floor beside Sugar. Her eyes were open and staring. There was no doubt that she was dead.

Harry, as calmly as if this were an everyday occurrence for him, picked up Homer's knife and sawed through the stocking that bound Brady's hands; then he squatted down and put the tip of it in Homer's ear.

"Are ya wantin' to live, or do I shove this knife in and tickle that rotten brain of yores?" Homer blinked his eyes rapidly. "Well, shucks. I was hopin' ya'd be contrary. Put yore hands behind yore back, ya sorry, sneakin' little bastard. Tie him with that other stockin', Alvin. Then yank off his belt and bind his feet."

People from the other cabins who had heard the commotion filled the doorway. They stared at the dead woman on the floor, at the cursing, spitting man being hog-tied and at the barefoot girl in the torn white nightgown.

"Someone call the police." Brady's arms were around Margie. He dabbed at the trickles of blood on her neck with the sleeve of his shirt.

"We already have."

"Are you all right, honey? Oh, God. I've never been so scared in all my life. I wanted to kill that vicious bastard. I wanted to stomp his guts out."

"I'm all . . . right . . . or will be in a minute. Go on and do what you have to do. I'll just sit down here."

"Get a wet cloth." Brady tossed the order over his shoulder, and in moments a wet towel was placed in his hand. He put it gently against the cuts on Margie's neck and eased her down on the edge of the bed.

"I guess I'd better go get Foley." Alvin stood close and spoke quietly to Brady. "She's still his wife. He'll have to bury her."

"I'm sure glad you came in when you did. I was just about to do something that more than likely would have got us both killed."

"Save your thanks for Harry."

Brady glanced down at the dead woman and then at Homer Persy sitting on the floor.

"You slimy piece of no-good shit. You got that woman killed."

"Hell, I didn't pull the trigger. He did." He jerked his head toward Harry, who was squatting on the floor beside him.

Harry looked up at Brady. "He's low-caliber. I been watchin' him behind us for three days. He wasn't even smart enough to hang back when we came into the campground. I figured he was after one of us — thought it was me. I've put away a few of his kind in my day."

"Yeah," Homer sneered. "I might be low-caliber, but I ain't never killed no woman, not even a slut like her."

"The woman saved your miserable life," Brady gritted.

"I never asked her to." He grinned cockily. "She was protectin' her stud. She'd hardly give me time to get my pants down."

"Shut your foul mouth! I'd like to be alone with you for just ten —"

"All right. What happened here?" A man with a star on his chest stepped in through the open door, his voice loud with authority.

Chapter 31

Margie was almost sure that no woman ever had or wanted a wedding night like the one she'd had. After she had dressed, she and Brady packed up and left the cabin where they had come so close to losing their lives. He took her back to the campground so that she would be among friends while he and Harry Wills explained to the county and state police what had happened.

Foley had come to claim the body of his wife and, tight-lipped and grim, had sent it away with the funeral director to be prepared for burial. He had been shocked speechless when he saw her and realized that she had taken up with one of the men who would have robbed them in Oklahoma.

It was after midnight when Brady and

Harry Wills returned. Harry went first to check on his wife and brought her, wrapped in an old housecoat, to the Putman camp, where they had all gathered and were talking in hushed tones.

The police had received a report that a Ford coupe had been reported stolen in Oklahoma and was possibly on Route 66 headed for California. A registration inside Homer's car was that of the stolen car.

Empty billfolds and purses in the car, along with nearly five hundred dollars taken from Homer Persy, led the police to believe the couple had been on a robbery spree. Evidence was also found to connect the body found in a ditch outside Amarillo to Homer. He was charged with the murder of his Uncle Chester.

Harry explained that he had been a lawman for fifteen years; but after he had married, his wife worried every time he left the house, and because her peace of mind was important to him, he had turned in his badge. He had been aware for three days that the Ford coupe was following, and when it circled the campground, he noticed that the two inside the car seemed unduly interested in the caravan. Uneasy and suspicious, he nosed around and discovered that the same car was parked next to the cabin

Brady had rented for the night.

On a hunch Harry spoke to Alvin, and the two of them had walked down to the motor court. It had not occurred to Harry that whoever was in the car was trailing Brady. He had made many enemies among the lawless and thought he was the one they were following. His intention had been to find out who was pursuing him and why.

It was while Harry and Alvin were standing in front of the cabin, trying to decide if it was safe to look in the car, that they heard Brady shout. Harry's fifteen years of law experience took over, and, with gun in hand, he threw open the door.

"Thank God it wasn't locked," Brady said. "It would have taken a little time to bust in, and in the meanwhile . . ."

Margie sat on a blanket in the shelter of Brady's arms. Mona sat beside Rusty, her eyes going often to her father. He had not said much since he and Jody returned from the funeral home. The burial would take place at ten o'clock day after tomorrow.

"Thank you for what you did, Mr. Wills," Margie said. "They were going to kill us."

"I'm sorry I shot the woman. I sure didn't intend to hit her. I meant to stop the man from throwing the knife. He would have nailed me if I had hesitated. The woman could have shot me. She had a gun in her hand, but she threw herself in front of that sorry little weasel."

"I understand how it was," Foley said slowly. "I think now that I didn't know her at all."

"It happens like that sometimes." Alvin passed behind Foley and put a reassuring hand on his shoulder.

The next day everyone moved around quietly, except for Anna Marie and Lucy. Totally unaware of the tragic events of the night before, they played happily. When they were not throwing the ball, they were tossing sticks for Blackie to chase.

Brady and Margie removed from the truck what she wanted to take with her. They unloaded Brady's car and repacked it. Brady thought it best to put the tin box containing the money in Margie's suitcase.

"We're going to stay in hotels or motor courts on the way home, and we'll take it inside at night." She nodded in agreement, glad to leave the decisions up to him.

In the late afternoon Brady and Margie left the campground and drove to the downtown area, where Brady registered them at a hotel. He had made arrangements for Mona to take care of Anna Marie one more time, and she was happy to do so.

He carried Margie's suitcase up a wide carpeted stairway and down a hall to the most luxurious room she had ever seen. The carpet was thick, and a big high bed dominated the room. The drapes were a rich wine and matched the bedspread. But best of all, there was a big white bathtub. Her eyes shone when she looked at her husband.

"How did you know that I wanted a bath more than anything?"

"I know you, sweetheart. You want to wash away every reminder of last night."

"Not every one. Some I want to remember as long as I live. This, for instance." She wound her arms around his neck and placed her lips on his.

"Margie, Margie." He said her name twice. "I love you so much. I died a thousand times last night."

"But you kept control." She stroked his cheeks.

"My heart almost stopped when I saw his hands on you, a knife at your throat." He kissed the small red marks made by the knife.

"I left that nightgown at the cabin. I never wanted to see it again."

"We'll buy you a new one."

"I . . . don't think I'll need it."

He laughed happily and hugged her tightly.

"I agree, sweetheart. Go take your bath. I'm going downstairs and order our dinner sent up. We're going to splurge. We deserve it."

Margie took a long, leisurely bath and washed her hair. When she came out of the bathroom with a towel wrapped around her, Brady was sitting in a chair beside the window.

"I was looking for something to put on, and I think I've found it." She snatched his shirt off the bed and fled to the bathroom.

"That might be all I'll let you wear from now on," he teased later as they ate the meal of roast beef, potatoes and creamed peas.

Margie looked into eyes that shone with pure happiness. Her pulse leaped, bringing color to her face. Her flushed cheeks made her soft brown eyes seem all the warmer.

After he had pushed the dinner cart out into the hallway, it was Brady's turn in the bathroom.

"Sweetheart," he whispered with a catch in his voice. "Be ready for me. I'm going to love you all night long."

When Margie heard the water running in the tub, she closed the window shades, turned down the bed and fluffed the pillows.

Then, more daring than she had ever been in her life, she hung Brady's shirt on the back of the chair and looked at her naked body in the long mirror beside the closet door.

Her breasts were high and firm but not very big. She had heard somewhere that men liked big breasts. Her stomach was flat, her hips slightly rounded. She wished that her thighs were not so skinny. Suddenly fearing Brady would come through the door and catch her standing naked before the mirror, she hurried to the bed and slid beneath the smooth, cool sheet.

When Brady came out of the bathroom, he had a bath towel wrapped around his middle. His face was freshly shaven, and his hair was wet. Margie's eyes clung to him. *He was so beautiful.*

He came to sit down on the edge of the bed.

"You smell good," she managed to say.

"It's the shaving lotion."

He moved, flipped off the towel and slid under the sheet. A choking sound came from his throat as he reached for her and clasped her naked length against him.

"You feel so good." She clutched him tightly, her hand biting into the warm, solid flesh of his back.

The feel of his body, the stroking of his hands, the warm moistness of his breath, the love filling and spilling from her heart, brought her mindless pleasure. Being here with him like this was more wonderful than she had ever imagined.

They were feverish in their desire for each other. Blindly, passionately, he kissed her lips, then her breasts, drawing sweetly on the nipple he took in his mouth. With her fingers tangled in his black hair, she held his head to her breasts, never wanting him to stop that glorious torment.

There was no room in her mind for anything but him. He was her universe, vibrating with all the love in the world, and he lifted her to undreamed-of sensual heights. Then he was there, inside her. She was part of him. He was part of her. Her own flesh splintered with an exquisite explosion, sending her into a void where fireworks brightened a blackened sky.

Brady shuddered, clasped her tightly, his mouth devouring hers. After a while he turned onto his back, bringing her with him. He pressed her head to his shoulder; she burrowed into the hollow of his arm, tasting the moisture that dewed his chest. Her whole body pulsated still.

"Oh, Lord. Oh, honey, was I too rough? I

wanted to make it last a long time." He trembled and buried his lips in her hair.

"If it had lasted any longer, I might not have made it."

"I wanted you to enjoy what we did together."

"I enjoyed it so much I . . . thought I had died," she whispered.

"Sweetheart, this is the first of many times for us. I love you, want you. I'll have to have you again before the night is over."

"You promised to love me all night long . . ."

He chuckled and kissed her lips again and again.

"Better get some sleep, darlin', 'cause you'll not get any after I get my wind back."

She placed her hand over his thumping heart. "Cross your heart?"

It was on the tip of his tongue to finish the rhyme: *hope to die, cut my throat if I tell a lie.* But it was too soon, the image still too real. He held her to him and smothered a moan. Life wouldn't be worth living without her.

The thought spiraled through his mind that he now had a better understanding of what his twin must have felt for his Becky.

While she lived, Sugar Luker had shown only contempt for the eleven people who stood, out of respect for the husband she had scorned, at the site of her final resting place.

Rusty played his guitar and sang "Rock of Ages." A prayer was said by the preacher connected to the funeral home, and the service was over. Sugar would forever be in this small piece of earth alongside the highway to California, where she had connived for so long to go.

The party followed Foley's car back to the campground, where he would hitch his trailer to his car and continue along the highway to the place that held so much hope. Margie and Brady would get Anna Marie, who with Lucy Taylor had stayed with Mrs. Wills, say their good-byes and head for Colorado.

Tears streamed from Margie's eyes as she hugged Grace.

"I'll never forget you. You have been the best friends I've ever had."

"Write, now. Hear? Brady gave us his address. I'll write and let you know as soon as we're settled."

Margie put her arms around Rusty. "I know you're going to be a big star in California. I'm going to be so proud that I know you."

"If it happens, I'll send you my autograph," he teased, his voice husky.

"Alvin, how can I thank you? You are as solid as a rock. If I'd have been able to choose my father, it would have been you."

"Well, now, that's mighty nice to hear. I know that Brady will take good care of you; and if you ever get the yen to see California, you know where you'll find a welcome."

"Mr. Luker, I never got to know you like I did Alvin. I'm sorry for the grief you've had to endure on this trip and wish you the very best from here on. You have two great kids who are lucky to have you for their father."

"I'm the lucky . . . one," he stammered.

"Jody, I'm going to hug you whether you like it or not."

"I'll like it a lot even if Brady breaks my head."

"I hope you are happy in California; but if you're not, come to see us, and Brady will make a cowboy out of you." Margie kissed him on the cheek.

She shook hands with the Taylors, then moved on to Harry Wills and his wife.

"If not for you, Mr. Wills, Brady and I might not have left that cabin alive. I'll always remember what you did." She looked down at Mrs. Wills seated in her chair and smiled. "Your husband is almost as wonderful as mine."

Mona was last. "Let me know how things turn out between you and Rusty," Margie whispered. "Oh, I wish I could be at your wedding like you were at mine. Write to me . . ."

Margie fled to the car. After the last handshake, Brady followed. As they left the campground, Margie, tears in her eyes, waved a last good-bye.

Anna Marie in the backseat stuck her head out the window. "Bye, Lucy. Bye, Aunt Grace."

Epilogue

June 1935
Rocking Horse Ranch

Margie drove the sedan along the lane that divided a stand of junipers. When she came out into the open, she could see the mountains, beautiful in their aloof loneliness. She rounded a low hill, crossed a rocky stream only a few inches deep, a few feet wide, the water clear and cold.

She loved this land, this way of life.

Anna Marie had not wanted to come along on this trip. She was enthralled with the new baby of one of the Mexican families who lived on the ranch and was eagerly awaiting the birth of her own little brother or sister.

Margie couldn't wait for Brady to return home to share the letter she had received from Grace. Ramon had gone to town early that morning and had just returned with the mail.

She knew that she would get a scolding from her husband for driving the car out over the rough trail when the time was so near for her to deliver their baby. He was so dear, so afraid something would happen to her or the baby. The scolding would be punctuated with kisses, as was his habit.

The house came into view, and she eased the car up close to the old truck and stopped. It was going to be beautiful with four big rooms downstairs and two beneath the roof that sloped down to cover the wide porch facing the mountains. A large cobblestoned chimney rose from each side of the house: one in the living area, the other in their bedroom.

Brady and a number of workers were on the roof. When she drove in, he started down the ladder. With a worried look on his face he hurried to the car.

"What's happened? Why are you here? Are you having pains?"

Margie got out of the car. "Nothing has happened. I'm here because I got a letter from Grace. No, I don't have any pains."

"Marjorie Hoyt. Someday I'm going to beat your butt —"

"Will you wait until after I have the

baby?" She put her arms around his neck and leaned against him.

"I'm all dirty, honey." He rubbed her back and nuzzled his face in the curve of her neck.

"Baby doesn't care." She took Brady's hand and placed it on her protruding stomach. "Feel him kicking? He's wantin' out of there."

"Sweetheart, I wish you'd be careful. I'll be out of my mind by the time he gets here."

"No, you won't. You'll scold and frown and look like you're mad, but you'll be just as happy as I am. Let's get in the car so you can read Grace's letter."

"We want to finish the roof by tonight. You get in the car and tell me about it."

Margie sat sideways on the seat, her feet on the running board.

"Grace said that the ice business is doing better than they expected. Isn't that great? She said that Jody had been talking about coming out this way, but he met a girl at the radio station where Rusty has his program. Mona and Foley like her and wish that he'd settle down there.

"Foley hasn't yet proposed to the lady he's been keeping company with. I bet he's afraid of being burnt again.

"Rusty's program on the radio is getting

to be more popular all the time. His song, 'What I See,' was sung by Woody Guthrie. Grace said that Rusty's records are selling. Oh, I wish we could get one. And . . . guess what?"

He smiled at her enthusiasm, even though he was still bothered because she had driven on the rough trail. Her happy nature never allowed him to stay upset with her for long.

"I'll never guess. Tell me."

"Mona's pregnant. Grace said that Alvin goes around with a grin on his face and that Rusty is walking on clouds."

"I know the feeling."

"She and Alvin will be good grandparents. They are the godparents of the little Wills boy. Who will be the godparents of our little boy?"

"Would you object to Ramon and Claudia?"

"Not at all. She's turned out to be a really good friend."

"Move over. I'm going to drive you home as soon as I tell the men that I'm knocking off for the day. There's only an hour or two of daylight left anyway."

"Can we stop along the way and smooch?"

He leaned into the car and kissed her. "You can bet your boots on it."

References

Oklahoma Route 66, by Jim Ross

Here It Is! Route 66: The Map Series, by Jim Ross and Jerry McClanahan

Route 66 Traveler's Guide, by Tom Snyder

Route 66: The Mother Road, by Michael Wallis